The Complete Cosmicomics

ITALO CALVINO

The Complete Cosmicomics

Translated by Martin McLaughlin, Tim Parks,
and William Weaver

 **MARINER** CLASSICS

New York   Boston

First U.S. edition

Copyright © 2002 by The Estate of Italo Calvino

Translation of 'The Distance of the Moon', 'At Daybreak', 'A Sign in Space',
'All at One Point', 'Without Colours', 'Games Without End', 'The Aquatic
Uncle', 'How Much Shall We Bet?', 'The Dinosaurs', 'The Form of Space', 'The
Light-Years', and 'The Spiral' copyright © HarperCollins Publishers
and Jonathan Cape Ltd, 1968
Translation of 'The Soft Moon', 'The Origin of the Birds', 'Crystals', 'Blood,
Sea', 'Mitosis', 'Meiosis', 'Death', 't zero', 'The Chase', 'The Night Driver', and
'The Count of Monte Cristo' copyright ©   HarperCollins Publi
and Jonathan Cape Ltd, 1969
Translation of 'World Memory', 'Nothing and Not Much', 'Implosion', and
'The Other Eurydice' copyright © Tim Parks, 1995
Introduction and translations of 'The Mushroom Moon', 'The Daughters of
the Moon', 'The Meteorites', 'The Stone Sky', 'As Long as the Sun Lasts', 'Solar
Storm', and 'Shells and Time' copyright © Martin McLaughlin, 2009

Mariner Books
An Imprint of HarperCollins Publishers, registered
in the United States of America and/or other jurisdictions.

www.marinerbooks.com

Introduction and stories 24–30 first published in the United Kingdom by Penguin
Books Ltd, 2009
Stories 1–23 first published in the United States by Harcourt, Inc., as *Cosmicomics*
and *t zero*, 1968, 1969
Stories 31–4 first published in the United States by Pantheon Books in *Numbers in
the Dark and Other Stories*, 1995

Library of Congress Cataloging-in-Publication Data
Calvino, Italo.
[Cosmicomiche. English]
The complete cosmicomics / Italo Calvino ; Translated by Martin McLaughlin,
Tim Parks, and William Weaver. — First U.S. Edition.
pages cm.
ISBN 978-0-544-14644-0 (hardback)   ISBN 978-0-544-57787-9 (pbk.)
I. McLaughlin, M. L. (Martin L.) translator. II. Parks, Tim, translator.
III. Weaver, William, 1923–2013. translator. IV. Title.
PQ4809.A45C6513 2014
853'.914 — dc23   2014001375

Printed in the United States of America
23 24 25 26 27 LBC 16 15 14 13 12

Contents

Contents

Introduction

Italo Calvino (1923–85) is best known in the English-speaking world for two kinds of fiction: his historical fantasy works of the 1950s, collected in the trilogy *Our Ancestors* (1960), and the semiotic and metafictional experiments of the 1970s, particularly the highly successful *Invisible Cities* (1972) and *If on a Winter's Night a Traveller* (1979). He chose these genres as radical alternatives to the realist narratives that he had embarked on as a young writer and which he regarded as the norm for Western fiction. But the 'cosmicomic' stories that Calvino began to write in 1963–4, although less well known in the Anglo-American world, were if anything even more original than any of the other kinds of narrative he produced. For a start, he invented this new genre himself: each 'cosmicomic' tale begins with a statement of a (genuine or apocryphal) scientific hypothesis, usually regarding the cosmos, and this is then followed by a first-person narrative, recounted by the unpronounceable but irrepressible protagonist, Qfwfq. Qfwfq has been described as a 'cosmic know-all', since he was present at all the key moments in the history of the universe from the Big Bang onwards, and his comic colloquialism undercuts the potential seriousness of the scientific themes. The neologism invented by Calvino encapsulated two ways in which traditional realism could be expanded: by a cosmic content and by a comic mode of writing. The cosmicomic stories are also significant because this new vein of writing initiated the second half of Calvino's career: in the twenty years from 1943 to 1963, he had alternated between the realism (initially neorealism) of his first fictions – including his debut novel, *The Path to the Spiders' Nests* (1947) – and the historical fantasy of *Our Ancestors*; but his first 'cosmicomic' volume, *Cosmicomics* (1965), inaugurated the second two decades of more experimental writing.

Despite the fact that these stories are less well known than others, Calvino clearly considered this genre a significant and fertile space for literary experiment, as he continued to use the form for the next two decades, publishing a total of thirty-four tales in all. The first volume to be published – *Cosmicomiche* (1965; 'Cosmicomics'), which later won the Asti d'Appello Prize – contained twelve fictions; the second collection – *Ti con zero* (1967; 'T zero', translated as *Time and the Hunter*) – contained eleven new stories, and both books were translated into English by William Weaver in the late 1960s. A little-known third collection – *La memoria del mondo e altre storie cosmicomiche* (1968; 'World Memory and Other Cosmicomic Stories'), a volume not available commercially – offered twenty fictions in all, twelve from the previous two collections and eight new pieces (seven of these new items are translated here for the first time into English; the other new 1968 tale, the title story, was translated by Tim Parks as 'World Memory' in the 1995 collection *Numbers in the Dark and Other Stories*). By 1968, then, Calvino had written thirty-one cosmicomic stories. Just before his untimely death, aged sixty-one, he put together an almost complete collection, entitled *Cosmicomiche vecchie e nuove* (1984; 'Cosmicomics Old and New') and containing thirty-one tales; but for this volume he deselected two stories ('World Memory' and 'Shells and Time') and in their place inserted two new pieces specially written for the 1984 edition: 'Nothing and Not Much' and 'Implosion'. In 1980 he published a variant of one of the 1968 tales, 'The Stone Sky', giving it an alternative title, 'The Other Eurydice' (although in fact the story must have been written about ten years earlier since it had appeared first in English translation in 1971). This rewrite and the last two tales written in 1984 brought the total of cosmicomic tales to thirty-four (all three of these later stories can be found translated by Tim Parks in *Numbers in the Dark*). A posthumous Italian volume containing the complete thirty-four stories appeared in an authoritative Mondadori edition as *Tutte le cosmicomiche* (1997; 'The Complete Cosmicomics'), edited by the Italian expert on these tales, Claudio Milanini. This English volume corresponds to Milanini's comprehensive edition: it contains the two volumes translated by William Weaver, the four stories translated by Tim Parks, plus seven newly translated tales, offering the English-speaking reader the chance to savour Calvino's entire output in a genre he cultivated for two decades.

Genesis

Why did Calvino write the cosmicomic stories? The main reason was that he felt that realist fiction was exhausted and that the writer had to turn elsewhere for inspiration. For Calvino in the early 1960s this place was science, initially books on the origins of the universe which created images in his head, including the *Encyclopaedia Britannica* and Raymond Queneau's *Encyclopédie de la Pléiade*. His ambition in inventing this new genre was that literature should keep pace with the enormous progress being made in scientific research. The fact that he wrote the vast majority of them in the five years between 1963 and 1968 and that these were the years when the 'space race' between the USA and the Soviet Union was at its peak explains the prominence of space and planetary science in the tales. Another probable source of inspiration was the volume of science fiction tales that Primo Levi was putting together in the early 1960s: Calvino, Levi's editor at the publishing house Einaudi at the time, had commented enthusiastically on these stories, which would be published in 1966 as *Storie naturali* ('Natural Histories', translated into English in 1990 in *The Sixth Day and Other Stories*). However, although some critics have talked of the cosmicomic tales in terms of science fiction, Calvino was keen to point out that his stories were very different, indeed the opposite of the traditional form of the genre: whereas the latter usually dealt with a dystopian future, with human protagonists pitted against other forces and creatures, his cosmicomic tales were set mostly in the remote past, at the dawn of the universe, with a protagonist, Qfwfq, who was clearly not always human. This was a typical example of Calvinian reversal of the reader's expectations of a genre.

Calvino was a notoriously eclectic writer, however, and one should not look for just one source of inspiration for any of his tales. Indeed his own semi-serious list of literary and visual influences on the cosmicomic stories is lengthy but probably not exhaustive: '*Cosmicomics* are indebted particularly to Leopardi, the Popeye comics, Samuel Beckett, Giordano Bruno, Lewis Carroll, the paintings of Matta and in some cases the works of Landolfi, Immanuel Kant, Borges, and Grandville's engravings' (Calvino's blurb from the publication of the first four cosmicomic tales, in *Il Caffè*, November 1964). One other source for these fictions, according to Calvino, was the work of the philosopher Giorgio de Santillana (1902–74), whose lecture 'Ancient and Modern

Ideas of Fate', given in Turin in 1963, struck Calvino mainly for its idea that the great cosmological myths were both the predecessors and the equivalent of modern science. Calvino wanted ancient cosmogonic myths to combine with the latest theories, the concrete images of the one counterbalancing the abstraction of the other.

The subject matter of the stories can be divided into four main strands:

1. The Moon, which appears in the first story in each collection ('The Distance of the Moon', 'The Soft Moon') but also elsewhere ('The Mushroom Moon', 'The Daughters of the Moon').

2. The Sun, stars and galaxies ('At Daybreak', 'A Sign in Space', 'All at One Point', 'Games Without End', 'The Form of Space', 'The Light-Years', 'As Long as the Sun Lasts', 'Solar Storm', 'Nothing and Not Much', 'Implosion').

3. The Earth ('Without Colours', 'Crystals', 'The Meteorites', 'The Stone Sky', 'The Other Eurydice').

4. Evolution and time ('The Aquatic Uncle', 'How Much Shall We Bet?', 'The Dinosaurs', 'The Spiral', 'The Origin of the Birds', 'Blood, Sea', the 'Priscilla' trilogy, 't zero', 'The Chase', 'The Night Driver', 'The Count of Monte Cristo', 'Shells and Time', 'World Memory').

Cosmicomics

The first volume begins with a tale of landing on the Moon, 'The Distance of the Moon', partly reflecting the major scientific obsession of the time, but also paying homage to the fact that early Italian literature is full of descriptions of the Earth's satellite, from Dante to Ariosto, Galileo and

Leopardi, all dear to the author's heart. Calvino himself was fascinated by the Moon and had offered a highly evocative description of its effects in 'Moon and Gnac', from another collection, *Marcovaldo*, published in 1963. This literary dimension, which cross-fertilizes the scientific content, is also present in a story such as 'Without Colours', which tells how the Earth's atmosphere allowed colours to be perceived, but is also a telluric version of the Orpheus and Eurydice myth: Qfwfq plays Orpheus, while his beloved Ayl refuses to follow him up to the Earth's now colourful surface, preferring instead the grey darkness inside the Earth. Calvino was so haunted by the myth that he subsequently rewrote this tale twice. First he reversed it in 'The Stone Sky' (1968) and then he produced a variant of this story, 'The Other Eurydice' (1971). In 'The Stone Sky' Qfwfq plays not Orpheus but Pluto, the god of the underworld, who is desolate when he loses his beloved Rdix (her name both suggests 'radix' or 'root' and 'Eurydice') to the Greek minstrel. In this tale the author defamiliarizes our notions of 'extraterrestrial' and 'superficial', for Qfwfq/Pluto uses both adjectives to describe us miserable creatures who merely inhabit the Earth's surface not its core. In 'The Other Eurydice' the main difference is Pluto's even more embittered attack on what men have done to the Earth, and a bravura central passage describing the plutonic cities that the god of the underworld planned to build in the Earth's core, each one a 'living-body-city-machine' (p. 396), a world of silence and Earth music, which would accomplish in a second what it has taken centuries of sweat for man to achieve. The reader can enjoy comparing Calvino's variations on this theme, and can observe in that evocation of the cities in the centre of the Earth the germs of the major work that was to follow the cosmicomic stories, *Invisible Cities* (1972).

Literary themes surface more briefly elsewhere in *Cosmicomics*, such as the allusion to Balzac's *Les Illusions perdues* in 'How Much Shall We Bet?', the character Lieutenant Fenimore, whom Qfwfq tries to shoot at the end of 'The Form of Space' (reflecting the subject matter of James Fenimore Cooper's most famous work, *The Last of the Mohicans*), and the appropriate mention of Herodotus, the 'father of history', in 'The Spiral', which has as its central theme the emergence of time and history. Apart from these literary tales, the first collection also contains some stories in which Calvino reflects on literature itself. One of the most significant is 'A Sign in Space', where, apart from the comedy of Qfwfq leaving his naïve first sign in the universe in order to recognize it the next time he passes by, there is also the serious reflection on how signs are still the system we use to communicate, especially the written word: it is no accident that the date of composition of the story (1963–4) coincides with the beginnings of the new science of semiotics. But the tale also refers to something more personal: that first sign, which Qfwfq leaves in space and which causes him such embarrassment when he comes back millions of years later to find it utterly simplistic and out of date, reflects also Calvino's attitude to his own first novel, *The Path to the Spiders' Nests*. Written in 1947, the novel was actually in the forefront of the author's mind at this time since in the same months he was writing 'A Sign in Space' he was also composing his lengthy 1964 preface to *The Path*, in which his own embarrassment and remorse regarding this earlier work are apparent. Similar metaliterary allusions are to be found in 'The Dinosaurs', where the outmoded creatures are equated with the old writers who have failed to move ahead with the times and are still writing in the old, realist way.

Along with the more serious literary reflections, there is

also plenty of comedy in the stories: perhaps the most 'comic' cosmic tale here is 'The Aquatic Uncle', in which Qfwfq's old uncle, N'ba N'ga, refuses to leave his pond to follow the other fish in developing into land mammals, insisting that this evolutionary thing will never catch on. Similar comic deflations of potentially portentous themes are in evidence elsewhere; for instance, in 'All at One Point', where the Big Bang and the creation of space are attributed to the wonderfully named Mrs Ph(i)Nk$_0$, who is seized by a generous urge to make tagliatelle for everyone. The basic technique throughout is to let Qfwfq's colloquial tone as a narrator offset the great cosmic events he describes to his family as if he were an elderly relative reminiscing about the good old days. The names of all the characters are meant to suggest scientific formulae but with a comic twist.

Another constant ingredient mingling with science in the stories is desire – indeed one of the desired females, Ursula H'x in 'The Form of Space', is partly a cosmicomic version of Ursula Andress, star of the 1965 film *She* – and many of the tales, starting with the first one, are love stories. In a number of these stories the female embodies the elusive, yearned-for opposite of the male protagonist and the structure of the tale is often a love triangle with two males competing for a female other ('The Distance of the Moon', 'Without Colours', 'The Aquatic Uncle', 'The Form of Space'). Calvino was well aware of the major role played by desire in the evolution of Western fiction, and combined this basic narrative structure with the new 'scientific' content in most of the tales in *Cosmicomics*. Even in the last tale, 'The Spiral', Qfwfq is the first mollusc to construct a spiral shell and is driven to do so by his desire to mate with a female mollusc. The collection is thus framed by desire as the key motive force of the universe, and is not simply a univocal work about science and evolution.

This last story is not placed where it is by accident: it is the most ambitious tale of this first collection both in terms of its tripartite form and in its content, for Qfwfq notes that by forming the shell this tiny creature also invents our very notion of time. The series of twelve stories thus moves from the Moon to molluscs, and this evolutionary theme provides a fitting end to the collection (the last words are 'without shores, without boundaries', p. 151) and points towards the thematics of the second collection of cosmicomic stories.

Time and the Hunter

Calvino's second collection won the prestigious Viareggio Prize in 1968, but in the context of the social upheaval of the times the author refused to accept the award. The eleven pieces in *Time and the Hunter* form a symmetrical volume, consisting as it does of four more stories about Qfwfq, then a trilogy of tales about a single cell, entitled 'Priscilla', and a concluding section of four tales of deductive logic. 'The Soft Moon' is the first of the four Qfwfq tales. Although the title reminds us of the title of the opening Moon story in the first collection, the story itself is quite different – about a past that is also a present and a future, with its setting a futuristic New York (Calvino's favourite city would also form the backdrop of 'Crystals' and 'The Daughters of the Moon'). Here too science is mingled with literature, in that the notion of the Moon falling to Earth owes much to a famous poetic fragment by Giacomo Leopardi, in which the Moon lands on a field and turns black like spent coals, a motif also taken up in 'The Daughters of the Moon', from the third collection, *World Memory and Other Cosmicomic Stories*. But other media are evident in a story such as 'The Origin of the Birds', in which Qfwfq recounts his meeting with the Queen of the

Birds in verbal summaries of a series of cartoon strips. Calvino's visual imagination had always been stimulated by the economy and immediacy of cartoons and some of his early stories were indebted to this medium (as indeed was 'The Mushroom Moon', from *World Memory*, clearly inspired by the Popeye cartoons). At one point when Qfwfq jumps on to the planet of the birds, he sees fishes with spiders' legs, worms with feathers, all the potential but discarded forms that the animal kingdom could have developed, but did not: here the visual stimulus comes not from cartoons but from Hieronymus Bosch's nightmarish paintings. This interest in an alternative visual medium for narrative would eventually lead to Calvino's highly experimental *The Castle of Crossed Destinies* (1973), where the Tarot cards are actually produced in the margin alongside the narrative text. The last story in this first section, 'Blood, Sea', is about cells rather than about more complex beings, and thus effects a transition to the tales of the second section, which are all about cellular organisms. In 'Blood, Sea' Qfwfq is a cell inside a passenger of a car on an Italian motorway: the final description of the car crash that ends the tale is given in a virtuoso sentence, which constitutes a verbal homage to yet another visual medium, the contemporary Jean-Luc Godard film *Weekend* (1967).

The second section, entitled 'Priscilla', consists of three tales, 'Mitosis', 'Meiosis' and 'Death', the first term referring to the division of cells within asexual reproduction, the second to cell division within sexual reproduction. 'Death' amounts almost to a history of the world in five pages, beginning with the first drops of life on Earth and ending with the links that extend from DNA to man's technological achievements in machines and computers. All three tales of this second section are in a sense one tale, since they have one overall title, 'Priscilla', and instead of having three individual epigraphs, the whole section begins with four pages of quotations from embryologists, computer experts, philosophers and Galileo. This structural ambivalence between the one story and the three reflects the thematics of the tales themselves, which deal with the development from monocellular to pluricellular beings.

The four stories that constitute the last section in *Time and the Hunter* are not really cosmicomic tales, but rather fictions inspired by mathematics and deductive logic. The narrator of the first of these, the title story 't zero', is called simply Q, who thus represents a transition from the earlier Qfwfq tales to the last three stories in which the narrator is not named at all. The formula t_0 expresses the point of time which marks the beginning of Q's speculations about whether his arrow, A, will hit the lion, L, leaping on him before t_0 becomes t_1, t_2, t_3, etc. The idea derives from one of Zeno's famous paradoxes, that an arrow in flight is actually stationary, since if space is infinitely divisible, then the arrow is always above just one piece of ground. While 't zero' was largely concerned with time, the second tale in the series, 'The Chase', concentrates more on space, and if that first deductive tale alluded to the elementary nature of all narrative, a man facing a challenge, this one is written in the vein of a sophisticated thriller, as the first-person narrator tries to escape from his would-be killer by driving into the gridlocked city centre. The penultimate story, 'The Night Driver', is one of Calvino's most revolutionary narratives, eliminating as it does characters, landscape (the action takes place by night) and plot. Again mathematics informs this story: the first-person protagonist, though not named, is presumably called X, since he tells us he is driving from A to B, where he hopes to meet his lover, Y, but is afraid that his rival, Z, will get to Y before him. Here Calvino tries to reach a degree zero of writing where everything anthropomorphic has been erased from the tale apart from the love triangle. The story is innovative in its attempt to integrate the clarity of mathematics with the ambiguity of literature (one of the ideals of the Parisian group OULIPO, Ouvroir de Littérature Potentielle, or Workshop of Potential Literature, of which Calvino was a member), and in its allusions to information theory and semiotics. The concluding tale, 'The Count of Monte Cristo', owes its position to its embracing of the many other themes in the rest of the collection as well as to its greater length and complexity. It is in effect a brief rewriting of Alexandre Dumas's famous novel, but centring on the contrast between the Abbé Faria's empirical attempts to escape from the Château d'If and Edmond Dantès's preference for theory and deductive logic: Dantès concludes that the only way to escape the condition of prisoner is to understand mentally how the perfect prison is structured and then compare it with the one where he is currently detained in order to find the loophole. The thematics of the prison-labyrinth are indebted to similar ideas in Franz Kafka and Jorge Luis Borges, but the notion of the loophole reflected Calvino's own notion that all the great totalizing systems of our time (those of Charles Darwin, Karl Marx, Sigmund Freud) still contain gaps. The final sentence suggests but does not guarantee an exit from the labyrinth, but it was a conclusion that Calvino found optimistic and regarded as his gnoseological testament.

World Memory and Other Cosmicomic Stories

The third volume of cosmicomic tales was never translated in a single volume in English. The twenty pieces (twelve from the previous two collections and eight new ones) are divided into five sections of four stories each, the title of each section articulating the ambitious, global scope of the work: 'Four Stories on the Moon' ('The Distance of the Moon', 'The Mushroom Moon', 'The Soft Moon', 'The Daughters of the Moon'); 'Four Stories on the Earth' ('Without Colours', 'The Meteorites', 'Crystals', 'The Stone Sky'); 'Four Stories on the Sun, the Stars, the Galaxies' ('At Daybreak', 'As Long as the Sun Lasts', 'Solar Storm', 'Games without End'); 'Four Stories on Evolution' ('The Aquatic Uncle', 'The Dinosaurs', 'The Origin of the Birds', 'Shells and Time'); 'Four Stories on Time and Space' ('World Memory', 'The Chase', 'The Night Driver', 'The Count of Monte Cristo').

Calvino claimed that this was the cosmicomic volume that he had wanted to write from the start, since it was a more 'organic' work than the previous two, the titles of the five sections suggesting comprehensive coverage. The first two stories, 'The Mushroom Moon' and 'The Daughters of the Moon', are linked in inspiration to previous tales such as 'The Soft Moon', while, as we have seen, 'The Stone Sky' is a rewrite of 'Without Colours' from the first collection. 'The Meteorites' contains one of the first mentions of the theme of order, disorder and rubbish, an obsession that looks forward to *Invisible Cities*, while 'As Long as the Sun Lasts' is the most humorous tale in this series. But perhaps the most interesting story here is 'Solar Storm', a fiction that mixes scientific theory with allusions to some of Joseph Conrad's most famous novels. Conrad had been a favourite author of Calvino ever since his university thesis on the Anglo-Polish writer in 1946.

In the story Qfwfq is the captain of the steamer *Halley*, returning towards Liverpool, when it is caught in a magnetic storm occasioned by Rah, daughter of the Sun and the captain's aerial lover, who wraps herself round the foremast, invisible to the rest of the crew. Although the ship's name obviously alludes to Halley's comet, it also comes from the protagonist of Conrad's 1902 story 'The End of the Tether', Captain Whalley, whose wife used to live on board with him, and who makes one last voyage on a Liverpool-built ship, trying to conceal his increasing blindness from the crew. In addition to this text, there are also clear echoes of two other Conrad tales. The opening movement from calm sea to electric storm owes something to a similar shift in the crucial third chapter of *Lord Jim* (1900), a novel Calvino knew well since he translated the first ten chapters of it into Italian. The other Conrad text lurking beneath this tale is *Heart of Darkness* (1899): the description of Rah gripping the foremast, with her hair flying in the wind, and the folds of her drapery blending with the sky, is a clear echo of Conrad's description of the African woman who appears at the climax of the novel, a passage quoted in its entirety and commented upon more than once by Calvino in his thesis. Apart from these textual echoes, the main themes of the story are also Conradian: ships, compasses, radios and maps all epitomize rationality and control, while Qfwfq's statement that he never departed from the line of conduct he had set himself is not just the articulation of a quintessentially Conradian ethic, but the phrase 'with Rah on my back' (p. 358) is in Italian ('*con Rah addosso*') a pun on the Anglo-Polish author's name. The reader can also enjoy in the second half of the tale counting the allusions to other classics of English literature (Samuel Taylor Coleridge, Charlotte Brontë, Jane Austen) in cameo form. 'Solar Storm', one of the last tales to be written in the five years between 1963 and 1968, is not just another cosmicomic fiction but a minimalist rewriting of fundamental Conrad narratives and a mini-pastiche of nineteenth-century English classics. Once again, it is clear that the cosmicomic stories are inspired as much by literature as by science.

One of the last two tales, 'Shells and Time', is an extension of 'The Spiral', but taking the discourse about time further: shells may have in a sense created time, but they too are superseded by the sand which eventually settles on them, since sand-time deposits layers of other shells on them. The final lesson is that man's history is like the mollusc's: archaeological findings show that what has been lost to man is the hand of the potter who made the vase, the pronunciation of the scribe who wrote the manuscript, the flesh of the mollusc that secreted the shell. The other story, 'World Memory', stands apart from all the other cosmicomic tales, notably in its lack of scientific epigraph, the absence of Qfwfq from the story, and in its cosmic but not comic tone. Set in an unspecified future, the tale is narrated by the outgoing director of an institute which is cataloguing for posterity information about every human, plant and animal in the world; but for the information to be manageable it has to be reduced to a meaningful minimum. The phrase in the centre of the tale used to define humanity at the moment of its extinction shows the much broader perspective that these tales have: 'What will the human race be at the moment of its extinction? A certain quantity of information about itself and the world . . .' (p. 368).

Cosmicomics Old and New

In 1984 Calvino collected almost all of his cosmicomic stories in an anthology which, like *World Memory and Other Cosmicomic Stories*, was never translated into English as a separate volume. The work is divided into four parts: first, fourteen tales on evolution, the Earth, the Moon and the Sun, entitled 'The Memory of Worlds', and consisting of most of the stories from the first four sections of *World Memory*; then eight pieces on the universe, in a section called 'Chasing Galaxies', containing six stories from *Cosmicomics* plus the two new tales written for this collection, 'Nothing and Not Much' and 'Implosion'; a third part entitled 'Biocomics', consisting of five tales ('The Spiral', 'Blood, Sea' and the 'Priscilla' trilogy); and a fourth section, 'Deductive Stories', comprising the final four narratives from *Time and the Hunter*. The two new tales, 'Nothing and Not Much' and 'Implosion', naturally show some differences from the stories of the 1960s. The first one opens with a cutting from the *Washington Post* declaring that the universe came into existence in an infinitesimal fraction of a second. Qfwfq of course remembers both the nothing that preceded the Big Bang and all that emerged from it (the universe, time, space, memory); he describes the 'sense of invincibility, of power, of pride' accompanying this 'vertiginous expansion' (pp. 377–8), but in the end he comes round to the point of view of his female antagonist, Nugkta, and sees the universe as flawed and fundamentally unstable, a system in collapse, therefore gravely inferior to the perfection of nothing. That description of the universe as a bungled construction, crumbling away on all sides, and the final sentence on the slaughter that takes place daily on our planet reflects Calvino's own more pessimistic outlook on the world at the start of the 1980s. 'Implosion' was one of the last fictions that Calvino wrote, though it was developed from an earlier piece on black holes that he had written but excluded from the volume *Palomar* (1983). Exploiting his favourite poetics of contrast, Qfwfq initiates his musings on black holes by parodying Hamlet's great soliloquy: 'To explode or to implode . . . that is the question' (p. 384). The conclusion of the whole tale – 'Any way time runs it leads to disaster . . .' (p. 388) – also reflects Calvino's dystopian vision in what were to be his last years.

However, although readers of *Cosmicomics Old and New* will notice the gradual darkening of Calvino's outlook from the 1960s to the early 1980s, they will also appreciate the way Calvino expanded the frontiers of fiction by making his own literary discourse embrace science (physics, embryology, DNA, computing theory), mathematics, philosophy and the visual arts (paintings, cartoons, cinema, architecture). The main thrust of his poetics was constantly to raise the target which literature sets itself: he challenges literature to describe the indescribable, from macrocosm to microcosm, from the Big Bang to the division of cells.

The cosmicomic tales are in one sense a product of their time, the 1960s, but in their cosmic content and ambition they try to move beyond such temporal limitations: it is significant that starting with *Cosmicomics* Calvino breaks his habit of placing the date of composition at the end of his books, as though to confirm the irrelevance of contemporary history to a narrative that occupies itself with larger and more significant swathes of time. Nor was it an accident that some critics compared these stories with the abstract, geometric narrations of *nouveau-roman* writers such as Alain Robbe-Grillet (1922–2008). But although these fictions may be less well known than others, they represent a crucial phase in Calvino's own development as a writer, as we see in them the seeds of later works such as *Invisible Cities* and *The Castle of Crossed Destinies*. Drawing from different media, his works have also had considerable influence on other art forms. If *Invisible Cities* inspired architects and visual artists, the cosmicomic fictions have been taken up by musical artists. Two important musical works have so far emerged: Giovanni Renzo's operatic version of 'The Distance of the Moon' (1996), inspired by the Moon music in the first cosmicomic story, and Jonathan Dove's of 'The Other Eurydice' (2001), which provides the Earth music mentioned in that tale. These operatic spin-offs are a tribute to the creative force of these stories; indeed the latter work is highly appropriate in that one of the very first operas, Monteverdi's *L'Orfeo* (1607), was based on the myth of Orpheus. The continuing validity of the cosmicomic project for the author himself is also demonstrated by the fact that during the course of his last summer, in 1985, Calvino made a little note of the topics of three book projects he wanted to give priority to in the future: 'The Senses', 'Objects' and 'Cosmicomics'. There is still, in fact, in Calvino's archive a drawer full of newspaper cuttings concerning scientific discoveries. As I write this introduction, a news item today talks about the fact that thanks to recent technological developments we can now hear the sounds the planets make as they revolve. Had Calvino still been alive today we could almost imagine his next story beginning: 'Sounds! – *exclaimed Qfwfq* – Of course we heard the sounds of the planets! Deafening they were, but not without a certain variety . . .'

This translator wishes to thank for their valuable help Esther Calvino, Peter Hainsworth, Christopher Holland, Claudio Milanini, Catherine, McLaughlin, Mairi McLaughlin, Claudia Nocentini, Andrew Smith, Elisabetta Tarantino.

Martin McLaughlin
Oxford, November 2008

A Note on the Translations

This edition corresponds to Claudio Milanini's comprehensive edition of the cosmicomic tales, *Tuttle le cosmicomiche*, published in 1997. It contains the two volumes translated by William Weaver, *Cosmicomics* (1968) and *Time and the Hunter* (1969), the four stories translated by Tim Parks ('World Memory', 'Nothing and Not Much', 'Implosion' and 'The Other Eurydice'), from *Numbers in the Dark* (1995), plus seven newly translated tales from *La memoria del mondo e altre storie cosmicomiche* (1968; 'World Memory and Other Cosmicomic Stories'). The two volumes translated by William Weaver were originally published in America; for this edition, minor changes have been made to standardize presentation, together with minor emendations to a sentence in certain stories ('At Daybreak', 'All at One Point', 'How Much Shall We Bet?', 'The Dinosaurs', 'The Form of Space', 'The Light Years', 'The Soft Moon', 'Blood, Sea', 'Mitosis', 'Meiosis', 'The Night Driver' and 'The Count of Monte Cristo') to reflect the original Italian.

Cosmicomics

The Distance of the Moon

At one time, according to Sir George H. Darwin, the Moon was very close to the Earth. Then the tides gradually pushed her far away: the tides that the Moon herself causes in the Earth's waters, where the Earth slowly loses energy.

How well I know! – *old Qfwfq cried* – the rest of you can't remember, but I can. We had her on top of us all the time, that enormous Moon: when she was full – nights as bright as day, but with a butter-coloured light – it looked as if she were going to crush us; when she was new, she rolled around the sky like a black umbrella blown by the wind; and when she was waxing, she came forward with her horns so low she seemed about to stick into the peak of a promontory and get caught there. But the whole business of the Moon's phases worked in a different way then: because the distances from the Sun were different, and the orbits, and the angle of something or other, I forget what; as for eclipses, with Earth and Moon stuck together the way they were, why, we had eclipses every minute: naturally, those two big monsters managed to put each other in the shade constantly, first one, then the other.

Orbit? Oh, elliptical, of course: for a while it would huddle against us and then it would take flight for a while. The tides, when the Moon swung closer, rose so high nobody could hold them back. There were nights when the Moon was full and very, very low, and the tide was so high that the Moon missed a ducking in the sea by a hair's-breadth; well, let's say a few yards anyway. Climb up on the Moon? Of course we did. All you had to do was row out to it in a boat and, when you were underneath, prop a ladder against her and scramble up.

The spot where the Moon was lowest, as she went by, was off the Zinc Cliffs. We used to go out with those little rowing boats they had in those days, round and flat, made of cork. They held quite a few of us: me, Captain Vhd Vhd, his wife, my deaf cousin, and sometimes little Xlthlx – she was twelve or so at that time. On those nights the water was very calm, so silvery it looked like mercury, and the fish in it, violet-coloured, unable to resist the Moon's attraction, rose to the surface, all of them, and so did the octopuses and the saffron medusas. There was always a flight of tiny creatures – little crabs, squid, and even some weeds, light and filmy, and coral plants – that broke from the sea and ended up on the Moon, hanging down from that lime-white ceiling, or else they stayed in midair, a phosphorescent swarm we had to drive off, waving banana leaves at them.

This is how we did the job: in the boat we had a ladder: one of us held it, another climbed to the top, and a third, at the oars, rowed until we were right under the Moon; that's why there had to be so many of us (I only mentioned the main ones). The man at the top of the ladder, as the boat approached the Moon, would become scared and start shouting: 'Stop! Stop! I'm going to bang my head!' That was the impression you had, seeing her on top of you, immense, and all rough with sharp spikes and jagged, saw-tooth edges. It may be different now, but then the Moon, or rather the bottom, the underbelly of the Moon, the part that passed closest to the Earth and almost scraped it, was covered with a crust of sharp scales. It had come to resemble the belly of a fish, and the smell too, as I recall, if not downright fishy, was faintly similar, like smoked salmon.

In reality, from the top of the ladder, standing erect on the last rung, you could just touch the Moon if you held your arms up. We had taken the measurements carefully (we didn't yet suspect that she was moving away from us); the only thing you had to be very careful about was where you put your hands. I always chose a scale that seemed fast (we climbed up in groups of five or six at a time), then I would cling first with one hand, then with both, and immediately I would feel ladder and boat drifting away from below me, and the motion of the Moon would tear me from the Earth's attraction. Yes, the Moon was so strong that she pulled you up; you realized this the moment you passed from one to the other: you had to swing up abruptly, with a kind of somersault, grabbing the scales, throwing your legs over your head, until your feet were on the Moon's surface. Seen from the Earth, you looked as if you were hanging there with your head down, but for you, it was the normal position, and the only odd thing was that when you raised your eyes you saw the sea above you, glistening, with the boat and the others upside down, hanging like a bunch of grapes from the vine.

My cousin, the Deaf One, showed a special talent for making those leaps. His clumsy hands, as soon as they touched the lunar surface (he was always the first to jump up from the ladder), suddenly became deft and sensitive. They found immediately the spot where he could hoist himself up; in fact just the pressure of his palms seemed enough to make him stick to the satellite's crust. Once I even thought I saw the Moon come towards him, as he held out his hands.

5

He was just as dextrous in coming back down to Earth, an operation still more difficult. For us, it consisted in jumping, as high as we could, our arms upraised (seen from the Moon, that is, because seen from the Earth it looked more like a dive, or like swimming downwards, arms at our sides), like jumping up from the Earth in other words, only now we were without the ladder, because there was nothing to prop it against on the Moon. But instead of jumping with his arms out, my cousin bent towards the Moon's surface, his head down as if for a somersault, then made a leap, pushing with his hands. From the boat we watched him, erect in the air as if he were supporting the Moon's enormous ball and were tossing it, striking it with his palms; then, when his legs came within reach, we managed to grab his ankles and pull him down on board.

Now, you will ask me what in the world we went up on the Moon for; I'll explain it to you. We went to collect the milk, with a big spoon and a bucket. Moon-milk was very thick, like a kind of cream cheese. It formed in the crevices between one scale and the next, through the fermentation of various bodies and substances of terrestrial origin which had flown up from the prairies and forests and lakes, as the Moon sailed over them. It was composed chiefly of vegetal juices, tadpoles, bitumen, lentils, honey, starch crystals, sturgeon eggs, moulds, pollens, gelatinous matter, worms, resins, pepper, mineral salts, combustion residue. You had only to dip the spoon under the scales that covered the Moon's scabby terrain, and you brought it out filled with that precious muck. Not in the pure state, obviously; there was a lot of refuse. In the fermentation (which took place as the Moon passed over the expanses of hot air above the deserts) not all the bodies melted; some remained stuck in it: fingernails and cartilage, bolts, sea horses, nuts and peduncles, shards of crockery, fish-hooks, at times even a comb. So this paste, after it was collected, had to be refined, filtered. But that wasn't the difficulty: the hard part was transporting it down to the Earth. This is how we did it: we hurled each spoonful into the air with both hands, using the spoon as a catapult. The cheese flew, and if we had thrown it hard enough, it stuck to the ceiling, I mean the surface of the sea. Once there, it floated, and it was easy enough to pull it into the boat. In this operation, too, my deaf cousin displayed a special gift; he had strength and a good aim; with a single, sharp throw, he could send the cheese straight into a bucket we held up to him from the boat. As for me, I occasionally misfired; the contents of the spoon would fail to overcome the Moon's attraction and they would fall back into my eye.

I still haven't told you everything about the things my cousin was good at. That job of extracting lunar milk from the Moon's scales was child's play to him: instead of the spoon, at times he had only to thrust his bare hand under the scales, or even one finger. He didn't proceed in any orderly way, but went to isolated places, jumping from one to the other, as if he were playing tricks on the Moon, surprising her, or perhaps tickling her. And wherever he put his hand, the milk spurted out as if from a nanny goat's teats. So the rest of us had only to follow him and collect with our spoons the substance that he was pressing out, first here, then there, but always as if by chance, since the Deaf One's movements seemed to have no clear, practical sense. There were places, for example, that he touched merely for the fun of touching them: gaps between two scales, naked and tender folds of lunar flesh. At times my cousin pressed not only his fingers but – in a carefully gauged leap – his big toe (he climbed on to the Moon barefoot) and this seemed to be the height of amusement for him, if we could judge by the chirping sounds that came from his throat as he went on leaping.

The soil of the Moon was not uniformly scaly, but revealed irregular bare patches of pale, slippery clay. These soft areas inspired the Deaf One to turn somersaults or to fly almost like a bird, as if he wanted to impress his whole body into the Moon's pulp. As he ventured further in this way, we lost sight of him at one point. On the Moon there were vast areas we had never had any reason or curiosity to explore, and that was where my cousin vanished; I had suspected that all those somersaults and nudges he indulged in before our eyes were only a preparation, a prelude to something secret meant to take place in the hidden zones.

We fell into a special mood on those nights off the Zinc Cliffs: gay, but with a touch of suspense, as if inside our skulls, instead of the brain, we felt a fish, floating, attracted by the Moon. And so we navigated, playing and singing. The Captain's wife played the harp; she had very long arms, silvery as eels on those nights, and armpits as dark and mysterious as sea urchins; and the sound of the harp was sweet and piercing, so sweet and piercing it was almost unbearable, and we were forced to let out long cries, not so much to accompany the music as to protect our hearing from it.

Transparent medusas rose to the sea's surface, throbbed there a moment, then flew off, swaying towards the Moon. Little Xlthlx amused herself by catching them in midair, though it wasn't easy. Once, as she stretched her little arms out to catch one, she jumped up slightly and was also set free. Thin as she was, she was an ounce or two short of the weight necessary for the Earth's gravity to overcome the Moon's attraction and bring her back: so she flew up among the medusas, suspended over the sea. She took fright, cried, then laughed and started playing, catching shellfish and minnows as they flew, sticking some into her mouth and chewing them. We rowed hard, to keep up with the child: the Moon ran off in her ellipse, dragging that swarm of marine fauna through the sky, and a train of long, entwined seaweeds, and Xlthlx hanging there in the midst. Her two wispy braids seemed to be flying on their own, outstretched towards the Moon; but all the while she kept wriggling and kicking at the air, as if she wanted to fight that influence, and her socks – she had lost her shoes in the fight – slipped off her feet and swayed, attracted by the Earth's force. On the ladder, we tried to grab them.

The idea of eating the little animals in the air had been a good one; the more weight Xlthlx gained, the more she sank towards the Earth; in fact, since among those hovering bodies hers was the largest, molluscs and seaweeds and plankton began to gravitate about her, and soon the child was covered with siliceous little shells, chitinous carapaces and fibres of sea plants. And the further she vanished into that tangle, the more she was freed of the Moon's influence, until she grazed the surface of the water and sank into the sea.

We rowed quickly, to pull her out and save her: her body had remained magnetized, and we had to work hard to scrape off all the things encrusted on her. Tender corals were wound about her head, and every time we ran the comb through her hair there was a shower of crayfish and sardines; her eyes were sealed shut by limpets clinging to the lids with their suckers; squids' tentacles were coiled around her arms and her neck; and her little dress now seemed woven only of weeds and sponges. We got the worst of it off her, but for weeks afterwards she went on pulling out fins and shells, and her skin, dotted with little diatoms, remained affected for ever, looking – to someone who didn't observe her carefully – as if it were faintly dusted with freckles.

This should give you an idea of how the influences of Earth and Moon, practically equal, fought over the space between them. I'll tell you something else: a body that descended to the Earth from the satellite was still charged for a while with lunar force and rejected the attraction of our world. Even I, big and heavy as I was: every time I had been up there, I took a while to get used to the Earth's up and its down, and the others would have to grab my arms and hold me, clinging in a bunch in the swaying boat while I still had my head hanging and my legs stretching up towards the sky.

'Hold on! Hold on to us!' they shouted at me, and in all that groping, sometimes I ended up by seizing one of Mrs Vhd Vhd's breasts, which were round and firm and the contact was good and secure and had an attraction as strong as the Moon's or even stronger, especially if I managed, as I plunged down, to put my other arm around her hips, and with this I passed back into our world and fell with a thud into the bottom of the boat, where Captain Vhd Vhd brought me around, throwing a bucket of water in my face.

This is how the story of my love for the Captain's wife began, and my suffering. Because it didn't take me long to realize whom the lady kept looking at insistently: when my cousin's hands clasped the satellite, I watched Mrs Vhd Vhd, and in her eyes I could read the thoughts that the deaf man's familiarity with the Moon were arousing in her; and when he disappeared in his mysterious lunar explorations, I saw her become restless, as if on pins and needles, and then it was all clear to me, how Mrs Vhd Vhd was becoming jealous of the Moon and I was jealous of my cousin. Her eyes were made of diamonds, Mrs Vhd Vhd's; they flared when she looked at the Moon, almost challengingly, as if she were saying: 'You shan't have him!' And I felt like an outsider.

The one who least understood all of this was my deaf

cousin. When we helped him down, pulling him – as I explained to you – by his legs, Mrs Vhd Vhd lost all her self-control, doing everything she could to take his weight against her own body, folding her long silvery arms around him; I felt a pang in my heart (the times I clung to her, her body was soft and kind, but not thrust forward, the way it was with my cousin), while he was indifferent, still lost in his lunar bliss.

I looked at the Captain, wondering if he also noticed his wife's behaviour; but there was never a trace of any expression on that face of his, eaten by brine, marked with tarry wrinkles. Since the Deaf One was always the last to break away from the Moon, his return was the signal for the boats to move off. Then, with an unusually polite gesture, Vhd Vhd picked up the harp from the bottom of the boat and handed it to his wife. She was obliged to take it and play a few notes. Nothing could separate her more from the Deaf One than the sound of the harp. I took to singing in a low voice that sad song that goes: 'Every shiny fish is floating, floating; and every dark fish is at the bottom, at the bottom of the sea . . .' and all the others, except my cousin, echoed my words.

Every month, once the satellite had moved on, the Deaf One returned to his solitary detachment from the things of the world; only the approach of the full moon aroused him again. That time I had arranged things so it wasn't my turn to go up, I could stay in the boat with the Captain's wife. But then, as soon as my cousin had climbed the ladder, Mrs Vhd Vhd said: 'This time I want to go up there, too!'

This had never happened before; the Captain's wife had never gone up on the Moon. But Vhd Vhd made no objection, in fact he almost pushed her up the ladder bodily, exclaiming: 'Go ahead then!' and we all started helping her, and I held her from behind, felt her round and soft on my arms, and to hold her up I began to press my face and the palms of my hands against her, and when I felt her rising into the Moon's sphere I was heartsick at that lost contact, so I started to rush after her, saying: 'I'm going to go up for a while, too, to help out!'

I was held back as if in a vice. 'You stay here; you have work to do later,' the Captain commanded, without raising his voice.

At that moment each one's intentions were already clear. And yet I couldn't figure things out; even now I'm not sure I've interpreted it all correctly. Certainly the Captain's wife had for a long time been cherishing the desire to go off privately with my cousin up there (or at least to prevent him from going off alone with the Moon), but probably she had a still more ambitious plan, one that would have to be carried out in agreement with the Deaf One: she wanted the two of them to hide up there together and stay on the Moon for a month. But perhaps my cousin, deaf as he was, hadn't understood anything of what she had tried to explain to him, or perhaps he hadn't even realized that he was the object of the lady's desires. And the Captain? He wanted nothing better than to be rid of his wife; in fact, as soon as she was confined up there, we saw him give free rein to his inclinations and plunge into vice, and then we understood why he had done nothing to hold her back. But had he known from the beginning that the Moon's orbit was widening?

None of us could have suspected it. The Deaf One perhaps, but only he: in the shadowy way he knew things, he may have had a presentiment that he would be forced to bid the Moon farewell that night. This is why he hid in his secret places and reappeared only when it was time to come back down on board. It was no use for the Captain's wife to try to follow him: we saw her cross the scaly zone various times, length and breadth, then suddenly she stopped, looking at us in the boat, as if about to ask us whether we had seen him.

Surely there was something strange about that night. The sea's surface, instead of being taut as it was during the full moon, or even arched a bit towards the sky, now seemed limp, sagging, as if the lunar magnet no longer exercised its full power. And the light, too, wasn't the same as the light of other full moons; the night's shadows seemed somehow to have thickened. Our friends up there must have realized what was happening; in fact, they looked up at us with frightened eyes. And from their mouths and ours, at the same moment, came a cry: 'The Moon's going away!'

The cry hadn't died out when my cousin appeared on the Moon, running. He didn't seem frightened, or even amazed: he placed his hands on the terrain, flinging himself into his usual somersault, but this time after he had hurled himself into the air he remained suspended, as little Xlthlx had. He hovered a moment between Moon and Earth, upside down, then laboriously moving his arms, like someone swimming against a current, he headed with unusual slowness towards our planet.

From the Moon the other sailors hastened to follow his example. Nobody gave a thought to getting the Moon-milk that had been collected into the boats, nor did the Captain scold them for this. They had already waited too long, the distance was difficult to cross by now; when they tried to imitate my cousin's leap or his swimming, they remained there groping, suspended in midair. 'Cling together! Idiots! Cling together!' the Captain yelled. At this command, the sailors tried to form a group, a mass, to push all together until they reached the zone of the Earth's attraction: all of a sudden a cascade of bodies plunged into the sea with a loud splash.

The boats were now rowing to pick them up. 'Wait! The Captain's wife is missing!' I shouted. The Captain's wife had also tried to jump, but she was still floating only a few yards from the Moon, slowly moving her long, silvery arms in the air. I climbed up the ladder, and in a vain attempt to give her something to grasp I held the harp out towards her. 'I can't reach her! We have to go after her!' and I started to jump up, brandishing the harp. Above me the enormous lunar disc no longer seemed the same as before: it had become much smaller, it kept contracting, as if my gaze were driving it away, and the emptied sky gaped like an abyss where, at the bottom, the stars had begun multiplying, and the night poured a river of emptiness over me, drowned me in dizziness and alarm.

'I'm afraid,' I thought. 'I'm too afraid to jump. I'm a coward!' and at that moment I jumped. I swam furiously through the sky, and held the harp out to her, and instead of coming towards me she rolled over and over, showing me first her impassive face and then her backside.

'Hold tight to me!' I shouted, and I was already overtaking her, entwining my limbs with hers. 'If we cling together we can go down!' and I was concentrating all my strength on uniting myself more closely with her, and I concentrated my sensations as I enjoyed the fullness of that embrace. I was so absorbed I didn't realize at first that I was, indeed, tearing her from her weightless condition, but was making her fall back on the Moon. Didn't I realize it? Or had that been my intention from the very beginning? Before I could think properly, a cry was already bursting from my throat. 'I'll be the one to stay with you for a month!' Or rather, 'On you!' I shouted, in my excitement: 'On you for a month!' and at that moment our embrace was broken by our fall to the Moon's surface, where we rolled away from each other among those cold scales.

I raised my eyes as I did every time I touched the Moon's crust, sure that I would see above me the native sea like an endless ceiling, and I saw it, yes, I saw it this time, too, but much higher, and much more narrow, bound by its borders of coasts and cliffs and promontories, and how small the boats seemed, and how unfamiliar my friends' faces and how weak their cries! A sound reached me from nearby: Mrs Vhd Vhd had discovered her harp and was caressing it, sketching out a chord as sad as weeping.

A long month began. The Moon turned slowly around the Earth. On the suspended globe we no longer saw our familiar shore, but the passage of oceans as deep as abysses and deserts of glowing lapilli, and continents of ice, and forests writhing with reptiles, and the rocky walls of mountain chains gashed by swift rivers, and swampy cities, and stone graveyards, and empires of clay and mud. The distance spread a uniform colour over everything: the alien perspectives made every image alien; herds of elephants and swarms of locusts ran over the plains, so evenly vast and dense and thickly grown that there was no difference among them.

I should have been happy: as I had dreamed, I was alone with her, that intimacy with the Moon I had so often envied my cousin and with Mrs Vhd Vhd was now my exclusive prerogative, a month of days and lunar nights stretched uninterrupted before us, the crust of the satellite nourished us with its milk, whose tart flavour was familiar to us, we raised our eyes up, up to the world where we had been born, finally traversed in all its various expanse, explored landscapes no Earth-being had ever seen, or else we contemplated the stars beyond the Moon, big as pieces of fruit, made of light, ripened on the curved branches of the sky, and everything exceeded my most luminous hopes, and yet, and yet, it was, instead, exile.

I thought only of the Earth. It was the Earth that caused each of us to be that someone he was rather than someone else; up there, wrested from the Earth, it was as if I were no longer that I, nor she that She, for me. I was eager to return to the Earth, and I trembled at the fear of having lost it. The fulfilment of my dream of love had lasted only that instant when we had been united, spinning between Earth and Moon; torn from its earthly soil, my love now knew only the heart-rending nostalgia for what it lacked: a where, a surrounding, a before, an after.

This is what I was feeling. But she? As I asked myself, I was torn by my fears. Because if she also thought only of the Earth, this could be a good sign, a sign that she had finally come to understand me, but it could also mean that everything had been useless, that her longings were directed still and only towards my deaf cousin. Instead, she felt nothing. She never raised her eyes to the old planet, she went off, pale, among those wastelands, mumbling dirges and stroking her harp, as if completely identified with her temporary (as I thought) lunar state. Did this mean I had won out over my rival? No; I had lost: a hopeless defeat. Because she had finally realized that my cousin loved only the Moon, and the only thing she wanted now was to become the Moon, to be assimilated into the object of that extrahuman love.

When the Moon had completed its circling of the planet, there we were again over the Zinc Cliffs. I recognized them with dismay: not even in my darkest previsions had I thought the distance would have made them so tiny. In that mud puddle of the sea, my friends had set forth again, without the now useless ladders; but from the boats rose a kind of forest of long poles; everybody was brandishing one, with a harpoon or a grappling hook at the end, perhaps in the hope of scraping off a last bit of Moon-milk or of lending some kind of help to us wretches up there. But it was soon clear that no pole was long enough to reach the Moon; and they dropped back, ridiculously short, humbled, floating on the sea; and in that confusion some of the boats were thrown off balance and overturned. But just then, from another vessel a longer pole, which till then they had dragged along on the water's surface, began to rise: it must have been made of bamboo, of many, many bamboo poles stuck one into the other, and to raise it they had to go slowly because – thin as it was – if they let it sway too much it might break. Therefore, they had to use it with great strength and skill, so that the wholly vertical weight wouldn't rock the boat.

Suddenly it was clear that the tip of that pole would touch the Moon, and we saw it graze, then press against the scaly terrain, rest there a moment, give a kind of little push, or rather a strong push that made it bounce off again, then come back and strike that same spot as if on the rebound, then move away once more. And I recognized, we both – the Captain's wife and I – recognized my cousin: it couldn't have been anyone else, he was playing his last game with the Moon, one of his tricks, with the Moon on the tip of his pole as if he were juggling with her. And we realized that his virtuosity had no purpose, aimed at no practical result, indeed you would have said he was driving the Moon away, that he was helping her departure, that he wanted to show her to her more distant orbit. And this, too, was just like him: he was unable to conceive desires that went against the Moon's nature, the Moon's course and destiny, and if the Moon now tended to go away from him, then he would take delight in this separation just as, till now, he had delighted in the Moon's nearness.

What could Mrs Vhd Vhd do, in the face of this? It was only at this moment that she proved her passion for the deaf man hadn't been a frivolous whim but an irrevocable vow. If what my cousin now loved was the distant Moon, then she too would remain distant, on the Moon. I sensed this, seeing that she didn't take a step towards the bamboo pole, but simply turned her harp towards the Earth, high in the sky, and plucked the strings. I say I saw her, but to tell the truth I only caught a glimpse of her out of the corner of my eye, because the minute the pole had touched the lunar crust, I had sprung and grasped it, and now, fast as a snake, I was climbing up the bamboo knots, pushing myself along with jerks of my arms and knees, light in the rarefied space, driven by a natural power that ordered me to return to the Earth, oblivious of the motive that had brought me here, or perhaps more aware of it than ever and of its unfortunate outcome; and already my climb up the swaying pole had reached the point where I no longer had to make any effort but could just allow myself to slide, head first, attracted by the Earth, until in my haste the pole broke into a thousand pieces and I fell into the sea, among the boats.

My return was sweet, my home refound, but my thoughts were filled only with grief at having lost her, and my eyes gazed at the Moon, for ever beyond my reach, as I sought her. And I saw her. She was there where I had left her, lying on a beach directly over our heads, and she said nothing. She was the colour of the Moon; she held the harp at her side and moved one hand now and then in slow arpeggios. I could distinguish the shape of her bosom, her arms, her thighs, just as I remember them now, just as now, when the Moon has become that flat, remote circle, I still look for her as soon as the first sliver appears in the sky, and the more it waxes, the more clearly I imagine I can see her, her or something of her, but only her, in a hundred, a thousand different vistas, she who makes the Moon the Moon and, whenever she is full, sets the dogs to howling all night long, and me with them.

At Daybreak

The planets of the solar system, G. P. Kuiper explains, began to solidify in the darkness, through the condensation of a fluid, shapeless nebula. All was cold and dark. Later the Sun began to become more concentrated until it was reduced almost to its present dimensions, and in this process the temperature rose and rose, to thousands of degrees, and the Sun started emitting radiations in space.

Pitch-dark it was – *old Qfwfq confirmed* – I was only a child, I can barely remember it. We were there, as usual, with Father and Mother, Granny Bb'b, some uncles and aunts who were visiting, Mr Hnw, the one who later became a horse, and us little ones. I think I've told you before the way we lived on the nebulae: it was like lying down, we were flat and very still, turning as they turned. Not that we were lying outside, you understand, on the nebula's surface; no, it was too cold out there. We were underneath, as if we had been tucked in under a layer of fluid, grainy matter. There was no way of telling time; whenever we started counting the nebula's turns there were disagreements, because we didn't have any reference points in the darkness, and we ended up arguing. So we preferred to let the centuries flow by as if they were minutes; there was nothing to do but wait, keep covered as best we could, doze, speak out now and then to make sure we were all still there; and, naturally, scratch ourselves; because – they can say what they like – all those particles spinning around had only one effect, a troublesome itching.

What we were waiting for, nobody could have said; to be sure, Granny Bb'b remembered back to the times when matter was uniformly scattered in space, and there was heat and light; even allowing for all the exaggerations there must have been in those old folks' tales, those times had surely been better in some ways, or at least different; but as far as we were concerned, we just had to get through that enormous night.

My sister G'd(w)^n fared the best, thanks to her introverted nature: she was a shy girl and she loved the dark. For herself, G'd(w)^n always chose to stay in places that were a bit removed, at the edge of the nebula, and she would contemplate the blackness, and toy with the little grains of dust in tiny cascades, and talk to herself, with faint bursts of laughter that were like tiny cascades of dust, and – waking or sleeping – she abandoned herself to dreams. They weren't dreams like ours (in the midst of the darkness, we dreamed of more darkness, because nothing else came into our minds); no, she dreamed – from what we could understand of her ravings – of a darkness a hundred times deeper and more various and velvety.

My father was the first to notice something was changing. I had dozed off, when his shout wakened me: 'Watch out! We're hitting something!'

Beneath us, the nebula's matter, instead of fluid as it had always been, was beginning to condense.

To tell the truth, my mother had been tossing and turning for several hours, saying: 'Uff, I just can't seem to make myself comfortable here!' In other words, according to her, she had become aware of a change in the place where she was lying: the dust wasn't the same as it had been before, soft, elastic, uniform, so you could wallow in it as much as you liked without leaving any print; instead, a kind of rut or furrow was being formed, especially where she was accustomed to resting all her weight. And she thought she could feel underneath her something like granules or blobs or bumps; which perhaps, after all, were buried hundreds of miles further down and were pressing through all those layers of soft dust. Not that we generally paid much attention to these premonitions of my mother's: poor thing, for a hypersensitive creature like herself, and already well along in years, our way of life then was hardly ideal for the nerves.

And then it was my brother Rwzfs, an infant at the time; at a certain point I felt him – who knows? – slamming or digging or writhing in some way, and I asked: 'What are you doing?' And he said: 'I'm playing.'

'Playing? With what?'

'With a thing,' he said.

You understand? It was the first time. There had never been things to play with before. And how could we have played? With that pap of gaseous matter? Some fun: that sort of stuff was all right perhaps for my sister G'd(w)^n. If Rwzfs was playing, it meant he had found something new: in fact, afterwards, exaggerating as usual, they said he had found a pebble. It wasn't a pebble, but it was surely a collection of more solid matter or – let's say – something less gaseous. He was never very clear on this point; that is, he told stories, as they occurred to him, and when the period came when nickel was formed and nobody talked of anything but nickel, he said: 'That's it: it was nickel. I was playing with some nickel!' So afterwards he was always called 'Nickel Rwzfs'. (It wasn't, as some say now, that he had turned into nickel, unable – retarded as he was – to go beyond the mineral phase; it was a different thing altogether, and I only mention this out of love for truth, not because he was my brother: he had always been a bit backward, true enough, but not of the metallic type, if anything a bit colloidal; in fact, when he was still very young, he married an alga, one of the first, and we never heard from him again.)

In short, it seemed everyone had felt something: except me. Maybe it's because I'm absent-minded. I heard – I don't know whether awake or asleep – our father's cry: 'We're hitting something!', a meaningless expression (since before then nothing had ever hit anything, you can be sure), but one that took on meaning at the very moment it was uttered, that is, it meant the sensation we were beginning to experience, slightly nauseating, like a slab of mud passing under us, something flat, on which we felt we were bouncing. And I said, in a reproachful tone: 'Oh, Granny!'

Afterwards I often asked myself why my first reaction was to become angry with our grandmother. Granny Bb'b, who clung to her habits of the old days, often did embarrassing things: she continued to believe that matter was in uniform expansion and, for example, that it was enough to throw refuse anywhere and it would rarefy and disappear into the distance. The fact that the process of condensation had begun some while ago, that is, that dirt thickened on particles so we weren't able to get rid of it – she couldn't get this into her head. So in some obscure way I connected this new fact of 'hitting' with some mistake my grandmother might have made and I let out that cry.

Then Granny Bb'b answered: 'What is it? Have you found my cushion?'

This cushion was a little ellipsoid of galactic matter Granny had found somewhere or other during the first cataclysms of the universe; and she always carried it around with her, to sit on. At a certain point, during the great night, it had been lost, and she accused me of having hidden it from her. Now, it was true I had always hated that cushion, it seemed so vulgar and out of place on our nebula, but the most Granny could blame me for was not having guarded it always as she had wanted me to.

Even my father, who was always very respectful towards her, couldn't help remarking: 'Oh, see here, Mamma, something is happening – we don't know what – and you go on about that cushion!'

'Ah, I told you I couldn't get to sleep!' my mother said: another remark hardly appropriate to the situation.

At that point we heard a great 'Pwack! Wack! Sgrr!' and we realized that something must have happened to Mr Hnw: he was hawking and spitting for all he was worth.

'Mr Hnw! Mr Hnw! Get hold of yourself! Where's he got to now?' my father started saying, and in that darkness, still without a ray of light, we managed to grope until we found him and could hoist him on to the surface of the nebula, where he caught his breath again. We laid him out on that external layer which was then taking on a clotted, slippery consistency.

'Wrrak! This stuff closes on you!' Mr Hnw tried to say, though he didn't have a great gift for self-expression. 'You go down and down, and you swallow! Skrrrack!' He spat.

There was another novelty: if you weren't careful, you could now sink on the nebula. My mother, with a mother's instinct, was the first to realize it. And she cried: 'Children: are you all there? Where are you?'

The truth was that we were a bit confused, and whereas before, when everything had been lying regularly for centuries, we were always careful not to scatter, now we had forgotten all about it.

'Keep calm. Nobody must stray,' my father said.

'G'd(w)^n! Where are you? And the twins? Has anybody seen the twins? Speak up!'

Nobody answered. 'Oh, my goodness, they're lost!' Mother shouted. My little brothers weren't yet old enough to know how to transmit any message: so they got lost easily and had to be watched over constantly. 'I'll go and look for them!' I said.

'Good for you, Qfwfq, yes, go!' Father and Mother said, then, immediately repentant: 'But if you do go, you'll be lost, too! No, stay here. Oh, all right, go, but let us know where you are: whistle!'

I began to walk in the darkness, in the marshy condensation of that nebula, emitting a constant whistle. I say 'walk'; I mean a way of moving over the surface, inconceivable until a few minutes earlier, and it was already an achievement to attempt it now, because the matter offered such little resistance that, if you weren't careful, instead of proceeding on the surface you sank sideways or even vertically and were buried. But in whatever direction I went and at whatever level, the chances of finding the twins remained the same: who could guess where the two of them had got to?

All of a sudden I sprawled; as if they had – we would say today – tripped me up. It was the first time I had fallen, I didn't know what 'to fall' was, but we were still on the softness and I didn't hurt myself. 'Don't trample here,' a voice said, 'I don't want you to, Qfwfq.' It was the voice of my sister G'd(w)^n.

'Why? What's there?'

'I made some things with things . . .' she said. It took me a while to realize, groping, that my sister, messing about with that sort of mud, had built up a little hill, all full of pinnacles, spires and battlements.

'What have you done there?'

G'd(w)^n never gave you a straight answer. 'An outside with an inside in it.'

I continued my walk, falling every now and then. I also stumbled over the inevitable Mr Hnw, who was stuck in the condensing matter again, head first. 'Come, Mr Hnw. Mr Hnw! Can't you possibly stay erect?' and I had to help him pull himself out once more, this time pushing him from below, because I was also completely immersed.

Mr Hnw, coughing and puffing and sneezing (it had never been so icy cold before), popped up on the surface at the very spot where Granny Bb'b was sitting. Granny flew into the air, immediately overcome with emotion: 'My grandchildren! My grandchildren are back!'

'No, no, Mamma. Look, it's Mr Hnw!' Everything was confused.

'But the grandchildren?'

'They're here!' I shouted, 'and the cushion is here, too!'

The twins must long before have made a secret hiding place for themselves in the thickness of the nebula, and they had hidden the cushion there, to play with. As long as matter had been fluid, they could float in there and do somersaults through the round cushion, but now they were imprisoned in a kind of spongy cream: the cushion's central hole was clogged up, and they felt crushed on all sides.

'Hang on to the cushion,' I tried to make them understand. 'I'll pull you out, you little fools!' I pulled and pulled and, at a certain point, before they knew what was happening, they were already rolling about on the surface, now covered with a scabby film like the white of an egg. The cushion, instead, dissolved as soon as it emerged. There was no use trying to understand the phenomena that took place in those days; and there was no use trying to explain to Granny Bb'b.

Just then, as if they couldn't have chosen a better moment, our visiting relatives got up slowly and said: 'Well, it's getting late; I wonder what our children are up to. We're a little worried about them. It's been nice seeing all of you again, but we'd better be getting along.'

Nobody could say they were wrong; in fact, they should have taken fright and run off long since; but these relations, perhaps because of the out-of-the-way place where they lived, were a bit gauche. Perhaps they had been on pins and needles all this time and hadn't dared say so.

My father said: 'Well, if you want to go, I won't try to keep you. But think it over: maybe it would be wiser to stay until the situation's cleared up a bit, because as things stand now, you don't know what sort of risk you might be running.' Good, common sense, in short.

But they insisted: 'No, no, thanks all the same. It's been a really nice get-together, but we won't intrude on you any longer,' and more nonsense of the sort. In other words, we may not have understood very much of the situation, but they had no notion of it at all.

There were three of them: an aunt and two uncles, all three very tall and practically identical; we never really understood which uncle was the husband and which the brother, or exactly how they were related to us: in those days there were many things that were left vague.

They began to go off, one at a time, each in a different direction, towards the black sky, and every now and then, as if to maintain contact, they cried: 'Oh! Oh!' They always acted like this: they weren't capable of behaving with any sort of system.

They had hardly left when their cries of 'Oh! Oh!' could be heard from very distant points, though they ought to have been still only a few paces away. And we could also hear some exclamations of theirs, whose meaning we couldn't understand: 'Why, it's hollow here!' 'You can't get past this spot!' 'Then why don't you come here?' 'Where are you?' 'Jump!' 'Fine! And what do I jump over?' 'Oh, but now we're heading back again!' In other words, everything was incomprehensible, except the fact that some enormous distances were stretching out between us and those relatives.

It was our aunt, the last to leave, whose yells made the most sense: 'Here I am, all alone, stuck on top of a piece of this stuff that's come loose . . .'

And the voices of the two uncles, weak now in the distance, repeated: 'Fool . . . Fool . . . Fool . . .'

We were peering into this darkness, criss-crossed with voices, when the change took place: the only real, great change I've ever happened to witness, and compared to it the rest is nothing. I mean this thing that began at the horizon, this vibration which didn't resemble those we then called sounds, or those now called the 'hitting' vibrations, or any others; a kind of eruption, distant surely, and yet, at the same time, it made what was close come closer; in other words, all the darkness was suddenly dark in contrast with something else that wasn't darkness, namely light. As soon as we could make a more careful analysis of the situation, it turned out that: first, the sky was dark as before but was beginning to be not so dark; second, the surface where we were was all bumpy and crusty, an ice so dirty it was revolting, which was rapidly dissolving because the temperature was rising at full speed; and, third, there was what we would later have called a source of light, that is, a mass that was becoming incandescent, separated from us by an enormous empty space, and it seemed to be trying out all the colours one by one, in iridescent fits and starts. And there was more: in the midst of the sky, between us and that incandescent mass, a couple of islands, brightly lit and vague, which whirled in the void with our uncles on them and other people, reduced to distant shadows, letting out a kind of chirping noise.

So the better part was done: the heart of the nebula, contracting, had developed warmth and light, and now there was the Sun. All the rest went on revolving nearby, divided and clotted into various pieces, Mercury, Venus, the Earth, and others further on, and whoever was on them, stayed where he was. And, above all, it was deathly hot.

We stood there, open-mouthed, erect, except for Mr Hnw, who was on all fours, to be on the safe side. And my grandmother! How she laughed! As I said before, Granny Bb'b dated from the age of diffused luminosity, and all through this dark time she had kept saying that any minute things would go back the way they had been in the old days. Now her moment seemed to have come; for a while she tried to act casual, the sort of person who accepts anything that happens as perfectly natural; then, seeing we paid her no attention, she started laughing and calling us: 'Bunch of ignorant louts . . . Know-nothings . . .'

She wasn't speaking quite in good faith, however; unless her memory by then had begun to fail her. My father, understanding what little he did, said to her, prudently as always: 'Mamma, I know what you mean, but really, this seems quite a different phenomenon . . .' And he pointed to the terrain: 'Look down!' he exclaimed.

We lowered our eyes. The Earth which supported us was still a gelatinous, diaphanous mass, growing more and more firm and opaque, beginning from the centre where a kind of yolk was thickening; but still our eyes managed to penetrate through it, illuminated as it was by that first Sun. And in the midst of this kind of transparent bubble we saw a shadow moving, as if swimming and flying. And our mother said: 'Daughter!'

We all recognized G'd(w)^n: frightened perhaps by the Sun's catching fire, following a reaction of her shy spirit, she had sunk into the condensing matter of the Earth, and now she was trying to clear a path for herself in the depths of the planet, and she looked like a gold and silver butterfly as she passed into a zone that was still illuminated and diaphanous or vanished into the sphere of shadow that was growing wider and wider.

'G'd(w)^n! G'd(w)^n!' we shouted and flung ourselves on the ground, also trying to clear a way, to reach her. But the Earth's surface now was coagulating more and more into a porous husk, and my brother Rwzfs, who had managed to stick his head into a fissure, was almost strangled.

Then she was seen no more: the solid zone now occupied the whole central part of the planet. My sister had remained in there, and I never found out whether she had stayed buried in those depths or whether she had reached safety on the other side until I met her, much later, at Canberra in 1912, married to a certain Sullivan, a retired railwayman, so changed I hardly recognized her.

We got up. Mr Hnw and Granny were in front of us, crying, surrounded by pale blue-and-gold flames.

'Rwzfs! Why have you set fire to Granny?' Father began to scold, but, turning towards my brother, he saw that Rwzfs was also enveloped in flames. And so was my father, and my mother, too, and I – we were all burning in the fire. Or rather: we weren't burning, we were immersed in it as in a dazzling forest; the flames shot high over the whole surface of the planet, a fiery air in which we could run and float and fly, and we were gripped by a kind of new joy.

The Sun's radiations were burning the envelopes of the

planets, made of helium and hydrogen: in the sky, where our uncles and aunt were, fiery globes spun, dragging after them long beards of gold and turquoise, as a comet drags its tail.

The darkness came back. By now we were sure that everything that could possibly happen had happened, and 'yes, this is the end,' Grandmother said, 'mind what us old folks say . . .' Instead, the Earth had merely made one of its turns. It was night. Everything was just beginning.

A Sign in Space

Situated in the external zone of the Milky Way, the Sun takes about two hundred million years to make a complete revolution of the galaxy.

Right, that's how long it takes, not a day less – *Qfwfq said* – once, as I went past, I drew a sign at a point in space, just so I could find it again two hundred million years later, when we went by the next time around. What sort of sign? It's hard to explain because if I say sign to you, you immediately think of a something that can be distinguished from a something else, but nothing could be distinguished from anything there; you immediately think of a sign made with some implement or with your hands, and then when you take the implement or your hands away, the sign remains, but in those days there were no implements or even hands, or teeth, or noses, all things that came along afterwards, a long time afterwards. As to the form a sign should have, you say it's no problem because, whatever form it may be given, a sign only has to serve as a sign, that is, be different or else the same as other signs: here again it's easy for you young ones to talk, but in that period I didn't have any examples to follow, I couldn't say I'll make it the same or I'll make it different, there were no things to copy, nobody knew what a line was, straight or curved, or even a dot, or a protuberance or a cavity. I conceived the idea of making a sign, that's true enough, or rather, I conceived the idea of considering a sign a something that I felt like making, so when, at that point in space and not in another, I made something, meaning to make a sign, it turned out that I really had made a sign, after all.

In other words, considering it was the first sign ever made in the universe, or at least in the circuit of the Milky Way, I must admit it came out very well. Visible? What a question! Who had eyes to see with in those days? Nothing had ever been seen by anything, the question never even arose. Recognizable, yes, beyond any possibility of error: because all the other points in space were the same, indistinguishable, and instead, this one had the sign on it.

So as the planets continued their revolutions, and the solar system went on in its own, I soon left the sign far behind me, separated from it by the endless fields of space. And I couldn't help thinking about when I would come back and encounter it again, and how I would know it, and how happy it would make me, in that anonymous expanse, after I had spent a hundred thousand light-years without meeting anything familiar, nothing for hundreds of centuries, for thousands of millennia; I'd come back and there it would be in its place, just as I had left it, simple and bare, but with that unmistakable imprint, so to speak, that I had given it.

Slowly the Milky Way revolved, with its fringe of constellations and planets and clouds, and the Sun along with the rest, towards the edge. In all that circling, only the sign remained still, in an ordinary spot, out of all the orbit's reach (to make it, I had leaned over the border of the galaxy a little, so it would remain outside and all those revolving worlds wouldn't crash into it), in an ordinary point that was no longer ordinary since it was the only point that was surely there, and which could be used as a reference point to distinguish other points.

I thought about it day and night; in fact, I couldn't think about anything else; actually, this was the first opportunity I had had to think something; or I should say: to think something had never been possible, first because there were no things to think about, and second because signs to think of them by were lacking, but from the moment there was that sign, it was possible for someone thinking to think of a sign, and therefore that one, in the sense that the sign was the thing you could think about and also the sign of the thing thought, namely, itself.

So the situation was this: the sign served to mark a place but at the same time it meant that in that place there was a sign (something far more important because there were plenty of places but there was only one sign) and also at the same time that sign was mine, the sign of me, because it was the only sign I had ever made and I was the only one who had ever made signs. It was like a name, the name of that point, and also my name that I had signed on that spot; in short, it was the only name available for everything that required a name.

Transported by the sides of the galaxy, our world went navigating through distant spaces, and the sign stayed where I had left it to mark that spot, and at the same time it marked me, I carried it with me, it inhabited me, possessed me entirely, came between me and everything with which I might have attempted to establish a relationship. As I waited to come back and meet it again, I could try to derive other signs from it and combinations of signs, series of similar signs and contrasts of different signs. But already tens and tens of thousands of millennia had gone by since the moment when I had made it (rather, since the few seconds in which I had scrawled it down in the constant movement of the Milky Way) and now, just when I needed to bear in mind its every detail (the slightest uncertainty about its form made uncertain the possible distinctions between it and other signs I might make), I realized that, though I recalled its general outline, its overall appearance, still something about it eluded me, I mean if I tried to break it down into its various elements, I couldn't remember whether, between one part and the other, it went like this or like that. I needed it there in front of me, to study, to consult, but instead it was still far away, I didn't yet know how far, because I had made it precisely in order to know the time it would take me to see it again, and until I had found it once more, I wouldn't know. Now, however, it wasn't my motive in making it that mattered to me, but how it was made, and I started inventing hypotheses about this how, and theories according to which a certain sign had to be perforce in a certain way, or else, proceeding by exclusion, I tried to eliminate all the less probable types of sign to arrive at the right one, but all these imaginary signs vanished inevitably because that first sign was missing as a term of comparison. As I racked my brain like this (while the galaxy went on turning wakefully in its bed of soft emptiness and the atoms burned and radiated) I realized I had lost by now even that confused notion of my sign, and I succeeded in conceiving only interchangeable fragments of signs, that is, smaller signs within the large one, and every change of these signs-within-the-sign changed the sign itself into a completely different one; in short, I had completely forgotten what my sign was like and, try as I might, it wouldn't come back to my mind.

Did I despair? No, this forgetfulness was annoying, but not irreparable. Whatever happened, I knew the sign was there waiting for me, quiet and still. I would arrive, I would find it again, and I would then be able to pick up the thread of my meditations. At a rough guess, I calculated we had completed half of our galactic revolution: I had only to be patient, the second half always seemed to go by more quickly. Now I just had to remember the sign existed and I would pass it again.

Day followed day, and then I knew I must be near. I was furiously impatient because I might encounter the sign at any moment. It's here, no, a little further on, now I'll count up to a hundred ... Had it disappeared? Had we already gone past it? I didn't know. My sign had perhaps remained who knows where, behind, completely remote from the revolutionary orbit of our system. I hadn't calculated the oscillations to which, especially in those days, the celestial bodies' fields of gravity were subject, and which caused them to trace irregular orbits, cut like the flower of a dahlia. For about a hundred millennia I tormented myself, going over my calculations: it turned out that our course touched that spot not every galactic year but only every three, that is, every six hundred million solar years. When you've waited two hundred million years, you can also wait six hundred; and I waited; the way was long but I wasn't on foot, after all; astride the galaxy I travelled through the light-years, galloping over the planetary and stellar orbits as if I were on a horse whose shoes struck sparks; I was in a state of mounting excitement; I felt I was going forth to conquer the only thing that mattered to me, sign and dominion and name ...

I made the second circuit, the third. I was there. I let out a yell. At a point which had to be that very point, in the place of my sign, there was a shapeless scratch, a bruised, chipped abrasion of space. I had lost everything: the sign, the point, the thing that caused me – being the one who had made the sign at that point – to be me. Space, without a sign, was once again a chasm, the void, without beginning or end, nauseating, in which everything – including me – was lost. (And don't come telling me that, to fix a point, my sign and the erasure of my sign amounted to the same thing; the erasure was the negation of the sign, and therefore didn't serve to distinguish one point from the preceding and successive points.)

I was disheartened and for many light-years I let myself be dragged along as if I were unconscious. When I finally raised my eyes (in the meanwhile, sight had begun in our world, and, as a result, also life), I saw what I would never have expected to see. I saw it, the sign, but not that one, a similar sign, a sign unquestionably copied from mine, but one I realized immediately couldn't be mine, it was so squat and careless and clumsily pretentious, a wretched counterfeit of what I had meant to indicate with that sign whose ineffable purity I could only now – through contrast – recapture. Who had played this trick on me? I couldn't figure it out. Finally, a plurimillennial chain of deductions led me to the solution: on another planetary system which performed its galactic revolution before us, there was a certain Kgwgk (the name I deduced afterwards, in the later era of names), a spiteful type, consumed with envy, who had erased my sign in a vandalistic impulse and then, with vulgar artifice, had attempted to make another.

It was clear that his sign had nothing to mark except Kgwgk's intention to imitate my sign, which was beyond all comparison. But at that moment the determination not to let my rival get the better of me was stronger than any other desire; I wanted immediately to make a new sign in space, a real sign that would make Kgwgk die of envy. About seven hundred millions of years had gone by since I had first tried to make a sign, but I fell to work with a will. Now things were different, however, because the world, as I mentioned, was beginning to produce an image of itself, and in everything a form was beginning to correspond to a function, and the forms of that time, we believed, had a long future ahead of them (instead, we were wrong: take – to give you a fairly recent example – the dinosaurs), and therefore in this new sign of mine you could perceive the influence of our new way of looking at things, call it style if you like, that special way that everything had to be, there, in a certain fashion. I must say I was truly satisfied with it, and I no longer regretted that first sign that had been erased, because this one seemed vastly more beautiful to me.

But in the duration of that galactic year we already began to realize that the world's forms had been temporary up until then, and that they would change, one by one. And this awareness was accompanied by a certain annoyance with the old images, so that even their memory was intolerable. I began to be tormented by a thought: I had left that sign in space, that sign which had seemed so beautiful and original to me and so suited to its function, and which now, in my memory, seemed inappropriate, in all its pretension, a sign chiefly of an antiquated way of conceiving signs and of my foolish acceptance of an order of things I ought to have been wise enough to break away from in time. In other words, I was ashamed of that sign which went on through the centuries, being passed by worlds in flight, making a ridiculous spectacle of itself and of me and of that temporary way we had had of seeing things. I blushed when I remembered it (and I remembered it constantly), blushes that lasted whole geological eras: to hide my shame I crawled into the craters of the volcanoes, in remorse I sank my teeth into the caps of the glaciations that covered the continents. I was tortured by the thought that Kgwgk, always preceding me in the circumnavigation of the Milky Way, would see the sign before I could erase it, and boor that he was, he would mock me and make fun of me, contemptuously repeating the sign in rough caricatures in every corner of the circumgalactic sphere.

Instead, this time the complicated astral timekeeping was in my favour. Kgwgk's constellation didn't encounter the sign, whereas our solar system turned up there punctually at the end of the first revolution, so close that I was able to erase the whole thing with the greatest care.

Now, there wasn't a single sign of mine in space. I could start drawing another, but I knew that signs also allow others to judge the one who makes them, and that in the course of a galactic year tastes and ideas have time to change, and the way of regarding the earlier ones depends on what comes afterwards; in short, I was afraid a sign that now might seem perfect to me, in two hundred or six hundred million years would make me look absurd. Instead, in my nostalgia, the first sign, brutally rubbed out by Kgwgk, remained beyond the attacks of time and its changes, the sign created before the beginning of forms, which was to contain something that would have survived all forms, namely the fact of being a sign and nothing else.

Making signs that weren't that sign no longer held any interest for me; and I had forgotten that sign now, billions of years before. So, unable to make true signs, but wanting somehow to annoy Kgwgk, I started making false signs, notches in space, holes, stains, little tricks that only an incompetent creature like Kgwgk could mistake for signs. And still he furiously got rid of them with his erasings (as I could see in later revolutions), with a determination that must have cost him much effort. (Now I scattered these false signs liberally through space, to see how far his simple-mindedness would go.)

Observing these erasures, one circuit after the next (the galaxy's revolutions had now become for me a slow, boring voyage without goal or expectation), I realized something: as the galactic years passed the erasures tended to fade in space, and beneath them what I had drawn at those points, my false signs – as I called them – began to reappear. This discovery, far from displeasing me, filled me with new hope. If Kgwgk's erasures were erased, the first he had made, there at that point, must have disappeared by now, and my sign must have returned to its pristine visibility!

So expectation was revived, to lend anxiety to my days. The galaxy turned like an omelette in its heated pan, itself both frying pan and golden egg; and I was frying, with it, in my impatience.

But, with the passing of the galactic years, space was no longer that uniformly barren and colourless expanse. The idea of fixing with signs the points where we passed – as it had come to me and to Kgwgk – had occurred to many, scattered over billions of planets of other solar systems, and I was constantly running into one of these things, or a pair, or even a dozen, simple two-dimensional scrawls, or else three-dimensional solids (polyhedrons, for example), or even things constructed with more care, with the fourth dimension and everything. So it happened that I reached the point of my sign, and I found five, all there. And I wasn't able to recognize my own. It's this one, no, that; no, no, that one seems too modern, but it could also be the most ancient; I don't recognize my hand in that one, I would never have wanted to make it like that . . . And meanwhile the galaxy ran through space and left behind those signs old and new and I still hadn't found mine.

I'm not exaggerating when I say that the galactic years that followed were the worst I had ever lived through. I went on looking, and signs kept growing thicker in space; from all the worlds anybody who had an opportunity invariably left his mark in space somehow; and our world, too, every time I turned, I found more crowded, so that world and space seemed the mirror of each other, both minutely adorned with hieroglyphics and ideograms, each of which might be a sign and might not be: a calcareous concretion on basalt, a crest raised by the wind on the clotted sand of the desert, the arrangement of the eyes in a peacock's tail (gradually, living among signs had led us to see signs in countless things that, before, were there, marking nothing but their own presence; they had been transformed into the sign of themselves and had been added to the series of signs made on purpose by those who meant to make a sign), the fire-streaks against a wall of schistose rock, the four-hundred-and-twenty-seventh groove – slightly crooked – of the cornice of a tomb's pediment, a sequence of streaks on a video during a thunderstorm (the series of signs was multiplied in the series of the signs of signs, of signs repeated countless times always the same and always somehow different because to the purposely made sign you had to add the sign that had happened there by chance), the badly inked tail of the letter *R* in an evening newspaper joined to a thready imperfection in the paper, one among the eight hundred thousand flakings of a tarred wall in the Melbourne docks, the curve of a graph, a skid-mark on the asphalt, a chromosome . . . Every now and then I'd start: that's the one! And for a second I was sure I had rediscovered my sign, on the Earth or in space, it made no difference, because through the signs a continuity had been established with no precise boundaries any more.

In the universe now there was no longer a container and a thing contained, but only a general thickness of signs superimposed and coagulated, occupying the whole volume of space; it was constantly being dotted, minutely, a network of lines and scratches and reliefs and engravings; the universe was scrawled over on all sides, along all its dimensions. There was no longer any way to establish a point of reference: the galaxy went on turning but I could no longer count the revolutions, any point could be the point of departure, any sign heaped up with the others could be mine, but discovering it would have served no purpose, because it was clear that, independent of signs, space didn't exist and perhaps had never existed.

All at One Point

Through the calculations begun by Edwin P. Hubble on the galaxies'
velocity of recession, we can establish the moment when all the
universe's matter was concentrated in a single point, before it began
to expand in space.

Naturally, we were all there – *old Qfwfq said* – where else
could we have been? Nobody knew then that there could be
space. Or time either: what use did we have for time, packed
in there like sardines?

I say 'packed like sardines', using a literary image: in reality
there wasn't even space to pack us into. Every point of each
of us coincided with every point of each of the others in a
single point, which was where we all were. In fact, we didn't
even bother one another, except for personality differences,
because when space doesn't exist, having somebody unpleasant like Mr Pber^t Pber^d underfoot all the time is the
most irritating thing.

How many of us were there? Oh, I was never able to
figure that out, not even approximately. To make a count,
we would have had to move apart, at least a little, and instead
we all occupied that same point. Contrary to what you
might think, it wasn't the sort of situation that encourages
sociability; I know, for example, that in other periods neighbours called on one another; but there, because of the fact

that we were all neighbours, nobody even said good morning or good evening to anybody else.

In the end each of us associated only with a limited number of acquaintances. The ones I remember most are Mrs Ph(i)Nk$_o$, her friend De XuaeauX, a family of immigrants by the name of Z'zu, and Mr Pber^t Pber^d, whom I just mentioned. There was also a cleaning woman – 'maintenance staff' she was called – only one, for the whole universe, since there was so little room. To tell the truth, she had nothing to do all day long, not even dusting – inside one point not even a grain of dust can enter – so she spent all her time gossiping and complaining.

Just with the people I've already named we would have been overcrowded; but you have to add all the stuff we had to keep piled up in there: all the material that was to serve afterwards to form the universe, now dismantled and concentrated in such a way that you weren't able to tell what was later to become part of astronomy (like the nebula of Andromeda) from what was assigned to geography (the Vosges, for example) or to chemistry (like certain beryllium isotopes). And on top of that, we were always bumping against the Z'zu family's household goods: camp beds, mattresses, baskets; these Z'zus, if you weren't careful, with the excuse that they were a large family, would begin to act as if they were the only ones in the world: they even wanted to hang lines across our point to dry their washing.

But the others also had wronged the Z'zus, to begin with, by calling them 'immigrants', on the pretext that, since the others had been there first, the Z'zus had come later. This was mere unfounded prejudice – that seems obvious to me – because neither before nor after existed, nor any place to immigrate from, but there were those who insisted that the concept of 'immigrant' could be understood in the abstract, outside of space and time.

It was what you might call a narrow-minded attitude, our outlook at that time, very petty. The fault of the environment in which we had been reared. An attitude that, basically, has remained in all of us, mind you: it keeps cropping up even today, if two of us happen to meet – at the bus stop, at the cinema, at an international dentists' convention – and start reminiscing about the old days. We say hello – at times somebody recognizes me, at other times I recognize somebody – and we promptly start asking about this one and that one (even if each remembers only a few of those remembered by the others), and so we start in again on the old disputes, the slanders, the denigrations. Until somebody mentions Mrs Ph(i)Nk$_0$ – every conversation finally gets around to her – and then, all of a sudden, the pettiness is put aside, and we feel uplifted, filled with a blissful, generous emotion. Mrs Ph(i)Nk$_0$, the only one that none of us has forgotten and that we all regret. Where has she ended up? I have long since stopped looking for her: Mrs Ph(i)Nk$_0$, her bosom, her thighs, her orange dressing gown – we'll never meet her again, in this system of galaxies or in any other.

Let me make one thing clear: this theory that the universe, after having reached an extremity of rarefaction, will be condensed again has never convinced me. And yet many of us are counting only on that, continually making plans for the time when we'll all be back there again. Last month, I went into the bar here on the corner and whom did I see? Mr Pber^t Pber^d. 'What's new with you? How do you happen to be in this neighbourhood?' I learned that he's the agent for a plastics firm, in Pavia. He's the same as ever, with his silver tooth, his loud braces. 'When we go back there,' he said to me, in a whisper, 'the thing we have to make sure of is, this time, certain people remain out . . . You know who I mean: those Z'zus . . .'

I would have liked to answer him by saying that I've heard a number of people make the same remark, concluding: 'You know who I mean . . . Mr Pber^t Pber^d . . .'

To avoid the subject, I hastened to say: 'What about Mrs Ph(i)Nk$_o$? Do you think we'll find her back there again?'

'Ah, yes . . . She, by all means . . .' he said, turning purple.

For all of us the hope of returning to that point means, above all, the hope of being once more with Mrs Ph(i)Nk$_o$. (This applies even to me, though I don't believe in it.) And in that bar, as always happens, we fell to talking about her, and were moved; even Mr Pber^t Pber^d's unpleasantness faded, in the face of that memory.

Mrs Ph(i)Nk$_o$'s great secret is that she never aroused any jealousy among us. Or any gossip, either. The fact that she went to bed with her friend Mr De XuaeauX was well known. But in a point, if there's a bed, it takes up the whole point, so it isn't a question of *going* to bed, but of *being* there, because anybody in the point is also in the bed. Consequently, it was inevitable that she should be in bed also with each of us. If she had been another person, there's no telling all the things that would have been said about her. It was the cleaning woman who always started the slander, and the others didn't have to be coaxed to imitate her. On the subject of the Z'zu family – for a change! – the horrible things we had to hear: father, daughters, brothers, sisters, mother, aunts: nobody showed any hesitation even before the most sinister insinuation. But with her it was different: the happiness I derived from her was the joy of being concealed, punctiform, in her, and of protecting her, punctiform, in me; it was at the same time vicious contemplation (thanks to the promiscuity of the punctiform convergence of us all in her) and also chastity (given her punctiform impenetrability). In short: what more could I ask?

And all of this, which was true of me, was true also for each of the others. And for her: she contained and was contained with equal happiness, and she welcomed us and loved and inhabited all equally.

We got along so well all together, so well that something extraordinary was bound to happen. It was enough for her to say, at a certain moment: 'Oh, if I only had some room, how I'd like to make some tagliatelle for you boys!' And in that moment we all thought of the space that her round arms would occupy, moving backwards and forwards with the rolling pin over the dough, her bosom leaning over the great mound of flour and eggs which cluttered the wide board while her arms kneaded and kneaded, white and shiny with oil up to the elbows; we thought of the space that the flour would occupy, and the wheat for the flour, and the fields to raise the wheat, and the mountains from which the water would flow to irrigate the fields, and the grazing lands for the herds of calves that would give their meat for the sauce; of the space it would take for the Sun to arrive with its rays, to ripen the wheat; of the space for the Sun to condense from the clouds of stellar gases and burn; of the quantities of stars and galaxies and galactic masses in flight through space which would be needed to hold suspended every galaxy, every nebula, every sun, every planet, and at the same time we thought of it, this space was inevitably being formed, at the same time that Mrs Ph(i)Nk$_0$ was uttering those words: '. . . ah, what tagliatelle, boys!' the point that contained her and all of us was expanding in a halo of distance in light-years and light-centuries and billions of light-millennia, and we were being hurled to the four corners of the universe (Mr

Pber^t Pber^d all the way to Pavia), and she, dissolved into I don't know what kind of energy-light-heat, she, Mrs Ph(i)Nk$_o$, she who in the midst of our closed, petty world had been capable of a generous impulse, 'Boys, the tagliatelle I would make for you!', a true outburst of general love, initiating at the same moment the concept of space and, properly speaking, space itself, and time, and universal gravitation, and the gravitating universe, making possible billions and billions of suns, and of planets, and fields of wheat, and Mrs Ph(i)Nk$_o$s, scattered through the continents of the planets, kneading with floury, oil-shiny, generous arms, and she lost at that very moment, and we, mourning her loss.

Without Colours

Before forming its atmosphere and its oceans, the Earth must have resembled a grey ball revolving in space. As the Moon does now; where the ultraviolet rays radiated by the Sun arrive directly, all colours are destroyed, which is why the cliffs of the lunar surface, instead of being coloured like Earth's, are of a dead, uniform grey. If the Earth displays a varicoloured countenance, it is thanks to the atmosphere, which filters that murderous light.

A bit monotonous – *Qfwfq confirmed* – but restful, all the same. I could go for miles and miles at top speed, the way you can move where there isn't any air about, and all I could see was grey upon grey. No sharp contrasts: the only really white white, if there was any, lay in the centre of the Sun and you couldn't even begin to approach it with your eyes; and as far as really black black is concerned, there wasn't even the darkness of night, because all the stars were constantly visible. Uninterrupted horizons opened before me with mountain chains just beginning to emerge, grey mountains, above grey rocky plains; and though I crossed continent after continent I never came to a shore, because oceans and lakes and rivers were still lying underground somewhere or other.

You rarely met anyone in those days: there were so few of us! To survive with that ultraviolet you couldn't be too demanding. Above all the lack of atmosphere asserted itself in many ways, you take meteors for example: they fell like hail from all the points of space, because then we didn't have the stratosphere where nowadays they strike, as if on a roof, and disintegrate. Then there was the silence: no use shouting! Without any air to vibrate, we were all deaf and dumb. The temperature? There was nothing around to retain the Sun's heat: when night fell it was so cold you could freeze stiff. Fortunately, the Earth's crust warmed us from below, with all those molten minerals which were being compressed in the bowels of the planet. The nights were short (like the days: the Earth turned around faster); I slept huddled up to a very warm rock; the dry cold all around was pleasant. In other words, as far as the climate went, to tell you the truth, I wasn't so badly off.

Among the countless indispensable things we had to do without, the absence of colours – as you can imagine – was the least of our problems; even if we had known they existed, we would have considered them an unsuitable luxury. The only drawback was the strain on your eyes when you had to hunt for something or someone, because with everything equally colourless no form could be clearly distinguished from what was behind it or around it. You could barely make out a moving object: a meteor fragment as it rolled, or the serpentine yawning of a seismic chasm, or a lapillus being ejected from a volcano.

That day I was running through a kind of amphitheatre of porous, spongy rocks, all pierced with arches beyond which other arches opened; a very uneven terrain where the absence of colour was streaked by distinguishable concave shadows. And among the pillars of these colourless arches I saw a kind of colourless flash running swiftly, disappearing, then reappearing further on: two flattened glows that appeared and disappeared abruptly; I still hadn't realized what they were, but I was already in love and running, in pursuit of the eyes of Ayl.

I went into a sandy wasteland: I proceeded, sinking down among dunes which were always somehow different and yet almost the same. Depending on the point from which you looked at them, the crests of the dunes seemed the outlines of reclining bodies. There you could almost make out the form of an arm folded over a tender breast, with the palm open under a resting cheek; further on, a young foot with a slender big toe seemed to emerge. As I stopped to observe those possible analogies, a full minute went by before I realized that, before my eyes, I didn't have a sandy ridge but the object of my pursuit.

She was lying, colourless, overcome with sleep, on the colourless sand. I sat down nearby. It was the season – as I know now – when the ultraviolet era was approaching its end on our planet; a way of life about to finish was displaying its supreme peak of beauty. Nothing so beautiful had ever run over the Earth, as the creature I had before my eyes.

Ayl opened her eyes. She saw me. At first I believe she couldn't distinguish me – as had happened to me, with her – from the rest of that sandy world; then she seemed to recognize in me the unknown presence that had pursued her and she was frightened. But in the end she became aware of our common substance and there was a half-timid, half-smiling palpitation in the look she gave me, which caused me to emit a silent whimper of happiness.

I started conversing, all in gestures. 'Sand. Not-sand,' I said, first pointing to our surroundings, then to the two of us.

She nodded yes, she had understood.

'Rock. Not-rock,' I said, to continue that line of reasoning.

It was a period in which we didn't have many concepts at our disposal: to indicate what we two were, for example, what we had in common and what was different, was not an easy undertaking.

'I. You-not-I,' I tried to explain, with gestures.

She was irked.

'Yes. You-like-me, but only so much,' I corrected myself.

She was a bit reassured, but still suspicious.

'I, you, together, run run,' I tried to say.

She burst out laughing and ran off.

We ran along the crest of the volcanoes. In the noon greyness Ayl's flying hair and the tongues of flame that rose from the craters were mingled in a wan, identical fluttering of wings.

'Fire. Hair,' I said to her. 'Fire same hair.'

She seemed convinced.

'Not beautiful?' I asked.

'Beautiful,' she answered.

The Sun was already sinking into a whitish sunset. On a crag of opaque rocks, the rays, striking sidelong, made some of the rocks shine.

'Stones there not same. Beautiful, eh?' I said.

'No,' she answered, and looked away.

'Stones there beautiful, eh?' I insisted, pointing to the shiny grey of the stones.

'No.' She refused to look.

'To you, I, stones there!' I offered her.

'No. Stones here!' Ayl answered and grasped a handful of the opaque ones. But I had already run ahead.

I came back with the glistening stones I had collected, but I had to force her to take them.

'Beautiful!' I tried to persuade her.

'No!' she protested, but she looked at them; removed now

from the Sun's reflections, they were opaque like the other stones; and only then did she say: 'Beautiful!'

Night fell, the first I had spent not embracing a rock, and perhaps for this reason it seemed cruelly shorter to me. The light tended at every moment to erase Ayl, to cast a doubt on her presence, but the darkness restored my certainty she was there.

The day returned, to paint the Earth with grey; and my gaze moved around and didn't see her. I let out a mute cry: 'Ayl! Why have you run off?' But she was in front of me and was looking for me, too; she couldn't see me and silently shouted: 'Qfwfq! Where are you?' Until our eyesight darkened, examining that sooty luminosity and recognizing the outline of an eyebrow, an elbow, a thigh.

Then I wanted to shower Ayl with presents, but nothing seemed to me worthy of her. I hunted for everything that was in some way detached from the uniform surface of the world, everything marked by a speckling, a stain. But I was soon forced to realize that Ayl and I had different tastes, if not downright opposite ones: I was seeking a new world beyond the pallid patina that imprisoned everything, I examined every sign, every crack (to tell the truth something was beginning to change: in certain points the colourlessness seemed shot through with variegated flashes); instead, Ayl was a happy inhabitant of the silence that reigns where all vibration is excluded; for her anything that looked likely to break the absolute visual neutrality was a harsh discord; beauty began for her only where the greyness had extinguished even the remotest desire to be anything other than grey.

How could we understand each other? Nothing in the world that lay before our eyes was sufficient to express what we felt for each other, but while I was in a fury to wrest

unknown vibrations from things, she wanted to reduce everything to the colourless beyond of their ultimate substance.

A meteorite crossed the sky, its trajectory passing in front
of the Sun; its fluid and fiery envelope for an instant acted as
a filter to the Sun's rays, and all of a sudden the world was
immersed in a light never seen before. Purple chasms gaped
at the foot of orange cliffs, and my violet hands pointed to
the flaming green meteor while a thought for which words
did not yet exist tried to burst from my throat:

'This for you! From me this for you, yes, yes, beautiful!'

At the same time I wheeled around, eager to see the new
way Ayl would surely shine in the general transfiguration;
but I didn't see her: as if in that sudden shattering of the
colourless glaze, she had found a way to hide herself, to slip
off among the crevices in the mosaic.

'Ayl! Don't be frightened, Ayl! Show yourself and look!'

But already the meteorite's arc had moved away from the
Sun, and the Earth was reconquered by its perennial grey,
now even greyer to my dazzled eyes, and indistinct, and
opaque, and there was no Ayl.

She had really disappeared. I sought her through a long
throbbing of days and nights. It was the era when the world
was testing the forms it was later to assume: it tested them
with the material it had available, even if it wasn't the most
suitable, since it was understood that there was nothing
definitive about the trials. Trees of smoke-coloured lava
stretched out twisted branches from which hung thin leaves
of slate. Butterflies of ash flying over clay meadows hovered
above opaque crystal daisies. Ayl might be the colourless
shadow swinging from a branch of the colourless forest or
bending to pick grey mushrooms under grey clumps of
bushes. A hundred times I thought I glimpsed her and a
hundred times I thought I lost her again. From the wastelands

I moved to the inhabited localities. At that time, sensing the changes that would take place, obscure builders were shaping premature images of a remote, possible future. I crossed a piled-up metropolis of stones; I went through a mountain pierced with passageways like an anchorite's retreat; I reached a port that opened upon a sea of mud; I entered a garden where, from sandy beds, tall menhirs rose into the sky.

The grey stone of the menhirs was covered with a pattern of barely indicated grey veins. I stopped. In the centre of this park, Ayl was playing with her female companions. They were tossing a quartz ball into the air and catching it.

Someone threw it too hard, the ball came within my reach, and I caught it. The others scattered to look for it; when I saw Ayl alone, I threw the ball into the air and caught it again. Ayl ran over; hiding, I threw the quartz ball, drawing Ayl further and further away. Finally I showed myself; she scolded me, then laughed; and so we went on, playing, through strange regions.

At that time the strata of the planet were laboriously trying to establish an equilibrium through a series of earthquakes. Every now and then the ground was shaken by one, and between Ayl and me crevasses opened across which we threw the quartz ball back and forth. These chasms gave the elements compressed in the heart of the Earth an avenue of escape, and now we saw outcroppings of rock emerge, or fluid clouds, or boiling jets spurt up.

As I went on playing with Ayl, I noticed that a gassy layer had spread over the Earth's crust, like a low fog slowly rising. A moment before it had reached our ankles, and now we were in it up to our knees, then to our hips . . . At that sight, a shadow of uncertainty and fear grew in Ayl's eyes; I didn't want to alarm her, and so, as if nothing were happening, I went on with our game; but I, too, was anxious.

It was something never seen before: an immense fluid bubble was swelling around the Earth and completely enfolding it; soon it would cover us from head to foot, and who could say what the consequences would be?

I threw the ball to Ayl beyond a crack opening in the ground, but my throw proved inexplicably shorter than I had intended and the ball fell into the gap; the ball must have become suddenly very heavy; no, it was the crack that had suddenly yawned enormously, and now Ayl was far away, beyond a liquid, wavy expanse that had opened between us and was foaming against the shore of rocks, and I leaned from this shore, shouting: 'Ayl, Ayl!' and my voice, its sound, the very sound of my voice spread loudly, as I had never imagined it, and the waves rumbled still louder than my voice. In other words: it was all beyond understanding.

I put my hands to my deafened ears, and at the same moment I also felt the need to cover my nose and mouth, so as not to breathe the heady blend of oxygen and nitrogen that surrounded me, but strongest of all was the impulse to cover my eyes, which seemed ready to explode.

The liquid mass spread out at my feet had suddenly turned a new colour, which blinded me, and I exploded in an articulate cry which, a little later, took on a specific meaning: 'Ayl! The sea is blue!'

The great change so long awaited had finally taken place. On the Earth now there was air, and water. And over that newborn blue sea, the Sun – also coloured – was setting, an absolutely different and even more violent colour. So I was driven to go on with my senseless cries, like: 'How red the Sun is, Ayl! Ayl! How red!'

Night fell. Even the darkness was different. I ran looking for Ayl, emitting cries without rhyme or reason, to express what I saw: 'The stars are yellow, Ayl! Ayl!'

I didn't find her that night or the days and nights that followed. All around, the world poured out colours, constantly new, pink clouds gathered in violet cumuli which unleashed gilded lightning; after the storms long rainbows announced hues that still hadn't been seen, in all possible combinations. And chlorophyll was already beginning its progress: mosses and ferns grew green in the valleys where torrents ran. This was finally the setting worthy of Ayl's beauty; but she wasn't there! And without her all this varicoloured sumptuousness seemed useless to me, wasted.

I ran all over the Earth, I saw again the things I had once known grey, and I was still amazed at discovering fire was red, ice white, the sky pale blue, the earth brown, that rubies were ruby-coloured, and topazes the colour of topaz, and emeralds emerald. And Ayl? With all my imagination I couldn't picture how she would appear to my eyes.

I found the menhir garden, now green with trees and grasses. In murmuring pools red and blue and yellow fish were swimming. Ayl's friends were still leaping over the lawn, tossing the iridescent ball: but how changed they were! One was blonde with white skin, one brunette with olive skin, one brown-haired with pink skin, one had red hair and was dotted with countless, enchanting freckles.

'Ayl!' I cried. 'Where is she? Where is Ayl? What does she look like? Why isn't she with you?'

Her friends' lips were red, their teeth white, and their tongues and gums were pink. Pink, too, were the tips of their breasts. Their eyes were aquamarine blue, cherry-black, hazel and maroon.

'Why . . . Ayl . . .' they answered. 'She's gone . . . we don't know . . .' and they went back to their game.

I tried to imagine Ayl's hair and her skin, in every possible colour, but I couldn't picture her; and so, as I looked for her, I explored the surface of the globe.

'If she's not up here,' I thought, 'that means she must be below,' and at the first earthquake that came along, I flung myself into a chasm, down down into the bowels of the Earth.

'Ayl! Ayl!' I called in the darkness. 'Ayl, come see how beautiful it is outside!'

Hoarse, I fell silent. And at that moment Ayl's voice, soft, calm, answered me. 'Sssh. I'm here. Why are you shouting so much? What do you want?'

I couldn't see a thing. 'Ayl! Come outside with me. If you only knew . . . Outside . . .'

'I don't like it, outside . . .'

'But you, before . . .'

'Before was before. Now it's different. All that confusion has come.'

I lied. 'No, no. It was just a passing change of light. Like that time with the meteorite! It's over now. Everything is the way it used to be. Come, don't be afraid . . .' If she comes out, I thought, after the first moment of bewilderment, she'll become used to the colours, she'll be happy, and she'll understand that I lied for her own good.

'Really?'

'Why should I tell you stories? Come, let me take you outside.'

'No, you go ahead. I'll follow you.'

'But I'm impatient to see you again.'

'You'll see me only the way I like. Go ahead and don't turn around.'

The telluric shocks cleared the way for us. The strata of rock opened fanwise and we advanced through the gaps. I heard Ayl's light footsteps behind me. One more quake and we were outside. I ran along steps of basalt and granite which turned like the pages of a book: already, at the end, the breach that would lead us into the open air was tearing wide, already the Earth's crust was appearing beyond the gap, sunny and green, already the light was forcing its way towards us. There: now I would see the colours brighten also on Ayl's face . . . I turned to look at her.

I heard her scream as she drew back towards the darkness, my eyes still dazzled by the earlier light could make out nothing, then the rumble of the earthquake drowned everything, and a wall of rock suddenly rose, vertically, separating us.

'Ayl! Where are you? Try to come over to this side, quickly, before the rock settles!' And I ran along the wall looking for an opening, but the smooth, grey surface was compact, without a fissure.

An enormous chain of mountains had formed at that point. As I had been projected outwards, into the open, Ayl had remained beyond the rock wall, closed in the bowels of the Earth.

'Ayl! Where are you? Why aren't you out here?' and I looked around at the landscape that stretched away from my feet. Then, all of a sudden, those pea-green lawns where the first scarlet poppies were flowering, those canary-yellow fields which striped the tawny hills sloping down to a sea full of azure glints, all seemed so trivial to me, so banal, so false, so much in contrast with Ayl's person, with Ayl's world, with Ayl's idea of beauty, that I realized her place could never have been out here. And I realized, with grief and fear, that I had remained out here, that I would never again be able to escape those gilded and silvered gleams, those little clouds that turned from pale blue to pink, those green leaves that yellowed every autumn, and that Ayl's perfect world was lost for ever, so lost I couldn't even imagine it any more, and nothing was left that could remind me of it, even remotely, nothing except perhaps that cold wall of grey stone.

Games Without End

When the galaxies become more remote, the rarefaction of the universe is compensated for by the formation of further galaxies composed of newly created matter. To maintain a stable median density of the universe it is sufficient to create a hydrogen atom every two hundred and fifty million years for forty cubic centimetres of expanding space. (This steady-state theory, as it is known, has been opposed to the other hypothesis, that the universe was born at a precise moment as the result of a gigantic explosion.)

I was only a child, but I was already aware of it – Qfwfq narrated – I was acquainted with all the hydrogen atoms, one by one, and when a new atom cropped up, I noticed it right away. When I was a kid, the only playthings we had in the whole universe were the hydrogen atoms, and we played with them all the time, I and another youngster my age whose name was Pfwfp.

What sort of games? That's simple enough to explain. Since space was curved, we sent the atoms rolling along its curve, like so many marbles, and the kid whose atom went furthest won the game. When you made your shot you had to be careful, to calculate the effects, the trajectories, you had to know how to exploit the magnetic fields and the fields of gravity, otherwise the ball left the track and was eliminated from the contest.

The rules were the usual thing: with one atom you could hit another of your atoms and send it further ahead, or else you could knock your opponent's atom out of the way. Of course, we were careful not to throw them too hard, because when two hydrogen atoms are knocked together, click! a deuterium atom might be formed, or even a helium atom, and for the purposes of the game, such atoms were out: what's more, if one of the two belonged to your opponent, you had to give him an atom of your own to pay him back.

You know how the curve of space is shaped: a little ball would go spinning along and then one fine moment it would start off down the slope and you couldn't catch it. So, as we went on playing, the number of atoms in the game kept getting smaller, and the first to run out of atoms was the loser.

Then, right at the crucial moment, these new atoms started cropping up. Obviously, there's quite a difference between a new atom and a used one: the new atoms were shiny, bright, fresh, and moist, as if with dew. We made new rules: one new was worth three old; and the new ones, as they were formed, were to be shared between us, fifty-fifty.

In this way our game never ended, and it never became boring either, because every time we found new atoms it seemed as if the game were new as well, as if we were playing it for the first time.

Then, what with one thing and another, as the days went by, the game grew less exciting. There were no more new atoms to be seen: the ones we lost couldn't be replaced, our shots became weak, hesitant, because we were afraid to lose the few pieces still in the game, in that barren, even space.

Pfwfp was changed, too: he became absent-minded, wandered off and couldn't be found when it was his turn to shoot; I would call him, but there was never an answer, and then he would turn up half an hour later.

'Go on, it's your turn. Aren't you in the game any more?'

'Of course I'm in the game. Don't rush me. I'm going to shoot now.'

'Well, if you keep going off by yourself, we might as well stop playing!'

'Hmph! You're only making all this fuss because you're losing.'

This was true: I hadn't any atoms left, whereas Pfwfp, somehow or other, always had one in reserve. If some new atoms didn't turn up for us to share, I hadn't a hope of getting even with him.

The next time Pfwfp went off, I followed him, on tiptoe. As long as I was present, he seemed to be strolling about aimlessly, whistling: but once he was out of my sight he started trotting through space, intent, like somebody who has a definite purpose in mind. And what this purpose of his was – this treachery, as you shall see – I soon discovered: Pfwfp knew all the places where new atoms were formed and every now and then he would take a little walk, to collect them on the spot the minute they were dished up, then he would hide them. This was why he was never short of atoms to play with!

But before putting them in the game, incorrigible cheat that he was, he set about disguising them as old atoms, rubbing the film of the electrons until it was worn and dull, to make me believe this was an old atom he had had all along and had just happened to find in his pocket.

And that wasn't the whole story: I made a quick calculation of the atoms played and I realized they were only a small part of those he had stolen and hid. Was he piling up a store of hydrogen? What was he going to do with it? What did he have in mind? I suddenly had a suspicion: Pfwfp wanted to build a universe of his own, a brand-new universe.

From that moment on, I couldn't rest easy: I had to get even with him. I could have followed his example: now that I knew the places, I could have gone there a little ahead of him and grabbed the new atoms the moment they were born, before he could get his hands on them! But that would have been too simple. I wanted to catch him in a trap worthy of his own perfidy. First of all, I started making fake atoms: while he was occupied with his treacherous raids, I was in a secret storeroom of mine, pounding and mixing and kneading all the material I had at my disposal. To tell you the truth, this material didn't amount to much: photoelectric radiations, scrapings from magnetic fields, a few neutrons collected in the road; but by rolling it into balls and wetting it with saliva, I managed to make it stick together. In other words, I prepared some little corpuscles that, on close inspection, were obviously not made of hydrogen or any other identifiable element, but for somebody in a hurry, like Pfwfp, who rushed past and stuck them furtively into his pocket, they looked like real hydrogen, and spanking new.

So while he still didn't suspect a thing, I preceded him in his rounds. I had made a careful mental note of all the places.

Space is curved everywhere, but in some places it's more curved than in others: like pockets or bottlenecks or niches, where the void is crumpled up. These niches are where, every two hundred and fifty million years, there is a slight tinkling sound and a shiny hydrogen atom is formed like a pearl between the valves of an oyster. I walked past, pocketed the atom, and set the fake atom in its place. Pfwfp didn't notice a thing: predatory, greedy, he filled his pockets with that rubbish, as I was accumulating all the treasures that the universe cherished in its bosom.

The fortunes of our games underwent a change: I always had new atoms to shoot, while Pfwfp's regularly misfired. Three times he tried a roll and three times the atom crumbled to bits as if crushed in space. Now Pfwfp found one excuse after another, trying to call off the game.

'Go on,' I insisted, 'if you don't shoot, the game's mine.'

And he said: 'It doesn't count. When an atom is ruined the game's null and void, and you start over again.' This was a rule he had invented at that very moment.

I didn't give him any peace, I danced around him, leaped on his back, and chanted:

> 'Throw it throw it throw it
> If not, you lose, you know it.
> For every turn that you don't take
> An extra throw for me to make.'

'That's enough of that,' Pfwfp said, 'let's change games.'

'Aha!' I said. 'Why don't we play at flying galaxies?'

'Galaxies?' Pfwfp suddenly brightened with pleasure. 'Suits me. But you . . . you don't have a galaxy!'

'Yes, I do.'

'So do I.'

'Come on! Let's see who can send his highest!'

And I took all the new atoms I was hiding and flung them into space. At first they seemed to scatter, then they thickened together into a kind of light cloud, and the cloud swelled and swelled, and inside it some incandescent condensations were formed, and they whirled and whirled and at a certain point became a spiral of constellations never seen before, a spiral that poised, opening in a gust, then sped away as I held on to its tail and ran after it. But now I wasn't the one who made the galaxy fly, it was the galaxy that was lifting me aloft, clinging to its tail; I mean, there wasn't any height or depth now but only space, widening, and the galaxy in its midst, also opening wide, and me hanging there, making faces at Pfwfp, who was already thousands of light-years away.

Pfwfp, at my first move, had promptly dug out all his hoard, hurling it with a balanced movement as if he expected to see the coils of an endless galaxy open in the sky. But instead, nothing happened. There was a sizzling sound of radiations, a messy flash, then everything died out at once.

'Is that the best you can do?' I shouted at Pfwfp, who was yelling curses at me, green with rage:

'I'll show you, Qfwfq, you pig!'

But in the meanwhile my galaxy and I were flying among thousands of other galaxies, and mine was the newest, the envy of the whole firmament, blazing as it was with young hydrogen and the youngest carbon and newborn beryllium. The old galaxies fled us, filled with jealousy, and we, prancing and haughty, avoided them, so antiquated and ponderous to look at. As that reciprocal flight developed, we sailed across spaces that became more and more rarefied and empty: and then I saw something appear in the midst of the void, like uncertain bursts of light. These were new galaxies, formed by matter just born, galaxies even newer than mine. Soon space became filled again, and dense, like a vineyard just before vintage time, and we flew on, escaping from one another, my galaxy fleeing the younger ones as it had the older, and young and old fleeing us. And we advanced to fly through empty skies, and these skies also became peopled, and so on and on.

In one of these propagations, I heard: 'Qfwfq, you'll pay for this now, you traitor!' and I saw a brand-new galaxy flying on our trail, and there leaning forward from the very tip of the spiral, yelling threats and insults at me, was my old playmate Pfwfp.

The chase began. Where space rose, Pfwfp's galaxy, young and agile, gained ground, but on the descents, my heavier galaxy plunged ahead again.

In any kind of race there's a secret: it's all in how you take the curves. Pfwfp's galaxy tended to narrow them, mine to swing out. And as it kept broadening the curves, we were finally flung beyond the edge of space, with Pfwfp after us. We kept up the pursuit, using the system one always uses in such circumstances, that is, creating space before us as we went forward.

So there I was, with nothingness in front of me, and that nasty-faced Pfwfp after me: an unpleasant sight either way. In any case, I preferred to look ahead, and what did I see? Pfwfp, whom my eyes had just left behind me, was speeding on his galaxy directly in front of me. 'Ah!' I cried, 'now it's my turn to chase you!'

'What?' Pfwfp said, from before me or behind me, I'm not really sure which, 'I'm the one who's chasing you!'

I turned around: there was Pfwfp, still at my heels. I looked ahead again: and he was there, racing off with his back turned to me. But as I looked more closely, I saw that in front of this galaxy of his that was preceding me there was another, and that other galaxy was mine, because there I was on it, unmistakable even though seen from behind. And I turned towards the Pfwfp following me and narrowed my eyes: I saw that his galaxy was being chased by another, mine, with me on top of it, turning at that same time to look back.

And so after every Qfwfq there was a Pfwfp, and after every Pfwfp a Qfwfq, and every Pfwfp was chasing a Qfwfq, who was pursuing him and vice versa. Our distances grew a bit shorter or a bit longer, but now it was clear that one would never overtake the other, nor the other overtake one. We had lost all pleasure in this game of chase, and we weren't children any more for that matter, but now there was nothing else we could do.

The Aquatic Uncle

The first vertebrates who, in the Carboniferous period, abandoned aquatic life for terrestrial descended from the osseous, pulmonate fish whose fins were capable of rotation beneath their bodies and thus could be used as paws on the Earth.

By then it was clear that the water period was coming to an end – *old Qfwfq recalled* – those who decided to make the great move were growing more and more numerous, there wasn't a family that didn't have some loved one up on dry land, and everybody told fabulous tales of the things that could be done there, and they called back to their relatives to join them. There was no holding the young fish; they slapped their fins on the muddy banks to see if they would work as paws, as the more talented ones had already discovered. But just at that time the differences among us were becoming accentuated: there might be a family that had been living on land, say, for several generations, whose young people acted in a way that wasn't even amphibious but almost reptilian already; and there were others who lingered, still living like fish, those who, in fact, became even more fishy than they had been before.

Our family, I must say, including grandparents, was all up on the shore, padding about as if we had never known how to do anything else. If it hadn't been for the obstinacy of our

69

great-uncle N'ba N'ga, we would have long since lost all contact with the aquatic world.

Yes, we had a great-uncle who was a fish, on my paternal grandmother's side, to be precise, of the Coelacanthus family of the Devonian period (the fresh-water branch: who are, for that matter, cousins of the others – but I don't want to go into all these questions of kinship, nobody can ever follow them anyhow). So as I was saying, this great-uncle lived in certain muddy shallows, among the roots of some proto-conifers, in that inlet of the lagoon where all our ancestors had been born. He never stirred from there: at any season of the year all we had to do was push ourselves over the softer layers of vegetation until we could feel ourselves sinking into the dampness, and there below, a few palms' lengths from the edge, we could see the column of little bubbles he sent up, breathing heavily the way old folk do, or the little cloud of mud scraped up by his sharp snout, always rummaging around, more out of habit than out of the need to hunt for anything.

'Uncle N'ba N'ga! We've come to pay you a visit! Were you expecting us?' we would shout, slapping our paws and tails in the water to attract his attention. 'We've brought you some insects that grow where we live! Uncle N'ba N'ga! Have you ever seen such fat cockroaches? Taste one and see if you like it . . .'

'You can clean those revolting warts you've got with your stinking cockroaches!' Our great-uncle's answer was always some remark of this sort, or perhaps even ruder: this is how he welcomed us every time, but we paid no attention because we knew he would mellow after a little while, accept our presents gladly, and converse in politer tones.

'What do you mean, Uncle? Warts? When did you ever see any warts on us?'

This business about warts was a widespread prejudice among the old fish: a notion that, from living on dry land, we would develop warts all over our bodies, exuding liquid matter: this was true enough for the toads, but we had nothing in common with them; on the contrary, our skin, smooth and slippery, was such as no fish had ever had; and our great-uncle knew this perfectly well, but he still couldn't stop larding his talk with all the slanders and intolerance he had grown up in the midst of.

We went to visit our great-uncle once a year, the whole family together. It also gave us an opportunity to have a reunion, since we were scattered all over the continent; we could exchange bits of news, trade edible insects, and discuss old questions that were still unsettled.

Our great-uncle spoke his mind even on questions that were removed from him by miles and miles of dry land, such as the division of territory for dragonfly hunting; and he would side with this one or that one, according to his own reasoning, which was always aquatic. 'But don't you know that it's always better to hunt on the bottom and not on the water's surface? So what are you getting all upset over?'

'But, Uncle, you see: it isn't a question of hunting on the bottom or on the surface. I live at the foot of a hill, and he lives halfway up the slope . . . You know what I mean by hill, Uncle . . .'

And he said: 'You always find the best crayfish at the foot of the cliffs.' It just wasn't possible to make him accept a reality different from his own.

And yet, his opinions continued to exert an authority over all of us; in the end we asked his advice about matters he didn't begin to understand, though we knew he could be dead wrong. Perhaps his authority stemmed from the fact that he was a leftover from the past, from his way of using old figures of speech, like: 'Lower your fins there, youngster!', whose meaning we didn't grasp very clearly.

We had made various attempts to get him up on land with us, and we went on making them; indeed, on this score, the rivalry among the various branches of the family never died out, because whoever managed to take our great-uncle home with him would achieve a position of pre-eminence over the rest of our relatives. But the rivalry was pointless, because our uncle wouldn't dream of leaving the lagoon.

'Uncle, if you only knew how sorry we feel leaving you all alone, at your age, in the midst of all that dampness . . . We've had a wonderful idea . . .' someone would begin.

'I was expecting the lot of you to catch on finally,' the old fish interrupted, 'now you've got over the whim of scraping around in that drought, so it's time you came back to live like normal beings. Here there's plenty of water for all, and when it comes to food, there's never been a better season for worms. You can all dive right in, and we won't have to discuss it any further.'

'No, no, Uncle N'ba N'ga, you've got it all wrong. We wanted to take you to live with us, in a lovely little meadow . . . You'll be nice and snug; we'll dig you a little damp hole. You'll be able to turn and toss in it, just like here. And you might even try taking a few steps around the place: you'll be very good at it, just wait and see. And besides, at your time of life, the climate on land is much more suitable. So come now, Uncle N'ba N'ga, don't wait to be coaxed. Won't you come home with us?'

'No!' was our great-uncle's sharp reply, and taking a nose-dive into the water, he vanished from our sight.

'But why, Uncle? What have you got against the idea? We simply don't understand. Anyone as broad-minded as you ought to be above certain prejudices . . .'

From an angry huff of water at the surface, before the final plunge with a still-agile jerk of his tail fin, came our uncle's final answer: 'He who has fleas in his scales swims with his belly in the mud!', which must have been an idiomatic expression (similar to our own, much more concise proverb: 'If you itch, scratch'), with that term 'mud' which he insisted on using where we would say 'land'.

That was about the time when I fell in love. Lll and I spent our days together, chasing each other; no one as quick as she had ever been seen before; in the ferns, which were as tall as trees in those days, she would climb to the top in one burst, and the tops would bend almost to the ground, then she would jump down and run off again; I, with slower and somewhat clumsier movements, followed her. We ventured into zones of the interior where no print had ever marked the dry and crusty terrain; at times I stopped, frightened at having come so far from the expanse of the lagoons. But nothing seemed so far from aquatic life as she, Lll, did: the deserts of sand and stones, the prairies, the thick forests, the rocky hillocks, the quartz mountains: this was her world, a world that seemed made especially to be scanned by her oblong eyes, to be trod by her darting steps. When you looked at her smooth skin, you felt that scales had never existed.

Her relatives made me a bit ill at ease; hers was one of those families who had become established on Earth in the earliest period and had finally become convinced they had never lived anywhere else, one of those families who, by now, even laid their eggs on dry terrain, protected by a hard shell, and Lll, if you looked at her when she jumped, at her flashing movements, you could tell she had been born the way she was now, from one of those eggs warmed by sand and sun, having completely skipped the swimming, wriggling phase of the tadpole, which was still obligatory in our less evolved families.

The time had come for Lll to meet my family: and since its oldest and most authoritative member was Great-Uncle N'ba N'ga, I couldn't avoid a visit to him, to introduce my fiancée. But every time an opportunity occurred, I postponed it, out of embarrassment; knowing the prejudices among which she had been brought up, I hadn't yet dared tell Lll that my great-uncle was a fish.

One day we had wandered off to one of those damp promontories that girdle the lagoon, where the ground is made not so much of sand as of tangled roots and rotting vegetation. And Lll came out with one of her usual dares, her challenges to feats: 'Qfwfq, how long can you keep your balance? Let's see who can run closest to the edge here!' And she darted forward with her Earth-creature's leap, now slightly hesitant, however.

This time I not only felt I could follow her, but also that I could win, because my paws got a better grip on damp surfaces. 'As close to the edge as you like!' I cried. 'And even beyond it!'

'Don't talk nonsense!' she said. 'How can you run beyond the edge? It's all water there!'

Perhaps this was the opportune moment to bring up the subject of my great-uncle. 'What of that?' I said to her. 'There are those who run on this side of the edge, and those who run on the other.'

'You're saying things that make no sense at all!'

'I'm saying that my great-uncle N'ba N'ga lives in the water the way we live on the land, and he's never come out of it!'

'Ha! I'd like to meet this N'ba N'ga of yours!'

She had no sooner finished saying this than the muddied

surface of the lagoon gurgled with bubbles, moved in a little eddy, and allowed a nose, all covered with spiky scales, to appear.

'Well, here I am. What's the trouble?' Great-Uncle said, staring at Lll with eyes as round and inexpressive as stones, flapping the gills at either side of his enormous throat. Never before had my great-uncle seemed so different from the rest of us: a real monster.

'Uncle, if you don't mind . . . this is . . . I mean, I have the pleasure to present to you my future bride, Lll,' and I pointed to my fiancée, who for some unknown reason had stood erect on her hind paws, in one of her most exotic poses, certainly the least likely to be appreciated by that boorish old relative.

'And so, young lady, you've come to wet your tail a bit, eh?' my great-uncle said: a remark that in his day no doubt had been considered courtly, but to us sounded downright indecent.

I looked at Lll, convinced I would see her turn and run off with a shocked twitter. But I hadn't considered how strong her training was, her habit of ignoring all vulgarity in the world around her. 'Tell me something: those little plants there . . .' she said, nonchalantly, pointing to some rushes growing tall in the midst of the lagoon, 'where do they put down their roots?'

One of those questions you ask just to make conversation: as if she cared about those rushes! But it seemed Uncle had been waiting only for that moment to start explaining the why and the wherefore of the roots of floating trees and how you could swim among them and, indeed, how they were the very best places for hunting.

I thought he would never stop. I huffed impatiently, I tried to interrupt him. But what did that saucy Lll do?

She encouraged him! 'Oh, so you go hunting among those underwater roots? How interesting!'

I could have sunk into the ground from shame.

And he said: 'I'm not fooling! The worms you find there! You can fill your belly, all right!' And without giving it a second thought, he dived. An agile dive such as I'd never seen him make before. Or rather, he made a leap into the air – his whole length out of the water, all dotted with scales – spreading the spiky fans of his fins; then, when he had completed a fine half-circle in the air, he plunged back, head-first, and disappeared quickly with a kind of screw-motion of his crescent-shaped tail.

At this sight, I recalled the little speech I had prepared hastily to apologize to Lll, taking advantage of my uncle's departure ('You really have to understand him, you know, this mania for living like a fish has finally even made him look like a fish'), but the words died in my throat. Not even I had ever realized the full extent of my grandmother's brother's fishiness. So I just said: 'It's late, Lll, let's go . . .' and already my great-uncle was re-emerging, holding in his shark's lips a garland of worms and muddy seaweed.

It seemed too good to be true, when we finally took our leave; but as I trotted along silently behind Lll, I was thinking that now she would begin to make her comments, that the worst was still to come. But then Lll, without stopping, turned slightly towards me: 'He's very nice, your uncle,' and that was all she said. More than once in the past her irony had disarmed me; but the icy sensation that filled me at this remark was so awful that I would rather not have seen her any more than to have to face the subject again.

Instead, we went on seeing each other, going together, and the lagoon episode was never mentioned. I was still uneasy: it was no use my trying to persuade myself she had forgotten; every now and then I suspected she was remaining silent in order to embarrass me later in some spectacular way, in front of her family, or else – and, for me, this was an even worse hypothesis – she was making an effort to talk about other things only because she felt sorry for me. Then, out of a clear sky, one morning she said curtly: 'See here, aren't you going to take me to visit your uncle any more?'

In a faint voice I asked: 'Are you joking?'

Not at all; she was in earnest, she couldn't wait to go back and have a little chat with old N'ba N'ga. I was all mixed up.

That time our visit to the lagoon lasted longer. We lay on a sloping bank, all three of us: my great-uncle was nearest the water, but the two of us were half in and half out, too, so anyone seeing us from the distance, all close together, wouldn't have known who was terrestrial and who was aquatic.

The fish started in with one of his usual tirades: the superiority of water respiration to air breathing, and all his repertory of denigration. 'Now Lll will jump up and give him what for!' I thought. Instead, that day Lll was apparently using a different tactic: she argued seriously, defending our point of view, but as if she were also taking old N'ba N'ga's notions into consideration.

According to my great-uncle, the lands that had emerged were a limited phenomenon: they were going to disappear just as they had cropped up or, in any event, they would be subject to constant changes: volcanoes, glaciations, earthquakes, upheavals, changes of climate and of vegetation. And our life in the midst of all this would have to face constant transformations, in the course of which whole races would disappear, and the only survivors would be those who were prepared to change the bases of their existence so radically that the reasons why living was beautiful would be completely overwhelmed and forgotten.

This prospect was in absolute contradiction to the optimism in which we children of the coast had been brought up, and I opposed the idea with shocked protests. But for me the true, living confutation of those arguments was Lll: in her I saw the perfect, definitive form, born from the conquest of the land that had emerged; she was the sum of the new boundless possibilities that had opened. How could my great-uncle try to deny the incarnate reality of Lll? I was aflame with polemical passion, and I thought that my fiancée was being all too patient and too understanding with our opponent.

True, even for me – used as I was to hearing only grumblings and abuse from my great-uncle's mouth – this logically arranged argumentation of his came as a novelty, though it was still spiced with antiquated and bombastic expressions and was made comical by his peculiar accent. It was also amazing to hear him display a detailed familiarity – though entirely external – with the continental lands.

But Lll, with her questions, tried to make him talk as much as possible about life underwater: and, to be sure, this was the theme that elicited the most tightly knit, even emotional discourse from my great-uncle. Compared to the uncertainties of earth and air, lagoons and seas and oceans represented a future with security. Down there, changes would be very few, space and provender were unlimited, the temperature would always be steady; in short, life would be maintained as it had gone on till then, in its achieved, perfect forms, without metamorphoses or additions with dubious outcome, and every individual would be able to develop his own nature, to arrive at the essence of himself and of all things. My great-uncle spoke of the aquatic future without embellishments or illusions, he didn't conceal the problems, even serious ones, that would arise (most worrying of all, the increase of saline content); but they were problems that wouldn't upset the values and the proportions in which he believed.

'But now we gallop over valleys and mountains, Uncle!' I cried, speaking for myself but especially for Lll, who remained silent.

'Go on with you, tadpole, when you're wet again, you'll be back home!' he apostrophized, to me, resuming the tone I had always heard him use with us.

'Don't you think, Uncle, that if we wanted to learn to breathe underwater, it would be too late?' Lll asked earnestly, and I didn't know whether to feel flattered because she had called my old relative uncle or confused because certain questions (at least, so I was accustomed to think) shouldn't even be asked.

'If you're game, sweetie,' the fish said, 'I can teach you in a minute!'

Lll came out with an odd laugh, then finally began to run away, to run on and on beyond all pursuit.

I hunted for her across plains and hills, I reached the top of a basalt spur which dominated the surrounding landscape of deserts and forests surrounded by the waters. Lll was there. What she had wanted to tell me – I had understood her! – by listening to N'ba N'ga and then by fleeing and taking refuge up here was surely this: we had to live in our world thoroughly, as the old fish lived in his.

'I'll live here, the way Uncle does down there,' I shouted, stammering a bit; then I corrected myself: 'The two of us will live here, together!' because it was true that without her I didn't feel secure.

But what did Lll answer me then? I blush when I remember it even now, after all these geological eras. She answered: 'Get along with you, tadpole; it takes more than that!' And I didn't know whether she was imitating my great-uncle, to mock him and me at once, or whether she had really assumed the old nut's attitude towards his nephew, and either hypothesis was equally discouraging, because both meant she considered me at a halfway stage, a creature not at home in the one world or in the other.

Had I lost her? Suspecting this, I hastened to woo her back. I took to performing all sorts of feats: hunting flying insects, leaping, digging underground dens, wrestling with the strongest of our group. I was proud of myself, but unfortunately whenever I did something brave, she wasn't there to see me: she kept disappearing, and no one knew where she had gone off to hide.

Finally I understood: she went to the lagoon, where my great-uncle was teaching her to swim underwater. I saw them surface together: they were moving along at the same speed, like brother and sister.

'You know?' she said, gaily, 'my paws work beautifully as fins!'

'Good for you! That's a big step forward,' I couldn't help remarking, sarcastically.

It was a game, for her: I understood. But a game I didn't like. I had to recall her to reality, to the future that was awaiting her.

One day I waited for her in the midst of a wood of tall ferns which sloped to the water.

'Lll, I have to talk to you,' I said as soon as I saw her, 'you've been amusing yourself long enough. We have more important things ahead of us. I've discovered a passage in the mountains: beyond it stretches an immense stone plain, just abandoned by the water. We'll be the first to settle there, we'll populate unknown lands, you and I, and our children.'

'The sea is immense,' Lll said.

'Stop repeating that old fool's nonsense. The world belongs to those with legs, not to fish, and you know it.'

'I know that he's somebody who is somebody,' Lll said.

'And what about me?'

'There's nobody with legs who is like him.'

'And your family?'

'We've quarrelled. They don't understand anything.'

'Why, you're crazy! Nobody can turn back!'

'I can.'

'And what do you think you'll do, all alone with an old fish?'

'Marry him. Be a fish again with him. And bring still more fish into the world. Goodbye.'

And with one of those rapid climbs of hers, the last, she reached the top of a fern frond, bent it towards the lagoon, and let go in a dive. She surfaced, but she wasn't alone: the sturdy, curved tail of Great-Uncle N'ba N'ga rose near hers and, together, they cleft the waters.

It was a hard blow for me. But, after all, what could I do about it? I went on my way, in the midst of the world's transformations, being transformed myself. Every now and then, among the many forms of living beings, I encountered one who 'was somebody' more than I was: one who announced the future, the duck-billed platypus who nurses its young, just hatched from the egg; or I might encounter another who bore witness to a past beyond all return, a dinosaur who had survived into the beginning of the Cenozoic, or else – a crocodile – part of the past that had discovered a way to remain immobile through the centuries. They all had something, I know, that made them somehow superior to me, sublime, something that made me, compared to them, mediocre. And yet I wouldn't have traded places with any of them.

How Much Shall We Bet?

The logic of cybernetics, applied to the history of the universe, is in the process of demonstrating how the galaxies, the solar system, the Earth, cellular life could not help but be born. According to cybernetics, the universe is formed by a series of feedbacks, positive and negative, at first through the force of gravity that concentrates masses of hydrogen in the primitive cloud, then through nuclear force and centrifugal force which are balanced with the first. From the moment that the process is set in motion, it can only follow the logic of this chain.

Yes, but at the beginning nobody knew it – *Qfwfq explained* – I mean, you could foretell it perhaps, but instinctively, by ear, guessing. I don't want to boast, but from the start I was willing to bet that there was going to be a universe, and I hit the nail on the head; on the question of its nature, too, I won plenty of bets, with old Dean (k)yK.

When we started betting there wasn't anything yet that might lead you to foresee anything, except for a few particles spinning around, some electrons scattered here and there at random, and protons all more or less on their own. I started feeling a bit strange, as if there was going to be a change of weather (in fact, it had grown slightly cold), and so I said: 'You want to bet we're heading for atoms today?'

And Dean (k)yK said: 'Oh, cut it out. Atoms! Nothing of the sort, and I'll bet anything you say.'

So I said: 'Would you even bet ix?'

The Dean answered: 'Ix raised to the power n!'

He had no sooner finished saying this than around each proton its electron started whirling and buzzing. An enormous hydrogen cloud was condensing in space. 'You see? Full of atoms!'

'Oh, if you call *that* stuff atoms!' (k)yK said; he had the bad habit of putting up an argument, instead of admitting he had lost a bet.

We were always betting, the Dean and I, because there was really nothing else to do, and also because the only proof I existed was that I bet with him, and the only proof he existed was that he bet with me. We bet on what events would or would not take place; the choice was virtually unlimited, because up till then absolutely nothing had happened. But since there wasn't even a way to imagine how an event might be, we designated it in a kind of code: Event A, Event B, Event C, and so on, just to distinguish one from the other. What I mean is: since there were no alphabets in existence then or any other series of accepted signs, first we bet on how a series of signs might be and then we matched these possible signs with various possible events, in order to identify with sufficient precision matters that we still didn't know a thing about.

We also didn't know what we were staking because there was nothing that could serve as a stake, and so we gambled on our word, keeping an account of the bets each had won, to be added up later. All these calculations were very difficult, since numbers didn't exist then, and we didn't even have the concept of number, to begin to count, because it wasn't possible to separate anything from anything else.

This situation began to change when, in the protogalaxies, the protostars started condensing, and I quickly realized where it would all end, with that temperature rising all the time, and so I said: 'Now they're going to catch fire.'

'Nuts!' the Dean said.

'Want to bet?' I said.

'Anything you like,' he said, and wham, the darkness was shattered by all these incandescent balls that began to swell out.

'Oh, but that isn't what catching fire means . . .' (k)yK began, quibbling about words in his usual way.

By that time I had developed a system of my own, to shut him up: 'Oh, no? And what does it mean then, in your opinion?'

He kept quiet: lacking imagination as he did, when a word began to have one meaning, he couldn't conceive of its having any other.

Dean (k)yK, if you had to spend much time with him, was a fairly boring sort, without any resources, he never had anything to tell. Not that I, on the other hand, could have told much, since events worth telling about had never happened, or at least so it appeared to us. The only thing was to frame hypotheses, or rather: hypothesize on the possibility of framing hypotheses. Now, when it came to framing hypotheses of hypotheses, I had much more imagination than the Dean, and this was both an advantage and a disadvantage, because it led me to make riskier bets, so that you might say our probabilities of winning were even.

As a rule, I bet on the possibility of a certain event's taking place, whereas the Dean almost always bet against it. He had a static sense of reality, old (k)yK, if I may express myself in these terms, since between static and dynamic at that time there wasn't the difference there is nowadays, or in any case you had to be very careful in grasping it, that difference.

For example, the stars began to swell, and I said: 'How

much?' I tried to lead our predictions into the field of numbers, where he would have less to argue about.

At that time there were only two numbers: the number *e* and the number *pi*. The Dean did some figuring, by and large, and answered: 'They'll grow to *e* raised to *pi*.'

Trying to act smart! Any fool could have told that much. But matters weren't so simple, as I had realized. 'You want to bet they stop, at a certain point?'

'All right. When are they going to stop?'

And with my usual bravado, I came out with my *pi*. He swallowed it. The Dean was dumbfounded.

From that moment on we began to bet on the basis of *e* and of *pi*.

'*Pi!*' the Dean shouted, in the midst of the darkness and the scattered flashes. But instead that was the time it was *e*.

We did it all for fun, obviously; because there was nothing in it for us, as far as earning went. When the elements began to be formed, we started evaluating our bets in atoms of the rarer elements, and this is where I made a mistake. I had seen that the rarest of all was technetium, so I started betting technetium and winning, and hoarding: I built up a capital of technetium. I hadn't foreseen it was an unstable element that dissolved in radiations: suddenly I had to start all over again, from zero.

Naturally, I made some wrong bets, too, but then I got ahead again and I could allow myself a few risky prognostications.

'Now a bismuth isotope is going to come out!' I said hastily, watching the newborn elements crackle forth from the crucible of a 'supernova' star. 'Let's bet!'

Nothing of the sort: it was a polonium atom, in mint condition.

In these cases (k)yK would snigger and chuckle as if his

victories were something to be proud of, whereas he simply benefited from overbold moves on my part. Conversely, the more I went ahead, the better I understood the mechanism, and in the face of every new phenomenon, after a few rather groping bets, I could calculate my previsions rationally. The order that made one galaxy move at precisely so many million light-years from another, no more and no less, became clear to me before he caught on. After a while it was all so easy I didn't enjoy it any more.

And so, from the data I had at my disposal, I tried mentally to deduce other data, and from them still others, until I succeeded in suggesting eventualities that had no apparent connection with what we were arguing about. And I just let them fall, casually, into our conversation.

For example, we were making predictions about the curve of the galactic spirals, and all of a sudden I came out with: 'Now listen a minute, (k)yK, what do you think? Will the Assyrians invade Mesopotamia?'

He laughed, confused. 'Meso- what? When?'

I calculated quickly and blurted a date, not in years and centuries of course, because then the units of measuring time weren't conceivable in lengths of that sort, and to indicate a precise date we had to rely on formulae so complicated it would have taken a whole blackboard to write them down.

'How can you tell?'

'Come on, (k)yK, are they going to invade or not? I say they do; you say no. All right? Don't take so long about it.'

We were still in the boundless void, striped here and there by a streak or two of hydrogen around the vortexes of the first constellations. I admit it required very complicated deductions to foresee the Mesopotamian plains black with men and horses and arrows and trumpets, but, since I had nothing else to do, I could bring it off.

Instead, in such cases, the Dean always bet no, not because he believed the Assyrians wouldn't do it, but simply because he refused to think there would ever be Assyrians and Mesopotamia and the Earth and the human race.

These bets, obviously, were long-term affairs, more than the others; not like some cases, where the result was immediately known. 'You see that Sun over there, the one being formed with an ellipsoid all around it? Quick, before the planets are formed: how far will the orbits be from one another?'

The words were hardly out of my mouth when, in the space of eight or nine – what am I saying? – six or seven hundred million years, the planets started revolving each in its orbit, not a whit more narrow nor a whit wider.

I got much more satisfaction, however, from the bets we had to bear in mind for billions and billions of years, without forgetting what we had bet on, and remembering the shorter-term bets at the same time, and the number (the era of whole numbers had begun, and this complicated matters a bit) of bets each of us had won, the sum of the stakes (my advantage kept growing; the Dean was up to his ears in debt). And in addition to all this I had to dream up new bets, further and further ahead in the chain of my deductions.

'On 8 February 1926, at Santhià, in the Province of Vercelli – got that? At number 18 in Via Garibaldi – you follow me? Signorina Giuseppina Pensotti, aged twenty-two, leaves her home at quarter to six in the afternoon: does she turn right or left?'

'Mmmmm . . .' (k)yK said.

'Come on, quickly. I say she turns right . . .' And through the dust nebulae, furrowed by the orbits of the constellations, I could already see the wispy evening mist rise in the streets of Santhià, the faint light of a street lamp barely outlining the pavement in the snow, illuminating for a moment the slim shadow of Giuseppina Pensotti as she turned the corner past the Customs House and disappeared.

On the subject of what was to happen among the celestial bodies, I could stop making new bets and wait calmly to pocket my winnings from (k)yK as my predictions gradually came true. But my passion for gambling led me, from every possible event, to foresee the interminable series of events that followed, even down to the most marginal and aleatory ones. I began to combine predictions of the most immediately and easily calculated events with others that required extremely complicated operations. 'Hurry, look at the way the planets are condensing: now tell me, which is the one where an atmosphere is going to be formed? Mercury? Venus? Earth? Mars? Come on: make up your mind! And while you're about it, calculate for me the index of demographic increase on the Indian subcontinent during the British raj. What are you puzzling over? Make it snappy!'

I had started along a narrow channel beyond which events were piling up with multiplied density; I had only to seize them by the handful and throw them in the face of my competitor, who had never guessed at their existence. Once I happened to drop, almost absently, the question: 'Arsenal–Real Madrid, semifinals. Arsenal playing at home. Who wins?' and in a moment I realized that with what seemed a casual jumble of words I had hit on an infinite reserve of new combinations among the signs which compact, opaque, uniform reality would use to disguise its monotony, and I realized that perhaps the race towards the future, the race I had been the first to foresee and desire, tended only – through time and space – towards a crumbling into alternatives like this, until it would dissolve in a geometry of invisible triangles and ricochets like the course of a football among the white lines of a field as I tried to imagine them, drawn at the bottom of the luminous vortex of the planetary system, deciphering the numbers marked on the chests and backs of the players at night, unrecognizable in the distance.

By now I had plunged into this new area of possibility, gambling everything I had won before. Who could stop me? The Dean's customary bewildered incredulity only spurred me to greater risks. When I saw I was caught in a trap it was too late. I still had the satisfaction – a meagre satisfaction, this time – of being the first to be aware of it: (k)yK seemed not to catch on to the fact that luck had now come over to his side, but I counted his bursts of laughter, once rare and now becoming more and more frequent . . .

'Qfwfq, have you noticed that Pharaoh Amenhotep IV had no male issue? I've won!'

'Qfwfq, look at Pompey! He lost out to Caesar after all! I told you so!'

And yet I had worked out my calculations to their conclusion, I hadn't overlooked a single component. Even if I were to go back to the beginning, I would bet the same way as before.

'Qfwfq, under the Emperor Justinian, it was the silkworm that was imported from China to Constantinople. Not gunpowder . . . Or am I getting things mixed up?'

'No, no, you win, you win . . .'

To be sure, I had let myself go, making predictions about fleeting, impalpable events, countless predictions, and now I couldn't draw back, I couldn't correct myself. Besides, correct myself how? On the basis of what?

'You see, Balzac doesn't make Lucien de Rubempré commit suicide at the end of *Les Illusions perdues*,' the Dean said, in a triumphant, squeaky little voice he had been developing of late. 'He has him saved by Carlos Herrera, alias Vautrin.

You know? The character who was also in *Père Goriot* . . . Now then, Qfwfq, how far have we got?'

My advantage was dropping. I had saved my winnings, converted into hard currency, in a Swiss bank, but I had constantly to withdraw big sums to meet my losses. Not that I lost every time. I still won a bet now and then, even a big one, but the roles had been reversed; when I won I could no longer be sure it wasn't an accident or that, the next time, my calculations wouldn't again be proved wrong.

At the point we had reached, we needed reference libraries, subscriptions to specialized magazines, as well as a complex of electronic computers for our calculations: everything, as you know, was furnished us by a Research Foundation, to which, when we settled on this planet, we appealed for funds to finance our research. Naturally, our bets figure as an innocent game between the two of us and nobody suspects the huge sums involved in them. Officially we live on our modest salaries as researchers for the Electronic Predictions Centre, with the added sum, for (k)yK, that goes with the position of Dean, which he intrigued to obtain from the Department, though he kept on pretending he wasn't lifting a finger. (His predilection for stasis has got steadily worse; he turned up here in the guise of a paralytic, in a wheelchair.) This title of Dean, I might add, has nothing to do with seniority, otherwise I'd be just as much entitled to it as he is, though of course it doesn't mean anything to me.

So this is how we reached our present situation. Dean (k)yK, from the porch of his building, seated in the wheelchair, his legs covered with a rug of newspapers from all over the world, which arrive with the morning post, shouts so loud you can hear him all the way across the campus: 'Qfwfq, the atomic treaty between Turkey and Japan wasn't signed today; they haven't even begun talks. You see? Qfwfq, that man in Termini Imerese who killed his wife was given three years, just as I said. Not life!'

And he waves the pages of the papers, black and white the way space was when the galaxies were being formed, and crammed – as space was then – with isolated corpuscles, surrounded by emptiness, containing no destination or meaning. And I think how beautiful it was then, through that void, to draw lines and parabolas, pick out the precise point, the intersection between space and time where the event would spring forth, undeniable in the prominence of its glow; whereas now events come flowing down without interruption, like cement being poured, one column next to the other, one within the other, separated by black and incongruous headlines, legible in many ways but intrinsically illegible, a doughy mass of events without form or direction, which surrounds, submerges, crushes all reasoning.

'You know something, Qfwfq? The closing quotations on Wall Street are down 2 per cent, not 6! And that building constructed illegally on the Via Cassia is twelve storeys high, not nine! Nearco IV wins at Longchamps by two lengths. What's our score now, Qfwfq?'

The Dinosaurs

*The causes of the rapid extinction of the Dinosaur remain mysteri-
ous; the species had evolved and grown throughout the Triassic
and the Jurassic, and for 150 million years the Dinosaur had been
the undisputed master of the continents. Perhaps the species was
unable to adapt to the great changes of climate and vegetation
which took place in the Cretaceous period. By its end all the
Dinosaurs were dead.*

All except me – *Qfwfq corrected* – because, for a certain period,
I was also a Dinosaur: about fifty million years, I'd say, and I
don't regret it; if you were a Dinosaur in those days, you
were sure you were in the right, and you made everyone
look up to you.

Then the situation changed – I don't have to tell you all
the details – and all sorts of trouble began, defeats, errors,
doubts, treachery, pestilences. A new population was growing up on the Earth, hostile to us. They attacked us on all
sides; there was no dealing with them. Now there are those
who say the pleasure of decadence, the desire to be destroyed
were part of the spirit of us Dinosaurs even before then. I
don't know: I never felt like that; if some of the others did,
it was because they sensed they were already finished.

I prefer not to think back to the period of the great death.
I never believed I'd escape it. The long migration that saved

me led me through a cemetery of fleshless carcasses, where only a crest or a horn or a scale of armour or a fragment of horny skin recalled the ancient splendour of the living creature. And over those remains worked the beaks, the bills, the talons, the suckers of the new masters of the planet. When at last I found no further traces, of the living or of the dead, then I stopped.

I spent many, many years on those deserted plateaux. I had survived ambushes, epidemics, starvation, frost: but I was alone. To go on staying up there for ever was impossible for me. I started the journey down.

The world had changed: I couldn't recognize the mountains any more, or the rivers, or the trees. The first time I glimpsed some living beings, I hid: it was a flock of the New Ones, small specimens, but strong.

'Hey, you!' They had spied me, and I was immediately amazed at this familiar way of addressing me. I ran off; they chased me. For millennia I had been used to striking terror all around me, and to feeling terror of the others' reactions to the terror I aroused. None of that now. 'Hey, you!' They came over to me casually, neither hostile nor frightened.

'Why are you running? What's come over you?' They only wanted me to show them the shortest path to I don't know where. I stammered out that I was a stranger there. 'What made you run off?' one of them said. 'You looked as if you'd seen . . . a Dinosaur!' And the others laughed. But in that laughter I sensed for the first time a hint of apprehension. Their good humour was a bit forced. Then one of them turned serious and added: 'Don't say that even as a joke. You don't know what they are . . .'

So, the terror of the Dinosaurs still continued in the New Ones, but perhaps they hadn't seen any for several generations and weren't able to recognize one. I travelled on, cautious but also impatient to repeat the experiment. At a spring a New One, a young female, was drinking; she was alone. I went up softly, stretched my neck to drink beside her; I could already imagine her desperate scream the moment she saw me, her breathless flight. She would spread the alarm, and the New Ones would come out in force to hunt me down . . . For a moment I repented my action; if I wanted to save myself, I should tear her limb from limb at once: start it all over again . . .

She turned and said: 'Nice and cool, isn't it?' She went on conversing amiably, the usual remarks one makes to strangers, asking me if I came from far away, if I had run into rain on the trip, or if it had been sunny. I would never have imagined it possible to talk like that with non-Dinosaurs, and I was tense and mostly silent.

'I always come here to drink,' she said, 'to the Dinosaur . . .'

I reacted with a start, my eyes widening.

'Oh, yes, that's what we call it. The Dinosaur's Spring . . . that's been its name since ancient times. They say that a Dinosaur hid here, one of the last, and whenever anybody came here for a drink the Dinosaur jumped on him and tore him limb from limb. My goodness!'

I wanted to drop through the earth. 'Now she'll realize who I am,' I was thinking, 'now she'll take a better look at me and recognize me!' And as one does, when one doesn't want to be observed, I kept my eyes lowered and coiled my tail, as if to hide it. It was such a strain that when, still smiling, she said goodbye and went on her way, I felt as tired as if I'd fought a battle, one of those battles we fought when we were defending ourselves with our claws and our teeth. I realized I hadn't even said goodbye back to her.

I reached the shore of a river, where the New Ones had their dens and fished for their living. To create a bend in the river, where the water would be less rapid and would hold the fish, they were constructing a dam of branches. As soon as they saw me, they glanced up from their work and stopped. They looked at me, then at each other, in silence, as if questioning one another. 'This is it,' I thought, 'all I can do is sell my life dearly.' And I prepared to leap to my defence.

Luckily, I stopped myself in time. Those fishermen had nothing against me: seeing how strong I was, they wanted to ask me if I could stay with them and work transporting wood.

'This is a safe place,' they insisted, when I seemed to hesitate. 'There hasn't been a Dinosaur seen here since the days of our grandfathers' grandfathers . . .'

Nobody suspected who I might be. I stayed. The climate was good, the food wasn't to my taste but it was all right, and the work wasn't too hard for one of my strength. They gave me a nickname: 'The Ugly One', because I was different from them, for no other reason. These New Ones, I don't know how in the world you call them, Pantotheres or whatever, were still a rather formless species; in fact, all the other species descended from it later; and already in those days there was the greatest variety of similarities and dissimilarities from one individual to the next, so, though I was an entirely different type, I was finally convinced I didn't stand out too much.

Not that I ever became completely used to this idea: I always felt like a Dinosaur in the midst of enemies, and every evening, when they started telling stories of the Dinosaurs, legends handed down from generation to generation, I hung back in the shadow, my nerves on edge.

The stories were terrifying. The listeners, pale, occasionally bursting out with cries of fear, hung on the lips of the storyteller, whose voice also betrayed an equally profound emotion. Soon it was clear to me that all of them already knew those stories (even though the repertory was very plentiful), but when they heard them, their fear was renewed every time. The Dinosaurs were portrayed as so many monsters, described with a wealth of detail that would never have helped anyone recognize them, and depicted as intent only on harming the New Ones, as if the New Ones from the very beginning had been the Earth's most important inhabitants and we had had nothing better to do than run after them from morning till night. For myself, when I thought about us Dinosaurs, I returned in memory to a long series of hardships, death agonies, mourning; the stories that the New Ones told about us were so remote from my experience that they should have left me indifferent, as if they referred to outsiders, strangers. And yet, as I listened, I realized I had never thought about how we appeared to others, and that, among all the nonsense, those tales, here and there, from the narrators' point of view, had hit on the truth. In my mind their stories of terrors we inflicted became confused with my memories of terror undergone: the more I learned how we had made others tremble, the more I trembled myself.

Each one told a story, in turn, and at a certain point they said: 'What does the Ugly One have to tell us? Don't you have any stories? Didn't anyone in your family have adventures with the Dinosaurs?'

'Yes, but . . .' I stammered, 'it was so long ago . . . ah, if you only knew . . .'

The one who came to my assistance at that juncture was Fern-flower, the young creature of the spring. 'Oh, leave him alone . . . He's a foreigner, he doesn't feel at home yet; he can't speak our language well enough . . .'

In the end they changed the subject. I could breathe again.

A kind of friendliness had grown up between Fern-flower

and me. Nothing too intimate: I had never dared touch her. But we had long talks. Or rather, she told me all sorts of things about her life; in my fear of giving myself away, of making her suspect my identity, I stuck always to generalities. Fern-flower told me her dreams: 'Last night I saw this enormous Dinosaur, terrifying, breathing smoke from his nostrils. He came closer, grabbed me by the nape, and carried me off. He wanted to eat me alive. It was a terrible dream, simply terrible, but – isn't this odd? – I wasn't the least frightened. No, I don't know how to say it . . . I liked him . . .'

That dream should have made me understand many things and especially one thing: that Fern-flower desired nothing more than to be assaulted. This was the moment for me to embrace her. But the Dinosaur they imagined was too different from the Dinosaur I was, and this thought made me even more different and timid. In other words, I missed a good opportunity. Then Fern-flower's brother returned from the season of fishing in the plains, the young one was much more closely watched, and our conversations became less frequent.

This brother, Zahn, started acting suspicious the moment he first saw me. 'Who's that? Where does he come from?' he asked the others, pointing to me.

'That's the Ugly One, a foreigner, who works with the timber,' they said to him. 'Why? What's strange about him?'

'I'd like to ask him that,' Zahn said, with a grim look. 'Hey, you! What's strange about you?' What could I answer? 'Me? Nothing.'

'So, you're not strange, eh?' and he laughed. That time it went no further, but I was prepared for the worst.

This Zahn was one of the most active ones in the village. He had travelled about the world and seemed to know many more things than the others. When he heard the usual talk about the Dinosaurs, he was seized by a kind of impatience.

'Fairy tales,' he said once, 'you're all telling fairy tales. I'd like to see you if a real Dinosaur turned up here.'

'There haven't been any for a long time now . . .' a fisherman said.

'Not all that long . . .' Zahn sniggered. 'And there might still be a herd or two around the countryside . . . In the plains, our bunch takes turns keeping watch, day and night. But there we can trust one another; we don't take in characters we don't know . . .' And he gave me a long, meaningful look.

There was no point dragging things out: better force him into the open right away. I took a step forward. 'Have you got something against me?' I asked.

'I'm against anybody when we don't know who gave him birth or where he came from, and when he wants to eat our food and court our sisters . . .'

One of the fishermen took up my defence: 'The Ugly One earns his keep; he's a hard worker . . .'

'He's capable of carrying tree-trunks on his back, I won't deny that,' Zahn went on, 'but if danger came, if we had to defend ourselves with claws and teeth, how can we be sure he would behave properly?'

A general argument began. The strange thing was that the possibility of my being a Dinosaur never occurred to anyone; the sin I was accused of was being Different, a Foreigner, and therefore Untrustworthy; and the argument was over how much my presence increased the danger of the Dinosaurs' ever coming back.

'I'd like to see him in battle, with that little lizard's mouth of his . . .' Zahn went on contemptuously, goading me.

I went over to him, abruptly, nose to nose. 'You can see me right now, if you don't run away.'

He wasn't expecting that. He looked around. The others formed a circle. There was nothing for us to do but fight.

I moved forward, brushed off his bite by twisting my neck; I had already given him a blow of my paw that knocked him on his back, and I was on top of him. This was a wrong move; as if I didn't know it, as if I had never seen Dinosaurs die, clawed and bitten on the chest and the belly, when they believed they had pinned down their enemy. But I still knew how to use my tail, to steady myself; I didn't want to let him turn me over; I put on pressure, but I felt I was about to give way . . .

Then one of the observers yelled: 'Give it to him, Dinosaur!' No sooner had they unmasked me than I became again the Dinosaur of the old days: since all was lost, I might as well make them feel their ancient terror. And I struck Zahn once, twice, three times . . .

They tore us apart. 'Zahn, we told you! The Ugly One has muscles. You don't try any tricks with him, not with old Ugly!' And they laughed and congratulated me, slapping me on the back with their paws. Convinced I had been discovered, I couldn't get my bearings; it was only later that I understood the cry 'Dinosaur' was a habit of theirs, to encourage the rivals in a fight, as if to say: 'Go on, you're the stronger one!' and I wasn't even sure whether they had shouted the word at me or at Zahn.

From that day on I was the most respected of all. Even Zahn encouraged me, followed me around to see me give new proofs of my strength. I must say that their usual talk about the Dinosaurs changed a bit, too, as always happens when you tire of judging things in the same old way and fashion begins to take a new turn. Now, if they wanted to criticize something in the village, they had got into the habit of saying that, among Dinosaurs, certain things were never done, that the Dinosaurs in many ways could offer an example, that the behaviour of the Dinosaurs in this or that situation (in their private life, for example) was beyond reproach, and so on. In short, there seemed to be emerging a kind of posthumous admiration for these Dinosaurs about whom no one knew anything precise.

Sometimes I couldn't help saying: 'Come, let's not exaggerate. What do you think a Dinosaur was, after all?'

They interrupted me: 'Shut up. What do you know about them? You've never seen one.'

Perhaps this was the right moment to start calling a spade a spade. 'I too have seen them!' I cried, 'and if you want, I can explain to you what they were like!'

They didn't believe me; they thought I was making fun of them. For me, this new way they had of talking about the Dinosaurs was almost as unbearable as the old one. Because – apart from the grief I felt at the sad fate that had befallen my species – I knew the life of the Dinosaurs from within, I knew how we had been governed by narrow-mindedness, prejudice, unable to adapt ourselves to new situations. And I now had to see them take as a model that little world of ours, so backward and so – to tell the truth – boring! I had to feel imposed on me, and by them, a kind of sacred respect for my species which I myself had never felt! But, after all, this was only right: what did these New Ones have that was so different from the Dinosaurs of the good old days? Safe in their village with their dams and their ponds, they had also taken on a smugness, a presumptuousness . . . I finally felt towards them the same intolerance I had had towards my own environment, and the more I heard them admiring the Dinosaurs the more I detested Dinosaurs and New Ones alike.

'You know something? Last night I dreamed that a Dinosaur was to go past my house,' Fern-flower said to me, 'a magnificent Dinosaur, a Prince or a King of Dinosaurs. I made myself pretty, I put a ribbon on my head, and I leaned out of the window. I tried to attract the Dinosaur's attention, I bowed to him, but he didn't even seem to notice me, didn't even deign to glance at me . . .'

This dream furnished me with a new key to the understanding of Fern-flower's attitude towards me: the young creature had mistaken my shyness for disdainful pride. Now, when I recall it, I realize that all I had to do was maintain that attitude a little longer, make a show of haughty detachment, and I would have won her completely. Instead, the revelation so moved me that I threw myself at her feet, tears in my eyes, and said: 'No, no, Fern-flower, it's not the way you think; you're better than any Dinosaur, a hundred times better, and I feel so inferior to you . . .'

Fern-flower stiffened, took a step backwards. 'What are you saying?' This wasn't what she expected: she was upset, and she found the scene a bit distasteful. I understood this too late; I hastily recovered myself, but a feeling of uneasiness now weighed heavily between us.

There was no time to ponder it, what with everything that happened a little later. Breathless messengers reached the village. 'The Dinosaurs are coming back!' A herd of strange monsters had been sighted, speeding fiercely over the plain. At this rate they would attack the village the following morning. The alarm was sounded.

You can imagine the flood of conflicting emotions that filled my breast at this news: my species wasn't extinct, I would be able to join my brothers, take up my old life! But the memory of the old life that returned to my mind was the endless series of defeats, of flights, of dangers; to begin again meant perhaps only a temporary extension of that death agony, the return to a phase I thought had already ended. Now, here in the village, I had achieved a kind of new tranquillity, and I was sorry to lose it.

The New Ones were also torn by conflicting feelings. On the one hand, there was panic; on the other, the wish to triumph over the ancient enemy; and at the same time, there was the conviction that if the Dinosaurs had survived and were now advancing vengefully it meant nobody could stop them and their victory, pitiless as it might be, could also perhaps be a good thing for all. It was as if the New Ones wanted at the same time to defend themselves, to flee, to wipe out the enemy, and to be defeated; and this uncertainty was reflected in the disorder of their defence preparations.

'Just a moment!' Zahn shouted. 'There is only one among us who is capable of taking command! The strongest of all, the Ugly One!'

'You're right! The Ugly One must command us!' the others shouted in chorus. 'Yes, yes, full power to the Ugly One!' And they placed themselves at my command.

'No, no, how can I, a foreigner? . . . I'm not up to it . . .' I parried. But it was impossible to convince them.

What was I to do? That night I couldn't close my eyes. The call of my blood insisted I should desert and join my brothers; loyalty towards the New Ones, who had welcomed and sheltered me and given me their trust, demanded I should consider myself on their side; and in addition I knew full well that neither Dinosaurs nor New Ones were worthy of my lifting a finger for them. If the Dinosaurs were trying to re-establish their rule with invasions and massacres, it meant they had learned nothing from experience, that they had survived only by mistake. And it was clear that the New Ones, turning the command over to me, had found the easiest solution: leave all responsibility to an outsider, who could be their saviour but also, in case of defeat, a scapegoat to hand over to the enemy to pacify him, or else a traitor who, putting them into the enemies' hands, could bring about their unconfessable dream of being mastered by the Dinosaurs. In short, I wanted nothing to do with either side: let them rip each other apart in turn! I didn't give a damn about any of them. I had to escape as fast as possible, let them stew in their own juice, have nothing more to do with these old stories.

That same night, slipping away in the darkness, I left the village. My first impulse was to get as far as possible from the battlefield, return to my secret refuges; but curiosity got the better of me: I had to see my counterparts, to know who would win. I hid on the top of some cliffs that overhung the bend of the river, and I waited for dawn.

As the light broke, some figures appeared on the horizon. They charged forward. Even before I could distinguish them clearly, I could dismiss the notion that Dinosaurs could ever run so gracelessly. When I recognized them I didn't know whether to laugh or to blush with shame. Rhinoceroses, a herd, the first ones, big and clumsy and crude, studded with horny bumps, but basically inoffensive, devoted only to cropping grass: this is what the others had mistaken for the ancient Lords of the Earth!

The rhinoceros herd galloped with the sound of thunder, stopped to lick some bushes, then ran on towards the horizon without even noticing the waiting squads of fishermen.

I ran back to the village. 'You got it all wrong! They weren't Dinosaurs!' I announced. 'Rhinoceroses, that's what they were! They've already gone. There isn't any more danger!' And I added, to justify my vanishing in the night: 'I went out scouting. To spy on them and report back.'

'We may not have understood they weren't Dinosaurs,' Zahn said calmly, 'but we have understood that you are no hero,' and he turned his back on me.

To be sure, they were all disappointed: about the Dinosaurs, about me. Now the stories of Dinosaurs became jokes, in which the terrible monsters played ridiculous roles. I no longer was affected by their petty wit. Now I recognized the greatness of spirit that had made us choose to disappear rather than live in a world no longer suited to us. If I survived it was only so that one of us could continue to feel himself a Dinosaur in the midst of these wretches who tried to conceal, with stupid teasing, the fear that still dominated them. And what choice did the New Ones have, beyond the choice between mockery and fear?

Fern-flower betrayed a new attitude when she narrated a dream to me: 'There was this Dinosaur, very funny, all green; and everybody was teasing him and pulling his tail. Then I stepped forward and protected him; I took him away and petted him. And I realized that, ridiculous as he was, he was the saddest of all creatures and a river of tears flowed from his red and yellow eyes.'

What came over me, at those words? A revulsion, a refusal to identify myself with the images of that dream, the rejection of a sentiment that seemed to have become pity, an intolerance of the diminished idea they had all conceived of the Dinosaurian dignity? I had a burst of pride; I stiffened and hurled a few contemptuous phrases in her face: 'Why do you bore me with these dreams of yours? They get more childish every time! You can't dream anything but sentimental nonsense!'

Fern-flower burst into tears. I went off, shrugging my shoulders.

This happened on the dam; we weren't alone; the fishermen hadn't heard our dialogue but they had noticed my angry reaction and the young creature's tears.

Zahn felt called upon to intervene. 'Who do you think you are?' he said, in a harsh voice. 'How dare you insult my sister?'

I stopped, but didn't answer. If he wanted to fight, I was ready. But the mood of the village had changed in recent times: they made a joke of everything. From the group of fishermen a falsetto cry was heard: 'Come off it, get along with you, Dinosaur!' This, as I well knew, was a mocking expression which had now come into use, as if to say: 'Don't exaggerate, don't get carried away,' and so on. But something stirred in my blood.

'Yes, I am one, if you care to know,' I shouted, 'a Dinosaur! That's what I am! Since you never have seen any Dinosaurs, here, take a look at me!'

General snickering broke out.

'I saw one yesterday,' an old fisherman said, 'he came out of the snow.' Silence immediately fell all around him.

The old fellow was just back from a journey in the mountains. The thaw had melted an ancient glacier and a Dinosaur's skeleton had come to light.

The news spread through the village. 'Let's go and see the Dinosaur!' They all ran up the mountain, and I went with them.

When we had passed a moraine of stones, uprooted trunks, mud, and dead birds, we saw a deep, shell-shaped valley. A veil of early lichens was turning the rocks green, now that they were freed from the ice. In the midst, lying as if asleep, his neck stretched by the widened intervals of the vertebrae, his tail sown in a long serpentine, a giant Dinosaur's skeleton was lying. The chest cavity was arched like a sail, and when the wind struck the flat slabs of the ribs an invisible heart seemed to be beating within them still. The skull was turned in an anguished position, mouth open as if in a last cry.

The New Ones ran down there, shouting gaily; facing the skull, they felt the empty eye sockets staring at them; they kept a few paces' distance, silently; then they turned and resumed their silly festiveness. If one of them had looked from the skeleton to me, as I stood there staring at it, he would have realized at once that we were identical. But nobody did this. Those bones, those claws, those murderous limbs spoke a language now become illegible; they no longer said anything to anyone, except that vague name which had remained unconnected with the experiences of the present.

I continued looking at the skeleton, the Father, the Brother, my Counterpart, my Self; I recognized my fleshless limbs, my lineaments carved in the stone, everything we had been and were no longer, our majesty, our faults, our ruin.

Now these remains would be used by the planet's new, heedless occupants to mark a spot in the landscape, they would follow the destiny of the name 'Dinosaur', becoming an opaque sound without meaning. I must not allow it. Everything that concerned the true nature of the Dinosaurs must remain hidden. In the night, as the New Ones slept around the skeleton, which they had decked with flags, I transported it, vertebra by vertebra, and buried my Dead.

In the morning the New Ones found not a trace of the skeleton. They didn't worry about it very long. It was another mystery added to the many mysteries concerning the Dinosaurs. They soon dismissed it from their thoughts.

But the appearance of the skeleton left its mark, for in all of them the idea of the Dinosaurs became bound to the idea of a sad end, and in the stories they now told the predominant tone was one of commiseration, of grief at our sufferings. I had no use for this pity of theirs. Pity for what? If ever a species had had a rich, full evolution, a long and happy reign, that species was ours. Our extinction had been a grandiose epilogue, worthy of our past. What could those fools understand of it? Every time I heard them become sentimental about the poor Dinosaurs I felt like making fun of them, telling invented, incredible stories. In any case, the real truth about the Dinosaurs would never be understood by anyone now; it was a secret I would keep for myself alone.

A band of vagabonds stopped at the village. Among them was a young female. When I saw her, I started with surprise. Unless my eyes were deceiving me, she didn't have only the blood of the New Ones in her veins: she was a Half-breed, a Dinosaur Half-breed. Was she aware of it? No, certainly not, judging by her nonchalance. Perhaps it hadn't been one of her parents but one of her grandparents or great-grandparents or a more remote ancestor who had been a Dinosaur; and the features, the movements of our stock were cropping out again in her in an almost shameless fashion, now unrecognizable to the others, and to herself. She was a pretty, gay creature; she immediately had a group of suitors after her, and among them the most constant and the most smitten was Zahn.

It was early summer. The young people were giving a feast on the river. 'Come with us,' Zahn invited me, trying to be my friend after all our disagreements; then he immediately went back to swim at the side of the Half-breed.

I went over to Fern-flower. Perhaps the moment had come for us to speak openly, to come to an understanding. 'What did you dream last night?' I asked, to break the ice.

She hung her head. 'I saw a wounded Dinosaur, writhing and dying. He had bowed his noble, delicate head, and he suffered and suffered . . . I looked at him, couldn't take my eyes off him, and I realized I was feeling a strange pleasure at seeing him suffer . . .'

Fern-flower's lips were taut, evil, in an expression I had never noticed in her. I wanted only to show her that in that play of ambiguous, grim feelings I had no part: I was one who enjoyed life, I was the heir of a happy race. I started to dance around her, I splashed river water on her, waving my tail.

'You can never talk about anything that isn't sad!' I said, frivolously. 'Stop it. Come and dance!'

She didn't understand me. She made a grimace.

'And if you don't dance with me, I'll dance with another!' I cried. I grasped the Half-breed by one paw, carrying her off under Zahn's nose. First he watched us move away without understanding, he was so lost in his amorous contemplation, then he was seized with jealous rage. Too late. The Half-breed and I had already dived into the river and were swimming towards the other bank, to hide in the bushes.

Perhaps I only wanted to show Fern-flower who I really was, to deny the mistaken notions she had of me. And perhaps I was also moved by an old bitterness towards Zahn; I wanted to reject, ostentatiously, his new offer of friendship. Or else, more than anything, it was the familiar and yet unusual form of the Half-breed which made me desire a natural, direct relationship, without secret thoughts, without memories.

The vagabond caravan would be leaving again in the morning. The Half-breed was willing to spend the night in the bushes. I stayed there, dallying with her, until dawn.

These were only ephemeral episodes in a life otherwise calm and uneventful. I had allowed the truth about myself and the era of our domination to vanish into silence. Now they hardly ever talked about the Dinosaurs any more; perhaps nobody believed they had ever existed. Even Fern-flower had stopped dreaming of them.

When she told me: 'I dreamed that in a cavern there was the sole survivor of a species whose name nobody remembered, and I went to ask it of him, and it was dark, and I knew he was there, and I couldn't see him, and I knew well who he was and what he looked like but I couldn't have expressed it, and I didn't understand if he was answering my questions or I was answering his . . .' for me this was a sign that finally an amorous understanding had begun between us, the kind I had wanted since I first stopped at the spring, when I didn't yet know if I would be allowed to survive.

Since then I had learned many things, and above all the way in which Dinosaurs conquer. First I had believed that disappearing had been, for my brothers, the magnanimous acceptance of a defeat; now I knew that the more the Dinosaurs disappear, the more they extend their dominion, and over forests far more vast than those that cover the continents: in the labyrinth of the survivors' thoughts. From the semi-darkness of fears and doubts of now ignorant generations, the Dinosaurs continued to extend their necks, to raise their taloned hoofs, and when the last shadow of their image had been erased, their name went on, superimposed on all meanings, perpetuating their presence in relations among living beings. Now, when the name too had been erased, they would become one thing with the mute and anonymous moulds of thought, through which thoughts take on form and substance: by the New Ones, and by those who would come after the New Ones, and those who would come even after them.

I looked around: the village that had seen me arrive as a stranger I could now rightfully call mine, and I could call Fern-flower mine, in the only way a Dinosaur could call something his. For this, with a silent wave, I said goodbye to Fern-flower, left the village, and went off for ever.

Along my way I looked at the trees, the rivers and the mountains, and I could no longer distinguish the ones that had been there during the Dinosaurs' time from those that had come afterwards. Around some dens a band of vagabonds was camping. From the distance I recognized the Half-breed, still attractive, only a little fatter. To avoid being seen, I headed for the woods and observed her. She was followed by a little son, barely able to stand on his legs and wag his tail. How long had it been since I had seen a little Dinosaur, so perfect, so full of his own Dinosaur essence, and so unaware of what the word 'Dinosaur' meant?

I waited for him in a clearing in the woods to watch him play, chase a butterfly, slam a pine cone against a stone to dig out the pine nuts. I went over. It was my son, all right.

He looked at me curiously. 'Who are you?' he asked.

'Nobody,' I said. 'What about you? Do you know who you are?'

'What a question! Everybody knows that: I'm a New One!' he said.

That was exactly what I had expected to hear him say. I patted his head, said: 'Good for you,' and went off.

I travelled through valleys and plains. I came to a station, caught the first train, and was lost in the crowd.

The Form of Space

The equations of the gravitational field which relate the curve of space to the distribution of matter are already becoming common knowledge.

To fall in the void as I fell: none of you knows what that means. For you, to fall means to plunge perhaps from the twenty-sixth floor of a skyscraper, or from an aeroplane which breaks down in flight: to fall headlong, grope in the air a moment, and then the Earth is immediately there, and you get a big bump. But I'm talking about the time when there wasn't any Earth underneath or anything else solid, not even a celestial body in the distance capable of attracting you into its orbit. You simply fell, indefinitely, for an indefinite length of time. I went down into the void, to the most absolute bottom conceivable, and once there I saw that the extreme limit must have been much, much further below, very remote, and I went on falling, to reach it. Since there were no reference points, I had no idea whether my fall was fast or slow. Now that I think about it, there weren't even any proofs that I was really falling: perhaps I had always remained immobile in the same place, or I was moving in an upward direction; since there was no above or below these were only nominal questions and so I might just as well go on thinking I was falling, as I was naturally led to think.

Assuming then that one was falling, everyone fell with the same speed and rate of acceleration; in fact we were always more or less on the same level: I, Ursula H'x, Lieutenant Fenimore. I didn't take my eyes off Ursula H'x: she was very beautiful to see, and in falling she had an easy, relaxed attitude. I hoped I would be able sometimes to catch her eye, but as she fell, Ursula H'x was always intent on filing and polishing her nails or running her comb through her long, smooth hair, and she never glanced towards me. Nor towards Lieutenant Fenimore, I must say, though he did everything he could to attract her attention.

Once I caught him – he thought I couldn't see him – as he was making some signals to Ursula H'x: first he struck his two index fingers, outstretched, one against the other, then he made a rotating gesture with one hand, then he pointed down. I mean, he seemed to hint at an understanding with her, an appointment for later on, in some place down there, where they were to meet. All nonsense, I knew perfectly well: there were no meetings possible among us, because our falls were parallel and the same distance always remained between us. But the mere fact that Lieutenant Fenimore had got such ideas into his head – and tried to put them into the head of Ursula H'x – was enough to get on my nerves, even though she paid no attention to him, indeed she made a slight blurting sound with her lips, directed – I felt there was no doubt – at him. (Ursula H'x fell, revolving with lazy movements as if she were turning in her bed and it was hard to say whether her gestures were directed at someone else or whether she was playing for her own benefit, as was her habit.)

I too, naturally, dreamed only of meeting Ursula H'x, but since, in my fall, I was following a straight line absolutely parallel to the one she followed, it seemed inappropriate to reveal such an unattainable desire. Of course, if I chose to be an optimist, there was always the possibility that, if our two parallels continued to infinity, the moment would come when they would touch. This eventuality gave me some hope; indeed, it kept me in a state of constant excitement. I don't mind telling you I had dreamed so much of a meeting of our parallels, in great detail, that it was now a part of my experience, as if I had actually lived it. Everything would happen suddenly, with simplicity and naturalness: after the long separate journey, unable to move an inch closer to each other, after having felt her as an alien being for so long, a prisoner of her parallel route, then the consistency of space, instead of being impalpable as it had always been, would become more taut and, at the same time, looser, a condensing of the void which would seem to come not from outside but from within us, and would press me and Ursula H'x together (I had only to shut my eyes to see her come forward, in an attitude I recognized as hers even if it was different from all her habitual attitudes: her arms stretched down, along her sides, twisting her wrists as if she were stretching and at the same time writhing and leaning forward), and then the invisible line I was following would become a single line, occupied by a mingling of her and me where her soft and secret nature would be penetrated or rather would enfold and, I would say, almost absorb the part of myself that till then had been suffering at being alone and separate and barren.

Even the most beautiful dreams can suddenly turn into nightmares, and it then occurred to me that the meeting point of our two parallels might also be the point at which all parallels existing in space eventually meet, and so it would mark not only my meeting with Ursula H'x but also – dreadful prospect – a meeting with Lieutenant Fenimore. At the very moment when Ursula H'x would cease to be alien to me, another alien with his thin black moustache would share our intimacies in an inextricable way: this thought was enough to plunge me into the most tormented jealous hallucinations: I heard the cry that our meeting – hers and mine – tore from us melt in a spasmodically joyous unison and then – I was aghast at the presentiment – from that sound burst her piercing cry as she was violated – so, in my resentful bias, I imagined – from behind, and at the same time the Lieutenant's vulgar shout of triumph, but perhaps – and here my jealousy became delirium – these cries of theirs, hers and his, might also not be so different or so dissonant, they might also achieve a unison, be joined in a single cry of downright pleasure, distinct from the sobbing, desperate moan that would burst from my lips.

In this alternation of hopes and apprehensions I continued to fall, constantly peering into the depths of space to see if anything heralded an immediate or future change in our condition. A couple of times I managed to glimpse a universe, but it was far away and seemed very tiny, well off to the right or to the left; I barely had time to make out a certain number of galaxies like shining little dots collected into superimposed masses which revolved with a faint buzz, when everything would vanish as it had appeared, upwards or to one side, so that I began to suspect it had only been a momentary glare in my eyes.

'There! Look! There's a universe! Look over there! There's something!' I shouted to Ursula H'x, motioning in that direction; but, tongue between her teeth, she was busy caressing the smooth, taut skin of her legs, looking for those very rare and almost invisible excess hairs she could uproot with a sharp tug of her pincer-like nails, and the only sign she had heard my call might be the way she stretched one leg upwards, as if to exploit – you would have said – for her methodical inspection the dim light reflected from that distant firmament.

I don't have to tell you the contempt Lieutenant Fenimore displayed towards what I might have discovered on those occasions: he gave a shrug – shaking his epaulettes, his bandolier and the decorations with which he was pointlessly arrayed – and turned in the other direction, snickering. Unless he was the one (when he was sure I was looking elsewhere) who tried to arouse Ursula's curiosity (and then it was my turn to laugh, seeing that her only response was to revolve in a kind of somersault, turning her behind to him: a gesture no doubt disrespectful but lovely to see, so that, after rejoicing in my rival's humiliation, I caught myself envying him this, as a privilege), indicating a labile point fleeing through space, shouting: 'There! There! A universe! This big! I saw it! It's a universe!'

I won't say he was lying: statements of that sort, as far as I know, were as likely to be true as false. It was a proven fact that, every now and then, we skirted a universe (or else a universe skirted us), but it wasn't clear whether these were a number of universes scattered through space or whether it was always the same universe we kept passing, revolving in a mysterious trajectory, or whether there was no universe at all and what we thought we saw was the mirage of a universe which perhaps had once existed and whose image continued to rebound from the walls of space like the rebounding of an echo. But it could also be that the universes had always been there, dense around us, and had no idea of moving, and we weren't moving, either, and everything was arrested for ever, without time, in a darkness punctuated only by rapid flashes when something or someone managed for a moment to free himself from that sluggish timelessness and indicate the semblance of a movement.

All these hypotheses were equally worth considering, but they interested me only in so far as they concerned our fall and the possibility of touching Ursula H'x. In other words, nobody really knew anything. So why did that pompous Fenimore sometimes assume a superior manner, as if he were certain of things? He had realized that when he wanted to infuriate me the surest system was to pretend to a long-standing familiarity with Ursula H'x. At a certain point Ursula took to swaying as she came down, her knees together, shifting the weight of her body this way and that, as if wavering in an ever-broader zigzag: just to break the monotony of that endless fall. And the Lieutenant then also started swaying, trying to pick up her rhythm, as if he were following the same invisible track, or rather as if he were dancing to the sound of the same music, audible only to the two of them, which he even pretended to whistle, putting into it, on his own, a kind of unspoken understanding, as if alluding to a private joke among old boozing companions. It was all a bluff – I knew that, of course – but still it gave me the idea that a meeting between Ursula H'x and Lieutenant Fenimore might already have taken place, who knows how long ago, at the beginning of their trajectories, and this suspicion gnawed at me painfully, as if I had been the victim of an injustice. On reflecting, however, I reasoned that if Ursula and the Lieutenant had once occupied the same point in space, this meant that their respective lines of fall had since been moving apart and presumably were still moving apart. Now, in this slow but constant removal from the Lieutenant, it was more than likely that Ursula was coming closer to me; so the Lieutenant had little to boast of in his past conjunctions: I was the one at whom the future smiled.

The process of reasoning that led me to this conclusion was not enough to reassure me at heart: the possibility that

Ursula H'x had already met the Lieutenant was in itself a wrong which, if it had been done to me, could no longer be redeemed. I must add that past and future were vague terms for me, and I couldn't make much distinction between them: my memory didn't extend beyond the interminable present of our parallel fall, and what might have been before, since it couldn't be remembered, belonged to the same imaginary world as the future, and was confounded with the future. So I could also suppose that if two parallels had ever set out from the same point, these were the lines that Ursula H'x and I were following (in this case it was nostalgia for a lost oneness that fed my eager desire to meet her); however, I was reluctant to believe in this hypothesis, because it might imply a progressive separation and perhaps her future arrival in the braid-festooned arms of Lieutenant Fenimore, but chiefly because I couldn't get out of the present except to imagine a different present, and none of the rest counted.

Perhaps this was the secret: to identify oneself so completely with one's own state of fall that one could realize the line followed in falling wasn't what it seemed but another, or rather to succeed in changing that line in the only way it could be changed, namely, by making it become what it had really always been. It wasn't through concentrating on myself that this idea came to me, though, but through observing, with my loving eye, how beautiful Ursula H'x was even when seen from behind, and noting, as we passed in sight of a very distant system of constellations, an arching of her back and a kind of twitch of her behind, but not so much the behind itself as an external sliding that seemed to rub past the behind and cause a not unpleasant reaction from the behind itself. This fleeting impression was enough to make me see our situation in a new way: if it was true that space with something inside is different from empty space because the matter causes a curving or a tautness which makes all the lines contained in space curve or tauten, then the line each of us was following was straight in the only way a straight line can be straight: namely, deformed to the extent that the limpid harmony of the general void is deformed by the clutter of matter, in other words, twisting all around this bump or pimple or excrescence which is the universe in the midst of space.

My point of reference was always Ursula and, in fact, a certain way she had of proceeding as if twisting could make more familiar the idea that our fall was like a winding and unwinding in a sort of spiral that tightened and then loosened. However, Ursula – if you watched her carefully – wound first in one direction, then in the other, so the pattern we were tracing was more complicated. The universe, therefore, had to be considered not a crude swelling placed there like a turnip, but as an angular, pointed figure where every dent or bulge or facet corresponded to other cavities and projections and notchings of space and of the lines we followed. This, however, was still a schematic image, as if we were dealing with a smooth-walled solid, a compenetration of poly-hedrons, a cluster of crystals; in reality the space in which we moved was all battlemented and perforated, with spires and pinnacles which spread out on every side, with cupolas and balustrades and peristyles, with rose windows, with double- and triple-arched fenestrations, and while we felt we were plunging straight down, in reality we were racing along the edge of mouldings and invisible friezes, like ants who, cross-ing a city, follow itineraries traced not on the street cobbles but along walls and ceilings and cornices and chandeliers. Now if I say city it amounts to suggesting figures that are, in some way, regular, with right angles and symmetrical proportions, whereas instead, we should always bear in mind how space breaks up around every cherry tree and every leaf of every bough that moves in the wind, and at every indentation of the edge of every leaf, and also it forms along every vein of the leaf, and on the network of veins inside the leaf, and on the piercings made every moment by the riddling arrows of light, all printed in negative in the dough of the void, so that there is nothing now that does not leave its print, every possible print of every possible thing, and together every transformation of these prints, instant by instant, so the pimple growing on a caliph's nose or the soap bubble resting on a laundress's bosom changes the general form of space in all its dimensions.

All I had to do was understand that space was made in this way and I realized there were certain soft cavities hollowed in it as welcoming as hammocks where I could lie joined with Ursula H'x, the two of us swaying together, biting each other in turn along all our persons. The properties of space, in fact, were such that one parallel went one way, and another in another way: I for example was plunging within a tortuous cavern while Ursula H'x was being sucked along a passage communicating with that same cavern so that we found ourselves rolling together on a lawn of algae in a kind of subspatial island, writhing, she and I, in every pose, upright and capsized, until all of a sudden our two straight lines resumed their distance, the same as always, and each continued on its own as if nothing had happened.

The grain of space was porous and broken with crevasses and dunes. If I looked carefully, I could observe when Lieutenant Fenimore's course passed through the bed of a narrow, winding canyon; then I placed myself on the top of a cliff and, at just the right moment, I hurled myself down on him, careful to strike him on the cervical vertebrae with my full weight. The bottom of such precipices in the void was stony as the bed of a dried-up stream, and Lieutenant Fenimore, sinking to the ground, remained with his head stuck between two spurs of rock; I pressed one knee into his stomach, but he meanwhile was crushing my knuckles against a cactus's thorns – or the back of a porcupine? (spikes, in any case, of the kind corresponding to certain sharp contractions of space) – to prevent me from grabbing the pistol I had kicked from his hand. I don't know how I happened, a moment later, to find myself with my head thrust into the stifling granulosity of the strata where space gives way, crumbling like sand; I spat, blinded and dazed; Fenimore had managed to collect his pistol; a bullet whistled past my ear, ricocheting off a proliferation of the void that rose in the shape of an anthill. And I fell upon him, my hands at his throat, to strangle him, but my hands slammed against each other with a 'plop!': our paths had become parallel again, and Lieutenant Fenimore and I were descending, maintaining our customary distance, ostentatiously turning our backs on each other, like two people who pretend they have never met, haven't even seen each other before.

What you might consider straight, one-dimensional lines were similar, in effect, to lines of handwriting made on a white page by a pen that shifts words and fragments of sentences from one line to another, with insertions and cross-references, in the haste to finish an exposition which has gone through successive, approximate drafts, always unsatisfactory; and so we pursued each other, Lieutenant Fenimore and I, hiding behind the loops of the *l*'s, especially the *l*'s of the word 'parallel', in order to shoot and take cover from the bullets and pretend to be dead and wait, say, till Fenimore went past in order to trip him up and drag him by his feet, slamming his chin against the bottoms of the *v*'s and the *u*'s and the *m*'s and the *n*'s which, written all evenly in an italic hand, became a bumpy succession of holes in the pavement (for example, in the expression 'one-dimensional universe'), leaving him stretched out in a place all trampled with erasings, then standing up there again, stained with clotted ink, to run towards Ursula H'x, who was trying to act sly, slipping behind the tails of the *f* which trail off until they become wisps, but I could seize her by the hair and bend her against a *d* or a *t* just as I write them now, in haste, bent, so you can recline against them, then we might dig a niche for ourselves down in a *g*, in the *g* of 'big', a subterranean den which can be adapted as we choose to our dimensions, being made more cosy and almost invisible or else arranged more horizontally so you can stretch out in it. Whereas naturally the same lines, rather than remain series of letters and words, can easily be drawn out in their black thread and unwound in continuous, parallel, straight lines which mean nothing beyond themselves in their constant flow, never meeting, just as we never meet in our constant fall: I, Ursula H'x, Lieutenant Fenimore, and all the others.

The Light-Years

The more distant a galaxy is, the more swiftly it moves away from us. A galaxy located at ten billion light-years from us would have a speed of recession equal to the speed of light, three hundred thousand kilometres per second. The 'quasars' recently discovered are already approaching this threshold.

One night I was, as usual, observing the sky with my telescope. I noticed that a sign was hanging from a galaxy a hundred million light-years away. On it was written: I SAW YOU. I made a quick calculation: the galaxy's light had taken a hundred million years to reach me, and since they saw up there what was taking place here a hundred million years later, the moment when they had seen me must date back two hundred million years.

Even before I checked my diary to see what I had been doing that day, I was seized by a ghastly presentiment: exactly two hundred million years before, not a day more nor a day less, something had happened to me that I had always tried to hide. I had hoped that with the passage of time the episode had been completely forgotten; it was in sharp contrast – at least, so it seemed to me – with my customary behaviour before and after that date: so, if ever anybody wanted to dig up that business again, I was ready to deny it quite calmly, and not only because it would have been impossible to furnish proof, but also because an action determined by such exceptional conditions – even if it was really verified – was so improbable that it could be considered untrue in all good faith, even by me. Instead, from a distant celestial body, here was somebody who had seen me, and the story was cropping up again, now of all times.

Naturally, I was in a position to explain everything that had happened, and what caused it to happen, and to make my own behaviour completely comprehensible, if not excusable. I thought of replying at once with a sign, using a phrase in my own defence, like LET ME EXPLAIN or else I'D LIKE TO HAVE SEEN YOU IN MY PLACE, but this wouldn't have been enough and the things that would have to be said were too many to be compressed into a short statement legible at such a distance. And above all, I had to be careful not to make a misstep, not to reinforce with an explicit admission what that I SAW YOU merely hinted at. In short, before leaving myself open with any declaration I would have to know exactly what they had seen from the galaxy and what they hadn't: and for this purpose all I could do was ask, using a sign on the order of DID YOU REALLY SEE EVERYTHING OR JUST A LITTLE BIT? or perhaps LET'S SEE IF YOU'RE TELLING THE TRUTH: WHAT WAS I DOING?, then I would have to wait long enough for them to be able to see my sign, and then an equally long period until I could see their answer and attend to the necessary rectifications. All this would take another two hundred million years, or rather a few million years more, because while the images were coming and going with the speed of light, the galaxies continued to move apart, therefore that constellation now was no longer where I had seen it, but a bit further on, and the image of my sign would have to chase it. I mean, it was a slow system, which would have obliged me to discuss again, more than four hundred million years after they had happened, those events that I wanted to make everyone forget in the shortest possible time.

I thought the best line to take was to act as if nothing had happened, minimize the importance of what they might have found out. So I hastened to expose, in full view, a sign on which I had written simply: WHAT OF IT? If up in the galaxy they had thought they would embarrass me with their I SAW YOU, my calm would disconcert them, and they would be convinced there was no point in dwelling on that episode. If, at the same time, they didn't have much information against me, a vague expression like WHAT OF IT? would be useful as a feeler, to see how seriously I should take their affirmation I SAW YOU. The distance separating us (from its dock of a hundred million light-years away the galaxy had sailed a million centuries before, journeying into the darkness) would perhaps make it less obvious that my WHAT OF IT? was replying to their I SAW YOU of two hundred million years before, but it didn't seem wise to include more explicit references in the new sign, because if the memory of that day, after three million centuries, was becoming dim, I certainly didn't want to be the one to refresh it.

After all, the opinion they might have formed of me, on that single occasion, shouldn't worry me too much. The facts of my life, the ones that had followed, after that day, for years and centuries and millennia, testified – at least the great majority of them – in my favour; so I had only to let the facts speak for themselves. If, from that distant celestial body, they had seen what I was doing one day two hundred million years ago, they must have seen me also the following day, and the day after that, and the next and the next, and they would gradually have modified the first negative opinion of me they might have formed, hastily, on the basis of an isolated episode. In fact, when I thought how many years had already gone by since that I SAW YOU, I was convinced the bad impression must now have been erased by time and followed by a probably positive evaluation, or one, in any case, that corresponded more to reality. However, this rational certainty was not enough to afford me relief: until I had the proof of a change of opinion in my favour, I would remain uneasy at having been caught in an embarrassing position and identified with it, nailed fast in that situation.

Now you will say I could very well have shrugged off the opinion of me held by some strangers living on a remote constellation. As a matter of fact, what worried me wasn't the limited opinion of this or that celestial body, but the suspicion that the consequences of their having seen me might be limitless. Around that galaxy there were many others, some with a radius shorter by a hundred million light-years, with observers who kept their eyes open: the I SAW YOU sign, before I had glimpsed it, had certainly been read by inhabitants of other celestial bodies, and the same thing would have happened afterwards on the gradually more distant constellations. Even if no one could know precisely to what specific situation that I SAW YOU referred, this indefiniteness would not in the least be to my advantage. On the contrary, since people are always ready to believe the worst, what I might really have been seen doing at a distance of a hundred million light-years was, after all, nothing compared to everything that elsewhere they might imagine had been seen. The bad impression I may have left during that moment of heedlessness two million centuries ago would then be enlarged and multiplied, refracted across all the galaxies of the universe, nor was it possible for me to deny it without making the situation worse, since, not knowing what extreme and slanderous deductions those who hadn't directly seen me might have come to, I had no idea where to begin and where to end my denials.

In this state of mind, I kept looking around every night with my telescope. And after two nights I noticed that on a galaxy at a distance of a hundred million years and one light-day they had also put up a sign: I SAW YOU. There could be no doubt that they were also referring to that time: what I had always tried to hide had been discovered not by only one celestial body but also by another located in quite a different zone in space. And by still others: in the nights that followed I continued to see new signs with I SAW YOU on them, set on different constellations every time. From a calculation of the light-years it emerged that the moment when they had seen me was always the same. To each of these I SAW YOUS I answered with signs marked by contemptuous indifference, such as OH REALLY? HOW NICE or else FAT LOT I CARE, or else by an almost provocative mockery, such as TANT PIS or else LOOK! IT'S ME!, but still retaining my reserve.

Though the logic of the situation led me to regard the future with reasonable optimism, the convergence of all those I SAW YOUS on a single point in my life, a convergence surely fortuitous, due to special conditions of interstellar visibility (the single exception was one celestial body where, corresponding to that same date, a sign appeared saying WE CAN'T SEE A DAMN THING), kept me in a constant state of nerves.

It was as if in the space containing all the galaxies the image of what I had done that day were being projected in the interior of a sphere that swelled constantly, at the speed of light: the observers of the celestial bodies that gradually came within the sphere's radius were enabled to see what had happened. Each of these observers could, in turn, be considered the centre of a sphere also expanding at the speed of light, projecting the words I SAW YOU on their signs all around. At the same time, all these celestial bodies belonged to galaxies moving away from one another in space at a speed proportional to the distance, and every observer who indicated he had received a message, before he could receive a second one, had already moved off through space at a constantly increasing speed. At a certain point the furthest galaxies that had seen me (or had seen the I SAW YOU sign from a galaxy closer to us, or the I SAW THE I SAW YOU from a bit further on) would reach the ten-billion-light-year threshold, beyond which they would move off at three hundred thousand kilometres per second, the speed of light, and no image would be able to overtake them after that. So there was the risk that they would remain with their temporary mistaken opinion of me, which from that moment on would become definitive, no longer rectifiable, beyond all appeal and therefore, in a sense, correct, corresponding to the truth.

So it was indispensable to clear up the misunderstanding as quickly as possible. And to clear it up, I could hope for only one thing: that, after that occasion, I had been seen other times, when I gave another image of myself, the one that was – I had no doubts on this score – the true image of me that should be remembered. In the course of the last two hundred million years, there had been no lack of opportunities, and for me just one, very clear, would be enough, to avoid confusion. Now, for example, I recalled a day when I had really been myself, I mean myself in the way I wanted others to see me. This day – I calculated rapidly – had been exactly one hundred million years ago. So, on the galaxy a hundred million light-years away they were seeing me at this very moment in that situation so flattering to my prestige, and their opinion of me was surely changing, modifying, or rather refuting, that first fleeting impression. Right now, or thereabouts: because now the distance that separated us was no longer a hundred million light-years, but a hundred and one; anyhow I had only to wait an equal number of years to allow the light there to arrive here (the date when that would happen was easily calculated, bearing Hubble's constant in mind) and then I would learn their reaction.

Those who had managed to see me at moment x would, all the more surely, have seen me at moment y, and since my image in y was much more convincing than in x – indeed, I would call it more inspiring, unforgettable – they would remember me in y, whereas what had been seen of me in x would be forgotten immediately, erased, perhaps after having been fleetingly recalled to mind, in a kind of dismissal, as if to say: Just think, one who is like y can by chance be seen as x and you might believe he *is* x although it's clear that he's absolutely y.

I was almost cheered by the number of I SAW YOUS still appearing all around, because it meant that interest in me was aroused and therefore my more radiant day would escape no one. It would have (or rather, was already having, beyond my knowledge) a much wider resonance than the sort – limited to given surroundings and, moreover, I must admit, rather marginal – which I, in my modesty, had formerly expected.

You must also consider those celestial bodies from which – through absent-mindedness or bad placing – they hadn't seen me but only a nearby I SAW YOU sign; they had also set up signs saying: LOOKS AS IF THEY'VE SEEN YOU or else FROM WHERE THEY ARE THEY CAN SEE YOU! (expressions in which I sensed a touch of curiosity or of sarcasm); on those bodies, too, there were eyes trained on me and now, precisely because they had missed one opportunity, they would hardly allow a second to escape them, and having received only indirect and hearsay information about x, they would be all the more ready to accept y as the only true reality concerning me.

So the echo of the moment y would be propagated through time and space, it would reach the most distant, the fastest galaxies, and they would elude all further images, racing at light's speed of three hundred thousand kilometres per second and taking that now definitive image of me beyond time and space, where it would become the truth containing in its sphere with unlimited radius all the other spheres with their partial and contradictory truths.

A hundred million centuries or so, after all, aren't an eternity, but to me they seemed never to go by. Finally the night arrived: I had long since aimed my telescope at that same galaxy of the first time. I moved my right eye, its lid half closed, to the eyepiece, I raised my eyelid slowly, and there was the constellation, perfectly framed, and there was a sign in its midst, the words as yet indistinct. I focused better . . . There was written: TRA-LA-LA-LA. Just that: TRA-LA-LA-LA. At the moment when I had expressed the essence of my personality, with abundant evidence and with no risk of misinterpretation, at the moment when I had furnished the key to interpreting all the acts of my past and future life and to forming an overall and objective opinion, what had they seen, they who had not only the opportunity but also the moral obligation to observe and note what I was doing? They hadn't seen anything, hadn't been aware of anything, hadn't observed anything special. To discover that such a great part of my reputation was at the mercy of a character who was so untrustworthy left me prostrate. That proof of myself, which – because of the various favourable circumstances that had accompanied it – I considered incapable of repetition, had gone by unobserved, wasted, definitely lost for a whole zone of the universe, only because that gentleman had allowed himself five minutes of idleness, of relaxation, we might as well say of irresponsibility, his head in the air like an idiot, perhaps in the euphoria of someone who has had a drop too much, and on his sign he had found nothing better to write than a meaningless scrawl, perhaps the silly tune that he had been whistling, forgetting his duties, TRA-LA-LA-LA.

Only one thought afforded me some comfort: the thought that on the other galaxies there were bound to be more diligent observers. Until then I had never been so pleased at the great number of spectators that the old, and unfortunate, episode had had; now they would be ready to perceive the new situation. I returned to the telescope, night after night. A few nights later a galaxy at the proper distance appeared to me in all its splendour. It had a sign. And on it was written this sentence: YOU HAVE A FLANNEL UNDERSHIRT.

Tears in my eyes, I racked my brain for an explanation. Perhaps in that place, with the passage of time, they had so perfected their telescopes that they amused themselves by observing the most insignificant details, the undershirt a person wore, whether it was flannel or cotton, and all the rest meant nothing to them, they paid no attention to it at all. And, for them, my honourable act, my – shall we say? – magnanimous and generous act, had gone for nothing; they had retained only one element, my flannel undershirt: an excellent undershirt, to be sure, and perhaps at another moment I would have been pleased at their noticing it, but not then, oh no, not then.

In any case, I had many other witnesses awaiting me: it was only natural that, out of the whole number, some should fail; I wasn't the sort of person to become distraught over such a little setback. In fact, from a galaxy a bit further on, I finally had the proof that someone had seen perfectly how I had behaved and had evaluated my action properly, that is, enthusiastically. Indeed, on a sign he had written: THAT CHARACTER'S REALLY ON THE BALL. I noted it with complete satisfaction – a satisfaction, mind you, which merely confirmed my expectation, or rather my certainty that my merits would be suitably recognized – but then the expression THAT CHARACTER attracted my attention. Why did they call me THAT CHARACTER, if they already knew me and had seen me, even in that unfortunate circumstance? Shouldn't I be quite familiar to them already? With some adjustment, I improved the focus of my telescope and discovered, at the bottom of the same sign, another sentence written in smaller letters: WHO THE HELL CAN HE BE? Can you imagine a worse stroke of luck? Those who held the key to understanding who I really was hadn't recognized me. They hadn't connected this praiseworthy episode with that deplorable incident two hundred million years earlier, so the deplorable incident was still attributed to me, and the other wasn't, the other remained an impersonal, anonymous anecdote, which didn't belong to anyone's history.

My first impulse was to brandish a sign: IT'S ME! I gave up the idea: what would be the good of it? They would see it more than a hundred million years after moment x had gone by; we were approaching the half-billion mark; to be sure of making myself understood I would have to specify, dig up that old business again, and this was just what I wanted most to avoid.

By now I had lost my self-confidence. I was afraid I wouldn't receive any greater amends from the other galaxies, either. Those who had seen me had seen me in a partial, fragmentary, careless way, or had understood only up to a point what was happening, missing the essential quality, not analysing the elements of my personality which, from one situation to the next, were thrown into relief.

Only one sign said what I had really been expecting: YOU
KNOW SOMETHING? YOU'RE REALLY ON THE BALL! I hastened
to leaf through my notebook, to see what reactions had come
from that galaxy at moment x. By coincidence, that was the
very place where the sign had appeared saying WE CAN'T SEE
A DAMN THING. In that zone of the universe, I surely enjoyed
a higher esteem, no denying that, and I ought to have rejoiced
at last, but instead I felt no satisfaction at all. I realized that,
since these admirers of mine weren't those who might earlier
have formed an unfavourable opinion of me, I didn't give a
damn about them. The assurance that moment y had re-
futed and erased moment x couldn't come to me from them,
and my uneasiness continued, exacerbated by the great length
of time and by my not knowing whether the causes of
my dismay were there and whether or not they would be
dispelled.

Naturally, for the observers scattered over the universe,
moment x and moment y were only two among countless
observable moments, and in fact, every night on the constellations located at the most varied distances signs appeared
referring to other episodes, signs saying KEEP GOING: YOU'RE
ON THE RIGHT TRACK, THERE YOU GO AGAIN, WATCH YOUR
STEP, I TOLD YOU SO. For each of them I could work out the
calculation, the light-years from here to there, the light-years
from there to here, and establish which episode they were
referring to: all the actions of my life, every time I picked my
nose, all the times I managed to jump down from a moving
tram, were still there, travelling from one galaxy to another,
and they were being considered, commented on, judged.
The comments and judgements were not always pertinent:
the sign TCHK TCHK applied to the time I gave a third of my
salary to a charity subscription; the sign THIS TIME I LIKE
YOU, to when I had forgotten in a train the manuscript of a

treatise that had cost me years of study; my famous prolusion at the University of Göttingen was commented on with the words: WATCH OUT FOR DRAUGHTS.

In a certain sense, I could set my mind at rest: no action of mine, good or bad, was completely lost. At least an echo of it was always saved; or rather, several echoes, which varied from one end of the universe to the other, and in that sphere which was expanding and generating other spheres; but the echoes were discontinuous, conflicting pieces of information, inessential, from which the nexus of my actions didn't emerge, and a new action was unable to explain or correct an old one, so they remained one next to the other, with a plus or minus sign, like a long, long polynomial which cannot be reduced to a more simple expression.

What could I do, at this point? To keep bothering with the past was useless; so far it had gone the way it had gone; I had to make sure the future went better. The important thing was that, in everything I did, it should be clear what was essential, where the stress should be placed, what was to be noted and what not. I procured an enormous directional sign, one of those huge hands with the pointing index finger. When I performed an action to which I wanted to call attention, I had only to raise that sign, trying to make the finger point at the most important detail of the scene. For the moments when, instead, I preferred not to be observed, I made another sign, a hand with the thumb pointing in the direction opposite the one I was turning, to distract attention.

All I had to do was carry those signs wherever I went and raise one or the other, according to the occasion. It was a long-term operation, naturally: the observers hundreds of thousands of light-years away would be hundreds of thousands of millennia late in perceiving what I was doing now, and I would have to wait more hundreds of thousands of millennia to read their reactions. This delay was inevitable; but there was, unfortunately, another drawback I hadn't foreseen: what could I do when I realized I had raised the wrong sign?

For example, at a certain moment I was sure I was about to do something that would give me dignity and prestige; I hastened to wave the sign with the index finger pointed at me; and at that very moment I happened to make a dreadful faux pas, something unforgivable, a display of human wretchedness to make you sink into the ground in shame. But it was done; that image, with the pointing sign, was already navigating through space, nobody could stop it, it was devouring the light-years, spreading among the galaxies, arousing in the millions of future centuries comments and laughter and turned-up noses, which from the depths of the millennia would return to me and would force me to still clumsier excuses, to more embarrassed attempts at correction . . .

Another day, instead, I had to face an unpleasant situation, one of those situations in life that one is obliged to live through, knowing that, whatever happens, there's no way of showing up well. I shielded myself with the sign with the thumb pointing in the other way, and I went off. Unexpectedly, in that delicate and ticklish situation, I displayed quick-wittedness, a balance, a tact, a decisiveness that no one – myself least of all – had ever suspected in me: I suddenly revealed hidden talents that implied a long ripening of character; and meanwhile the sign was deflecting the observers' gaze, making them look at a pot of peonies nearby.

Cases like these, which at first I considered exceptions, the result of my inexperience, kept happening to me more and more frequently. Too late I realized I should have pointed out what I hadn't wanted seen and should have hidden what

I had instead pointed out: there was no way to arrive before the image and to warn them not to pay attention to the sign.

I tried making a third sign with the word CORRECTION, to raise when I wanted to annul the preceding sign, but in every galaxy this image would have been seen only after the one it was meant to correct, and by then the harm was done and I would only seem doubly ridiculous, and to neutralize that with another sign, IGNORE CORRECTION, would have been equally useless.

I went on living, waiting for the remote moment when, from the galaxies, the comments on the new episodes would arrive, charged for me with embarrassment and uneasiness; then I would be able to rebut, sending off my messages of reply, which I was already pondering, each dictated by the situation. Meanwhile, the galaxies for whom I was most compromised were already revolving around the threshold of the billions of light-years at such speeds that, to reach them, my messages would have to struggle across space, clinging to their accelerating flight: then, one by one, they would disappear from the last ten-billion-light-year horizon beyond which no visible object can be seen, and they would bear with them a judgement by then irrevocable.

And, thinking of this judgement I would no longer be able to change, I suddenly felt a kind of relief, as if peace could come to me only after the moment when there would be nothing to add and nothing to remove in that arbitrary ledger of misunderstandings, and the galaxies which were gradually reduced to the last tail of the last luminous ray, winding from the sphere of darkness, seemed to bring with them the only possible truth about myself, and I couldn't wait until all of them, one after the other, had followed this path.

The Spiral

For the majority of molluscs, the visible organic form has little importance in the life of the members of a species, since they cannot see one another and have, at most, only a vague perception of other individuals and of their surroundings. This does not prevent brightly coloured stripings and forms which seem very beautiful to our eyes (as in many gastropod shells) from existing independently of any relationship to visibility.

I

Like me, when I was clinging to that rock, you mean? – *Qfwfq asked* – With the waves rising and falling, and me there, still, flat, sucking what there was to suck and thinking about it all the time? If that's the time you want to know about, there isn't much I can tell you. Form? I didn't have any; that is, I didn't know I had one, or rather I didn't know you *could* have one. I grew more or less on all sides, at random; if this is what you call radial symmetry, I suppose I had radial symmetry, but to tell you the truth I never paid any attention to it. Why should I have grown more on one side than on the other? I had no eyes, no head, no part of the body that was different from any other part; now I try to persuade myself that the two holes I had were a mouth and an anus, and that I therefore already had my bilateral symmetry, just like the trilobites and the rest of you, but in my memory I really can't tell those holes apart, I passed stuff from whatever side I felt like, inside or outside was the same, differences and repugnances came along much later. Every now and then I was seized by fantasies, that's true; for example, the notion of scratching my armpit, or crossing my legs, or once even of growing a moustache. I use these words here with you, to make myself clear; then there were many details I couldn't foresee: I had some cells, one more or less the same as another, and they all did more or less the same job. But since I had no form I could feel all possible forms in myself, and all actions and expressions and possibilities of making noises, even rude ones. In short, there were no limitations to my thoughts, which weren't thoughts, after all, because I had no brain to think them; every cell on its own thought every thinkable thing all at once, not through images, since we had no images of any kind at our disposal, but simply in that indeterminate way of feeling oneself there, which did not prevent us from feeling ourselves equally there in some other way.

It was a rich and free and contented condition, my condition at that time, quite the contrary of what you might think. I was a bachelor (our system of reproduction in those days didn't require even temporary couplings), healthy, without too many ambitions. When you're young, all evolution lies before you, every road is open to you, and at the same time you can enjoy the fact of being there on the rock, flat mollusc-pulp, damp and happy. If you compare yourself with the limitations that came afterwards, if you think of how having one form excludes other forms, of the monotonous routine where you finally feel trapped, well, I don't mind saying, life was beautiful in those days.

To be sure, I lived a bit withdrawn into myself, that's true, no comparison with our interrelated life nowadays; and I'll also admit that – partly because of my age and partly under the influence of my surroundings – I was what they call a narcissist to a slight extent; I mean I stayed there observing myself all the time, I saw all my good points and all my defects, and I liked myself for the former and for the latter; I had no terms of comparison, you must remember that, too.

But I wasn't so backward that I didn't know something else existed beyond me: the rock where I clung, obviously, and also the water that reached me with every wave, but other stuff, too, further on: that is, the world. The water was a source of information, reliable and precise: it brought me edible substances which I absorbed through all my surface, and other inedible ones which still helped me form an idea of what there was around. The system worked like this: a wave would come, and I, still sticking to the rock, would raise myself up a little bit, imperceptibly – all I had to do was loosen the pressure slightly – and, splat, the water passed beneath me, full of substances and sensations and stimuli. You never knew how those stimuli were going to turn out, sometimes a tickling that made you die laughing, other times a shudder, a burning, an itch; so it was a constant seesaw of amusement and emotion. But you mustn't think I just lay there passively, dumbly accepting everything that came: after a while I had acquired some experience and I was quick to analyse what sort of stuff was arriving and to decide how I should behave, to make the best use of it or to avoid the more unpleasant consequences. It was all a kind of game of contractions, with each of the cells I had, or of relaxing at the right moment: and I could make my choices, reject, attract, even spit.

And so I learned that there were *the others*, the element surrounding me was filled with traces of them, *others* hostile and different from me or else disgustingly similar. No, now I'm giving you a disagreeable idea of my character, which is all wrong. Naturally, each of us went about on his own business, but the presence of *the others* reassured me, created an inhabited zone around me, freed me from the fear of being an alarming exception, which I would have been if the fact of existing had been my fate alone, a kind of exile.

So I knew that some of the *others* were female. The water transmitted a special vibration, a kind of brrrum brrrum brrrum, I remember when I became aware of it the first time, or rather, not the first, I remember when I became aware of being aware of it as a thing I had always known. At the discovery of these vibrations' existence, I was seized with a great curiosity, not so much to see them, or to be seen by them either – since, first, we hadn't any sight, and secondly, the sexes weren't yet differentiated, each individual was identical with every other individual and in looking at one or another I would have felt no more pleasure than in looking at myself – but a curiosity to know whether something would happen between me and them. A desperation filled me, a desire not to do anything special, which would have been out of place, knowing that there was nothing special to do, or non-special either, but to respond in some way to that vibration with a corresponding vibration, or rather, with a personal vibration of my own, because, sure enough, there was something there that wasn't exactly the same as the other, I mean now you might say it came from hormones, but for me it was very beautiful.

So then, one of them, shlup shlup shlup, emitted her eggs, and I, shlup shlup shlup, fertilized them: all down inside the sea, mingling in the water tepid from the sun; oh, I forgot to tell you, I could feel the sun, which warmed the sea and heated the rock.

One of them, I said. Because, among all those female messages that the sea slammed against me like an indistinct soup at first where everything was all right with me and I grubbed about paying no attention to what one was like or another, suddenly I understood what corresponded best to my tastes, tastes which I hadn't known before that moment, of course. In other words, I had fallen in love. What I mean is: I had begun to recognize, to isolate the signs of one of those from the others, in fact I waited for these signs I had begun to recognize, I sought them, responded to those signs I awaited with other signs I made myself, or rather it was I who aroused them, these signs from her, which I answered with other signs of my own, I mean I was in love with her and she with me, so what more could I want from life?

Now habits have changed, and it already seems inconceivable to you that one could love a female like that, without having spent any time with her. And yet, through that unmistakable part of her still in solution in the sea water, which the waves placed at my disposal, I received a quantity of information about her, more than you can imagine: not the superficial, generic information you get now, seeing and smelling and touching and hearing a voice, but essential information, which I could then develop at length in my imagination. I could think of her with minute precision, thinking not so much of how she was made, which would have been a banal and vulgar way of thinking of her, but of how from her present formlessness she would be transformed into one of the infinite possible forms, still remaining herself, however. I didn't imagine the forms that she might assume, but I imagined the special quality that, in taking them, she would give to those forms.

I knew her well, in other words. And I wasn't sure of her. Every now and then I was overcome with suspicion, anxiety, rage. I didn't let anything show, you know my character, but beneath that impassive mask passed suppositions I can't bring myself to confess even now. More than once I suspected she was unfaithful to me, that she sent messages not only to me but also to others; more than once I thought I had intercepted one, or that I had discovered a tone of insincerity in a message addressed to me. I was jealous, I can admit it now, not so much out of distrust of her as out of unsureness of myself: who could assure me that she had really understood who I was? Or that she had understood the fact that I was? This relationship achieved between us thanks to the sea water – a full, complete relationship, what more could I ask for? – was for me something absolutely personal, between two unique and distinct individualities; but for her? Who could assure me that what she might find in me she hadn't also found in another, or in another two or three or ten or a hundred like me? Who could assure me that her abandon in our shared relations wasn't an indiscriminate abandon, slapdash, a kind of 'who's next?' collective ecstasy?

The fact that these suspicions did not correspond to the truth was confirmed, for me, by the subtle, soft, private vibration, at times still trembling with modesty, in our correspondences; but what if, precisely out of shyness and inexperience, she didn't pay enough attention to my characteristics and others took advantage of this innocence to worm their way in? And what if she, a novice, believed it was still I and couldn't distinguish one from the other, and so our most intimate play was extended to a circle of strangers . . . ?

It was then that I began to secrete calcareous matter. I wanted to make something to mark my presence in an unmistakable fashion, something that would defend this individual presence of mine from the indiscriminate instability of all the rest. Now it's no use my piling up words, trying to explain the novelty of this intention I had; the first word I said is more than enough: *make*, I wanted to *make*, and considering the fact that I had never made anything or thought you could make anything, this in itself was a big event. So I began to make the first thing that occurred to me, and it was a shell. From the margin of that fleshy cloak on my body, using certain glands, I began to give off secretions which took on a curving shape all around, until I was covered with a hard and variegated shield, rough on the outside and smooth and shiny inside. Naturally, I had no way of controlling the form of what I was making: I just stayed there all huddled up, silent and sluggish, and I secreted. I went on even after the shell covered my whole body; I began another turn; in short, I was getting one of those shells all twisted into a spiral, which you, when you see them, think are so hard to make, but all you have to do is keep working and giving off the same matter without stopping, and they grow like that, one turn after the other.

Once it existed, this shell was also a necessary and indispensable place to stay inside of, a defence for my survival; it was a lucky thing I had made it, but while I was making it I had no idea of making it because I needed it; on the contrary, it was like when somebody lets out an exclamation he could perfectly well not make, and yet he makes it, like 'Ha' or 'hmph!', that's how I made the shell: simply to express myself. And in this self-expression I put all the thoughts I had about her, I released the anger she made me feel, my amorous way of thinking about her, my determination to exist for her, the desire for me to be me, and for her to be her, and the love for myself that I put in my love for her – all the things that could be said only in that conch shell wound into a spiral.

At regular intervals the calcareous matter I was secreting came out coloured, so a number of lovely stripes were formed running straight through the spirals, and this shell was a thing different from me but also the truest part of me, the explanation of who I was, my portrait translated into a rhythmic system of volumes and stripes and colours and hard matter, and it was the portrait of her as she was, because at the same time she was making herself a shell identical to mine and without knowing it I was copying what she was doing and she without knowing it was copying what I was doing, and all the others were copying all the others, so we would be back where we had been before except for the fact that in saying these shells were the same I was a bit hasty, because when you looked closer you discovered all sorts of little differences that later on might become enormous.

So I can say that my shell made itself, without my taking any special pains to have it come out one way rather than another, but this doesn't mean that I was absent-minded during that time; I applied myself, instead, to that act of secreting, without allowing myself a moment's distraction, never thinking of anything else, or rather: thinking always of something else, since I didn't know how to think of the shell, just as, for that matter, I didn't know how to think of anything else either, but I accompanied the effort of making the shell with the effort of thinking I was making something, that is anything: that is, I thought of all the things it would be possible to make. So it wasn't even a monotonous task, because the effort of thinking which accompanied it spread towards countless types of thoughts which spread, each one, towards countless types of actions that might each serve to make countless things, and making each of these things was implicit in making the shell grow, turn after turn . . .

II

(And so now, after five hundred million years have gone by, I look around and, above the rock, I see the railway embankment and the train passing along it with a party of Dutch girls looking out of the window and, in the last compartment, a solitary traveller reading Herodotus in a bilingual edition, and the train vanishes into the tunnel under the highway, where there is a sign with the Pyramids and the words 'VISIT EGYPT', and a little ice-cream van tries to pass a big truck laden with instalments of Rh-Stijl, a periodical encyclopedia that comes out in paperback, but then it puts its brakes on because its visibility is blocked by a cloud of bees which crosses the road coming from a row of hives in a field from which surely a queen bee is flying away, drawing behind her a swarm in the direction opposite to the smoke of the train, which has reappeared at the other end of the tunnel, so you can see hardly anything thanks to the cloudy stream of bees and coal smoke, except a few yards further up there is a peasant breaking the ground with his mattock and, unaware, he brings to light and reburies a fragment of a Neolithic mattock similar to his own, in a garden that surrounds an astronomical observatory with its telescopes aimed at the sky and on whose threshold the keeper's daughter sits reading the horoscopes in a weekly whose cover displays the face of the star of Cleopatra: *I see all this and I feel no amazement because making the shell implied also making the honey in the wax comb and the coal and the telescopes and the reign of Cleopatra and the films about Cleopatra and the Pyramids and the design of the zodiac of the Chaldean astrologers and the wars and empires Herodotus speaks of and the words written by Herodotus and the works written in all languages, including those of Spinoza in Dutch, and the fourteen-line summary of Spinoza's life and works in the instalment of the encyclopedia in the truck passed by the*

ice-cream van, and so I feel as if, in making the shell, I had also made the rest.

I look around, and whom am I looking for? She is still the one I seek; I've been in love for five hundred million years, and if I see a Dutch girl on the sand with a beachboy wearing a gold chain around his neck and showing her the swarm of bees to frighten her, there she is: I recognize her from her inimitable way of raising one shoulder until it almost touches her cheek, I'm almost sure, or rather I'd say absolutely sure if it weren't for a certain resemblance that I find also in the daughter of the keeper of the observatory, and in the photograph of the actress made up as Cleopatra, or perhaps in Cleopatra as she really was in person, for that part of the true Cleopatra they say every representation of Cleopatra contains, or in the queen bee flying at the head of the swarm with that forward impetuousness, or in the paper woman cut out and pasted on the plastic windscreen of the little ice-cream van, wearing a bathing suit like the Dutch girl on the beach now listening over a little transistor radio to the voice of a woman singing, the same voice that the encyclopedia truck driver hears over his radio, and the same one I'm now sure I've heard for five million years, it is surely she I hear singing and whose image I look for all around, seeing only gulls volplaning on the surface of the sea where a school of anchovies glistens and for a moment I am certain I recognize her in a female gull and a moment later I suspect that instead she's an anchovy, though she might just as well be any queen or slave-girl named by Herodotus or only hinted at in the pages of the volume left to mark the seat of the reader who has stepped into the corridor of the train to strike up a conversation with the party of Dutch tourists; I might say I am in love with each of those girls and at the same time I am sure of being in love always with her alone.

And the more I torment myself with love for each of them, the less I can bring myself to say to them: 'Here I am!', afraid of being mistaken and even more afraid that she is mistaken, taking me for *somebody else, for somebody who, for all she knows of me, might easily take my place, for example the beachboy with the gold chain, or the director of the observatory, or a gull, or a male anchovy, or the reader of Herodotus, or Herodotus himself, or the vendor of ice cream, who has come down to the beach along a dusty road among the prickly pears and is now surrounded by the Dutch girls in their bathing suits, or Spinoza, or the truck driver who is transporting the life and works of Spinoza summarized and repeated two thousand times, or one of the drones dying at the bottom of the hive after having fulfilled his role in the continuation of the species.)*

III

... Which doesn't mean that the shell wasn't, first and foremost, a shell, with its particular form, which couldn't be any different because it was the very form I had given it, the only one I could or would give it. Since the shell had a form, the form of the world was also changed, in the sense that now it included the form of the world as it had been without a shell plus the form of the shell.

And that had great consequences: because the waving vibrations of light, striking bodies, produce particular effects from them, colour first of all, namely, that matter I used to make stripes with which vibrated in a different way from the rest; but there was also the fact that a volume enters into a special relationship of volumes with other volumes, all phenomena I couldn't be aware of, though they existed.

The shell in this way was able to create visual images of shells, which are things very similar – as far as we know – to the shell itself, except that the shell is here, whereas the images of it are formed elsewhere, possibly on a retina. An image therefore presupposes a retina, which in turn presupposes a complex system stemming from an encephalon. So, in producing the shell, I also produced its image – not one, of course, but many, because with one shell you can make as many shell-images as you want – but only potential images because to form an image you need all the requisites I mentioned before: an encephalon with its optic ganglia, and an optic nerve to carry the vibrations from outside to inside, and this optic nerve, at the other extremity, ends in something made purposely to see what there is outside, namely the eye. Now it's ridiculous to think that, having an encephalon, one would simply drop a nerve like a fishing line cast into the darkness; until the eyes crop up, one can't know whether there is something to be seen outside or not. For myself, I had none of this equipment, so I was the least authorized to speak of it; however, I had conceived an idea of my own, namely that the important thing was to form some visual images, and the eyes would come later in consequence. So I concentrated on making the part of me that was outside (and even the interior part of me that conditioned the exterior) give rise to an image, or rather to what would later be called a lovely image (when compared to other images considered less lovely, or rather ugly, or simply revoltingly hideous).

When a body succeeds in emitting or in reflecting luminous vibrations in a distinct and recognizable order – I thought – what does it do with these vibrations? Put them in its pocket? No, it releases them on the first passer-by. And how will the latter behave in the face of vibrations he can't utilize and which, taken in this way, might even be annoying? Hide his head in a hole? No, he'll thrust it out in that direction until the point most exposed to the optic vibrations becomes sensitized and develops the mechanism for exploiting them in the form of images. In short, I conceived of the eye–

encephalon link as a kind of tunnel dug from the outside by the force of what was ready to become image, rather than from within by the intention of picking up any old image.

And I wasn't mistaken: even today I'm sure that the project – in its overall aspect – was right. But my error lay in thinking that sight would also come to us, that is to me and to her. I elaborated a harmonious, coloured image of myself to enter her visual receptivity, to occupy its centre, to settle there, so that she could utilize me constantly, in dreaming and in memory, with thought as well as with sight. And I felt at the same time she was radiating an image of herself so perfect that it would impose itself on my foggy, backward senses, developing in me an interior visual field where it would blaze forth definitely.

So our efforts led us to become those perfect objects of a sense whose nature nobody quite knew yet, and which later became perfect precisely through the perfection of its object, which was, in fact, us. I'm talking about sight, the eyes; only I had failed to foresee one thing: the eyes that finally opened to see us didn't belong to us but to others.

Shapeless, colourless beings, sacks of guts stuck together carelessly, peopled the world all around us, without giving the slightest thought to what they should make of themselves, to how to express themselves and identify themselves in a stable, complete form, such as to enrich the visual possibilities of whoever saw them. They came and went, sank a while, then emerged, in that space between air and water and rock, wandering about absently; and we in the meanwhile, she and I and all those intent on squeezing out a form of ourselves, were there slaving away at our dark task. Thanks to us, that badly defined space became a visual field; and who reaped the benefit? These intruders, who had never before given a thought to the possibility of eyesight (ugly as they were, they wouldn't have gained a thing by seeing one another), these creatures who had always turned a deaf ear to the vocation of form. While we were bent over, doing the hardest part of the job, that is creating something to be seen, they were quietly taking on the easiest part: adapting their lazy, embryonic receptive organs to what there was to receive: our images. And they needn't try telling me now that their job was toilsome too: from that gluey mess that filled their heads anything could have come out, and a photosensitive mechanism doesn't take all that much trouble to put together. But when it comes to perfecting it, that's another story! How can you, if you don't have visible objects to see, gaudy ones even, the kind that impose themselves on the eyesight? To sum it up in a few words: they developed eyes at our expense.

So sight, *our* sight, which we were obscurely waiting for, was the sight that the others had of us. In one way or another, the great revolution had taken place: all of a sudden, around us, eyes were opening, and corneas and irises and pupils: the swollen, colourless eye of polyps and cuttlefish, the dazed and gelatinous eyes of bream and mullet, the protruding and peduncled eyes of crayfish and lobsters, the bulging and faceted eyes of flies and ants. A seal now comes forward, black and shiny, winking little eyes like pinheads. A snail extends ball-like eyes at the end of long antennae. The inexpressive eyes of the gull examine the surface of the water. Beyond a glass mask the frowning eyes of an underwater fisherman explore the depths. Through the lens of a spyglass a sea captain's eyes and the eyes of a woman bathing converge on my shell, then look at each other, forgetting me. Framed by far-sighted lenses I feel on me the far-sighted eyes of a zoologist, trying to frame me in the eye of a Rolleiflex. At that moment a school of tiny anchovies, barely born, passes before me, so tiny that in each little white fish it seems there is room only for the eye's black dot, and it is a kind of eye-dust that crosses the sea.

All these eyes were mine. I had made them possible; I had had the active part; I furnished them the raw material, the image. With eyes had come all the rest, so everything that the others, having eyes, had become, their every form and function, and the quantity of things that, thanks to eyes, they had managed to do, in their every form and function, came from what I had done. Of course, they were not just casually implicit in my being there, in my having relations with others, male and female, et cetera, in my setting out to make a shell, et cetera. In other words, I had foreseen absolutely everything.

And at the bottom of each of those eyes I lived, or rather another me lived, one of the images of me, and it encountered the image of her, the most faithful image of her, in that beyond which opens up, past the semi-liquid sphere of the irises, in the darkness of the pupils, the mirrored hall of the retinas, in our true element which extends without shores, without boundaries.

Time and the Hunter

PART ONE

More of Qfwfq

The Soft Moon

According to the calculations of H. Gerstenkorn, later developed by H. Alfven, the terrestrial continents are simply fragments of the Moon which fell upon our planet. According to this theory, the Moon originally was a planet gravitating around the Sun, until the moment when the nearness of the Earth caused it to be derailed from its orbit. Captured by terrestrial gravity, the Moon moved closer and closer, contracting its orbit around us. At a certain moment the reciprocal attraction began to alter the surface of the two celestial bodies, raising very high waves from which fragments were detached and sent spinning in space, between Earth and Moon, especially fragments of lunar matter which finally fell upon Earth. Later, through the influence of our tides, the Moon was impelled to move away again, until it reached its present orbit. But a part of the lunar mass, perhaps half of it, had remained on Earth, forming the continents.

She was coming closer – *Qfwfq recalled* – I noticed it as I was going home, raising my eyes between the walls of glass and steel, and I saw her, no longer a light like all the others that shine in the evening: the ones they light on Earth when at a certain hour they pull down a lever at the power station, or those of the sky, further away but similar, or at least not out of harmony with the style of all the rest – I speak in the present tense, but I am still referring to those remote times

– I saw her breaking away from all the other lights of the sky and the streets, standing out in the concave map of darkness, no longer occupying a point, perhaps a big one on the order of Mars and Venus, like a hole through which the light spreads, but now becoming an out-and-out portion of space, and she was taking form, not yet clearly identifiable because eyes weren't used to identifying it, but also because the outlines weren't sufficiently precise to define a regular figure. Anyway I saw it was becoming a thing.

And it revolted me. Because it was a thing that, though you couldn't understand what it was made of, or perhaps precisely because you couldn't understand, seemed different from all the things in our life, our good things of plastic, of nylon, of chrome-plated steel, ducotone, synthetic resins, plexiglass, aluminium, vinyl, formica, zinc, asphalt, asbestos, cement, the old things among which we were born and bred. It was something incompatible, extraneous. I saw it approaching as if it were going to slip between the skyscrapers of Madison Avenue (I'm talking about the avenue we had then, beyond comparison with the Madison of today), in that corridor of night sky glowing with light from above the jagged line of the cornices; and it spread out, imposing on our familiar landscape not only its light of an unsuitable colour, but also its volume, its weight, its incongruous substantiality. And then, all over the face of the Earth – the surfaces of metal plating, iron armatures, rubber pavements, glass domes – over every part of us that was exposed, I felt a shudder pass.

As fast as the traffic allowed, I went through the tunnel, drove towards the Observatory. Sibyl was there, her eye glued to the telescope. As a rule she didn't like me to visit her during working hours, and the moment she saw me she would make a vexed face; but not that evening: she didn't even look up, it was obvious she was expecting my visit.

'Have you seen it?' would have been a stupid question, but I had to bite my tongue to keep from asking it, I was so impatient to know what she thought about it all.

'Yes, the planet Moon has come still closer,' Sibyl said, before I had asked her anything, 'the phenomenon was foreseen.'

I felt a bit relieved. 'Do you foresee that it'll move away again?' I asked.

Sibyl still had one eyelid half closed, peering into the telescope. 'No,' she said, 'it won't move away any more.'

I didn't understand. 'You mean that the Earth and the Moon have become twin planets?'

'I mean the Moon isn't a planet any more and the Earth has a Moon.'

Sibyl had a casual way of dismissing matters; it irritated me every time she did it. 'What kind of thinking is that?' I complained. 'One planet's just as much a planet as the others, isn't it?'

'Would you call this a planet? I mean, a planet the way the Earth's a planet? Look!' And Sibyl moved from the telescope, motioning me to approach it. 'The Moon could never manage to become a planet like ours.'

I wasn't listening to her explanation: the Moon, enlarged by the telescope, appeared to me in all its details, or rather many of its details appeared to me at once, so mixed up that the more I observed it the less sure I was of how it was made, and I could only vouch for the effect this sight caused in me, an effect of fascinated disgust. First of all, I could note the green veins that ran over it, thicker in certain zones, like a network, but to tell the truth this was the most insignificant detail, the least showy, because what you might call the general properties eluded the grasp of my glance, thanks perhaps to the slightly viscous glistening that transpired from a myriad of pores, one would have said, or opercula, and also in certain points from extended tumefactions of the surface, like buboes or suckers. There, I'm concentrating again on the details, a more picturesque method of description apparently, though in reality of only limited efficiency, because only by considering the details within the whole – such as the swelling of the sublunar pulp which stretched its pale external tissues but made them also fold over on themselves in inlets or recesses looking like scars (so it, this Moon, might also have been made of pieces pressed together and stuck on carelessly) – it is, as I say, only by considering the whole, as in diseased viscera, that the single details can also be considered: for example, a thick forest as of black fur which jutted out of a rift.

'Does it seem right to you that it should go on revolving around the Sun, like us?' Sibyl said. 'The Earth is far stronger: in the end it'll shift the Moon from its orbit and make it turn around the Earth. We'll have a satellite.'

I was quite careful not to express the anguish I was feeling. I knew how Sibyl reacted in these cases: assuming an attitude of blatant superiority, if not of downright cynicism, acting like a person who is never surprised by anything. She behaved this way to provoke me, I believe (that is, I hope; I would certainly have felt even greater anguish at the thought that she acted out of real indifference).

'And . . . and . . .' I started to say, taking care to formulate a question that would show nothing but objective curiosity and yet would force Sibyl to say something to appease my anxiety (so I still hoped for this from her, I still insisted that her calm reassure me), '. . . and will we always have it in sight like this?'

'This is nothing,' she answered. 'It'll come even closer.' And for the first time, she smiled. 'Don't you like it? Why, seeing it there like that, so different, so far from any known form, and knowing that it's ours, that the Earth has captured it and is keeping it there . . . I don't know, I like it, it seems beautiful to me.'

At this point I no longer cared about hiding my mood. 'But won't it be dangerous for us?' I asked.

Sibyl tensed her lips in the expression of hers I liked least. 'We are on the Earth, the Earth has a force which means it can keep planets around itself, on its own, like the Sun. What can the Moon oppose, in the way of mass, field of gravity, orbit stability, consistency? Surely you don't mean to compare the two? The Moon is all soft, the Earth is hard, solid, the Earth endures.'

'What about the Moon? If it doesn't endure?'

'Oh, the Earth's force will keep it in its place.'

I waited till Sibyl had finished her shift at the Observatory, to drive her home. Just outside the city there is that cloverleaf where all the motorways spread out, rushing over bridges that cross one another in spiral patterns, held up by cement pillars of different heights; you never know in what direction you're going as you follow the white arrows painted on the asphalt, and now and then you find the city you're leaving suddenly facing you, coming closer, patterned with squares of light among the pillars and the curves of the spiral. There was the Moon just above us: and the city seemed fragile to me, suspended like a cobweb, with all its little tinkling panes, its threadlike embroidery of light, under that excrescence that swelled the sky.

Now, I have used the word 'excrescence' to indicate the Moon, but I must at once fall back on the same word to describe the new thing I discovered at that moment: namely, an excrescence emerging from that Moon-excrescence, stretching towards the Earth like the drip of a candle.

'What's that? What's happening?' I asked, but by now a new curve had set our automobile journeying towards the darkness.

'It's the terrestrial attraction causing solid tides on the Moon's surface,' Sibyl said. 'What did I tell you? Call that consistency?'

The unwinding of the motorway brought us again face to face with the Moon, and that candle dripping had stretched still further towards the Earth, curling at its tip like a moustache hair, and then, as its point of attachment thinned to a peduncle, it had almost the appearance of a mushroom.

We lived in a cottage, in a line with others along one of the many avenues of a vast Green Belt. We sat down as always on the rocking chairs on the porch with a view of the backyard, but this time we didn't look at the half-acre of glazed tiles that formed our share of green space; our eyes were staring above, magnetized by that sort of polyp hanging over us. Because now the Moon's drippings had become numerous, and they extended towards the Earth like slimy tentacles, and each of them seemed about to start dripping in its turn a matter composed of gelatin and hair and mould and slaver.

'I ask you, is that any way for a celestial body to disintegrate?' Sibyl insisted. 'Now you must realize the superiority of our planet. What if the Moon does come down? Let it come: the time will come also for it to stop. This is the sort of power the Earth's field of gravity has: after it's attracted the Moon almost on top of us, all of a sudden it stops the Moon, carries it back to a proper distance, and keeps it there, making it revolve, pressing it into a compact ball. The Moon has us to thank if it doesn't fall apart completely!'

I found Sibyl's reasoning convincing, because to me, too, the Moon seemed something inferior and revolting; but her words still couldn't relieve my apprehension. I saw the lunar outcrops writhing in the sky with sinuous movements, as if they were trying to reach or enfold something: there was the city, below, where we could see a glow of light on the horizon with the jagged shadow of the skyline. Would it stop in time, the Moon, as Sibyl had said, before one of its tentacles had succeeded in clutching the spire of a skyscraper? And what if, sooner, one of these stalactites that kept stretching and lengthening should break off, plunge down upon us?

'Something may come down,' Sibyl admitted, without waiting for a question from me, 'but what does that matter? The Earth is all sheathed in waterproof, crushproof, dirtproof materials; even if a bit of this Moon mush drips on to us, we can clean it up in a hurry.'

As if Sibyl's assurance had enabled me to see something that had surely been taking place for a while, I cried: 'Look, stuff is coming down!' and I raised my arm to point out a suspension of thick drops of a creamy pap in the air. But at that same moment a vibration came from the Earth, a tinkling; and through the sky, in the direction opposite to the falling clumps of planetary secretion, a very minute flight of solid fragments rose, the scales of the Earth's armour which was being shattered: unbreakable glass and plates of steel and sheaths of non-conducting material, drawn up by the Moon's attraction as in an eddy of grains of sand.

'Only minimal damage,' Sibyl said, 'and just on the surface. We can repair the gaps in no time. It's only logical that the capture of a satellite should cost us some losses: but it's worth it, there's simply no comparison!'

That was when we heard the first crack of a lunar meteorite falling to the Earth: a very loud 'splat!', a deafening noise and, at the same time, a disgustingly spongy one, which didn't remain alone but was followed by a series of apparently explosive splashes, of flabby whip strokes falling on every side. Before our eyes became accustomed to perceiving what was falling, a little time went by: to tell the truth, I was the slow one because I expected the pieces of the Moon to be luminous too; whereas Sibyl already saw them and commented on them in her contemptuous tone but also with an unusual indulgence: 'Soft meteorites, now really, who's ever seen such a thing? Stuff worthy of the Moon . . . interesting, though, in its way . . .'

One remained stuck on the wire hedge, half crushed under its weight, spilling over on the ground and immediately mixing with it, and I began to see what it was, that is I began to assemble some sensations that would allow me to form a visual image of what I had before me, and then I became aware of other, smaller spots scattered all over the tile pavement: something like a mud of acid mucus which penetrated into the terrestrial strata, or rather a kind of vegetal parasite that absorbed everything it touched, incorporating it into its own gluey pulp, or else like a serum in which colonies of whirling and ravenous micro-organisms were agglomerated, or else a pancreas cut in pieces trying to join together again, opening like suckers the cells of its cut edges, or else . . .

I would have liked to close my eyes and I couldn't; but when I heard Sibyl's voice say: 'Of course, I find it revolting too, but when you think that the fact is finally established: the Earth is definitely different and superior and we're on this side, I believe that for a moment we can even enjoy sinking into it, because anyway afterwards . . .' I wheeled around towards her. Her mouth was open in a smile I had never seen before: a damp smile, slightly animal . . .

The sensation I felt on seeing her like that became confused with the fear caused almost at the same moment by the fall of the great lunar fragment, the one that submerged and destroyed our cottage and the whole avenue and the residential suburb and a great part of the county, in a single, hot, syrupy, stunning blow. After digging through the lunar matter all night, we managed to see the sky again. It was dawn; the storm of meteorites was over; the Earth around us was unrecognizable, covered by a deep layer of mud, a paste of green proliferations and slippery organisms. Of our former terrestrial materials not a trace was visible. The Moon was moving off in the sky, pale, also unrecognizable: narrowing my eyes, I could see it was covered with a thick mass of rubble and shards and fragments, shiny, sharp, clean.

The sequel is familiar. After hundreds of thousands of centuries we are trying to give the Earth its former natural appearance, we are reconstructing the primitive terrestrial crust of plastic and cement and metal and glass and enamel and imitation leather. But what a long way we have to go! For a still incalculable amount of time we will be condemned to sink into the lunar discharge, rotten with chlorophyll and gastric juices and dew and nitrogenous gases and cream and tears. We still have much to do, soldering the shiny and precise plates of the primordial terrestrial sheath until we have erased – or at least concealed – the alien and hostile additions. And with today's materials, too, concocted haphazardly, products of a corrupt Earth, trying in vain to imitate the prime substances, which cannot be equalled.

The true materials, those of the past, are said to be found now only on the Moon, unexploited and lying there in a mess, and they say that for this reason alone it would be worthwhile going there: to recover them. I don't like to seem the sort who always says disagreeable things, but we all know what state the Moon is in, exposed to cosmic storms, full of holes, corroded, worn. If we go there, we'll only have the disappointment of learning that even our material of the old days – the great reason and proof of terrestrial superiority – was inferior goods, not made to last, which can no longer be used even as scrap. There was a time when I would have been careful not to show suspicions of this sort to Sibyl. But now, when she's fat, dishevelled, lazy, greedily eating cream puffs, what can Sibyl say to me?

The Origin of the Birds

The appearance of Birds comes relatively late, in the history of evolution, following the emergence of all the other classes of the animal kingdom. The progenitor of the Birds – or at least the first whose traces have been found by palaeontologists – is the Archaeopteryx (still endowed with certain characteristics of the Reptiles from which he descends), who dates from the Jurassic period, tens of millions of years after the first Mammals. This is the only exception to the successive appearance of animal groups progressively more developed in the zoological scale.

In those days we weren't expecting any more surprises – *Qfwfq narrated* – by then it was clear how things were going to proceed. Those who existed, existed; we had to work things out for ourselves: some would go further, some would remain where they were, and some wouldn't manage to survive. The choice had to be made from a limited number of possibilities.

But instead, one morning I hear some singing, outside, that I have never heard before. Or rather (since we didn't yet know what singing was), I hear something making a sound that nobody has ever made before. I look out. I see an unknown animal singing on a branch. He had wings feet tail claws spurs feathers plumes fins quills beak teeth crop horns crest wattles and a star on his forehead. It was a bird; you've realized that already, but I didn't; they had never been seen before. He sang: 'Koaxpf . . . Koaxpf . . . Koaaacch . . .', he beat his wings, striped with iridescent colours, he rose in flight, he came to rest a bit further on, resumed his singing.

Now these stories can be told better with strip drawings than with a story composed of sentences one after the other. But to make a cartoon with the bird on the branch and me looking out and all the others with their noses in the air, I would have to remember better how a number of things were made, things I've long since forgotten; first the thing I now call bird, second what I now call I, third the branch, fourth the place where I was looking out, fifth all the others. Of these elements I remember only that they were very different from the way we would draw them now. It's best for you to try on your own to imagine the series of cartoons with all the little figures of the characters in their places, against an effectively outlined background, but you must try at the same time not to imagine the figures, or the background either. Each figure will have its little balloon with the words it says, or with the noises it makes, but there's no need for you to read everything written there letter for letter, you only need a general idea, according to what I'm going to tell you.

To begin with, you can read a lot of exclamation marks and question marks spurting from our heads, and these mean we were looking at the bird full of amazement – festive amazement, with desire on our part also to sing, to imitate that first warbling, and to jump, to see the bird rise in flight – but also full of consternation, because the existence of birds knocked our traditional way of thinking into a cocked hat.

In the strip that follows, you see the wisest of us all, old U(h), who moves from the group of the others and says: 'Don't look at him! He's a mistake!' and he holds out his hands as if he wanted to cover the eyes of those present. 'Now I'll erase him!' he says, or thinks, and to depict this desire of his we could have him draw a diagonal line across the frame. The bird flaps his wings, eludes the diagonal, and flies to safety in the opposite corner. U(h) is happy because, with that diagonal line between them, he can't see the bird any more. The bird pecks at the line, breaks it, and flies at old U(h). Old U(h), to erase him, tries to draw a couple of crossed lines over him. At the point where the two lines meet, the bird alights and lays an egg. Old U(h) pulls the lines from under him, the egg falls, the bird darts off. There is one frame all stained with egg yolk.

I like telling things in cartoon form, but I would have to alternate the action frames with idea frames, and explain for example this stubbornness of U(h)'s in not wanting to admit the existence of the bird. So imagine one of those little frames all filled with writing, which are used to bring you up to date on what went before: *After the failure of the Pterosauria, for millions and millions of years all trace of animals with wings had been lost.* ('Except for Insects', a footnote can clarify.)

The question of winged creatures was considered closed by now. Hadn't we been told over and over that everything capable of being born from the Reptiles had been born? In the course of millions of years there was no form of living creature that hadn't had its opportunity to come forth, populate the Earth, and then – in ninety-nine cases out of a hundred – decline and vanish. On this point we were all agreed: the remaining species were the only deserving ones, destined to give life to more and more highly selected progeny, better suited to their surroundings. For some time we had been tormented by doubts as to who was a monster and who wasn't, but that too could be considered long settled: all of us who existed were non-monsters, while the monsters were all those who could exist and didn't, because the succession of causes and effects had clearly favoured us, the non-monsters, rather than them.

But if we were going to begin again with strange animals, if the Reptiles, antiquated as they were, started to pull out limbs and teguments they had never felt any need for previously, in other words if a creature impossible by definition such as a bird was instead possible (and what's more if it could be a handsome bird like this one, pleasing to the sight when he poised on the fern leaves, and to the hearing when he released his warbling), then the barrier between monsters and non-monsters was exploded and everything was possible again.

The bird flew far off. (In the drawing you see a black shadow against the clouds in the sky: not because the bird is black but because that's the way distant birds are drawn.) And I ran after him. (You see me from behind, as I enter a vast landscape of mountains and forests.) Old U(h) is shouting at me: 'Come back, Qfwfq!'

I crossed unfamiliar zones. More than once I thought I was lost (in the drawing it only has to be depicted once), but then I would hear a 'Koaxpf . . .' and, raising my eyes, I would see the bird perched on a plant, as if he were waiting for me.

Following him like that, I reached a spot where the bushes blocked my view. I opened a path for myself: beneath my feet I saw the void. The Earth ended there; I was balanced on the brink. (The spiral line rising from my head represents my dizziness.) Below, nothing could be seen: a few clouds. And the bird, in that void, went flying off, and every now and then he twisted his neck towards me as if inviting me to follow him. Follow him where, when there was nothing further on?

And then from the white distance a shadow rose, like a

horizon of mist, which gradually became clearer, with more distinct outlines. It was a continent, coming forward in the void: you could see its shores, its valleys, its heights, and already the bird was flying above them. But what bird? He was no longer alone, the whole sky over there was a flapping of wings of every colour and every form.

Leaning out from the brink of our Earth, I watched the continent drift towards me. 'It's crashing into us!' I shouted, and at that moment the ground trembled. (A 'bang!' written in big letters.) The two worlds, having touched, bounced apart again, then were rejoined, then separated once more. In one of these clashes I found myself flung to the other side, while the empty abyss yawned again and separated me from my world.

I looked around: I didn't recognize anything. Trees, crystals, animals, grasses – everything was different. Not only did birds inhabit the branches, but so did fish (after a manner of speaking) with spiders' legs or (you might say) worms with feathers. Now it's not that I want to describe to you the forms of life over there; imagine them any way you can, more or less strange, it doesn't much matter. What matters is that around me there were displayed all the forms the world could have taken in its transformations but instead hadn't taken, for some casual reason or for some basic incompatibility: the rejected forms, unusable, lost.

(To give an idea this strip of drawings should be done in negative: with figures not unlike the others but in white on black; or else upside down – assuming that it can be decided, for any of these figures, which is up and which is down.)

Alarm froze my bones (in the cartoon, drops of cold sweat spurt from my figure) at seeing those images, all of them in some way familiar and all in some way distorted in their proportions or their combinations (my very tiny figure in white, superimposed on the black shadows that occupy the whole frame), but I couldn't refrain from exploring eagerly all around me. You would have said that my gaze, rather than avoid those monsters, sought them out, as if to be convinced they weren't monsters entirely, and at a certain point my horror was replaced by a not unpleasant sensation (represented in the drawing by luminous rays crossing the black background): beauty existed even there, if one could recognize it.

This curiosity had led me away from the coast, and I moved among hills that were spiky like enormous sea urchins. By now I was lost in the heart of the unknown continent. (The figure that represents me has become minuscule.) The birds, which a short time before had been for me the strangest of apparitions, were already becoming the most familiar of presences. There were so many that they formed a kind of dome around me, raising and lowering their wings all together (frame crammed with birds; my outline barely glimpsed). Others were resting on the ground, perched on the bushes, and gradually as I advanced they moved. Was I their prisoner? I turned to run off, but I was surrounded by walls of birds who left me no passage, except in one direction. They were driving me where they wanted, all their movements were leading me to one point. What was there, at the end? I could discern only a kind of enormous egg lying on its side, which opened slowly, like a shell.

All of a sudden it was flung open. I smiled. My eyes filled with tears of emotion. (I'm depicted alone, in profile; what I'm looking at remains outside the frame.) Before me there was a creature of a beauty never seen before. A *different* beauty, which couldn't be compared to all the forms in which we had recognized beauty (in the frame it is still placed in such a way that only I have it before me, not the reader), and yet *ours*, the most *ours* thing of our world (in the frame a symbolical depiction could be used: a feminine hand, or a foot, or a breast, emerging from a great cloak of feathers); without it our world would always have lacked something. I felt I had arrived at the point where everything converged (an eye could be drawn, an eye with long radial lashes which are transformed into a vortex) and where I was about to be swallowed (or a mouth, the parting of two finely drawn lips, tall as I, and me flying, sucked towards the tongue rising from the darkness).

All around me, birds: flapping of beaks, wings that flutter, claws extended, and the cry: 'Koaxpf ... Koaxpf ... Koaaacch ...'

'Who are you?' I asked.

A title explains: *Qfwfq before the beautiful Org-Onir-Ornit-Or*, and makes my question pointless; the balloon that contains it is covered by another, also rising from my mouth, with the words 'I love you!' – an equally superfluous affirmation – promptly followed by another balloon containing the question: 'Are you a prisoner?' to which I don't await an answer, and in a fourth balloon which makes its way among the others I add, 'I'll rescue you. Tonight we'll flee together.'

The following strip is entirely dedicated to the preparations for the flight, to the sleep of the birds and the monsters in a night illuminated by an unknown firmament. A dark little frame, and my voice: 'Are you following me?' Or's voice answered: 'Yes.'

Here you can imagine for yourselves a series of adventurous strips: *Qfwfq and Or in flight across the Continent of the Birds*. Alarms, pursuit, dangers: I leave these to you. To tell the story I should somehow describe what Or was like; and I can't. Imagine a figure somehow towering over mine, but which I somehow hide and protect.

We reached the edge of the chasm. It was dawn. The sun was rising, pale, to reveal our continent now disappearing in the distance. How were we to reach it? I turned towards Or: Or opened her wings. (You hadn't noticed she had them, in the previous frames: two wings broad as sails.) I clung to her cloak. Or flew.

In the next cartoons Or is seen flying among the clouds, with my head peeping out from her bosom. Then, a triangle of little black triangles in the sky: a swarm of birds pursuing us. We are still in the midst of the void; our continent is approaching, but the swarm is faster. They are birds of prey, with curved beaks, fiery eyes. If Or is quick to reach Earth, we will be among our own kind, before the raptors can attack us. Hurry, Or, a few more flaps of your wings: in the next strip we can reach safety.

Not a chance: now the swarm has surrounded us. Or is flying among the raptors (a little white triangle drawn in another triangle full of little black triangles). We are flying over my village: Or would have only to fold her wings and let herself drop, and we would be free. But Or continues flying high, along with the birds. I shouted: 'Or, move lower!' She opened her cloak and let me fall. ('Plop!') The swarm, with Or in their midst, turns in the sky, goes back, becomes tiny on the horizon. I find myself flat on the ground, alone.

(Title: *During Qfwfq's absence, many changes had taken place.*) Since the existence of birds had been discovered, the ideas that governed our world had come to a crisis. What everyone had thought he understood before, the simple and regular way in which things were as they were, was no longer valid; in other words: this was nothing but one of the countless possibilities; nobody excluded the possibility that things could proceed in other, entirely different ways. You would have said that now each individual was ashamed of being the way he was expected to be, and was making an effort to show some irregular, unforeseen aspect: a slightly more birdlike aspect, or if not exactly birdlike, at least sufficiently so to keep him from looking out of place alongside the strangeness of the birds. I no longer recognized my neighbours. Not that they were much changed: but those who had some inexplicable characteristic which they had formerly tried to conceal now put it on display. And they all looked as if they were expecting something any moment: not the punctual succession of causes and effects as in the past, but the unexpected.

I couldn't get my bearings. The others thought I had stuck to the old ideas, to the time before the birds; they didn't understand that to me their birdish whims were only laughable: I had seen much more than that, I had visited the world of the things that could have been, and I couldn't drive it from my mind. And I had known the beauty kept prisoner in the heart of that world, the beauty lost for me and for all of us, and I had fallen in love with it.

I spent my days on the top of a mountain, gazing at the sky in case a bird flew across it. And on the peak of another mountain nearby there was old U(h), also looking at the sky. Old U(h) was still considered the wisest of us all, but his attitude towards the birds had changed. He believed the birds were no longer a mistake, but the truth, the only truth of the world. He had taken to interpreting the birds' flight, trying to read the future in it.

'Seen anything?' he shouted to me, from his mountain.

'Nothing in sight,' I said.

'There's one!' we would shout at times, he or I.

'Where was it coming from? I didn't have time to see from what part of the sky it appeared. Tell me: where from?' he asked, all breathless. U(h) drew his auguries from the source of the flight.

Or else it was I who asked: 'What direction was it flying in? I didn't see it! Did it vanish over here or over there?' because I hoped the birds would show me the way to reach Or.

There's no use my telling you in detail the cunning I used to succeed in returning to the Continent of the Birds. In the strips it would be told with one of those tricks that work well only in drawings. (The frame is empty. I arrive. I spread paste on the upper right-hand corner. I sit down in the lower left-hand corner. A bird enters, flying, from the left, at the top. As he leaves the frame, his tail becomes stuck. He keeps flying and pulls after him the whole frame stuck to his tail, with me sitting at the bottom, allowing myself to be carried along. Thus I arrive at the Land of the Birds. If you don't like this story you can think up another one: the important thing is to have me arrive there.)

I arrived and I felt my arms and legs clutched. I was surrounded by birds; one had perched on my head, one was pecking at my neck. 'Qfwfq, you're under arrest! We've caught you, at last!' I was shut up in a cell.

'Will they kill me?' I asked the jailer bird.

'Tomorrow you'll be tried and then you'll know,' he said, perched on the bars.

'Who's going to judge me?'

'The Queen of the Birds.'

The next day I was led into the throne room. But I had seen before that enormous shell-egg that was opening. I started.

'Then you're not a prisoner of the birds!' I exclaimed.

A beak dug into my neck. 'Bow down before Queen Org-Onir-Ornit-Or!'

Or made a sign. All the birds stopped. (In the drawing you see a slender, beringed hand which rises from an arrangement of feathers.)

'Marry me and you'll be safe,' Or said.

Our wedding was celebrated. I can't tell you anything about this either: the only thing that's remained in my memory is a feathery flutter of iridescent images. Perhaps I was paying for my happiness by renouncing any understanding of what I was living through.

I asked Or.

'I would like to understand.'

'What?'

'Everything, all this.' I gestured towards my surroundings.

'You'll understand when you've forgotten what you understood before.'

Night fell. The shell-egg served both as throne and as nuptial bed.

'Have you forgotten?'

'Yes. What? I don't know what, I don't remember anything.'

(Frame of Qfwfq's thoughts: *No, I still remember, I'm about to forget everything, but I'm forcing myself to remember!*)

'Come.'

We lay down together.

(Frame of Qfwfq's thoughts: *I'm forgetting . . . It's beautiful to forget . . . No, I want to remember . . . I want to forget and remember at the same time . . . Just another second and I feel I'll have forgotten . . . Wait . . . Oh!* An explosion marked with the word 'Flash!' or else 'Eureka!' in capital letters.)

For a fraction of a second between the loss of everything I knew before and the gain of everything I would know afterwards, I managed to embrace in a single thought the world of things as they were and of things as they could have been, and I realized that a single system included all. The world of birds, of monsters, of Or's beauty was the same as the one where I had always lived, which none of us had understood wholly.

'Or! I understand! You! How beautiful! Hurrah!' I exclaimed and I sat up in the bed.

My bride let out a cry.

'Now I'll explain it to you!' I said, exultant. 'Now I'll explain everything to everyone!'

'Be quiet!' Or shouted. 'You must be quiet!'

'The world is single and what exists can't be explained without . . .' I proclaimed. Now she was over me, she was trying to suffocate me (in the drawing: a breast crushing me): 'Be quiet! Be quiet!'

Hundreds of beaks and claws were tearing the canopy of the nuptial bed. The birds fell upon me, but beyond their wings I could recognize my native landscape, which was becoming fused with the alien continent.

'There's no difference. Monsters and non-monsters have always been close to one another! What hasn't been continues to be . . .' – I was speaking not only to the birds and the monsters but also to those I had always known, who were rushing in on every side.

'Qfwfq! You've lost me! Birds! He's yours!' and the Queen pushed me away.

Too late, I realized how the birds' beaks were intent on separating the two worlds that my revelation had united. 'No, wait, don't move away, the two of us together, Or . . . where are you?' I was rolling in the void among scraps of paper and feathers.

(The birds, with beaks and claws, tear up the page of strips. Each flies off with a scrap of printed paper in his beak. The page below is also covered with strip drawings; it depicts the world as it was before the birds' appearance and its successive, predictable developments. I'm among the others, with a bewildered look. In the sky there are still birds, but nobody pays attention to them any more.)

Of what I understood then, I've now forgotten everything. What I've told you is all I can reconstruct, with the help of conjectures in the episodes with the most gaps. I have never stopped hoping that the birds might one day take me back to Queen Or. But are they real birds, these ones that have remained in our midst? The more I observe them, the less they suggest what I would like to remember. (The last strip is all photographs: a bird, the same bird in close-up, the head of the bird enlarged, a detail of the head, the eye . . .)

Crystals

If the substances that made up the terrestrial globe in its incandescent state had had at their disposal a period of time long enough to allow them to grow cold and also sufficient freedom of movement, each of them would have become separated from the others in a single, enormous crystal.

It could have been different, I know – *Qfwfq remarked* – you're telling me: I believed so firmly in that world of crystal that was supposed to come forth that I can't resign myself to living still in this world, amorphous and crumbling and gummy, which has been our lot, instead. I run all the time like everybody else, I take the train each morning (I live in New Jersey) to slip into the cluster of prisms I see emerging beyond the Hudson, with its sharp cusps; I spend my days there, going up and down the horizontal and vertical axes that criss-cross that compact solid, or along the obligatory routes that graze its sides and its edges. But I don't fall into the trap: I know they're making me run among smooth transparent walls and between symmetrical angles so I'll believe I'm inside a crystal, so I'll recognize a regular form there, a rotation axis, a constant in the dihedrons, whereas none of all this exists. The contrary exists: glass, those are glass solids that flank the streets, not crystal, it's a paste of haphazard molecules which has invaded and cemented the world, a layer of suddenly chilled lava, stiffened into forms imposed from the outside, whereas inside it's magma just as in the Earth's incandescent days.

I don't pine for them surely, those days: I feel discontented with things as they are, but if, for that reason, you expect me to remember the past with nostalgia, you're mistaken. It was horrible, the Earth without any crust, an eternal incandescent winter, a mineral bog, with black swirls of iron and nickel that dripped down from every crack towards the centre of the globe, and jets of mercury that gushed up in high spurts. We made our way through a boiling haze, Vug and I, and we could never manage to touch a solid point. A barrier of liquid rocks that we found before us would suddenly evaporate in our path, disintegrating into an acid cloud; we would rush to pass it, but already we could feel it condensing and striking us like a storm of metallic rain, swelling the thick waves of an aluminium ocean. The substance of things changed around us every minute; the atoms, that is, passed from one state of disorder to another state of disorder and then another still: or rather, practically speaking, everything remained always the same. The only real change would have been the atoms' arranging themselves in some sort of order: this is what Vug and I were looking for, moving in the mixture of the elements without any points of reference, without a before or an after.

Now the situation is different, I admit: I have a wristwatch, I compare the angle of its hands with the angle of all the hands I see; I have an engagement book where the hours of my business appointments are marked down; I have a chequebook on whose stubs I add and subtract numbers. At Penn Station I get off the train, I take the subway, I stand and grasp the strap with one hand to keep my balance while I hold my newspaper up in the other, folded so I can glance over the figures of the stock market quotations: I play the game, in other words, the game of pretending there's an order in the dust, a regularity in the system, or an interpenetration of different systems, incongruous but still measurable, so that every graininess of disorder coincides with the faceting of an order which promptly crumbles.

Before it was worse, of course. The world was a solution of substances where everything was dissolved into everything and the solvent of everything. Vug and I kept on getting lost in its midst, losing our lost places, where we had been lost always, without any idea of what we could have found (or of what could have found us) so as to be lost no more.

We realized it all of a sudden. Vug said: 'There!'

She was pointing, in the midst of a lava flow, at something that was taking form. It was a solid with regular, smooth facets and sharp corners; and these facets and corners were slowly expanding, as if at the expense of the surrounding matter, and also the form of the solid was changing, while still maintaining symmetrical proportions . . . And it wasn't only the form that was distinct from all the rest: it was also the way the light entered inside, passing through it and refracted by it. Vug said: 'They shine! Lots of them!'

It wasn't the only one, in fact. On the incandescent expanse where once only ephemeral gas bubbles had risen, expelled from the Earth's bowels, cubes now were coming to the surface and octahedrons, prisms, figures so transparent they seemed airy, empty inside, but instead, as we soon saw, they concentrated in themselves an incredible compactness and hardness. The sparkle of this angled blossoming was invading the Earth, and Vug said: 'It's spring!' I kissed her.

Now you can understand me: if I love order, it's not – as with so many others – the mark of a character subjected to an inner discipline, a repression of the instincts. In me the idea of an absolutely regular world, symmetrical and methodical, is associated with that first impulse and burgeoning of nature, that amorous tension – what you call eros – while all the rest of your images, those that according to you associate passion with disorder, love with intemperate overflow – river fire whirlpool volcano – for me are memories of nothingness and listlessness and boredom.

It was a mistake on my part, it didn't take me long to understand that. Here we are at the point of arrival: Vug is lost; of the diamond eros only dust remains; the simulated crystal that imprisons me now is base glass. I follow the arrows on the asphalt, I line up at the traffic light, and I start again (today I came into New York by car) when the green comes on (as I do every Wednesday because I take) shifting into first (Dorothy to her psychoanalyst), I try to maintain a steady speed which allows me to pass all the green lights on Second Avenue. This, which you call order, is a threadbare patch over disintegration; I found a parking space but in two hours I'll have to go down again to put another coin in the meter; if I forget they'll tow my car away.

I dreamed of a world of crystal, in those days: I didn't dream it, I saw it, an indestructible frozen springtime of quartz. Polyhedrons grew up, tall as mountains, diaphanous: the shadow of the person beyond pierced through their thickness. 'Vug, it's you!' To reach her I flung myself against walls smooth as mirrors; I slipped back; I clutched the edges, wounding myself; I ran along treacherous perimeters, and at every turn there was a different light – diffused, milky, opaque – that the mountain contained.

'Where are you?'

'In the woods!'

The silver crystals were filiform trees, with branches at

every right angle. Skeletal fronds of tin and of lead thickened the forest in a geometric vegetation.

In the middle there was Vug, running. 'Qfwfq! It's different over there!' she cried. 'Gold, green, blue!'

A valley of beryllium opened out, surrounded by ridges of every colour, from aquamarine to emerald. I followed Vug with my spirit torn between happiness and fear: happiness at seeing how every substance that made up the world was finding its definitive and solid form, and a still vague fear that this triumph of order in such various fashions might reproduce on another scale the disorder we had barely left behind us. A total crystal I dreamed, a topaz world that would leave out nothing: I was impatient for our Earth to detach itself from the wheel of gas and dust in which all the celestial bodies were whirling, ours should be the first to escape that useless dispersal which is the universe.

Of course, if he chooses, a person can also take it into his head to find an order in the stars, the galaxies, an order in the lighted windows of the empty skyscrapers where between nine and midnight the cleaning women wax the floors of the offices. Rationalize, that's the big task: rationalize if you don't want everything to come apart. Tonight we're dining in town, in a restaurant on the terrace of a twenty-fourth floor. It's a business dinner: there are six of us; there is also Dorothy, and the wife of Dick Bemberg. I eat some oysters, I look at a star that's called (if I have the right one) Betelgeuse. We make conversation: we husbands talk about production; the ladies, about consumption. Anyway, seeing the firmament is difficult: the lights of Manhattan spread out a halo that becomes mixed with the luminosity of the sky.

The wonder of crystals is the network of atoms that is constantly repeated: this is what Vug wouldn't understand. What she liked – I quickly realized – was to discover in crystals some differences, even minimal ones, irregularities, flaws.

'But what does one atom out of place matter to you, an exfoliation that's a bit crooked,' I said, 'in a solid that's destined to be enlarged infinitely according to a regular pattern? It's the single crystal we're working towards, the gigantic crystal . . .'

'I like them when there're lots of little ones,' she said. To contradict me, surely; but also because it was true that crystals were popping up by the thousands at the same time and were interpenetrating one another, arresting their growth where they came in contact, and they never succeeded in taking over entirely the liquid rock from which they received their form: the world wasn't tending to be composed into an ever-simpler figure but was clotting in a vitreous mass from which prisms and octahedrons and cubes seemed to be struggling to be free, to draw all the matter to themselves . . .

A crater exploded: a cascade of diamonds spread out.

'Look! Aren't they big?' Vug exclaimed.

On every side there were erupting volcanoes: a continent of diamond refracted the Sun's light in a mosaic of rainbow chips.

'Didn't you say the smaller they are the more you like them?' I reminded her.

'No! Those enormous ones – I want them!' and she darted off.

'There are still bigger ones,' I said, pointing above us. The sparkle was blinding: I could already see a mountain-diamond, a faceted and iridescent chain, a gem-plateau, a Koh-i-noor-Himalaya.

'What can I do with them? I like the ones that can be picked up. I want to have them!' and in Vug there was already the frenzy of possession.

'The diamond will have us, instead. It's the stronger,' I said.

I was mistaken, as usual: the diamond was had, not by us. When I walk past Tiffany's, I stop to look at the windows, I contemplate the diamond prisoners, shards of our lost kingdom. They lie in velvet coffins, chained with silver and platinum; with my imagination and my memory I enlarge them, I give them again the gigantic dimensions of fortress, garden, lake, I imagine Vug's pale blue shadow mirrored there. I'm not imagining it: it really is Vug who now advances among the diamonds. I turn: it's the girl looking into the window over my shoulder, from beneath the hair falling across her forehead.

'Vug!' I say. 'Our diamonds!'

She laughs.

'Is it really you?' I ask. 'What's your name?'

She gives me her telephone number.

We are among slabs of glass: I live in simulated order, I would like to say to her, I have an office on the East Side, I live in New Jersey, for the weekend Dorothy has invited the Bembergs, against simulated order simulated disorder is impotent, the diamond would be necessary, not for us to possess it but for it to possess us, the free diamond in which Vug and I were free . . .

'I'll call you,' I say to her, only out of the desire to resume my arguing with her.

In an aluminium crystal, where chance scatters some chrome atoms, the transparency is coloured a dark red: so the rubies flowered beneath our footsteps.

'You see?' Vug said. 'Aren't they beautiful?'

We couldn't walk through a valley of rubies without starting to quarrel again.

'Yes,' I said, 'because the regularity of the hexagon . . .'

'Uff!' she said. 'Would they be rubies without the intrusion of extraneous atoms? Answer me that!'

I became angry. More beautiful? Or less beautiful? We could go on arguing to infinity, but the only sure fact was that the Earth was moving in the direction of Vug's preferences. Vug's world was in the fissures, the cracks where lava rises, dissolving the rock and mixing the minerals in unpredictable concretions. Seeing her caress walls of granite, I regretted what had been lost in that rock, the exactness of the feldspars, the micas, the quartzes. Vug seemed to take pleasure only in noting how minutely variegated the face of the world appeared. How could we understand each other? For me all that mattered was homogeneous growth, indiscerptibility, achieved serenity; for her, everything had to be separation and mixture, one or the other, or both at once. Even the two of us had to take on an aspect (we still possessed neither form nor future): I imagined a slow uniform expansion, following the crystals' example, until the me-crystal would have interpenetrated and fused with the her-crystal and perhaps together we would have become a unity within the world-crystal; she already seemed to know that the law of living matter would be infinite separating and rejoining. Was it Vug, then, who was right?

It's Monday; I telephone her. It's almost summer already. We spend a day together, on Staten Island, lying on the beach. Vug watches the grains of sand trickle through her fingers.

'All these tiny crystals . . .' she says.

The shattered world that surrounds us is, for her, still the world of the past, the one we expected to be born from the incandescent world. To be sure, the crystals still give the world form, breaking up, being reduced to almost imperceptible fragments rolled by the waves, encrusted with all the elements dissolved in the sea which kneads them together again in steep cliffs, in sandstone reefs, a hundred times dissolved and recomposed, in schists, slates, marbles of glabrous whiteness, simulacra of what they once could have been and now can never be.

And again I am gripped by my stubbornness as I was when it began to be clear that the game was lost, that the Earth's crust was becoming a congeries of disparate forms, and I didn't want to resign myself, and at every irregularity in the porphyry that Vug happily pointed out to me, at every vitrescence that emerged from the basalt, I wanted to persuade myself that these were only apparent flaws, that they were all part of a much vaster regular structure, in which every asymmetry we thought we observed really corresponded to a network of symmetries so complicated we couldn't comprehend it, and I tried to calculate how many billions of sides and dihedral corners this labyrinthine crystal must have, this hypercrystal that included within itself crystals and non-crystals.

Vug has brought a little transistor radio along to the beach with her.

'Everything comes from crystal,' I say, 'even the music we're hearing.' But I know full well that the transistor's crystal is imperfect, flawed, veined with impurities, with rents in the warp of the atoms.

She says: 'It's an obsession with you.' And it is our old quarrel, continuing. She wants to make me admit that real order carries impurity within itself, destruction.

The boat lands at the Battery, it is evening; in the illuminated network of the skyscraper-prisms I now look only at the dark rips, the gaps. I see Vug home; I go up with her. She lives downtown, she has a photography studio. As I look around I see nothing but perturbations of the order of the atoms: luminescent tubes, TV, the condensing of tiny silver crystals on the photographic plates. I open the icebox, I take out the ice for our whisky. From the transistor comes the sound of a saxophone. The crystal which has succeeded in becoming the world, in making the world transparent to itself, in refracting it into infinite spectral images, is not mine: it is a corroded crystal, stained, mixed. The victory of the crystals (and of Vug) has been the same thing as their defeat (and mine). I'll wait now till the Thelonious Monk record ends, then I'll tell her.

Blood, Sea

The conditions that obtained when life had not yet emerged from the oceans have not subsequently changed a great deal for the cells of the human body, bathed by the primordial wave which continues to flow in the arteries. Our blood in fact has a chemical composition analogous to that of the sea of our origins, from which the first living cells and the first multicellular beings derived the oxygen and the other elements necessary to life. With the evolution of more complex organisms, the problem of maintaining a maximum number of cells in contact with the liquid environment could not be solved simply by the expansion of the exterior surface: those organisms endowed with hollow structures, into which the sea water could flow, found themselves at an advantage. But it was only with the ramification of these cavities into a system of blood circulation that distribution of oxygen was guaranteed to the complex of cells, thus making terrestrial life possible. The sea where living creatures were at one time immersed is now enclosed within their bodies.

Basically not much has changed: I swim, I continue swimming in the same warm sea – *Qfwfq said* – or rather, the inside isn't changed, what was formerly the outside, where I used to swim under the Sun, and where I now swim in darkness, is inside; what's changed is the outside, the present outside, which was the inside before, that's changed all right;

however, it doesn't matter very much. I say it doesn't matter very much and you promptly reply: What do you mean, the outside doesn't matter much? What I mean is that if you look at it more closely, from the point of view of the old outside, that is from the present inside, what is the present outside? It's simply where it's dry, where there is no flux or reflux, and as far as mattering goes, of course, that matters too, in as much as it's the outside, since it's been on the outside, since that outside has been outside, and people believe it's more deserving of consideration than the inside. When all is said and done, however, even when it was inside it mattered, though in a more restricted range or so it seemed then. This is what I mean: less deserving of consideration. Well, let's start talking right now about the others, those who are not I, our neighbour: we know our neighbour exists because he's outside, agreed? Outside like the present outside. But before, when the outside was what we swam in, the very dense and very warm ocean, even then there were the others, slippery things, in that old outside, which is like the present inside, and so it is now when I've changed places and given the wheel to Signor Cècere, at the Codogno service station, and in front, next to him, Jenny Fumagalli has taken the passenger's seat, and I've moved into the back with Zylphia: the outside, what is the outside? A dry environment, lacking in meaning, a bit crammed (there are four of us in a Volkswagen), where all is indifferent and interchangeable, Jenny Fumagalli, Codogno, Signor Cècere, the service station, and as far as Zylphia is concerned, at the moment when I placed my hand on her knee, at perhaps ten miles from Casalpusterlengo, or else she was the one who started touching me, I don't remember, since outside events tend to be confused, what I felt, I mean the sensation that came from outside, was really a weak business compared to what went through my blood and to what I have felt ever since then, since the time when we were swimming together in the same torrid, blazing ocean, Zylphia and I.

The underwater depths were red like the colour we see now only inside our eyelids, and the Sun's rays penetrated to brighten them in flashes or else in sprays. We undulated with no sense of direction, drawn by an obscure current so light that it seemed downright impalpable and yet strong enough to drag us up in very high waves and down in their troughs. Zylphia would plunge headlong beneath me in a violet, almost black whirlpool, then soar over me rising towards the more scarlet stripes that ran beneath the luminous vault. We felt all this through the layers of our former surface dilated to maintain the most extended possible contact with that nourishing sea, because at every up and down of the waves there was stuff that passed from outside of us to our inside, all sustenance of every sort, even iron, healthful stuff, in short, and in fact I've never been so well as I was then. Or, to be more precise: I was well since in dilating my surface I increased the possibilities of contact between me and this outside of me that was so precious, but as the zones of my body soaked in marine solution were extended, my volume also increased at the same time, and a more and more voluminous zone within me became unreachable by the element outside, it became arid, dull, and the weight of this dry and torpid thickness I carried within me was the only shadow on my happiness, our happiness, Zylphia's and mine, because the more she splendidly took up space in the sea, the more the inert and opaque thickness grew in her too, unlaved and unlavable, lost to the vital flux, not reached by the messages I transmitted to her through the vibration of the waves. So perhaps I could say I'm better off now than I was then, now that the layers of our former surface, then stretched on the outside, have been turned inside out like a glove, now that all the outside has been turned inwards and has entered and pervaded us through filiform ramifications, yes, I could really say this, were it not for the fact that the dull arid zone has been projected outwards, has expanded to the extent of the distance between my tweed suit and the fleeting landscape of the Lodi plain, and it surrounds me, swollen with undesired presences such as Signor Cècere's, with all the thickness that Signor Cècere, formerly, would have enclosed within himself – in his foolish manner of dilating uniformly like a ball – now unfolded before me in a surface unsuitably irregular and detailed, especially in his pudgy neck dotted with pimples, taut in his half-starched collar at this moment when he is saying: 'Oh, you two on the back seat!' and he has slightly shifted the rear-view mirror and has certainly glimpsed what our hands are doing, mine and Zylphia's, our diminutive outside hands, our diminutively sensitive hands that pursue the memory of ourselves swimming, or rather our swimming memory, or rather the presence of what in me and Zylphia continues swimming or being swum, together, as then.

This is a distinction I might bring up to give a clearer idea of before and now: before, we swam, and now we are swum. But on sober reflection I prefer not to go into this, because in reality even when the sea was outside I swam in it the same way I do now, without any intervention of my will, that is to say I was swum even then, no more nor less than now, there was a current that enfolded me and carried me this way and that, a gentle and soft fluid, in which Zylphia and I wallowed, turning on ourselves, hovering over abysses of ruby-coloured transparence, hiding among turquoise-coloured filaments that wriggled up from the depths; but these sensations of movement – wait and I'll explain it to you

– were due only to what? They were due to a kind of general pulsation, no, I don't want to confuse things with the way they are now, because since we've been keeping the sea closed inside us it's natural that in moving it should make this piston effect, but in those days you certainly couldn't have talked about pistons, because you would have had to imagine a piston without walls, a combustion chamber of infinite volume as the sea appeared infinite to us, or rather the ocean, in which we were immersed, whereas now everything is pulsation and beating and rumble and crackling, inside the arteries and outside, the sea within the arteries that accelerates its course as soon as I feel Zylphia's hand seeking mine, or rather, as soon as I feel the acceleration in the course of Zylphia's arteries as she feels my hand seeking hers (the two flows which are still the same flow of a same sea and which are joined beyond the contact of the thirsty fingertips); and also outside, the opaque thirsty outside that seeks dully to imitate the beat and rumble and crackling of inside, and vibrates in the accelerator under Signor Cècere's foot, and the whole line of cars stopped at the exit from the motorway tries to repeat the pulsing of the ocean now buried inside us, of the red ocean that was once without shores, under the Sun.

It is a false sense of movement that this now-motionless line of spluttering cars transmits; then it moves and it's as if it were still, the movement is false, it merely repeats signs and white stripes and roadbeds; and the whole journey has been nothing but false movement in the immobility and indifference of everything that is outside. Only the sea moved and moves, outside or inside, only in that movement did Zylphia and I become aware of each other's presence, even if then we didn't so much as graze each other, even if I was undulating in this direction and she in that, but the sea had only to quicken its rhythm and I became aware of Zylphia's presence, her presence which was different, for example, from Signor Cècere, who was however also around even then and I could sense him as I felt an acceleration of the same sort as that other one but with a negative charge, that is the acceleration of the sea (and now of the blood) with regard to Zylphia was (is) like swimming towards each other, or else like swimming and chasing each other in play, while the acceleration (of the sea and now of the blood) with regard to Signor Cècere was (is) like a swimming away to avoid him, or else like swimming towards him to make him go away, all of this involving no change in the relationship of our respective distances.

Now it is Signor Cècere who accelerates (the words used are the same but the meanings change) and passes an Alfa Romeo in a curve, and it is with regard to Zylphia that he accelerates, to distract her with a risky manoeuvre, a false risky manoeuvre, from the swimming that unites her and me: false, I say, as a manoeuvre, not as a risk because the risk may well be real, that is to our inside which in a crash could spurt outside; whereas the manoeuvre in itself changes nothing at all, the distances between Alfa, curve, Volkswagen can assume different values and relationships but nothing essential happens, as nothing essential happens in Zylphia, who doesn't care a bit about Signor Cècere's driving, at most it is Jenny Fumagalli who exults: 'My, isn't this car fast?' and her exultation, in the presumption that Signor Cècere's bold driving is for her benefit, is doubly unjustified, first because her inside transmits nothing to her that justifies exultation, and secondly because she is mistaken about Signor Cècere's intentions as he in turn is mistaken, believing he is achieving God knows what with his showing off, just as she, Jenny Fumagalli, was mistaken before about my intentions, when

I was at the wheel and she at my side, and there in the back next to Zylphia Signor Cècere, too, was mistaken, both concentrating – he and Jenny – on the reverse arrangement of dry layers of surface, unaware – dilated into balls as they were – that the only real things that happen are those that happen in the swimming of our immersed parts; and so this silly business of passing Alfas meaning nothing, like a passing of fixed, immobile, nailed-down objects, continues to be superimposed on the story of our free and real swimming, continues to seek meaning by interfering with it, in the only silly way it knows, in this story of the risk of blood, of the possibility of our blood returning to a sea of blood, of a false return to a sea of blood which would no longer be blood or sea.

Here I must hasten to make clear – before by another idiotic passing of a trailer truck Signor Cècere makes all clarification pointless – the way that the common blood-sea of the past was common and at the same time individual to each of us and how we can continue swimming in it as such and how we can't: I don't know if I can make this sort of explanation in a hurry because, as always, when this general substance is discussed, the talk can't be in general terms but has to vary according to the relationship between one individual and the others, so it amounts practically to beginning all over again at the beginning. Now then: this business of having the vital element in common was a beautiful thing in as much as the separation between me and Zylphia was so to speak overcome and we could feel ourselves at the same time two distinct individuals and a single whole, which always has its advantages, but when you realize that this single whole also included absolutely insipid presences such as Jenny Fumagalli, or worse, unbearable ones such as Signor Cècere, then thanks all the same, the thing loses much of its interest. This is the point where the reproductive instinct comes into play: we had a great desire, Zylphia and I, or at least I had a great desire, and I think she must have had it too, since she was willing, to multiply our presence in the sea-blood so that there would be more and more of us to profit from it and less and less of Signor Cècere, and as we had our reproductive cells all ready for that very purpose, we fell to fertilizing with a will, that is to say I fertilized everything of hers that was fertilizable, so that our presence would increase in both absolute number and in percentage, and Signor Cècere – though he too made feverish clumsy efforts at reproducing himself – would remain in a minority – this was the dream, the virtual obsession that gripped me – a minority that would become smaller and smaller, insignificant, zero point zero zero et cetera per cent, until he vanished into the dense cloud of our progeny as in a school of rapid and ravenous anchovies who would devour him bit by bit, burying him inside our dry inner layers, bit by bit, where the sea's flow would never reach him again, and then the sea-blood would have become one with us, that is, all blood would finally be our blood.

This is in fact the secret desire I feel, looking at the stiff collar of Signor Cècere up front: make him disappear, eat him up, I mean: not eat him up myself, because he turns my stomach slightly (in view of the pimples), but emit, project, outside myself (outside the Zylphia-me unit), a school of ravenous anchovies (of me-sardines, of Zylphia-sardines) to devour Signor Cècere, deprive him of the use of a circulatory system (as well as of a combustion engine, as well as the illusory use of an engine foolishly combustive), and while we're at it, devour also that pain in the neck Fumagalli, who because of the simple fact that I sat next to her before has got it into her head that I flirted with her somehow, when I wasn't paying the slightest attention to her, and now she says in that whiny little voice of hers: 'Watch out, Zylphia' (just to cause trouble), 'I know that gentleman back there . . .' just to suggest I behaved with her before as I'm behaving now with Zylphia, but what can la Fumagalli know about what is really happening between me and Zylphia, about how Zylphia and I are continuing our ancient swim through the scarlet depths?

I'll go back to what I was saying earlier, because I have the impression things have become a bit confused: to devour Signor Cècere, to ingurgitate him was the best way to separate him from the blood-sea when the blood was in fact the sea, when our present inside was outside and our outside, inside; but now, in reality, my secret desire is to make Signor Cècere become pure outside, deprive him of the inside he illicitly enjoys, make him expel the lost sea within his pleonastic person; in short, my dream is to eject against him not so much a swarm of me-anchovies as a hail of me-projectiles, rat-tat-tat to riddle him from head to foot, making him spurt his black blood to the last drop, and this idea is linked also to the idea of reproducing myself with Zylphia, of multiplying with her our blood circulation in a platoon or battalion of vindictive descendants armed with automatic rifles to riddle Signor Cècere, this in fact now prompts my sanguinary instinct (in all secrecy, given my constant mien as a civil, polite person just like the rest of you), the sanguinary instinct connected to the meaning of blood as 'our blood' which I bear in me just as you do, civilly and politely.

Thus far everything may seem clear: however, you must bear in mind that to make it clear I have so simplified things that I'm not sure whether the step forward I've made is really a step forward. Because from the moment when blood becomes 'our blood', the relationship between us and blood changes, that is, what counts is the blood in so far as it is 'ours', and all the rest, us included, counts less. So there was in my impulse towards Zylphia, not only the drive to have all the ocean for us, but also the drive to lose it, the ocean, to annihilate ourselves in the ocean, to destroy ourselves, to torment ourselves, or rather – as a beginning – to torment her, Zylphia my beloved, to tear her to pieces, to eat her up. And with her it's the same: what she wanted was to torment me, devour me, swallow me, nothing but that. The orange stain of the Sun seen from the water's depths swayed like a medusa, and Zylphia darted among the luminous filaments devoured by the desire to devour me, and I writhed in the tangles of darkness that rose from the depths like long strands of seaweed beringed with indigo glints, raving and longing to bite her. And finally there on the back seat of the Volkswagen in an abrupt swerve I fell on her and I sank my teeth into her skin just where the 'American cut' of her sleeves left her shoulder bare, and she dug her sharp nails between the buttons of my shirt, and this is the same impulse as before, the impulse that tended to remove her (or remove me) from marine citizenship and now instead tends to remove the sea from her, from me, in any case to achieve the passage from the blazing element of life to the pale and opaque element which is our absence from the ocean and the absence of the ocean from us.

The same impulse acts then with amorous obstinacy between her and me and with hostile obstinacy against Signor Cècere: for each of us there is no other way of entering into a relationship with the others; I mean, it's always this impulse that nourishes our own relationship with the others in the most different and unrecognizable forms, as when Signor Cècere passes cars of greater horsepower than his, even a Porsche, through intentions of mastery towards these superior cars and through ill-advised amorous intentions towards Zylphia and also vindictive ones towards me and also self-destructive ones towards himself. So, through risk, the insignificance of the outside manages to interfere with the essential element, the sea where Zylphia and I continue our nuptial flights of fertilization and destruction: since the risk aims directly at the blood, at our blood, for if it were a matter only of the blood of Signor Cècere (a driver, after all, heedless of the traffic laws) we should hope that at the very least he would run off the road, but in effect it's a question of all of us, of the risk of a possible return of our blood from darkness to the Sun, from the separate to the mixed, a false return, as all of us in our ambiguous game pretend to forget, because our present inside once it is poured out becomes our present outside and it can no longer return to being the outside of the old days.

So Zylphia and I in falling upon each other in the curves play at provoking vibrations in the blood, that is at permitting the false thrills of the insipid outside to be added to those that vibrated from the depths of the millennia and of the marine abysses, and then Signor Cècere said: 'Let's have a nice plate of spaghetti at the truck drivers' café,' masking as generous love of life his constant torpid violence, and Jenny Fumagalli, acting clever, spoke up: 'But you have to get to the spaghetti first, before the truck drivers, otherwise they won't leave you any,' clever and always working in the service of the blackest destruction, and the black truck with the number plate Udine 38 96 21 was there ahead, roaring at its forty mph along the road that was nothing but curves, and Signor Cècere thought (and perhaps said): 'I'll make it,' and he swung out to the left, and we all thought (and didn't say): 'You can't make it,' and in fact, from the curve the Jaguar was already arriving full tilt, and to avoid it the

Volkswagen scraped the wall and bounced back to scrape its side against the curved chrome bumper and, bouncing, it struck the plane tree, then went spinning down into the precipice, and the sea of common blood which floods over the crumpled metal isn't the blood-sea of our origin but only an infinitesimal detail of the outside, of the insignificant and arid outside, a number in the statistics of accidents over the weekend.

PART TWO

Priscilla

In asexual reproduction, the simplest entity which is the cell divides at a point in its growth. The nucleus divides into two equal parts, and from a single entity, two result. But we cannot say that a first entity has given birth to a second. The two new entities are, to the same degree, the products of the first. The first has disappeared. Essentially, it is dead, since only the two entities it has produced survive. It does not decompose in the way sexed animals die, but it ceases to be. It ceases to be, in the sense that it is discontinuous. But, in a point of the reproduction, there was continuity. There exists a point where the primitive *one* becomes *two*. When there are two, there is again discontinuity in each of the entities. But the passage implies an *instant* of continuity between the two. The first dies, but *in its death* appears a fundamental instant of continuity.

Georges Bataille, *L'Érotisme* (from the introduction)

All genes of the same chromosome are not always pulled into the same daughter cell, and so are not always inherited together, though they do tend to be. For two homologous filaments, during their synapsis with one another, are apt to break, at identical points, and to become joined up again with their corresponding pieces interchanged, a process called *crossing-over*. Thus a given gene of paternal origin may in the mature germ cell find itself in the same chromosome with some other gene of maternal origin, instead of with its former associate gene.

Encyclopaedia Britannica, 'Gene'

. . . in the midst of the Aeneases who carry their Anchiseses on their backs, I pass from one shore to another, alone, hating these invisible parents astride their sons for all their life . . .

J.-P. Sartre, *Les Mots*

Suddenly I became aware that an adenine-thymine pair held together by two hydrogen bonds was identical in shape to a guanine-cytosine pair held together by at least two hydrogen bonds. All the hydrogen bonds seemed to form naturally; no fudging was required to make the two types of base pairs identical in shape. Quickly I called Jerry over to ask him whether this time he had any objection to my new base pairs. When he said no, my morale skyrocketed . . . this type of double helix suggested a replication scheme much more satisfactory . . . Given the base sequence of one chain, that of its partner was automatically determined. Conceptually, it was thus very easy to visualize how a single chain could be the template for the synthesis of a chain with the complementary sequence. Upon his arrival Francis did not get more than halfway through the door before I let loose that the answer to everything was in our hands . . .

James D. Watson, *The Double Helix: A Personal Account of the Discovery of the Structure of DNA*, Chap. 26

Everything summons us to death; nature, as if envious of the good she had done us, announces to us often and reminds us that she cannot leave us for long that bit of matter she lends us, which must not remain in the same hands, and which must eternally be in circulation: she needs it for other forms, she asks it back for other works.

Bossuet, *Sermon sur la mort*

One need not worry about how a fixed automaton of this sort can produce others which are larger and more complex than itself. In this case the greater size and the higher complexity of the object to be constructed will be reflected in a presumably still greater size of the instructions I that have to be furnished . . . In what follows, all automata for whose construction the facility A will be used are going to share with A this property. All of them will have a place for an instruction I, that is, a place where such an instruction can be inserted . . . It is quite clear that the instruction I is roughly effecting the function of a gene. It is also clear that the copying mechanism B performs the fundamental act of reproduction, the duplication of the genetic material, which is clearly the fundamental operation in the multiplication of living cells.

Johann von Neumann,
Theory of Automata (in *Collected Works*, Vol. 5)

As for those who so exalt incorruptibility, inalterability, I believe they are brought to say these things through their great desire to live a long time and through the terror they have of death. And not considering that, if men were immortal, these men would not have had an opportunity to come into the world. They would deserve to encounter a Medusa's head, which would transform them into statues of jasper or of diamond, to make them more perfect than they are . . . And there is not the slightest doubt that the Earth is far more perfect, being, as it is, alterable, changeable, than if it were a mass of stone, even if it were a whole diamond, hard and impenetrable.

Galileo Galilei, *Dialogo sopra i due massimi sistemi*, giornata I

I. Mitosis

. . . And when I say 'dying of love' – *Qfwfq went on* – I mean
something you have no idea of, because you think falling in
love has to signify falling in love with another person, or
thing, or what have you, in other words I'm here and what
I'm in love with is there, in short a relationship connected to
the life of relationships, whereas I'm talking about the times
before I had established any relationships between myself
and anything else, there was a cell and the cell was me, and
that was that. Now we needn't wonder whether there were
other cells around too, it doesn't matter, there was the cell
that was me and it was already quite an achievement, such a
thing is more than enough to fill one's life, and it's this very
sense of fullness I want to talk to you about. I don't mean
fullness because of the protoplasm I had, because even if it
had increased to a considerable degree it wasn't anything
exceptional, cells of course are full of protoplasm, what else
could they be full of; no, I'm talking about a sense of fullness that was, if you'll allow the expression, quote spiritual
unquote, namely the awareness that this cell was me, this
sense of fullness, this fullness of being aware was something
that kept me awake nights, something that made me beside
myself, in other words the situation I mentioned before,
I was 'dying of love'.

Now I know all of you will raise a flock of objections

because being in love presupposes not only self-awareness but also awareness of the other, et cetera, et cetera, and all I can answer is thanks a lot I know that much myself but if you aren't going to be patient there's no use in my trying to explain, and above all you have to forget for a minute the way you fall in love nowadays, the way I do too now, if you'll permit me confidences of this sort, I say confidences because I know if I told you about my falling in love at present you could accuse me of being indiscreet, whereas I can talk without any scruples about the time when I was a unicellular organism, that is I can talk about it objectively as the saying goes, because it's all water under the bridge now, and it's a feat on my part even to remember it, and yet what I do remember is still enough to disturb me from head to foot, so when I use the word 'objectively' it's a figure of speech, as it always is when you start out saying you're objective and then what with one thing and another you end up being subjective, and so this business I want to tell you about is difficult for me precisely because it keeps slipping into the subjective, in my subjective state of those days, which though I recall it only partially still disturbs me from head to foot like my subjective of the present, and that's why I've used expressions that have the disadvantage of creating confusion with what is different nowadays while they have the advantage of bringing to light what is common between the two times.

First of all I must be more specific about what little I remember, or rather I should warn you that if certain parts of my story are narrated less fully than others it doesn't mean they're less important but only that they are less firm in my memory, since what I remember well is my love story's initial phase if you want to call it that, I would almost say the preceding phase; at the climax of the love story my memory dissolves, frays, goes to pieces, and there's no way for me to remember then what happens afterwards. I say this not to ward off objections that I'm trying to make you listen to a love story I don't even remember, but to clarify the fact that not remembering it is at a certain point necessary to make the story this one and not another, in other words while a story usually consists in the memory you have of it, here not remembering the story becomes the very story itself.

So I am speaking then of the initial phase of a love story which afterwards is probably repeated in an interminable multiplication of initial phases just like the first and identified with the first, a multiplication or rather a squaring, an exponential growth of stories which is always tantamount to the first story, but it isn't as if I were so very sure of all this, I assume it as you can also assume it. I'm referring to an initial phase that precedes the other initial phases, a first phase which must surely have existed, because it's logical to expect it to exist, and also because I remember it very well, and when I say it's the first I don't in the least mean first in the absolute sense, that's what you'd like me to mean but I don't; I mean first in the sense that we can consider any of these identical initial phases the first, and the one I refer to is the one I remember, the one I remember as first in the sense that before it I don't remember anything. And as for the first in the absolute sense, your guess is as good as mine, I'm not interested.

Let's begin this way, then: there is a cell, and this cell is a unicellular organism, and this unicellular organism is me, and I know it, and I'm pleased about it. Nothing special so far. Now let's try to represent this situation for ourselves in space and time. Time passes, and I, more and more pleased with being in it and with being me, am also more and more pleased that there is time, and that I am in time, or rather that time passes and I pass time and time passes me, or rather I am pleased to be contained in time, to be the content of time, or the container, in short, to mark by being me the passing of time. Now you must admit this begins to arouse a sense of expectation, a happy and hopeful waiting, a happy youthful impatience, and also an anxiety, a youthful excited anxiety also basically painful, a painful unbearable tension and impatience. In addition you must keep in mind that existing also means being in space, and in fact I was dished out into space to my full width, with space all around, and even though I had no knowledge it obviously continued on all sides. There's no point in bothering now about what else this space contained, I was closed in myself and I minded my own business, and I didn't even have a nose so I couldn't stick my nose out, or an eye to take an interest in outside, in what was and what wasn't; however, I had the sense of occupying space within space, of wallowing in it, of growing with my protoplasm in various directions, but as I said, I don't want to insist on this quantitative and material aspect, I want to talk above all about the satisfaction and the burning desire to do something with space, to have time to extract enjoyment from space, to have space to make something in the passing of time.

Up until now I've kept time and space separated to help you to understand me better, or rather so that I could understand better what I should make you understand, but in those days I didn't really distinguish too clearly what one of them was from what the other was: there was me, in that point and at that moment – right? – and then there was an outside which seemed to me a void I might occupy in another moment or point, in a series of other points or moments, in short a potential projection of me where, however, I wasn't present, and therefore a void which was actually the world and the future, but I didn't know that yet; it was void because perception was still denied me, and as for imagination I was even further behind, and when it came to mental categories I was a total loss, but I had this contentment because outside of me there was this void that wasn't me, which perhaps could become me because 'me' was the only word I knew, the only word I could have declined, a void that could become me, however, wasn't me at that moment and basically never would be: it was the discovery of something else that wasn't yet something but anyhow wasn't me, or rather wasn't me at that moment and in that point and therefore was something else, and this discovery aroused an exhilarating enthusiasm in me, no, a torment, a dizzying torture, the dizziness of a void which represented everything possible, the complement of that fullness that was for me all, and there I was brimming over with love for this elsewhere, this other time, this otherwise, silent and void.

So you see that when I spoke of being 'in love' I wasn't saying something so far-fetched, and you were always on the point of interrupting me to say: 'In love with yourself, um-hum, in love with yourself,' and I was wise to pay no attention and not use or let you use that expression; there, you see that being in love was even then searing passion for what was outside me, it was the writhing of one who yearns to escape outside himself as I then went rolling around in time and space, dying of love.

To tell properly the way things proceeded I must remind you of how I was made, a mass of protoplasm like a kind of pulpy dumpling with a nucleus in the middle. Now I'm not just trying to make myself sound interesting, but I must say that in that nucleus I led a very intense life. Physically I was an individual in his full flowering, all right, on this point

I feel it would be indiscreet to insist: I was young, healthy, at the peak of my strength, but by that I certainly don't want to deny that another who might have been in worse shape, with his cytoplasm fragile or watery, could have revealed even greater talents. What's important to my story is how much of this physical life of mine was reflected in the nucleus; I say physical not because there was a distinction between physical life and some other kind of life, but to allow you to understand how physical life had, in the nucleus, its point of greatest concentration, sensitivity and tension, so that while all around it I was perhaps calm and blissful in my whitish pulp, the nucleus shared in this cytoplasmic calm and bliss in its nucleic way, that is, accentuating and thickening the tangled grain and speckling that adorned it, and so I concealed in myself an intense nucleic labour which then corresponded only to my exterior well-being, so that, we might say, the more I was happy to be me, the more my nucleus became charged with this thick impatience, and everything I was and everything I was gradually becoming ended up being nucleus, absorbed there and registered and accumulated in a serpentine twisting of spirals, in the gradually different way that they were forming a skein and unravelling, so I would say that everything I knew I knew in the nucleus, if that wouldn't involve the danger of making you believe in a separate or perhaps even opposing function of the nucleus with respect to the rest, whereas if there's an agile and impulsive organism where you can't make all these distinctions that is the unicellular organism. However, I don't want to exaggerate in the other direction either, as if to give you the idea of a chemical homogeneity like an inorganic drop spilled there; you know better than I how many differentiations there are within the cell, and even within the nucleus, and mine was in fact all speckled, freckled, dotted with filaments or strokes or lines, and each of these filaments or strokes or lines or chromosomes had a specific relationship to some characteristic of the cell that was me. Now I might attempt a somewhat risky assertion and say I was nothing but the sum of those filaments or lines or strokes, an assertion which can be disputed because of the fact that I was I entirely and not a part of myself, but one that can also be sustained by explaining that those strokes were myself translated into strokes, to then be retranslated back into me. And therefore when I speak of the intense life of the nucleus I don't mean so much the rustle or scraping of all those lines inside the nucleus as the nervousness of an individual who knows he has all those lines, he is all those lines, but also knows there's something that can't be represented with those lines, a void of which those lines succeed only in feeling the emptiness. Or rather the tension towards the outside, the elsewhere, the otherwise, which is what is then called a state of desire.

I had better be more precise about this state of desire business: a state of desire takes place when from a state of satisfaction one passes to a state of mounting satisfaction and then, immediately thereafter, to a state of dissatisfying satisfaction, namely, of desire. It isn't true that the state of desire takes place when something is missing; if something is missing, too bad, you do without it, and if the something is indispensable, in doing without it you do without some vital function, and therefore you proceed rapidly towards certain extinction. I mean that from a pure and simple state of lack nothing can be born, nothing good and nothing bad, only other lacks including finally the lack of life, a condition notoriously neither good nor bad. But a state of lack pure and simple doesn't exist, as far as I know, in nature: the state of lack is experienced always in contrast with a previous state of satisfaction, and it is from the state of satisfaction that everything which can grow, grows. And it isn't true that a state of desire presupposes necessarily a desired something; the desired something begins to exist only when there is the state of desire; not because before that something wasn't desired but because before who knew it existed? So once there's the state of desire it's precisely that something which begins to be, something which if all goes well will be the desired something but which could also remain just a something through lack of the desirer who in desiring might also cease to be, as in the present case of 'dying of love', which we still don't know the end of. Then, to go back to the point where we were before, I must tell you that my state of desire tended simply towards an elsewhere, another time, an otherwise that might contain something (or, let's say, the world) or contain only me, or me in relation to something (or to the world), or something (the world) without me any more.

To make this point clear, I realize now, I have gone back to talking in general terms, losing the ground gained with my previous clarifications; this often happens in love stories. I was becoming aware of what was happening around me through what was happening to the nucleus and especially to the chromosomes of the nucleus; through them I gained the awareness of a void beyond me and beyond them, the fitful awareness that through them forced me to something, a state of desire which, however little we can move, becomes immediately a movement of desire. This movement of desire remained basically a desire for movement, as usually happens when you can't move towards some place because the world doesn't exist or you don't know it exists, and in these cases desire moves you to want to do, to do something, or rather to do anything. But when you can do nothing because of the lack of an outside world, the only doing you can allow yourself with the scant means at your disposal is that special kind of doing that is saying. In short, I was moved to express: my state of desire, my state-motion-desire of motion-desire-love moved me to say, and since the only thing I had to say was myself, I was moved to say myself, to express myself. I'll be more precise: before, when I said that very few means suffice for expressing, I wasn't telling the exact truth, and therefore I'll correct myself: for expressing you need a language, and that's no trifle. As language I had all those specks or twigs called chromosomes, and therefore all I had to do was repeat those specks or twigs and I was repeating myself, obviously repeating myself in so far as language was concerned, which as you will see is the first step towards repeating myself as such, which as you will also see isn't repetition at all. But you'd better see what you're going to see when the right time comes, because if I keep making clarifications within other clarifications I'll never find my way out again.

It's true that at this point we must proceed with great care to avoid falling into errors. All this situation I've tried to narrate and which at the beginning I defined as being 'in love', explaining then how this phrase must be understood – all this, in short, had repercussions inside the nucleus in a quantitative and energetic enrichment of the chromosomes, indeed in their joyful doubling, because each of the chromosomes was repeated in a second chromosome. Speaking of the nucleus, I naturally tend to identify it with awareness, which is only a rather crude simplification, but even if things really were like that, it wouldn't imply awareness of possessing a double number of lines, because since each line had a function, each being – to return to the language metaphor – a word, the fact that one word was to be found twice didn't change what I was, since I consisted of the assortment or the vocabulary of the different words or functions at my disposal and the fact of having double words was felt in that sense of fullness which I earlier called quote spiritual unquote, and now you see how the quotation marks alluded to the fact that we were dealing with a basically quite material business of filaments or lines or twigs, though none the less joyful and energetic.

So far I remember everything very well, because the memories of the nucleus, awareness or no awareness, retain a greater clarity. But this tension I was telling you about, as time went by, was transmitted to the cytoplasm: I was seized with a need to stretch to my full width, to a kind of intermittent stiffening of the nerves I didn't have: and so the cytoplasm had become more elongated as if the two extremes wanted to run away from each other, in a bundle of fibrous matter which was all trembling no more and no less than the nucleus. In fact, it was now hard to distinguish between nucleus and cytoplasm: the nucleus had so to speak dissolved and the little sticks were poised there halfway along this shaft of tense and fitful fibres, but without scattering, turning upon themselves all together like a merry-go-round.

To tell the truth, I had hardly noticed the explosion of the nucleus: I felt I was all myself in a more total way than ever before, and at the same time that I wasn't myself any longer, that all this me was a place where there was everything except me: what I mean is, I had the sense of being inhabited, no, of inhabiting myself. No, of inhabiting a me inhabited by others. No, I had the sense that another was inhabited by others. Instead, what I realized only then was that fact of redoubling which before as I said I hadn't seen clearly: then and there I found myself with an exorbitant number of chromosomes, all mixed together at the time because the pairs of twin chromosomes had become unstuck and I couldn't make head or tail of anything. In other words: faced by the mute unknown void into which I had gradually and amorously submerged myself I had to say something that would re-establish my presence, but at that moment the words at my disposal seemed so many to me, too many to be arranged into something to say that was still me, my name, my new name.

I remember another thing: how from this state of chaotic congestion I tended to pass, in a vain search for relief, to a more balanced and neat congestion, to have a complete assortment of chromosomes arranged on one side and another on the other side, so the nucleus – or rather that whirligig of strokes that had taken the place of the exploded nucleus – at a certain point finally assumed a symmetrical, mirrored appearance, as if divaricating its strength to dominate the challenge of the silent unknown void, so the redoubling which first concerned the individual twigs now involved the nucleus as a whole, or rather what I went on considering a sole nucleus and went on operating as such, though it was simply an eddy of stuff separating into two distinct eddies.

Here I must explain that this separation wasn't a matter of old chromosomes on one side and new chromosomes on the other, because if I haven't already told you I'll tell you now, every twig after thickening had divided lengthwise, so they were all equally old and equally new; this is important because I used before the verb 'to repeat', which as always was rather approximate and might give the mistaken idea that there was an original twig and a copy, and also the verb 'to say' was a bit out of place, although that expression about saying myself worked out fairly well, out of place in that to say something you have to have someone who says and something that's said, and this wasn't actually the case at that time.

It's difficult, in other words, to define in precise terms the imprecision of amorous moods, which consist in a joyous impatience to possess a void, in a greedy expectation of what might come to me from the void, and also in the pain of being still deprived of what I am impatiently and greedily expecting, in the tormenting pain of feeling myself already potentially doubled to possess potentially something potentially mine, and yet forced not to possess, to consider not mine and therefore potentially another's what I potentially possess. The pain of having to bear the fact that the potentially mine is also potentially another's, or, for all I know, actually another's; this greedy jealous pain is a state of such fullness that it makes you believe being in love consists entirely and only in pain, that the greedy impatience is nothing but jealous desperation, and the emotion of impatience is only the emotion of despair that twists within itself, becoming more and more desperate, with the capacity that each particle of despair has for redoubling and arranging itself symmetrically alongside the analogous particle and for tending to move from its own state to enter another, perhaps worse state which rends and lacerates the former.

In this tug of war between the two eddies, an interval was being formed, and this was the moment when my state of doubling began to be clear to me, first as a branching of awareness, as a kind of squinting of the sense of presence of all of me, because it wasn't only the nucleus which was affected by these phenomena; as you already know, everything going on there in the little sticks of the nucleus was reflected in what was happening in the extension of my tapering physical person, commanded in fact by those sticks. So my cytoplasm fibres were also becoming concentrated in two opposing directions and were growing thin in the middle until the moment came when I seemed to have two equal bodies, one on one side and one on the other, joined by a bottleneck that was becoming finer and finer until it was only a thread, and at that instant I was for the first time aware of plurality, for the first and last time because it was late by then, I felt the plurality in me as the image and destiny of the world's plurality, and the sense of being part of the world, of being lost in the innumerable world, and at the same time the still-sharp sense of being me; I say 'sense' and no longer 'awareness' because if we agree to call awareness what I felt in the nucleus, then the nuclei were two, and each was tearing at the last fibres that kept it bound to the other, and by now they were both transmitting on their own, on my own now, on my own in a repeated fashion, each independent, awareness as if stammering ripped away the last fibres of my memory my memories.

I say that the sense of being me no longer came from the nuclei but from that bit of plasma strangled and wrung out there in the middle, and it was still like a filiform zenith of fullness, like a delirium where I saw all the diversities of the plural world filiformly radiating from my former, singular continuity. And at the same moment I realized that my moving out of myself was an exit with no return, without possible restitution of the me that now I realize I'm throwing away without its possible restitution to me ever, and then comes the death agony that precipitates triumphantly because life is already elsewhere, already the flashes of another's memory of the other cell which are split not superimposed establish the relationship of the novice cell, the relationship with its novice self and with the rest.

Everything that came afterwards is lost in the memory, shattered and multiplied like the propagation and repetition in the world of unremembering and mortal individuals, but already an instant before that afterwards began I understood everything that was to happen, the future or the soldering of the link that now or already then happens or tended desperately to happen, I understood that this picking up and moving out of oneself which is birth-death would make the circuit, would be transformed from strangling and fracture into interpenetration and mingling of asymmetrical cells that add up the messages repeated through trillions of trillions of mortal loves, I saw my mortal love return to seeking the original soldering or the final one, and all the words that weren't exact in the narration of my love story became exact and yet their meaning remained the exact meaning of before, and the loves kindled in the forest of the plurality of the sexes and of the individuals and of the species, the empty dizziness filled with the form of the species and individuals and sexes, and yet there was always the repetition of that wrench of myself, of that picking up and moving out, picking myself up and moving out of myself, the yearning towards that impossible doing which leads to saying, that impossible saying that leads to expressing oneself, even when the self will be divided into a self that says and will surely die and a self that is said and that at times risks living on, in a multicellular and unique self that retains in its cells the one that, repeating itself, repeats the secret words of the vocabulary that we are, and in a unicellular and countlessly plural unicellular self which can be poured out in countless cell-words of which only the one that encounters the complementary cell-word that is its asymmetrical self will try to continue the continuous and fragmentary story, but if it doesn't encounter it, no matter; in fact in the story which I'm about to tell there was no plan for the encounter at all, indeed at the beginning we'll try to avoid its taking place, because what matters is the initial or rather preceding phase which repeats every initial or rather preceding phase, the encounter with oneself loving and mortal, in the best of cases loving and in any case mortal; what matters is the moment when wrenching yourself from yourself you feel in a flash the union of past and future, just as I, in the wrenching from myself which I have just now finished narrating to you, saw what was to happen, finding myself today in love, in a today perhaps in the future perhaps in the past but also surely contemporaneous with that last unicellular and self-contained instant. I saw who was coming forward towards me from the void of the elsewhere, the other time, the otherwise with first and last name address red coat little black boots fringe freckles: Priscilla Langwood, chez Madame Lebras, cent-quatre-vingt-treize Rue Vaugirard, Paris quinzième.

II. Meiosis

Narrating things as they are means narrating them from the beginning, and even if I start the story at a point where the characters are multicellular organisms, for example the story of my relationship with Priscilla, I have first to define clearly what I mean when I say me and what I mean when I say Priscilla, then I can go on to establish what this relationship was. So I'll begin by saying that Priscilla is an individual of my same species and of the sex opposite mine, multicellular as I now find myself, too; but having said this I still haven't said anything, because I must specify that by multicellular individual is meant a complex of about fifty trillion cells very different among themselves but marked by certain chains of identical acids in the chromosomes of each cell of each individual, acids that determine various processes in the proteins of the cells themselves.

So narrating the story of me and Priscilla means first of all defining the relations established between my proteins and Priscilla's proteins, commanded, both mine and hers, by chains of nucleic acids arranged in identical series in each of her cells and in each of mine. Then narrating this story becomes still more complicated than when it was a question of a single cell, not only because the description of the relationship must take into account so many things that happen at the same time but above all because it's necessary to establish who is having relations with whom, before specifying what sort of relations they are. Actually, when you come right down to it, defining the sort of relations isn't after all as important as it seems, because saying we have mental relations, for example, or else, for example, physical relations doesn't change much, since a mental relationship involves several billion special cells called neurons which, however, function by receiving stimuli from such a great number of other cells that we might just as well consider all the trillions of cells of the organism at once as we do when we talk about a physical relationship.

In saying how difficult it is to establish who's having relations with whom we must first clear the decks of a subject that often crops up in conversation: namely, the fact that from one moment to the next I am no longer the same I nor is Priscilla any longer the same Priscilla, because of the continuous renewal of the protein molecules in our cells through, for example, digestion or also respiration which fixes the oxygen in the bloodstream. This kind of argument takes us completely off our course because while it's true that the cells are renewed, in renewing themselves they go on following the programme established by those that were there before and so in this sense you could reasonably insist that I continue to be I and Priscilla, Priscilla. This in other words is not the problem, but perhaps it was of some use to raise it because it helps us realize that things aren't as simple as they seem and so we slowly approach the point where we will realize how complicated they are.

Well then, when I say I, or when I say Priscilla, what do I mean? I mean that special configuration which my cells and her cells assume through a special relationship between the environment and a special genetic heritage which from the beginning seemed invented on purpose to cause my cells to be mine and Priscilla's cells to be Priscilla's. As we proceed we'll see that nothing is made on purpose, that nobody has invented anything, that the way I am and Priscilla is really doesn't matter in the least to anyone: all a genetic heritage has to do is to transmit what was transmitted to it for transmitting, not giving a damn about how it's received. But for the moment let's limit ourselves to answering the question if I, in quotes, and Priscilla, in quotes, are our genetic heritage, in quotes, or our form, in quotes. And when I say form I mean both what is seen and what isn't seen, namely, all her way of being Priscilla, the fact that fuchsia or orange is becoming to her, the scent emanating from her skin not only because she was born with a glandular constitution suited to giving off that scent but also because of everything she has eaten in her life and the brands of soap she has used, in other words because of what is called, in quotes, culture, and also her way of walking and of sitting down which comes to her from the way she has moved among those who move in the cities and houses and streets where she's lived, all this but also the things she has in her memory, after having seen them perhaps just once and perhaps at the movies, and also the forgotten things which still remain recorded somewhere in the back of the neurons like all the psychic trauma a person has to swallow from infancy on.

Now, both in the form you see and don't see and in our genetic heritage, Priscilla and I have absolutely identical elements – common to the two of us, or to the environment, or to the species – and also elements which establish a difference. Then the problem begins to arise whether the relationship between me and Priscilla is the relationship only between the differential elements, because the common ones can be overlooked in both – that is, whether by 'Priscilla' we must understand 'what is peculiar to Priscilla as far as the other members of the species are concerned' – or whether the relationship is between the common elements, and then we must decide if it's the ones common to the species or to the environment or to the two of us as distinct from the rest of the species and perhaps more beautiful than the others.

On closer examination, if individuals of opposite sex enter into a particular relationship it clearly isn't we who decide but the species, or rather not so much the species as the animal condition, or the vegetable-animal condition of the animal-vegetives distinguished into distinct sexes. Now, in the choice I make of Priscilla to have with her relations whose nature I don't yet know – and in the choice that Priscilla makes of me, assuming that she does choose me and doesn't change her mind at the last moment – no one knows what order of priority comes first into play, therefore no one knows how many I's precede the I that I think I am, and how many Priscillas precede the Priscilla towards whom I believe I am running.

In short, the more you simplify the terms of the question the more they become complicated: once we've established that what I call 'I' consists of a certain number of amino acids which line up in a certain way, it's logical that inside these molecules all possible relations are foreseen, and from outside we have nothing but the exclusion of some of the possible relations in the form of certain enzymes which block certain processes. Therefore you can say that it's as if everything possible had already happened to me, including the possibility of its not happening: once I am I the cards are all dealt, I dispose of a finite number of possibilities and no more, what happens outside counts for me only if it's translated into operations already foreseen by my nucleic acids, I'm walled up within myself, chained to my molecular programme: outside of me I don't have and won't have relations with anything or with anybody. And neither will Priscilla; I mean the *real* Priscilla, poor thing. If around me and around her there's some stuff that seems to have relations with other stuff, these are facts that don't concern us: in reality for me and for her nothing substantial can happen.

Hardly a cheerful situation, therefore: and not because I was expecting to have a more complex individuality than the one given me, beginning with a special arrangement of an acid and of four basic substances which in their turn command the disposition of about twenty amino acids in the forty-six chromosomes of each cell I have; but because this individuality repeated in each of my cells is mine only after a manner of speaking, since out of forty-six chromosomes twenty-three come to me from my father and twenty-three from my mother, that is, I continue carrying my parents with me in all my cells, and I'll never be able to free myself of this burden.

What my parents programmed me to be in the beginning is what I am: that and nothing else. And in my parents' instructions are contained the instructions of my parents' parents handed down in turn from parent to parent in an endless chain of obedience. The story I wanted to narrate therefore is not only impossible to narrate but first of all impossible to live, because it's all there already, contained in a past that can't be narrated since, in turn, it's included in its own past, in the many individual pasts – so many that we can't really be sure they aren't the past of the species and of what existed before the species, a general past to which all individual pasts refer but which no matter how far you go back doesn't exist except in the form of individual cases, such as Priscilla and I might be, between which, however, nothing happens, individual or general.

What each of us really is and has is the past; all we are and have is the catalogue of the possibilities that didn't fail, of the experiences that are ready to be repeated. A present doesn't exist, we proceed blindly towards the outside and the after-wards, carrying out an established programme with materials we fabricate ourselves, always the same. We don't tend towards any future, there's nothing awaiting us, we're shut within the system of a memory which foresees no task but remembering itself. What now leads me and Priscilla to seek each other isn't an impulse towards the afterwards: it's the final action of the past that is fulfilled through us. Goodbye, Priscilla, our encounter, our embrace are useless, we remain distant, or finally near, in other words for ever apart.

Separation, the impossibility of meeting, has been in us from the very beginning. We were born not from a fusion but from a juxtaposition of distinct bodies. Two cells grazed each other: one is lazy and all pulp, the other is only a head and a darting tail. They are egg and seed: they experience a certain timidity; then they rush – at their different speeds – and hurry towards each other. The seed plunges headlong into the egg; the tail is left outside; the head – all full of nucleus – is shot at the nucleus of the egg; the two nuclei are shattered: you might expect heaven knows what fusion or mingling or exchange of selves; instead, what was written in one nucleus and in the other, those spaced lines, fall in and arrange themselves, on each side, in the new nucleus, very closely printed; the words of both nuclei fit in, whole and clearly separate. In short, nobody was lost in the other, nobody has given in or has given himself; the two cells now one are packaged together but just as they were before: the first thing they feel is a slight disappointment. Meanwhile the double nucleus has begun its sequence of duplications, printing the combined messages of father and mother in each of the offspring cells, perpetuating not so much the union as the unbridgeable distance that separates in each couple the two companions, the failure, the void that remains in the midst of even the most successful couple.

Of course, on every disputed issue our cells can follow the instructions of a single parent and thus feel free of the other's command, but we know what we claim to be in our exterior form counts for little compared to the secret programme we carry printed in each cell, where the contradictory orders of father and mother continue arguing. What really counts is this incompatible quarrel of father and mother that each of us drags after him, with the rancour of every point where one partner has had to give way to the other, who then raises his voice still louder in his victory as dominant mate. So the characteristics that determine my interior and exterior form, when they are not the sum or the average of the orders received from father and mother together, are orders denied in the depth of the cells, counterbalanced by different orders which have remained latent, sapped by the suspicion that perhaps the other orders were better. So at times I'm seized with uncertainty as to whether I am really the sum of the dominant characteristics of the past, the result of a series of operations that produced always a number bigger than zero, or whether instead my true essence isn't rather what descends from the succession of defeated characteristics, the total of the terms with the minus sign, of everything that in the tree of derivations has remained excluded, stifled, interrupted: the weight of what hasn't been weighs on me, no less crushing than what has been and couldn't not be.

Void, separation and waiting, that's what we are. And such we remain even on the day when the past inside us rediscovers its original forms, clustering into swarms of seed-cells or concentrated ripening of the egg-cells, and finally the words written in the nuclei are no longer the same as before but are no longer part of us either, they're a message beyond us, which already belongs to us no more. In a hidden point in ourselves the double series of orders from the past is divided in two and the new cells find themselves with a simple past, no longer double, which gives them lightness and the illusion of being really new, of having a new past that almost seems a future.

Now, I've said it hastily like this but it's a complicated process, there in the darkness of the nucleus, in the depth of the sex organs, a succession of phases some a bit jumbled with others, but from which there's no turning back. At first the pairs of maternal and paternal messages which thus far had remained separate seem to remember they're couples and they join together two by two, so many fine little threads that become interwoven and confused; the desire to copulate outside myself now leads me to copulate within myself, at the depths of the extreme roots of the matter I'm made of, to couple the memory of the ancient pair I carry within me, the first couple, that is both the one that comes immediately before me, mother and father, and the absolute first one, the couple at the animal-vegetal origins of the first coupling on Earth, and so the forty-six filaments that an obscure and secret cell bears in the nucleus are knotted two by two, still not giving up their old disagreement, since in fact they immediately try to disentangle themselves but remain stuck at some point in the knot, so when in the end they do succeed, with a wrench, in separating – because meanwhile the mechanism of separation has taken possession of the whole cell, stretching out its pulp – each chromosome dis-covers it's changed, made of segments that first belonged some to one and some to the other, and it moves from the other, now changed too, marked by the alternate exchanges of the segments, and already two cells are being detached each with twenty-three chromosomes, the chromosomes in one cell different from those in the other, and in each case different from those that were in the previous cell, and at the next doubling there will be four cells all different, each with twenty-three chromosomes, in which what was the father's and the mother's, or rather the fathers' and the mothers', is mingled.

So finally the encounter of the pasts which can never take place in the present of those who believe they are meeting does take place in the form of the past of him who comes afterwards and who cannot live that encounter in his own present. We believe we're going towards our marriage, but it is still the marriage of the fathers and the mothers which is celebrated through our expectation and our desire. What seems to us our happiness is perhaps only the happiness of the others' story which ends just where we thought ours began.

And it's pointless for us to run, Priscilla, to meet each other and follow each other: the past disposes of us with blind indifference, and once it has moved those fragments of itself and of us, it doesn't bother afterwards how we spend them. We were only the preparation, the envelope, for the encounter of pasts which happens through us but which is already part of another story, the story of the afterwards: the encounters always take place before and after us, and in them the elements of the new, forbidden to us, are active: chance, risk, improbability.

This is how we live, not free, surrounded by freedom, driven, acted on by this constant wave which is the combination of the possible cases and which passes through those points of space and of time in which the range of the pasts is joined to the range of the futures. The primordial sea was a soup of beringed molecules traversed at intervals by the

messages of the similarity and of the difference that surrounded us and imposed new combinations. So the ancient
tide rises at intervals in me and in Priscilla following the
course of the Moon; so the sexed species respond to the old
conditioning which prescribes ages and seasons of loves and
also grants extensions and postponements to the ages and
the seasons and at times becomes involved in obstinacies
and coercions and vices.

In other words, Priscilla and I are only meeting places
for messages from the past: not only for messages among
themselves, but for messages meeting answers to messages.
And as the different elements and molecules answer messages
in different ways – imperceptibly or boundlessly different –
so the messages vary according to the world that receives
them and interprets them, or else, to remain the same, they
are forced to change. You might say, then, that the messages
are not messages at all, that a past to transmit doesn't exist,
and only so many futures exist which correct the course of
the past, which give it form, which invent it.

The story I wanted to tell is the encounter of two individuals who don't exist, since they are definable only with
regard to a past or a future, a past and future whose reality
is reciprocally doubted. Or else it's a story that cannot be
separated from the story of all the rest of what exists, and
therefore from the story of what doesn't exist and, not
existing, causes what does exist to exist. All we can say is that
in certain points and moments that interval of void which is
our individual presence is grazed by the wave which continues to renew the combinations of molecules and to complicate them or erase them, and this is enough to give us the
certitude that somebody is 'I' and somebody is 'Priscilla' in
the temporal and spatial distribution of the living cells, and
that something happens or has happened or will happen

which involves us directly and – I would dare say – happily and totally. This is in itself enough, Priscilla, to cheer me, when I bend my outstretched neck over yours and I give you a little nip on your yellow fur and you dilate your nostrils, bare your teeth and kneel on the sand, lowering your hump to the level of my breast so that I can lean on it and press you from behind, bearing down on my rear legs, oh how sweet those sunsets in the oasis you remember when they loosen the burden from the packsaddle and the caravan scatters and we camels feel suddenly light and you break into a run and I trot after you, overtaking you in the grove of palm trees.

III. Death

The risk we ran was living: living for ever. The threat of continuing weighed, from the very start, on anyone who had by chance begun. The crust that covers the Earth is liquid: one drop among the many thickens, grows, little by little absorbs the substances around it, it is a drop-island, gelatinous, that contracts and expands, that occupies more space at each pulsation, it's a drop-continent that spreads its branches over the oceans, makes the poles coagulate, solidifies its mucus-green outlines on the equator, if it doesn't stop in time it gobbles up the globe. The drop will live, only that drop, for ever, uniform and continuous in time and in space, a mucilaginous sphere with the Earth as its kernel, a gruel that contains the matter for the lives of us all, because we are all arrested in this drop that will never let us be born or die, so life will belong to it and to nobody else.

Luckily it is shattered. Each fragment is a chain of molecules arranged in a certain order, and thanks to the mere fact of having an order, it has only to float in the midst of the disordered substance and immediately around it other chains of molecules are formed, lined up in the same way. Each chain spreads order around itself, or rather it repeats itself over and over again, and the copies in turn are repeated, always in that geometrical arrangement. A solution of living crystals, all the same, covers the face of the Earth, it is born and dies in every moment without being aware of it, living a discontinuous and perpetual life, always identical to itself in a shattered time and space. Every other form remains shut out for ever; including ours.

Up to the moment when the material necessary for self-repetition shows signs of becoming scarce, and then each chain of molecules begins to collect around itself a kind of reserve supply of substances, kept in a kind of packet with everything it needs inside. This cell grows; it grows up to a certain point; it divides in two; the two cells divide into four, into eight, into sixteen; the multiplied cells instead of undulating each by itself stick to one another like colonies or shoals or polyps. The world is covered with a forest of sponges; each sponge multiplies its cells in a network of full and empty spaces which spreads out its mesh and stirs in the currents of the sea. Each cell lives on its own and, all united, they live the unity of their lives. In the winter frost the tissues of the sponge are rent, but the newer cells remain there and start dividing again, they repeat the same sponge in spring. Now we're close to the point and the die is cast: the sea will be drunk by their pores, it will flow into their dense passages; they will live, for ever, not we, we who wait vainly for the moment to be generated by them.

But in the monstrous agglomerations of the sea's depths, in the viscous mushroom-beds that begin to crop up from the soft crust of the emergent lands, not all the cells continue to grow superimposed on one another: every now and then a swarm breaks loose, undulates, flies, comes to rest further on; they begin to divide again, they repeat that sponge or polyp or fungus from which they came. Time now repeats itself in cycles: the phases alternate, always the same. The mushrooms scatter their spores in the wind slightly, and they grow a bit like the perishable mycelium, until other spores ripen which will die, as such, on opening. The great division within living beings has begun: the funguses that do not know death last a day and are reborn in a day, but between the part that transmits the orders of reproduction and the part that carries them out an irreconcilable gap has opened.

By now the battle is joined between those that exist and would like to be eternal and us who don't exist and would like to, at least for a little while. Fearing that a casual mistake might open the way to diversity, those who exist increase their control devices: if the reproduction orders derive from the confrontation of two distinct and identical messages, errors of transmission are more easily eliminated. So the alternation of the phases becomes complicated: from the branches of the polyp attached to the sea-bed transparent medusas are detached, which float halfway to the surface; love among the medusas begins, ephemeral play and luxury of continuity through which the polyps confirm their eternity. On the lands that have emerged, vegetable monsters open fans of leaves, spread out mossy carpets, arch their boughs on which hermaphrodite flowers blossom; so they hope to grant death only a small and hidden part of themselves, but by now the play of crossing messages has invaded the world: that will be the breach through which the crowd of us who do not exist will make our overflowing entrance.

The sea is covered with undulating eggs; a wave lifts them, mixes them with clouds of seed. Each swimming creature that slips from a fertilized egg repeats not one but two beings that were swimming there before him; he will not be the one or the other of those two but yet another, a third; that is, the original two for the first time will die, and the third for the first time has been born.

In the invisible expanse of the programme-cells where all

the combinations are formed or undone within the species, the original continuity still flows; but between one combination and another the interval is occupied by individuals who are mortal and sexed and different.

The dangers of life without death are avoided – they say – for ever. Not because from the mud of the boiling swamps the first clot of undivided life cannot again emerge, but because we are all around now – above all, those of us who act as micro-organisms and bacteria – ready to fling ourselves on that clot and devour it. Not because the chains of the viruses don't continue repeating themselves in their exact crystalline order, but because this can happen only within our bodies and tissues, in us, the more complex animals and vegetables; so the world of the eternals has been incorporated into the world of the perishable, and their immunity to death serves to guarantee us our mortal condition. We still go swimming over depths of corals and sea anemones, we still walk and make our way through ferns and mosses under the boughs of the original forest, but sexual reproduction has now somehow entered the cycle of even the most ancient species, the spell is broken, the eternals are dead, nobody seems prepared any longer to renounce sex, even the little share of sex that falls to his lot, in order to have again a life that repeats itself interminably.

The victors – for the present – are we, the discontinuous. The swamp-forest, defeated, is still around us; we have barely opened a passage with blows of our machete in the thicket of mangrove roots; finally a glimpse of free sky opens over our heads, we raise our eyes shielding them from the Sun: above us stretches another roof, the hull of words we secrete constantly. As soon as we are out of the primordial matter, we are bound in a connective tissue that fills the hiatus between our discontinuities, between our deaths and births, a collection of signs, articulated sounds, ideograms, morphemes, numbers, punched cards, magnetic tapes, tattoos, a system of communication that includes social relations, kinship, institutions, merchandise, advertising posters, napalm bombs, namely everything that is language, in the broad sense. The danger still isn't over. We are in a state of alarm, in the forest losing its leaves. Like a duplicate of the Earth's crust, the cap is hardening over our heads: it will be a hostile envelope, a prison, if we don't find the right spot to break it, to prevent its perpetual self-repetition.

The ceiling that covers us is all jutting iron gears; it's like the belly of an automobile under which I have crawled to repair a fault, but I can't come out from under it because, while I'm stretched out there with my back on the ground, the car expands, extends, until it covers the whole world. There is no time to lose, I must understand the mechanism, find the place where we can get to work and stop this uncontrolled process, press the buttons that guide the passage to the following phase: that of the machines that reproduce themselves through crossed male and female messages, forcing new machines to be born and the old machines to die.

Everything at a certain point tends to cling around me, even this page where my story is seeking a finale that doesn't conclude it, a net of words where a written I and a written Priscilla meet and multiply into other words and other thoughts, where they may set into motion the chain reaction through which things done or used by men, that is, the elements of their language, can also acquire speech, where machines can speak, exchange the words by which they are constructed, the messages that cause them to move. The circuit of vital information that runs from the nucleic acids to writing is prolonged in the punched tapes of the automata, children of other automata: generations of machines, perhaps better than we, will go on living and speaking lives and words that were also ours; and translated into electronic instructions, the word 'I' and the word 'Priscilla' will meet again.

PART THREE

t zero

t zero

I have the impression this isn't the first time I've found myself in this situation: with my bow just slackened in my outstretched left hand, my right hand drawn back, the arrow A suspended in midair at about a third of its trajectory, and, a bit further on, also suspended in midair, and also at about a third of his trajectory, the lion L in the act of leaping upon me, jaws agape and claws extended. In a second I'll know if the arrow's trajectory and the lion's will or will not coincide at a point X crossed both by L and by A at the same second t_x, that is, if the lion will slump in the air with a roar stifled by the spurt of blood that will flood his dark throat pierced by the arrow, or whether he will fall unhurt upon me knocking me to the ground with both forepaws which will lacerate the muscular tissue of my shoulders and chest, while his mouth, closing with a simple snap of the jaws, will rip my head from my neck at the level of the first vertebra.

So many and so complex are the factors that condition the parabolic movement both of arrows and of felines that I am unable for the moment to judge which of the eventualities is the more probable. I am therefore in one of those situations of uncertainty and expectation where one really doesn't know what to think. And the thought that immediately occurs to me is this: it doesn't seem the first time to me.

With this I don't mean to refer to other hunting experiences of mine: an archer, the moment he thinks he's experienced, is lost; every lion we encounter in our brief life is different from every other lion; woe to us if we stop to make comparisons, to deduce our movements from norms and premises. I am speaking of this lion L and of this arrow A which have now reached a third, roughly, of their respective trajectories.

Nor am I to be included among those who believe in the existence of a first and absolute lion, of which all the various individual and approximate lions that jump on us are only shadows or simulacra. In our hard life there is no room for anything that isn't concrete, that can't be grasped by the senses.

Equally alien to me is the view of those who assert that each of us carries within himself from birth a memory of lion that weighs upon his dreams, inherited by sons from fathers, and so when he sees a lion he immediately and spontaneously says: Ha, a lion! I could explain why and how I have come to exclude this idea, but this doesn't seem to me the right moment.

Suffice it to say that by 'lion' I mean only this yellow clump that has sprung forth from a bush in the savannah, this hoarse grunt that exhales an odour of bloody flesh, and the white fur of the belly and the pink of the under-paws and the sharp angle of the retractile claws just as I see them over me now with a mixture of sensations that I call 'lion' in order to give it a name though I want it to be clear it has nothing to do with the word 'lion' nor even with the idea of lion which one might form in other circumstances.

If I say this moment I am living through is not being lived for the first time by me, it's because the sensation I have of it is one of a slight doubling of images, as if at the same time I were seeing not one lion or one arrow but two or more lions and two or more arrows superimposed with a barely perceptible overlapping, so the sinuous outlines of the lion's form and the segment of the arrow seem underlined or rather haloed by finer lines and a more delicate colour. The doubling, however, could be only an illusion through which I depict to myself an otherwise indefinable sense of thickness, whereby lion arrow bush are something more than this lion this arrow this bush, namely, the interminable repetition of lion arrow bush arranged in this specific relationship with an interminable repetition of myself in the moment when I have just slackened the string of my bow.

I wouldn't want this sensation as I have described it, however, to resemble too much the recognition of something already seen, arrow in that position, lion in that other and reciprocal relation between the positions of arrow and of lion and of me rooted here with the bow in my hand; I would prefer to say that what I have recognized is only the space, the point of space where the arrow is which would be empty if the arrow weren't there, the empty space which now contains the lion and the space which now contains me, as if in the void of the space we occupy or rather cross – that is, which the world occupies or rather crosses – certain points had become recognizable to me in the midst of all the other points equally empty and equally crossed by the world. And bear this in mind: it isn't that this recognition occurs in relation, for example, to the configuration of the terrain, the distance of the river or the forest: the space that surrounds us is a space that is always different, I know this quite well, I know the Earth is a heavenly body that moves in the midst of other moving heavenly bodies, I know that no sign, on the Earth or in the sky, can serve me as an absolute point of reference, I also remember that the stars turn in the wheel of the galaxy and the galaxies move away from one another at speeds proportional to the distance. But the suspicion that has gripped me is precisely this: that I have come to find myself in a space not new to me, that I have returned to a point where we had already passed by. And since it isn't merely a question of me but also of an arrow and a lion, it's no good thinking this is just chance: here time is involved, which continues to cover a trail it has already followed. I could then define as time and not as space that void I felt I recognized as I crossed it.

The question I now ask myself is if a point of time's trail can be superimposed on points of preceding passages. In this case, the impression of the images' thickness would be explained by the repeated beating of time on an identical instant. It might also be, in certain points, an occasional slight overlapping between one passage and the next: images slightly doubled or unfocused would then be the clue that the trail of time is a little worn by use and leaves a narrow margin of play around its obligatory channels. But even if it were simply a momentary optical effect, the accent remains, as of a cadence I seem to feel beating on the instant I am living through. I still wouldn't like what I have said to make this moment seem endowed with a special temporal consistency in the series of moments that precede it and follow it: from the point of view of time it is actually a moment that lasts as long as the others, indifferent to its content, suspended in its course between past and future; what it seems to me I've discovered is only its punctual recurrence in a series that is repeated, identical to itself every time.

In short, the whole problem, now that the arrow is hissing through the air and the lion arches in his spring and I still can't tell if the arrowhead dipped in serpent's venom will pierce the tawny skin between the widened eyes or will miss, abandoning my helpless viscera to the rending that will separate them from the framework of bones to which they are now anchored and will drag and scatter them over the bloodied, dusty ground until before night the vultures and the jackals will have erased the last trace, the whole problem for me is to know if the series of which this second is a part is open or closed. Because if, as I seem to have heard maintained sometimes, it is a finite series, that is if the universe's time began at a certain moment and continues in an explosion of stars and nebulae, more and more rarefied, until the moment when the dispersion will reach the extreme limit and stars and nebulae will start concentrating again, the consequence I must draw is that time will retrace its steps, that the chain of minutes will unroll in the opposite direction, until we are back at the beginning, only to start over again, and all of this will occur infinite times – and it may just be, then, that time did have a beginning: the universe does nothing but pulsate between two extreme moments, forced to repeat itself for ever – just as it has already repeated itself infinite times and just as this second where I now find myself is repeated.

Let's try to look at it all clearly, then: I find myself in a random space-time intermediary point of a phase of the universe; after hundreds of millions of billions of seconds here the arrow and the lion and I and the bush have found ourselves as we now find ourselves, and this second will be promptly swallowed up and buried in the series of the hundreds of millions of billions of seconds that continues, independently of the outcome, a second from now, of the convergent or divergent flight of the lion and of the arrow; then at a certain point the course will reverse its direction, the universe will repeat its vicissitude backwards, from the effects the causes will punctually arise, so also from these effects I am waiting for and don't know, from an arrow that ploughs into the ground raising a yellow cloud of dust and tiny fragments of flint or else which pierces the palate of the beast like a new, monstrous tooth, we'll come back to the moment I am now living, the arrow returning to fit itself to the taut bow as if sucked back, the lion falling again behind the bush on his rear legs tensed like a spring, and all the afterwards will gradually be erased second by second by the return of the before, it will be forgotten in the dispersal of billions of combinations of neurons within the lobes of brains, so that no one will know he's living in reversed time just as I myself am not now sure in which direction the time I move in is moving, and if the then I'm waiting for hasn't in reality already happened just a second ago, bearing with it my salvation or my death.

What I ask myself is whether, seeing that at this point we have to go back in any case, it wouldn't be wise for me to stop, to stop in space and in time, while the string of the barely slackened bow bends in the direction opposite to the one where it was previously tautened, and while my right foot barely lightened of the weight of the body is lifted in a ninety-degree twist, and to let it be motionless like that to wait until, from the darkness of space-time, the lion emerges again and sets himself against me with all four legs in the air, and the arrow goes back to its place in its trajectory at the exact point where it is now. What, after all, is the use of continuing if sooner or later we will only find ourselves in this situation again? I might as well grant myself a few dozen billion years' repose, and let the rest of the universe continue its spatial and temporal race to the end, and wait for the return trip to jump on again and go back in my story and the universe's to the origin, and then begin once more to find myself here – or else let time go back by itself and let it approach me again while I stand still and wait – and then see if the right moment has come for me to make up my mind and take the next step, to go and have a look at what will happen to me in a second, or on the other hand if it's best for me to remain here definitively. For this there is no need for my material particles to be removed from their spatio-temporal course, from the bloody ephemeral victory of the hunter or of the lion: I'm sure that in any case a part of us remains entangled with each single intersection of time and space, and therefore it would be enough not to separate ourselves from this part, to identify with it, letting the rest go on turning as it must turn to the end.

In short, I am offered this possibility: to constitute a fixed point in the oscillating phases of the universe. Shall I seize the opportunity or is it best to skip it? As far as stopping goes, I might well stop not just myself, which I realize wouldn't make much sense, but stop along with me what serves to define this moment for me, arrow lion archer suspended just as we are, for ever. It seems to me in fact that if the lion knew clearly how things stand, he too would surely agree to remain where he is now, at about a third of the trajectory of his furious leap, to separate himself from that self-projection which in another second will encounter the rigid jerks of the death agony or the angry crunching of a still-warm human skull. I can speak therefore not only for myself, but also in the name of the lion. And in the name of the arrow, because an arrow can wish for nothing but to be an arrow as it is in this rapid moment, postponing its destiny as blunted scrap which awaits it whichever target it may strike.

Having established, then, that the situation in which we now find ourselves, lion arrow and I in this moment t_0, will occur twice for each coming and going of time, identical to the other times, and that it has been so repeated as often as the universe has repeated its diastole and its systole in the past – if it really makes sense to speak of past and future for the succession of these phases, when we know that it doesn't make sense within the phases – an uncertainty still remains about the situation in the successive seconds t_1, t_2, t_3, et cetera, just as things were uncertain in the preceding t_{-1}, t_{-2}, t_{-3}, et cetera.

The alternatives, on closer examination, are these:

either the space-time lines that the universe follows in the phases of its pulsation coincide at every point;

or else they coincide only in certain exceptional points, such as the second I am now living in, diverging then in the others.

If the latter of these alternatives is correct, from the space-time point where I now am there extends a bundle of possibilities which, the more they proceed in time, the more they diverge, cone-like, towards futures which are completely different from one another, and each time I find myself here with the arrow and the lion in the air will correspond to a different point X of intersection in their trajectories, each time the lion will be wounded in a different way, he will have a different agony or will find to a different extent new strength to react, or he won't be wounded at all and will fling himself upon me each time in a different way leaving me possibilities of self-defence or not leaving them, and my victories and my defeats in the struggle with the lion prove to be potentially infinite, so the more times I am disembowelled the more probabilities I'll have of hitting the target the next time I find myself here billions and billions of years later, thus I can express no opinion on this present situation of mine because in the event that I am living the fraction of time immediately preceding the clawing of the beast this would be the last moment of a happy period, whereas if what awaits me is the triumph with which the tribe welcomes the victorious lion hunter, what I'm now living is the climax of anguish, the blackest point of the descent to hell which I must make in order to deserve the coming apotheosis. Therefore it's best for me to flee from this situation whatever may be in store for me, because if there's one interval of time that really counts for nothing it's this very moment, definable only in relation to what follows it, that is to say this second in itself doesn't exist, and so there is no possibility not only of staying in it but even of crossing it for the duration of a second, in short it is a jump of time between the moment in which the lion and the arrow took flight and the moment when a spurt of blood will burst from the lion's veins or from mine.

Consider, too, that if from this second infinite lines of possible futures move out in a cone, the same lines arrive obliquely from a past that is also a cone of infinite possibilities, therefore the I who is now here with the lion plunging on him from above and with the arrow cutting its way through the air is a different I every time because past mother father tribe language age experience are different each time, the lion is always another lion even if I see him just like this each time, with his tail which has curved in the leap till the tuft is near the right flank in a movement that could be a lash or a caress, with the mane so open that it covers a great part of the breast and the torso from my sight and allows only the forepaws to emerge laterally raised as if preparing for me a joyous embrace but in reality ready to plunge the claws in my shoulders with all their strength, and the arrow is made of material that is always different, tipped with different heads, poisoned by dissimilar serpents, though always crossing the air in the same parabola and with the same hiss. What doesn't change is the relation between me arrow lion in this moment of uncertainty which is repeated exactly, an uncertainty whose stake is death, but we must agree that if this menacing death is the death of a me with a different past, of a me that yesterday morning didn't go out to gather roots with my girl cousin, that is rightly speaking another me, a stranger, perhaps a stranger who yesterday morning went gathering roots with my girl cousin, therefore an enemy, in any case if here in my place the other times instead of me there was somebody else, it doesn't then matter much to know if the time before or the time after the arrow struck the lion or not.

In this case, then, it's out of the question that stopping in t_0 for the whole cycle of space and time could have any interest for me. However, the other hypothesis still remains: as in the old geometry lines had only to coincide in two points to coincide in all, so it may be that the spatio-temporal lines drawn by the universe in its alternating phases coincide in all their points and therefore not only t_0 but also t_1 and t_2 and everything that will come afterwards will coincide with the respective t_1 t_2 t_3 of the other phases, and likewise all the preceding and following seconds, and I will be reduced to having a sole past and a sole future repeated infinite times before and after this moment. One might, however, wonder whether there is any sense in speaking of repetition when time consists in a single series of points not allowing variations in their nature or in their succession: it would then suffice to say that time is finite and always equal to itself, and can thus be considered as given contemporaneously in all its extent forming a pile of layers of present; in other words, we have a time that is absolutely full, since each of the moments into which it can be broken down constitutes a kind of layer that stays there continuously present, inserted among other layers also continuously present. In short, the second t_0 in which we have the arrow A_0 and a bit further on the lion L_0

and here the me Q_0 is a space-time layer that remains motion-less and identical for ever, and next to it there is placed t_1 with the arrow A_1 and the lion L_1 and the me Q_1 who have slightly changed their positions, and beside that there is t_2 which contains A_2 and L_2 and Q_2 and so on. In one of these seconds placed in line it is clear who lives and who dies between the lion L_n and the me Q_n, and in the following seconds there are surely taking place either the tribe's festivities for the hunter who returns with the lion's remains or the funeral of the hunter as through the savannah spreads the terror of the prowling murderous lion. Each second is definitive, closed, without interferences from the others, and I, Q_0, here in my territory t_0 can be absolutely calm and take no interest in what is simultaneously happening to Q_1 Q_2 Q_3 Q_n in the respective seconds near mine, because in reality the lions L_1 L_2 L_3 L_n can never take the place of the familiar and still-inoffensive though menacing L_0, held at bay by an arrow in flight A_0 still containing in itself that mortal power that might prove wasted by A_1 A_2 A_3 A_n in their arrangement in segments of the trajectory more and more distant from the target, ridiculing me as the most clumsy archer of the tribe, or rather ridiculing as clumsy that Q_{-n} who in t_{-n} takes aim with his bow.

I know the comparison with the frames of a movie film emerges spontaneously, but if I've avoided using it so far you can be sure I've had my reasons. It's true that each second is closed in itself and incommunicable with the others exactly as in a film frame, but to define its content the points Q_0 L_0 A_0 are not enough: with them we would limit it to a little lion-hunting scene, dramatic if you like but surely not displaying a very broad horizon; what must be considered contemporaneously is the totality of the points contained in the universe in that second t_0 not excluding even one, and then it's best to put the film frame right out of your head because it just confuses things.

So now that I have decided to inhabit for ever this second t_0 – and if I hadn't decided to it would be the same thing because as Q_0 I can inhabit no other – I have ample leisure to look around and to contemplate my second to its full extent. It encompasses on my right a river blackish with hippopotamuses, on my left the savannah blackish-white with zebras, and scattered at various points along the horizon some baobab trees blackish-yellow with toucans, each of these elements marked by the positions occupied respectively by the hippopotamuses $H(a)_0$, $H(b)_0$, $H(c)_0$ et cetera, by the zebras $Z(a)_0$, $Z(b)_0$, $Z(c)_0$ et cetera, the toucans $T(a)_0$, $T(b)_0$, $T(c)_0$ et cetera. It further embraces hut villages and warehouses of importers and exporters, plantations that conceal underground thousands of seeds at different moments of the process of germination, endless deserts with the position of each grain of sand $G(a)_0$, $G(b)_0$ ... $G(n^n)_0$ transported by the wind, cities at night with lighted windows and dark windows, cities during the day with red and yellow and green traffic lights, production graphs, price indices, stock market figures, epidemics of contagious diseases with the position of each virus, local wars with volleys of bullets $B(a)_0$ $B(b)_0$ ... $B(z)_0$ $B(zz)_0$ $B(zzz)_0$ ... suspended in their trajectory, bullets which may strike the enemies $E(a)_0$ $E(b)_0$ $E(c)_0$ hidden among the leaves, aeroplanes with clusters of just-released bombs suspended beneath them, aeroplanes with clusters of bombs waiting to be released, total war implicit in the international situation $(IS)_0$ which at some unknown moment $(IS)_x$ will become explicit total war, explosions of supernovae which might change radically the configuration of our galaxy ...

Each second is a universe, the second I live is the second I live in, *la seconde que je vis c'est la seconde où je demeure*,

I must get used to conceiving my speech simultaneously in all possible languages if I want to live my universe-instant extensively. Through the combination of all contemporaneous data I could achieve an objective knowledge of the universe-instant t_0 in all its spatial extension, me included, since inside t_0 I, Q_0, am not in the least determined by my past Q_{-1} Q_{-2} Q_{-3} et cetera but by the system composed of all the toucans T_0, bullets B_0, viruses V_0, without which the fact that I am Q_0 could not be established. For that matter, since I no longer have to worry about what will happen to Q_1 Q_2 Q_3 et cetera, there's no use in my assuming the subjective point of view that has guided me so far, now I can identify myself with myself as well as with the lion or with the grain of sand or the cost-of-living index or with the enemy or with the enemy's enemy.

To do this I must establish exactly the co-ordinates of all these points and I must calculate certain constants. I could for example emphasize all the components of suspense and uncertainty that obtain both for me and for the lion the arrow the bombs the enemy and the enemy's enemy, and define t_0 as a moment of universal suspense and uncertainty. But this still tells me nothing substantial about t_0 because granted it is indeed a terrifying moment as I believe is now proved, it could also be just one terrifying moment in a series of moments of mounting terror or equally a terrifying moment in a series of decreasing and therefore illusory terror. In other words this established but relative terror of t_0 can assume completely different values, since t_1 t_2 t_3 can transform the substance of t_0 in a radical manner, or to put it more clearly there are the various t_1's of Q_1, L_1, $E(a)_1$, $E(\frac{1}{4})_1$ which have the power to determine the fundamental qualities of t_0.

And here, it seems to me, things start becoming complicated: my line of conduct is to close myself in t_0 and to know nothing of what happens outside of this second, giving up a limited personal point of view in order to live t_0 in all its global objective configuration, but this objective configuration can be grasped not from within t_0 but only by observing it from another universe-instant, for example from t_1 or from t_2, and not from all their extension contemporaneously but by adopting decisively one point of view, that of the enemy or of the enemy's enemy, that of the lion or that of myself.

To sum up: to stay in t_0 I must establish an objective configuration of t_0; to establish an objective configuration of t_0 I must move to t_1; to move into t_1 I must adopt some kind of subjective viewpoint so I might as well keep my own. To sum up further: to stay still in time I must move with time, to become objective I must remain subjective.

Now let's see how I must behave practically: it remains established that I as Q_0 retain my residence in t_0, but I could meanwhile make the quickest possible dash into t_1 and if that isn't enough proceed on to t_2 and t_3, identifying myself temporarily with Q_1 Q_2 Q_3, all this naturally in the hope that the Q series continues and isn't prematurely cut off by the curved claws of L_1 L_2 L_3, because only in this way could I realize how my position of Q_0 in t_0 is really constituted which is the only thing that should matter to me.

But the danger I risk is that the content of t_1, of the universe-instant t_1, is so much more interesting, so much richer than t_0, in emotions and surprises either triumphant or disastrous, that I might be tempted to devote myself entirely to t_1, turning my back on t_0, forgetting that I had moved to t_1 only to gain more information on t_0. And in this curiosity about t_1, in this illegitimate desire for knowledge about a universe-instant that isn't mine, in wanting to discover if I would really be making a good bargain trading my stable and secure citizenship of t_0 for that modicum of novelty that t_1 could offer me, I might take a step into t_2 just to have a more objective notion of t_1; and that step into t_2 might, in turn . . .

If this is how things stand I realize that my situation won't change in the least even if I abandon the hypotheses from which I set out: that is, supposing time knows no repetitions and consists of an irreversible series of seconds each different from the other, and each second happens once and for all, and living in it for its exact length of one second means living in it for ever, and t_0 interests me only with regard to the t_1 t_2 t_3's that follow it with their content of life or death in consequence of the movement I performed in shooting the arrow and the movement that the lion performed in making his leap and also of the other movements the lion and I will make in the next seconds and of the fear that for the whole duration of an interminable second keeps me petrified and keeps petrified the lion in midair and the arrow in my sight and the second t_0 swift as it came now swiftly clicks into the following second and traces with no further doubts the trajectory of the lion and of the arrow . . .

The Chase

That car that is chasing me is faster than mine; inside there is one man, alone, armed with a pistol, a good shot, as I have seen from the bullets which missed me by fractions of an inch. In my escape I have headed for the centre of the city; it was a healthy decision; the pursuer is constantly behind me but we are separated by several other cars; we have stopped at a traffic signal, in a long column.

The signal is regulated in such a way that on our side the red light lasts a hundred and eighty seconds and the green light a hundred and twenty, no doubt based on the premise that the perpendicular traffic is heavier and slower. A mistaken premise: calculating the cars I see going by transversely when it is green for them, I would say they are about twice the number of those that in an equally long period manage to break free of our column and pass the signal. This doesn't mean that, once beyond it, they speed: in reality they go on forward with exasperating slowness, which can be considered speed only compared to us since we are virtually motionless with red and green alike. It is also partially the fault of this slowness of theirs that we don't succeed in moving, because when the green goes off for them and comes on for us the intersection is still occupied by their wave, blocked there in the centre, and thus at least thirty of our hundred and twenty seconds are lost before a single tyre can revolve once here on our side. It must be said that the transverse flow does indeed inflict this delay on us but then it is compensated for by a loss of forty and sometimes sixty seconds before starting again when the green comes on once more for them, thanks to the trail of traffic jams that each of our slow waves drags after it: a loss for them which doesn't actually mean a gain for us because every final delay on our side (and initial delay on the other) corresponds to a greater final delay on the other side (and initial on ours), and this in mounting proportion, so that the green light period remains a deadlock for a longer and longer time on both sides, and this deadlock works more against our progress than theirs.

I realize that when, in this description, I oppose 'us' and 'them' I include in the term 'us' both myself and the man who is chasing me in order to kill me, as if the boundary line of enmity passed not between me and him but rather between those in our column and those in the transverse one. But for all who are here immobilized and impatient, with their feet on the clutch, thoughts and feelings can follow no other course but the one imposed by the respective situations in the currents of traffic; it is therefore admissible to suppose that a community of intention is established between me, who cannot wait to dash away, and him who is waiting for a repetition of his previous opportunity, when in a street on the city's outskirts he managed to fire at me two shots that missed me by sheerest luck, since one bullet shattered the glass of the left side window and the other lodged here in the roof.

It should be added that the community implied in the term 'us' is only apparent, because in practice my enmity extends not only to the cars that cross our column but also those in it; and inside our column I feel definitely more hostile towards the cars that precede me and prevent me from advancing than towards those following me, which, however, would make themselves declared enemies if they tried to pass me, a difficult undertaking in view of the dense jam where every car is stuck fast among the others with a minimum freedom of movement.

In short, the man who at this moment is my mortal enemy is now lost among many other solid bodies where my chafing aversion and fear are also perforce distributed, just as his murderous will though directed exclusively against me is somehow scattered and deflected among a great number of intermediary objects. It is certain in any case that he too, in the calculations he is making simultaneously with me, calls our column 'us' and calls 'them' the column that crosses ours, just as it is certain that our calculations, though aiming finally at opposite results, have many elements and developments in common.

I want our column to have first a fast movement, then a very slow one, or in other words that the cars in front of me should suddenly start speeding and then after them I too could pass the intersection on the last flicker of green; so then immediately behind my back the line would be blocked for a period of time long enough to allow me to vanish, turn off into a secondary cross street. In all likelihood my pursuer's calculations tend instead to foresee whether he will manage to pass the signal in the same wave with me, if he will succeed in keeping behind me until the cars that separate us are scattered in various directions or at least more thinned out, and if his car will then be able to take its place immediately behind or beside mine, for example in the column at another signal, in a good position to empty his pistol at me (I am unarmed) a second before the green comes on to give him a clear avenue of escape.

In other words, I am relying on the irregularity with which

the column's periods of immobility alternate with periods of movement; he on the other hand is counting on the regularity which can be found on an average between periods of movement and periods of immobility for each automobile in the column. The problem then is whether the column is divisible into a series of segments each endowed with a life of its own or whether it must be considered a single indivisible body where the only change one can hope for is a decrease in density as the hours of night approach, to an extreme of rarefaction where only our two cars will remain headed in the same direction and the distance will tend to disappear . . . What our calculations surely have in common is that in both of them the elements that determine the individual motion of our automobiles – power of the respective motors and ability of the drivers – count almost for nothing now, and what decides everything is the general movement of the column, or rather the combined movement of the various columns that intersect one another in the city. In short, I and the man commissioned to kill me are as if immobilized in a space that moves on its own, we are soldered to this pseudo-space which breaks up and re-forms and on whose combinations our fate depends.

To evade this situation the simplest method would be to get out of the car. If one or both of us left our automobiles and proceeded on foot, then space would exist again and the possibility of our moving in space. But we are in a street where parking is forbidden; we would have to leave the cars in the midst of the traffic (both his and mine are stolen cars, destined to be abandoned at random when they are no longer of use to us); I could slip away on all fours among the automobiles to keep from exposing myself to his aim, but such an escape would attract attention and I would immediately have the police on my heels. Now I not only cannot seek the protection of the police, but I must also avoid in every way arousing their curiosity; so obviously I mustn't get out of my car even if he leaves his.

My first fear, the moment we found ourselves trapped here, was of seeing him come forward on foot, alone and free in the midst of hundreds of people nailed to their wheels, calmly reviewing the row of cars and, on reaching mine, firing at me whatever bullets remain in his magazine, then running off and escaping. My fears were not unfounded: in the rear-view mirror I was not long in seeing the form of my pursuer extending from the half-open door of his car and stretching his neck above the expanse of metal roofs like someone trying to understand the reason for such an unnaturally prolonged stop; indeed, after a little while I saw his slender figure slip from the vehicle, move a few steps crosswise among the cars. But at that moment the column stirred in one of its intermittent hints of movement; from the line behind his empty car an angry honking rose, and already drivers and passengers were jumping out yelling and making threatening gestures. Certainly they would have chased him and brought him back by force to bend his head over the wheel if he hadn't hastened to resume his seat and put the car in gear, allowing the rest of the line to benefit from the new step forward, short as it was. On this score I can rest assured then: we cannot separate ourselves from our cars, not for a single moment, my pursuer will never dare overtake me on foot because even if he were in time to shoot me he couldn't then elude the fury of the other drivers, ready perhaps even to lynch him, not so much for the homicide in itself as for the traffic jam the two cars – his and the dead man's – would cause, stopped in the middle of the street.

I try to explore every hypothesis because the more details I can foresee the more probabilities I have of saving myself.

For that matter what else could I do? We aren't moving, not an inch. So far I have considered the column as a linear continuum or else as a fluid current where the individual automobiles flow in disorder. The moment has come to make it clear that in our column the cars are arranged side by side in three lanes and that the alternation of periods of immobility and of movement in each of the three does not correspond with the other two, so that there are moments when only the right-hand line goes forward, or else the centre line which is in fact the line where both I and my potential murderer are. If I have neglected such an outstanding element so far it isn't only because the three lines have gradually come to a regular arrangement and I myself was late in noticing it, but also because in reality this fact doesn't modify the situation for better or for worse. Certainly the difference in speed among the various lines would be decisive if the pursuer at a certain point could, for example advancing with the right-hand line, bring his car up beside mine, shoot, and continue on his way. This, however, is also an eventuality that can be excluded: even admitting that from the centre line he might manage to force his way into one of the side lines (the cars proceed almost with their bumpers touching but if you know how you can exploit the moment when a little interval opens in the next line between a nose and a tail and can stick your own nose in without minding the protests of dozens of horns), keeping my eye on him in my rear-view mirror I would notice his manoeuvre before it was completed and I would have plenty of time, given the distance between us, to find a hasty solution with a similar move. I could, that is, slip into the same line, left or right, where he had moved, and thus I would go on preceding him at the same speed; or else I could shift my position to the outside line on the other side, if he moved to the left I could go to the right, and then we would be separated not only by a distance in the direction of traffic but also by a latitudinal division which would immediately become an insuperable barrier.

Let's assume in any case that we could finally be abreast in two adjacent lines; shooting at me isn't just something that he could do at any moment, without risking being blocked in the line waiting for the police with a corpse at the wheel of the neighbouring car. Before the opportunity arose for rapid safe actions the pursuer would have to stick to my side for God knows how long; and in the meanwhile since the relative speeds of the various lines change irregularly our cars would not stay long at the same level; I could regain my advantage and that wouldn't be too bad because we would go back to our previous position; the greatest risk for my pursuer would be for his line to advance while mine remained behind.

With the pursuer preceding me, I would no longer be pursued. And I could also, to make my new situation conclusive, move into his same line, putting a certain number of cars between him and me. He would be forced to follow the stream, with no possibility of reversing his direction, and by falling in behind him I would be definitively safe. At the signal, seeing him go in one direction, I would take the other, and we would be separated for ever.

Anyway, all these hypothetical manoeuvres should take into account the fact that, on reaching the signal, those in the right-hand line are obliged to turn right, and those in the left, to turn left (the jam at the intersection allows no second thoughts), whereas those in the centre are able at the last moment to choose what they want to do. This is the real reason why both he and I are quite careful not to leave the centre line: I want to retain my freedom of choice to the last minute, he wants to be ready to turn in the direction where he sees I have turned.

Suddenly I feel gripped by a gust of enthusiasm: we are really the most alert, my pursuer and I, having placed ourselves in the centre line. It's wonderful to know that freedom still exists and at the same time to feel oneself surrounded and protected by a blockade of solid and impenetrable bodies, and to have no concern beyond raising the left foot from the clutch, pressing the right foot on the accelerator for an instant and immediately raising it and lowering the left again on the clutch, actions which above all are not decided by us but dictated by the traffic's general pace.

I am experiencing a moment of well-being and optimism. Basically our movement is equivalent to all other movement, that is, it consists in occupying the space before us and in causing it to flow behind us, and so the moment an empty space is formed in front of me I occupy it, otherwise somebody else would hasten to occupy it; the only possible action on space is the negation of space, I negate it the moment it gives a sign of forming and then I allow it to be formed again behind me where there is immediately somebody else who negates it. In short, this space is never seen and perhaps it doesn't exist, it is only an extension of objects and a measure of distances, the distance between me and my pursuer consists in the number of cars in the line between me and him, and since this number is constant our pursuit is only a pursuit after a manner of speaking, just as it would be difficult to establish that two travellers seated in two coaches of the same train are pursuing each other.

If, however, the number of these interval-cars were to increase or diminish, then our pursuit would once again be a real pursuit, independently of our speeds or our freedom of movement. Now I must once again pay close attention: both eventualities have some likelihood of taking place. Between the position where I am now and the intersection controlled by the signal I notice that a secondary street debouches, almost an alley, from which comes a thin but steady trickle of cars. It would suffice for some of these incoming cars to be inserted between me and him, and immediately my separation would increase, it would be as if I had spurted forward in sudden flight. On our left, instead, in the middle of the street a narrow island set aside for parking now begins; if there are free places or if places become free it would suffice for some of the interval-cars to decide to park and then all of a sudden my pursuer would find the distance separating us shortened.

I must discover a solution in a hurry, and since the only field open to me is the field of theory, I can only go on extending my theoretical knowledge of the situation. Reality, ugly or beautiful as it may be, is something I cannot change: that man has been given the job of overtaking me and killing me, whereas I have been told I can do nothing but run away; these instructions remain valid even in the event that space is abolished in one or in all of its dimensions whereby motion would remain impossible; this doesn't mean I would stop being the pursued or he the pursuer.

I must bear in mind at the same time two types of relationship: on one hand the system that includes all the vehicles simultaneously moving in the centre of a city where the total surface of the automobiles equals and perhaps exceeds the total surface of the streets; on the other hand the system created between an armed pursuer and an unarmed pursued man. Now these two types of relationship tend to become identified in the sense that the second is contained in the first as in a recipient which gives it its form and makes it invisible, so that an outside observer is unable to distinguish in the river of identical cars the two which are involved in a lethal pursuit, in a mad race that is hidden within this unbearable stasis.

Let's try to examine each element calmly: a pursuit should consist in the confrontation of the speeds of two bodies moving in space, but since we have seen that a space does not exist independently of the bodies that occupy it, the pursuit will consist only in a series of variations in the relative positions of such bodies. It is the bodies therefore that determine the surrounding space, and if this affirmation seems to contradict both my experience and my pursuer's – since the two of us can't determine anything at all, neither space to flee in nor space to pursue in – it is because we are dealing with a property not of single bodies but of the whole complex of bodies in their reciprocal relationships, in their moments of initiative and of indecision, of starting the motor, in their flashing of lights and honking and biting nails and constant angry shifts of gear: neutral, first, second, neutral; neutral, first, second, neutral . . .

Now that we have abolished the concept of space (I think my pursuer in these periods of waiting must also have reached the same conclusions as I) and now that the concept of motion no longer implies the continuous passage of a body through a series of points but only disconnected and irregular displacements of bodies that occupy this point or that, perhaps I will succeed in accepting more patiently the slowness of the line, because what counts is the relative space that is defined and transformed around my car as around every other car in this traffic jam. In short, each car is in the centre of a system of relationships which in practice is the equivalent of another, that is, the cars are interchangeable, I mean the cars each with its driver inside; each driver could perfectly well change places with another driver, I with my neighbours and my pursuer with his.

In these shifts of position preferred directions can be discerned locally: for example our line's direction of movement, which even if it doesn't really imply it is moving nevertheless excludes the possibility that one can move in the opposite direction. For us two, then, the direction of pursuit is the preferred one, in fact the only exchange of positions that cannot take place is an exchange between us, or any other exchange in contradiction with our chase. This demonstrates that in this world of interchangeable appearances the pursuer-pursued relationship continues to be the only reality we can rely on.

The point is this: if every car – direction of movement and direction of pursuit remaining constant – is equal to every other car, the properties of any one car can also be attributed to the others. Therefore nothing rules out the possibility that these lines of cars are all formed of cars being pursued, that each of these cars is fleeing as I am fleeing the threat of an aimed pistol in any one of the cars that follow. Nor can I exclude the further possibility that each car is pursuing another car with homicidal intentions, and that all of a sudden the centre of the city will be transformed into a battlefield or the scene of a massacre. Whether this is true or not, the behaviour of the cars around me would be no different from what it is now, therefore I am entitled to insist on my hypothesis and to follow the relative positions of any two cars in their various moments, attributing to one the role of the pursued and to the other that of the pursuer. Above all, it is a game that can serve very well to while away the waiting: I have only to interpret every change of position in the lines as an episode in a hypothetical pursuit. For example, now as one of the interval-cars starts indicating left because it has seen a free space in the parking island, instead of being concerned only with my advantage which is about to be reduced, I can very easily think this is a manoeuvre in another pursuit, the move of one pursued or of one pursuer among the countless others who surround me, and thus the situation in which so far I have lived subjectively, nailed to my solitary fear, is projected outside me, extended to the general system of which we are all parts.

This isn't the first time that an interval-car has abandoned its place; on one side the parking area and on the other the right-hand line, slightly faster, seem to exercise a strong attraction on the automobiles behind me. As I have continued following the thread of my deductions, the relative space that surrounds me has undergone various changes: at a certain point even my pursuer moved to the right and, exploiting an advance of that line, passed a couple of cars in the central line; then I moved to the right, too; he went back into the central line and I too went back to the centre, but I had to drop one car behind whereas he moved forward three. These are all things that before would have made me very uneasy, whereas now they interest me chiefly as special elements in the general system of pursuits whose properties I am trying to establish.

On thinking it over, I deduce that if all the cars are involved in pursuits, the pursuing property would have to be commutative, and anyone who pursues would have to be in his turn pursued and anyone who is pursued would also be pursuing. Among the cars, then, a uniformity and symmetry of relationships would be achieved, where the only difficult element to determine would be the pursued-pursuer interval in each chain of pursuits. In fact this interval could be perhaps twenty cars or perhaps forty, or else none, as – from what I see in the mirror – is now my case: at this very moment my pursuer has gained the position directly behind mine.

I should therefore consider myself defeated and admit that I now have left only a few minutes to live, unless in developing my hypothesis I can come upon some saving solution. For example, let's suppose the car pursuing me has behind it a chain of pursuing cars: exactly one second before my pursuer shoots, the pursuer of my pursuer could overtake him and kill him, saving my life. But if two seconds before that happened the pursuer of my pursuer were overtaken and killed by his pursuer, my pursuer would then be saved and free to kill me. A perfect system of pursuits should be based on a simple concatenation of functions: each pursuer has the job of preventing the pursuer ahead of him from shooting his victim, and he has one single means of doing this, namely, by shooting him. The whole problem then lies in knowing at which link the chain will break, because starting from the point where one pursuer succeeds in killing another, then the following pursuer, no longer having to prevent that homicide since it has already been committed, will give up the idea of shooting, and the pursuer who comes after him will have no further reason for shooting since the murder he was to prevent will no longer take place, and thus going back along the chain there will be no more pursued or pursuers.

But if I admit the existence of a chain of pursuits behind me there is no reason why this chain should not also continue through me into the part of the line that precedes me. Now that the signal is turning green and it is probable that in this very period of free movement I can succeed in pushing my way into the intersection where my fate will be decided, I realize the decisive element is not behind me but in my relationship with the man ahead of me. So the only significant alternative is whether my condition of pursued man is destined to remain terminal and asymmetrical (which would seem proved by the fact that in the relationship with my pursuer I am unarmed) or if I too in my turn am a pursuer. If I examine the data of the question more closely one of the hypotheses that occurs is this: I may have been given the assignment of killing a person but not the possibility of using weapons against anyone else for whatever reason: in this case I would be armed only for my victim and disarmed for all the others.

To discover if this hypothesis corresponds to the truth, I have only to extend my hand: if in the glove compartment of my car there is a pistol it is a sign that I too am a pursuer. I have time to check this: I have been unable to take advantage of the green light because the car ahead of me was blocked by the diagonal flow and now the red light has come on again. The perpendicular flow resumes; the car preceding me is in a nasty position, having passed the line of the signal; the driver turns to see if he can back up, he sees me, has an expression of terror. He is the enemy whom I have hunted through all the city and whom I have patiently followed in this long slow line. My right hand, gripping the pistol with its silencer, rests on the gearshift. In the little mirror I see my pursuer aiming at me.

The green comes on, I put the car into gear, racing the engine, I pull down hard with my left hand and at the same time I raise my right to the window and I shoot. The man I was pursuing slumps over the wheel. The man who was pursuing me lowers his pistol, now useless. I have already turned into the cross street. Absolutely nothing has changed: the line moves in little, irregular shifts of position, I am still prisoner of the general system of moving cars, where neither pursuers nor pursued can be distinguished.

The Night Driver

As soon as I am outside the city I realize night has fallen. I turn on my headlights. I am driving from A to B, along a three-lane motorway, the kind where the centre lane is used for passing in both directions. For night driving our eyes, too, must remove one kind of inner transparency and fit on another, because they no longer have to make an effort to distinguish among the shadows and the fading colours of the evening landscape the little speck of the distant cars which are coming towards us or preceding us, but they have to check a kind of black slate which requires a different method of reading, more precise but also simplified, since the darkness erases all the picture's details which might be distracting and underlines only the indispensable elements, the white stripes on the asphalt, the headlights' yellow glow and the little red dots. It's a process that occurs automatically, and if I am led to reflect on it this evening it's because now that the external possibilities of distraction diminish, the internal ones get the upper hand within me, and my thoughts race on their own in a circuit of alternatives and doubts I can't disengage; in other words, I have to make a special effort to concentrate on my driving.

I climbed into the car suddenly, after a quarrel over the telephone with Y. I live in A, Y lives in B. I wasn't planning to visit her this evening. But during our daily phone call we said dire things to each other; in the end, carried away by my exasperation, I told Y that I wanted to break off our affair; Y answered that it didn't matter to her and that she would immediately telephone Z, my rival. At this point one of us – I don't remember whether it was she or I – hung up. Before a minute had passed I realized the motive of our quarrel was trifling compared to the consequences it was creating. To call Y back on the telephone would have been a mistake; the only way to resolve the question was to dash over to B and have a face-to-face explanation with her. So here I am on this motorway I have driven over hundreds of times at every hour in every season but which never seemed so long to me before.

Or, to put it more clearly, I feel as if I had lost all sense of space and of time: the glowing cones projected by the headlights make the outlines of places sink into vagueness; the numbers of the miles on the signs and the numbers that click over on the dashboard are data that mean nothing to me, that do not respond to the urgency of my questions about what Y is doing at this moment, about what she is thinking. Did she really mean to call Z or was it only a threat, blurted out like that, out of pique? And if she was serious, did she do it immediately after our telephone conversation, or is she thinking it over for a moment, letting her anger subside before she makes up her mind? Like me, Z lives in A; for years he has loved Y hopelessly; if she has telephoned him and invited him over, he has surely set out at top speed towards B in his car; therefore he too is speeding along this motorway; every car that passes me could be his, as well as every car I pass. It is difficult to be certain: the cars going in the same direction as mine are two red lights when they precede me and two yellow eyes when I see them following me in my rear-view mirror. At the moment of passing I can make out at most what kind of car it is and how many people are inside it, but the cars carrying only their driver are the great majority, and as far as the model is concerned I don't believe Z's automobile is particularly recognizable.

As if that weren't enough, it's begun to rain. My field of vision is reduced to the semicircle of glass swept by the windscreen wiper, all the rest is streaked or opaque darkness, the information I receive from outside consists only of yellow and red flashes distorted by a tumult of drops. The only thing I can do with Z is try to pass him and not let him pass me, in whatever car he is, but I won't be able to know if he is here and which car is his. I feel all the cars heading towards B are equally hostile: every car faster than mine that knocks on my mirror insistently with its indicator asking me to give way causes me a pang of jealousy; and every time I see ahead of me the distance diminish between me and the rear lights of a rival, with an upsurge of triumph I hurl myself into the centre lane to reach Y before him.

Only a few minutes' advantage would be enough for me: seeing how promptly I have rushed to her, Y will immediately forget the causes of our quarrel; everything between us will again be as it was before; when Z arrives he will realize he was called into question only because of a kind of game between the two of us; he'll feel he's an intruder. Or perhaps Y at this moment has already regretted everything she said to me, has tried to call me back on the phone, or else she, like me, has decided the best thing was to come in person and has got into her car and is now racing in the direction opposite mine along this motorway.

Now I have stopped paying attention to the cars going in my direction and I keep looking at those coming towards me which for me consist only in a double star of headlights which dilates until it sweeps the darkness from my field of vision then suddenly disappears behind me dragging a kind of underwater luminescence after it. Y's car is a very common model; like mine, for that matter. Each of these luminous apparitions could be Y speeding towards me, at each one I feel my blood stir as if in an intimacy destined to remain secret, the amorous message addressed exclusively to me is mingled with all the other messages speeding along the motorway, and yet I couldn't desire from her a message different from this one.

I realize that in rushing towards Y what I desire most is not to find Y at the end of my race: I want Y to be racing towards me, this is the answer I need; what I mean is, I want her to know I'm racing towards her but at the same time I want to know she's racing towards me. The sole thought that comforts me is also the thought that torments me most: the thought that if Y at this moment is speeding towards A, then each time she sees the headlights of a car speeding towards B she will ask herself whether it's me racing towards her, and she will desire it to be me, and she will never be sure. Now two cars going in opposite directions have found themselves for a moment side by side, a flash has illuminated the raindrops, the sound of the motors has become fused as in an abrupt gust of wind: perhaps it was the two of us, or rather it is certain that one car was I and the other car could be she, that is the one I want to be she, the sign in which I want to recognize her, though it is this very sign that makes her unrecognizable to me. Speeding along the motorway is the only method we have left, she and I, to express what we have to say to each other, but we cannot communicate it or receive the communication as long as we are speeding.

Of course I took my place behind the wheel in order to reach her as fast as possible; but the more I go forward the more I realize that the moment of arrival is not the real end of my race. Our meeting, with all the inessential details a meeting involves, the minute network of sensations and meanings and memories that would spread out before me – the room with the philodendron, the opaline lamp, the earrings – and the things I would say to her, some of which would surely be mistaken or mistakable, and the things she would say, to some extent surely jarring or in any case not what I expect, and all the succession of unpredictable consequences that each gesture and each word involved would raise around the things that we have to say to each other, or rather that we want to hear each other say, a storm of such noise that our communication already difficult over the telephone would become even more hazardous, stifled, buried as if under an avalanche of sand. This is why, rather than go on talking, I felt the need to transform the things to be said into a cone of light hurled at a hundred miles an hour, to transform myself into this cone of light moving over the motorway, because it is certain that such a signal can be received and understood by her without being lost in the ambiguous disorder of secondary vibrations, just as I, to receive and understand the things she has to say to me, would like them to be only (rather, I would like her to be only) this cone of light I see advancing on the motorway at a speed (I'm guessing, at a glance) of eighty or ninety. What counts is communicating the indispensable, skipping all the superfluous, reducing ourselves to essential communication, to a luminous signal that moves in a given direction, abolishing the complexity of our personalities and situations and facial expressions, leaving them in the shadowy container that the headlights carry behind them and conceal. The Y I love is really that moving band of luminous rays, and all the rest of her can remain implicit; and the me that she can love, the me that has the power of entering that circuit of exaltation which is her affective life, is the flashing of this pass which, through love of her and with a certain risk, I am now attempting.

And also with Z (I haven't forgotten Z for a moment) I can establish the proper relationship only if he is for me simply the flash and glare that follow me, or the tail-lights I follow: because if I start taking into consideration his person, with its pathetic – shall we say – element but also with its undeniably unpleasant aspect, though it is – I must admit – also excusable, with all his boring story of unhappy love and his way of behaving which is always a bit questionable . . . well, there's no telling where I would end. Instead, while things continue like this, all is well: Z trying to pass me or allowing himself to be passed by me (but I don't know if it is he), Y hastening towards me (but I don't know if it's she) repentant and again in love, I hurrying to her, jealous and eager (but I'm unable to let her or anyone else know).

Naturally, if I were absolutely alone on this motorway, if I saw no other cars speeding in either direction, then everything would be much clearer, I would be certain that Z hasn't moved to supplant me, nor has Y moved to make peace with me, facts I might register as positive or negative in my accounting, but which would in any case leave no room for doubt. And yet if I had the power of exchanging my present state of uncertainty for such a negative certainty, I would refuse the bargain without hesitation. The ideal condition for excluding every doubt would prevail if in this part of the world there existed only three automobiles: mine, Y's and Z's; then no other car could proceed in my direction except Z's, and the only car heading in the opposite direction would surely be Y's. Instead, among the hundreds of cars that the night and the rain reduce to anonymous glimmers, only a motionless observer situated in a favourable position could distinguish one car from the other and perhaps recognize who is inside. This is the contradiction in which I find myself: if I want to receive a message I must give up being a message myself, but the message I want to receive from Y – namely, that Y has made herself into a message – has value only if I in turn am a message, and on the other hand the message I am has meaning only if Y doesn't limit herself to receiving it like any ordinary receiver of messages but if she also is that message I am waiting to receive from her.

By now to arrive in B, go up to Y's house, find that she has remained there with her headache brooding over the causes of our quarrel, would give me no satisfaction; if then Z were to arrive also a scene would be the result, histrionic and loathsome; and if instead I were to find out that Z has prudently stayed at home or that Y didn't carry out her threat to telephone him, I would feel I had acted the fool. On the other hand, if I had remained in A, and Y had gone there to apologize to me, I would have found myself in an embarrassing position: I would have seen Y through different eyes, a weak woman, clinging to me, and something between us would have changed. I can no longer accept any situation other than this transformation of ourselves into the messages of ourselves. And what about Z? Even Z must not escape our fate, he too must be transformed into the message of himself; it would be terrible if I were to run to Y jealous of Z and if Y were running to me, repentant, avoiding Z, while actually Z hasn't remotely thought of stirring from his house . . .

Halfway along the motorway there is a service station. I stop, I run to the bar, I get a handful of change, I dial the B area code, then Y's number. No answer. I allow the rain of returned coins to pour down with joy: it's clear Y couldn't overcome her impatience, she got into her car, she has rushed towards A. Now I have gone back to the motorway, but on the other side: I too am rushing towards A. All the cars I pass could be Y, or else all the cars that pass me. On the opposite lane all the cars advancing in the other direction could be Z, in his self-delusion. Or else Y too has stopped at a service station, has telephoned my house in A; not finding me in she has realized I am going to B, she has turned around. Now we are speeding in opposite directions, moving away from each other, and the car I pass or that passes me is Z, who also tried telephoning Y at the halfway point.

Everything is more uncertain than ever but I feel I've now reached a state of inner serenity: as long as we can check our telephone numbers and there is no answer then we will continue, all three of us, speeding back and forth along these white lines, with no points of departure or of arrival to threaten with their sensations and meanings the single-mindedness of our race, freed finally from the awkward thickness of our persons and voices and moods, reduced to luminous signals, the only appropriate way of being for those who wish to be identified with what they say, without the distorting buzz our presence or the presence of others transmits to our messages.

To be sure, the price paid is high but we must accept it: to be indistinguishable from all the other signals that pass along this road, each with his meaning that remains hidden and undecipherable because outside of here there is no one capable of receiving us now and understanding us.

The Count of Monte Cristo

I

From my cell, I can say little about the construction of this Château d'If where I have been imprisoned for so many years. The tiny barred window is at the end of a shaft that pierces the thickness of the wall: it frames no view; from the greater or lesser luminosity of the sky I can recognize approximately the hours and the seasons; but I do not know if, beneath that window, there is the open sea or the ramparts or one of the inner courtyards of the fortress. The shaft narrows in the form of a chute; to look out I would have to advance, crawling, to the very end; I have tried, it is impossible, even for a man reduced, as I am, to a mere shadow. The opening perhaps is further than it seems: estimation of the distance is confused by the funnel-like perspective and by the contrast of the light.

The walls are so thick they could contain other cells, stairways, casemates and powder magazines; or else the fortress could be all wall, a full and compact solid, with one live man buried in the middle. The images you summon up when you are imprisoned follow one another without any reciprocal exclusion: the cell, the aperture, the corridors along which the jailer comes twice a day with the soup and the bread could be simply tiny pores in a rock of spongy consistency.

You hear the sea pounding, especially on stormy nights; at times it seems almost that the waves are breaking here against the very wall to which I put my ear; at times they seem to be digging below, under the rocks of the foundations, and my cell seems to be at the top of the tallest tower, and the rumble rises through the prison, a prisoner too, as in the horn of a conch shell.

I prick up my ears: the sounds describe variable, jagged spaces and forms around me. From the jailers' shuffling I try to establish the network of the corridors, the turns, the openings, the straight lines broken by the dragging of the meal-container to the threshold of each cell and by the creak of the locks: I succeed only in fixing a succession of points in time, without any correspondence in space. At night the sounds become more distinct, but more uncertain in marking places and distances: somewhere a rat is gnawing, an ill man groans, a boat's siren announces its entry into the Marseilles roads, and Abbé Faria's spade continues digging its way among these stones.

I don't know how many times Abbé Faria has attempted to escape: each time he has worked for months prising up the stone slabs, crumbling the seams of mortar, perforating the rock with rudimentary awls; but at the moment when the pick's last blow should open his way to the rocky shore, he realizes he has come out in a cell that is even deeper in the fortress than the one from which he set out. It requires only a little error of calculation, a slight deviation in the incline of a tunnel and he is penetrating into the prison's viscera with no hope of finding his way again. After every failure, he goes back to correcting the plans and formulas with which he has frescoed the walls of his cell; he goes back to improving his arsenal of improvised tools; and then he resumes his scraping.

2

I too have thought and still think about a method of escape; in fact, I have made so many surmises about the topography of the fortress, about the shortest and surest way to reach the outer bastion and dive into the sea, that I can no longer distinguish between my conjectures and the data based on experience. Working with hypotheses, I can at times construct for myself such a minute and convincing picture of the fortress that in my mind I can move through it completely at my ease; whereas the elements I derive from what I see and what I hear are confused, full of gaps, more and more contradictory.

In the early days of my imprisonment, when my desperate acts of rebellion hadn't yet brought me to rot in this solitary cell, the routine tasks of prison life had caused me to climb up and down stairs and bastions, cross the entrance halls and posterns of the Château d'If; but from all the images retained by my memory, which now I keep arranging and rearranging in my conjectures, there is not one that fits neatly with another, none that helps explain to me the shape of the fortress or the point where I now am. Too many thoughts tormented me then – about how I, Edmond Dantès, poor but honest sailor, could have run afoul of the law's severity and suddenly lost my freedom – too many thoughts to allow my attention to concern itself with the plan of my surroundings.

The bay of Marseilles and its islands have been familiar to me since boyhood; and every embarkation of my not long life as a sailor, the departures and the arrivals, had this background; but the seaman's eye, every time it encounters the black fort of If, shifts away in an instinctive fear. So when they brought me here chained in a boat filled with gendarmes, and this cliff and the walls then loomed on the horizon, I understood my fate and bowed my head. I didn't see – or I don't remember – the pier where the boat docked, the steps they made me climb, the door that closed behind my back.

Now that, with the passage of years, I have stopped brooding over the chain of infamy and ill-luck that caused my imprisonment, I have come to understand one thing: the only way to escape the prisoner's state is to know how the prison is built.

If I feel no desire to imitate Faria, it is because the very knowledge that someone is seeking an avenue of escape is enough to convince me that such an avenue exists or, at least, that one can set himself the problem of seeking it. So the sound of Faria's digging has become a necessary complement to the concentration of my thoughts. I feel not only that Faria is a man attempting his own escape but also that he is a part of my plan; and not because I am hoping for an avenue to safety opened by him – he has been wrong so many times by now I have lost all faith in his intuition – but because the only information I have concerning this place where I am has come to me from the series of his mistakes.

3

The walls and the vaults have been pierced in every direction by the Abbé's pick, but his itineraries continue to wind around themselves like a ball of yarn, and he constantly goes through my cell as he follows, each time, a different course. He has long since lost his sense of orientation: Faria no longer recognizes the cardinal points, indeed he cannot recognize even the zenith and the nadir. At times I hear scratching at the ceiling; a rain of plaster falls on me; a breach opens; Faria's head appears, upside down. Upside down for me, not for him; he crawls out of his tunnel, he walks head down, while nothing about his person is ruffled, not his white hair, nor his beard green with mould, nor the tatters of sackcloth that cover his emaciated loins. He walks across the ceiling and the walls like a fly, he sinks his pick into a certain spot, a hole opens; he disappears.

Sometimes he has hardly disappeared through one wall when he pops out again from the wall opposite: he hasn't yet drawn his heel through the hole here when his beard is already appearing over there. He emerges again, more weary, skeletal, aged, as if years had passed since the last time I saw him.

At other times, however, he has hardly slipped into his tunnel when I hear him make the sound of a long aspiration like somebody preparing to sneeze loudly: in the labyrinth of the fortress there is much cold and damp; but the sneeze never comes. I wait: I wait for a week, for a month, for a year; Faria doesn't come back; I persuade myself he is dead. All of a sudden the wall opposite trembles as if shaken by an earthquake; from the shower of stones Faria looks out, completing his sneeze.

We exchange fewer and fewer words; or we continue conversations I cannot remember ever having begun. I realize Faria has trouble distinguishing one cell from another among the many he crosses in his mistaken journeys. Each cell contains a pallet, a pitcher, a wooden slops bucket, a man standing and looking at the sky through a narrow slit. When Faria appears from underground, the prisoner turns around: he always has the same face, the same voice, the same thoughts.

His name is the same: Edmond Dantès. The fortress has no favoured points: it repeats in space and time always the same combination of figures.

4

In all my hypotheses of escape, I try to imagine Faria as the protagonist. Not that I tend to identify myself with him: Faria necessarily plays his role so that I can mentally envisage my escape in an objective light, as I could not do if I were living it: I mean, dreaming it in the first person. By now I no longer know if the man I hear digging like a mole is the real Faria opening breaches in the walls of the real fortress of Château d'If or whether it is the hypothesis of a Faria dealing with a hypothetical fortress. It amounts to the same thing in any case: it is the fortress that wins. It is as if, in the contests between Faria and the fortress, I pressed my impartiality so far as to side with the fortress against him . . . no, now I am exaggerating: the contest does not take place only in my mind, but between two real contenders, independently of me; my efforts are directed towards seeing it with detachment, in a performance without anguish.

If I can come to observe fortress and Abbé from a perfectly equidistant point of view, I will be able to discern not only the particular errors Faria makes time after time, but also the error in method which continually defeats him and which I, thanks to my correct setting of the problem, will be able to avoid.

Faria proceeds in this way: he becomes aware of a difficulty, he studies a solution, he tries out the solution, encounters a new difficulty, plans a new solution, and so on and on.

For him, once all possible errors and unforeseen elements are eliminated, his escape can only be successful: it all lies in planning and carrying out the perfect escape.

I set out from the opposite premise: there exists a perfect fortress, from which one cannot escape; escape is possible only if in the planning or building of the fortress some error or oversight was made. While Faria continues taking the fortress apart, sounding out its weak points, I continue putting it back together, conjecturing more and more insuperable barriers.

The images of the fortress that Faria and I create are becoming more and more different: Faria, beginning with a simple figure, is complicating it extremely to include in it each of the single unforeseen elements he encounters in his path; I, setting out from the jumble of these data, see in each isolated obstacle the clue to a system of obstacles, I develop each segment into a regular figure, I fit these figures together as the sides of a solid, polyhedron or hyperpolyhedron, I inscribe these polyhedrons in spheres or hyperspheres, and so the more I enclose the form of the fortress the more I simplify it, defining it in a numerical relation or in an algebraic formula.

But to conceive a fortress in this way I need the Abbé Faria constantly combating landslides of rubble, steel bolts, sewers, sentry boxes, leaps into nothingness, recesses in the sustaining walls, because the only way to reinforce the imagined fortress is to put the real one continously to the test.

5

Therefore: each cell seems separated from the outside only by the thickness of a wall, but Faria as he excavates discovers that in between there is always another cell, and between this cell and the outside, still another. The image I derive is this: a fortress that grows around us, and the longer we remain shut up in it the more it removes us from the outside. The Abbé digs, digs, but the walls increase in thickness, the battlements and the buttresses are multiplied. Perhaps if he can succeed in advancing faster than the fortress expands, Faria at a certain point will find himself outside unawares. It would be necessary to invert the relative speeds so that the fortress, contracting, would expel the Abbé like a cannonball.

But if the fortress grows with the speed of time, to escape one would have to move even faster, retrace time. The moment in which I would find myself outside would be the same moment I entered here: I look out on the bay at last, and what do I see? A boat full of gendarmes is landing at If; in the midst is Edmond Dantès, in chains.

There, I have gone back to imagining myself as the protagonist of the escape, and I have immediately risked not only my future but my past, my memories. Everything that is unclear in the relationship between an innocent prisoner and his prison continues to cast shadows on images and decisions. If the prison is surrounded by *my* outside, that outside would bring me back inside each time I succeeded in reaching it: the outside is nothing but the past, it is useless to try to escape.

I must conceive of the prison either as a place that is only inside itself without an outside – that is, giving up the idea of leaving it – or I must conceive of it not as *my* prison but as a place with no relation to me inside or outside; that is, I must study an itinerary from inside to outside that precludes the import that 'inside' and 'outside' have acquired in my emotions; valid, that is, even if instead of 'outside' I say 'inside' and vice versa.

6

If outside there is the past, perhaps the future is concentrated at the innermost point of the island of If, in other words the avenue of escape is an avenue towards the inside. In the graffiti with which Abbé Faria covers his walls, two maps with ragged outlines alternate, constellated with arrows and marks: one is meant to be the plan of If, the other of an island of the Tuscan archipelago where a treasure is hidden: Monte Cristo.

It is, in fact, to seek this treasure that Abbé Faria wants to escape. To succeed in his intention he has to draw a line that in the map of the island of If carries him from inside to outside and in the map of the island of Monte Cristo carries him from outside to that point which is further inland than all the other points, the treasure cave. Between an island he cannot leave and an island he cannot enter there must be a relation: therefore in Faria's hieroglyphics the two maps can be superimposed and are almost identical.

It is hard for me to understand whether Faria is now digging in order to dive into the open sea or to penetrate the cave full of gold. In either case, if one looks closely, he is tending towards the same point of arrival: the place of the multiplicity of possible things. At times I visualize this multiplicity as concentrated in a gleaming underground cavern, at times I see it as an irradiating explosion. The treasure of Monte Cristo and the escape from If are two phases of the same process, perhaps successive perhaps periodical as in a pulsation.

The search for the centre of If-Monte Cristo does not lead to results that are more sure than those of the march towards its unreachable circumference: in whatever point I find myself the hypersphere stretches out around me in every direction; the centre is all around where I am; going deeper means descending into myself. You dig and dig and you do nothing but retrace the same path.

7

Once he has come into possession of the treasure, Faria intends to liberate the Emperor from Elba, give him the means to put himself again at the head of his army . . . The plan of escape-search on the island of If-Monte Cristo is therefore not complete if it does not include also the search-escape of Napoleon from the island where he is confined. Faria digs; he penetrates once again into the cell of Edmond Dantès; he sees the prisoner from behind, looking as usual at the sky through the slit-window; at the sound of the pick the prisoner turns: it is Napoleon Bonaparte. Faria and Dantès-Napoleon together excavate a tunnel in the fortress. The map of If-Monte Cristo-Elba is drawn in such a way that by turning it a certain number of degrees the map of Saint Helena is obtained: the escape is reversed into an exile beyond return.

The confused reasons for which both Faria and Edmond Dantès were imprisoned have, in different ways, something to do with the Bonapartist cause. That hypothetical geometric figure called If-Monte Cristo coincides in certain of its points with another figure called Elba-Saint Helena. There are points of the past and of the future in which Napoleonic history intervenes in our poor prisoners' history, and other points where Faria and I can or could influence a possible return of the Empire.

These intersections make any calculation of predictions even more complicated; there are points where the line that one of us is following bifurcates, ramifies, fans out; each branch can encounter branches that set out from other lines. Along one jagged line Faria goes by, digging; and only a few seconds keep him from bumping into the baggage wagons and cannon of the Imperial Army reconquering France.

We proceed in the dark; only the way our paths twist upon themselves warns us that something has changed in the paths of the others. We may say that Waterloo is the point where the path of Wellington's army might intersect the path of Napoleon; if the two lines meet, the segments beyond that point are cut off; in the map where Faria digs his tunnel, the projection of the Waterloo angle forces him to turn back.

8

The intersections of the various hypothetical lines define a series of planes arranged like the pages of a manuscript on a novelist's desk. Let us call Alexandre Dumas the writer who must deliver to his publisher as soon as possible a novel in twelve volumes entitled *The Count of Monte Cristo*. His work proceeds in this fashion: two assistants (Auguste Maquet and P. A. Fiorentino) develop one by one the various alternatives that depart from each single point, and they furnish Dumas with the outline of all the possible variants of an enormous supernovel; Dumas selects, rejects, cuts, pastes, interposes; if a given solution is preferred for well-founded reasons but omits an episode he would find it useful to include, he tries to put together the stub-ends of disparate provenance, he joins them with makeshift links, racks his brain to establish an apparent continuity among divergent segments of future. The final result will be the novel *The Count of Monte Cristo* to be handed to the printer.

The diagrams Faria and I draw on the walls of the prison resemble those Dumas pens on his papers to establish the order of the chosen variants. One bundle of sheets of paper can already be passed for printing: it contains the Marseilles of my youth; moving over the closely written lines I can fight my way on to the docks of the harbour, climb up the Rue de la Canebière in the morning sun, reach the Catalan village perched on the hill, see Mercedes again . . . Another bundle of papers is awaiting the final touches: Dumas is still revising the chapters of the imprisonment in the Château d'If; Faria and I are struggling inside there, ink-stained, in a tangle of revisions . . . At the edges of the desk there are piles of paper, the suggestions for the story's continuation which the two assistants are methodically compiling. In one of them, Dantès escapes from prison, finds Faria's treasure, transforms himself into the Count of Monte Cristo with his ashen, impassive face, devotes his implacable will and his boundless wealth to revenge; and the Machiavellian Villefort, the greedy Danglars, the grim Caderousse pay the price of their foul deeds; just as, for so many years among these walls, I had foreseen in my angry daydreams, in my longings for revenge.

Beside this, other sketches for the future are arranged on the desk. Faria opens a breach in the wall, bursts into the study of Alexandre Dumas, casts an impartial dispassionate look on the expanse of pasts and presents and futures – as I could not do, I who would try to recognize myself with tenderness in the young Dantès just promoted to his captaincy, with pity in the imprisoned Dantès, with delirious grandeur in the Count of Monte Cristo who makes his regal entrance into the proudest salons of Paris; I who in their place would find with dismay so many strangers – Faria takes a page here, a page there, like a monkey he moves his long hairy arms, hunts for the escape chapter, the page without which all the possible continuations of the novel outside the fortress become impossible. The concentric fortress, If-Monte Cristo-Dumas's desk, contains us prisoners, the treasure, and the supernovel *Monte Cristo* with its variants and combinations of variants in the nature of billions of billions but still in a finite number. Faria has set his heart on one page among the many, and he does not despair of finding it; I am interested in seeing the accumulation of rejected sheets increase, the solutions which need not be taken into account, which already form a series of piles, a wall . . .

Arranging one after the other all the continuations which allow the story to be extended, probable or improbable as they may be, you obtain the zigzag line of the *Monte Cristo* of Dumas; whereas connecting the circumstances that prevent the story from continuing you outline the spiral of a novel in negative, a *Monte Cristo* preceded by the minus sign. A spiral can wind upon itself towards the inside or towards the outside: if it twists towards the inside of itself, the story closes without any possible development; if it turns in widening curves it could, at every turn, include a segment of the *Monte Cristo* with the plus sign, finally coinciding with the novel Dumas will give to the printer, or perhaps even surpassing it in its wealth of lucky chances. The decisive difference between the two books – sufficient to cause one to be defined as true and the other as false, even if they are identical – lies entirely in the method. To plan a book – or an escape – the first thing to know is what to exclude.

9

And so we go on dealing with the fortress, Faria sounding out the weak points of the wall and coming up against new obstacles, I reflecting on his unsuccessful attempts in order to conjecture new outlines of walls to add to the plan of my fortress-conjecture.

If I succeed in mentally constructing a fortress from which it is impossible to escape, this conceived fortress either will be the same as the real one – and in this case it is certain we shall never escape from here, but at least we will achieve the serenity of one who knows he is here because he could be nowhere else – or it will be a fortress from which escape is even more impossible than from here – and this, then, is a sign that here an opportunity of escape exists: we have only to identify the point where the imagined fortress does not coincide with the real one and then find it.

From *World Memory and Other Cosmicomic Stories*

The Mushroom Moon

According to Sir George Darwin, a solar tide caused the Moon to detach itself from the Earth. The attraction of the Sun acted on the lightest covering of rock (granite) as if that were a fluid, lifting up part of it and tearing it away from our planet. The waters that then covered the Earth entirely were largely swallowed up by the huge chasm that the Moon's departure had opened up (that is, the Pacific Ocean), leaving the remaining granite uncovered: this then fragmented and hardened into the continents. Without the Moon, the evolution of life on Earth would have been very different, if indeed it had happened at all.

Yes, yes, now you mention it, it all comes back to me! – *exclaimed old Qfwfq* – Of course. It began to sprout up like a mushroom, the Moon, from underwater: I happened to be passing by in a boat just at that spot, when I suddenly felt something pushing me from below. 'Damn! A sandbank!' I shouted, but I'd already been hoisted in the air on top of a sort of white lump, my boat high and dry as well, my fishing line dangling above the water and my hook in the air.

It's easy to talk about it now, but I'd like to have seen you in my position then, trying to predict all those phenomena. Of course in those days too there were some people who warned us of the dangers the future had in store; and now we can see they had understood a lot of things, not about

297

the Moon – no, that was a surprise for all of us – but about the lands that would surface. Inspector Oo, from the High and Low Tides Observatory, gave many lectures on this topic but nobody ever paid him any attention. Just as well, because later he made a huge error in his calculations and paid for it in person.

At that time the surface of the globe was entirely covered by water, with no land visible. Everything in the world was flat and devoid of contours, the sea was a shallow fresh-water pond, and as for us, we went about in our canoes, fishing for sole.

From his calculations at the Observatory, Inspector Oo had become convinced that huge changes were about to happen on Earth. His theory was that the globe would soon divide into two zones: one made up of continents and one of oceans. On the continental areas mountains and watercourses would form, and lush vegetation would grow. For those of us who ended up on the continent there would be infinite possibilites for becoming rich; whereas in the meantime the oceans would become uninhabitable for everyone except their own special fauna, and our fragile boats would be blown away by enormous storms.

But who could take these apocalyptic prophecies seriously? Our whole life took place on the tiny layer of water, and we could not imagine a different existence. Everyone sailed on their own little boat, I engrossed in the patient labour of the fisherman, the pirate Bm Bn setting traps for the duck-shepherds behind the clumps of reeds, that slip of a girl Flw paddling along in her kayak. Could any of us have imagined that that stretch of water as smooth as a millpond would produce a wave – not a wave of water, but a hard wave of granite – which would whisk us away with it?

But one thing at a time. The first to end up high and dry

was myself, suddenly perched there with my boat beached. I heard my friends' cries rising up from the sea: they were shouting to each other, pointing at me, mocking me, and their words reached me as if from another world: 'Look at Qfwfq up there, ha ha!'

The hump I was hoisted on would not stay still: it careered across the sea, rolling like a marble; no, I didn't explain that well, it was a subterranean wave which, wherever it rolled, lifted up the carpet of rock and then dropped it again back in its own place. The great thing was that I was transported by this solid tide, and instead of falling back into the water as soon as it moved on, I stayed hovering up there, advancing with it as it moved forward, and all around I could see more and more fish getting stuck on dry land, struggling and gasping for air on the hard, whitish surface that was slowly emerging.

What did I think? Well, I certainly didn't think about Inspector Oo's theories (I had hardly heard him mentioned), but only about the new fishing possibilities that had unexpectedly opened up for me: all I had to do was stretch out my hand and I could fill my boat with sole. In the other boats, the cries of amazement and mockery turned into curses and threats. The fishermen called me a thief, a pirate: our rule was that each of us had to fish in the area that had been allocated; straying into someone else's territory was considered a crime. But now, who could stop this self-propelled reef? It was not my fault if my boat filled up while theirs stayed empty.

So the scene looked like this: there was the ball of granite speeding across the stretch of water and continually expanding, surrounded by a cloud of quivering sole; me catching fish in midair; behind me, in hot pursuit, were the boats of my friends, jealously trying to attack my fortress; after them, the ever-increasing distance that none of the new hordes of pursuers managed to make up; and after that was the twilight descending on them, and the darkness of the night gradually swallowing them up, whereas there where I was the Sun never ceased to beat down in an everlasting midday.

It was not only the fishes that got beached on the wave of rock; everything that floated round us ended up being shipwrecked on it: flotillas of canoes laden with archers, ordinary barges full of provisions, royal barges conveying kings and princesses and their courtiers. As we advanced, we saw towns built on wooden piles standing out on the horizon, high above the waters; and immediately they were overthrown in a crashing of broken wood and straw and squawking of hens. These were already revealing indications of the nature of the phenomenon: the fragile layer of things covering the world could be negated, replaced by a mobile desert at whose passage every living presence was overwhelmed and eliminated. This alone should have been enough to warn all of us, especially the Inspector. But, I repeat, I was not making any hypotheses about the future: I had quite enough to do to keep my balance, and try to maintain a more general, more widespread equilibrium, which I could see was being shaken to its foundations.

Each time the wave of rock shattered an obstacle into pieces, I got covered by a shower of knick-knacks, tools, diadems. An unscrupulous person in my place (as would clearly be seen later) would have immediately made off with the stuff. Me? No, you know me, I didn't. On the contrary, I was actually seized by the opposite urge: I started to chuck back to the poor fishermen the sole that I had caught so easily. I'm not saying this to make it sound as if I'm especially good; the only way I could find to counter what was happening was to try to repair the damage, to give the victims a hand. I shouted from the top of the advancing mountain: 'Every man for himself! Run! Get out of the way!' I tried to support the wavering piles that my hands managed to reach, so that once the wave had passed they would remain upright. And to the castaways floundering about down below I distributed everything that the collisions and crashes dropped within my hands' reach. What I hoped was this: that a new equilibrium would emerge from the fact that it was I who was up there on top. I would have liked the wave of rock to sweep away both the evil of its squalid emergence and the good of the actions to which I devoted so much effort, both of which were aspects of the same natural phenomenon, more powerful than my will and that of anyone else.

Instead, none of this transpired: the people didn't understand my cries and did not get out of the way, the piles crumpled the minute I touched them, the stuff I chucked out set off riots in the water and increased the confusion.

My only successful good deed was to save a gaggle of ducks from falling prey to the pirate Bm Bn. Their shepherd was advancing unaware between the reeds in his tranquil canoe, and failed to see the lance that was poised to transfix him. I arrived on the wave of stone, just in time to block the bandit's arm. I went 'Shoo! Shoo!' to the ducks, which flew to safety. But the minute I was on top of Bm Bn, he clung on to me: from then on there were two of us on top of the wave of rock, and the balance between good and evil that I still hoped to preserve was definitively compromised.

For Bm Bn, finding himself there was simply an opportunity for new acts of piracy, poaching and destruction. The wave of granite continued wiping out the world, ruthless and impassive; but over it now reigned a mind that turned this destruction to his own profit. I was now no longer the victim of a blind, telluric upheaval, but of that pirate; what could I do to halt those two unstoppable forces? Between the rock and the pirate I felt myself decidedly on the side of the rock; I felt it was in some mysterious way my ally, but I did not know how to combine my weak strength with it in order to prevent Bm Bn from wreaking violence and destruction.

Nor did things change when Flw too ended up on the rock-wave. I was obliged to witness her kidnapping without being able to move a finger to stop it, because Bm Bn had tied me up like a salami. The girl Flw was paddling along in her kayak between the water lilies and daffodils; Bm Bn whirled a long lasso in the air and captured her; but she was a young girl, kind and submissive, and she soon resigned herself to being that brute's prisoner.

I couldn't accept it, however, and I said so: 'I'm not here to be your sidekick, Bm Bn. Untie me and I'll go.'

Bm Bn barely turned his head. 'Are you still there?' he said. 'Whether you're there or not, you matter less to me than a flea. Go on, throw yourself in the sea, go and drown yourself,' and he untied me.

'I'm going, but this is not the last you'll hear of me,' I said, and beneath my breath I added for Flw to hear: 'Wait for me: I'll come back and release you.'

I got ready to dive in. Just at that moment I spotted someone on the horizon striding over the sea on stilts. As our wave approached, far from getting out of the way he actually came towards us. His stilts went up in pieces, and he crashed down on to the lump of granite.

'My calculations were exact,' he said. 'Allow me to introduce myself: Inspector Oo, from the High and Low Tides Observatory.'

'You've arrived just at the right moment, Inspector, to give me advice on what to do,' I replied. 'The situation up here has reached the point where I was just about to leave.'

'You would be making a huge mistake,' the Inspector objected, 'and I'll tell you why.'

He began to expound his theory, which was now confirmed by the evidence: the expected emergence of the continents was in fact beginning with this swelling landmass on which we found ourselves; an era of new, unlimited possibilities was opening up before us. I listened openmouthed: the outlook had changed; instead of riding a nucleus of destruction and devastation, I was on the cusp of a new possibility for a life on Earth that would be infinitely more plentiful than before.

'And that is why,' the Inspector triumphantly concluded, 'I wanted to join you.'

'That will depend on whether I want you to stay!' sneered Bm Bn.

'I'm sure we'll become friends,' Oo declared. 'We're heading towards huge cataclysms and my researches and forecasts will allow us to take them in hand; in fact to turn them to our advantage.'

'Not only *our* advantage, I hope!' I exclaimed. 'If what you say is true, Inspector, if this great stroke of good luck has really happened to us, how can we exclude our fellow-beings from it? We must tell everyone we meet! Get them to come up here with us!'

'Shut up there, you idiot!' – and Bm Bn grabbed me by the stomach – 'unless you want me to chuck you back headlong into the slime you came from! I'm here and so is whoever I want with me! End of story. Isn't that right, Inspector?'

I turned to Oo, confident I'd find in him an ally against the pirate's arrogance: 'Inspector, I'm sure you didn't devote yourself to your studies out of selfishness! You won't allow Bm Bn to profit from this for personal gain . . .'

The Inspector shrugged. 'Well, as a matter of fact, I don't really want to interfere in your internal squabbles: I don't know the background; I only deal with the technical side. If, as I seem to understand, the person in charge here is this man' – and he nodded in the direction of Bm Bn – 'then it's to his attention that I would like to submit the results of my calculations . . .'

The disillusionment I felt on hearing these words, which seemed like the most unexpected betrayal, was caused not so much by the Inspector himself as by his predictions for the future. He continued describing life as it would develop on the emerging lands: cities that would rise on stone foundations, roads travelled by camels, horses, carts, cats, caravans; and gold and silver mines, and forests of sandalwood and molucca wood, and elephants, and pyramids, and towers, and clocks, and lightning-conductors, and tramways, cranes, lifts, skyscrapers, bunting and flags on national holidays; luminous signs in all sorts of colours on the theatre and cinema façades, reflecting on pearl necklaces on grand gala evenings. We were all listening to him, Flw with an enchanted smile, Bm Bn with his nostrils dilated by his greed for possessions; but by now these fabulous prophecies no longer stirred any hope in me, because they only meant the perpetuation of my enemy's rule, and that was enough to cloak every marvel with a shiny, false, vulgar patina.

I said as much to Flw, in a moment when the other two were busy with their plans. 'Better to stay with our poor aquatic life as sole-fishers,' I told her, 'than all these splendours whose price is being subject to Bm Bn!' and I suggested we escape together, abandoning the bandit and the Inspector on their continent: 'Let's see how they manage on their own . . .'

Did I persuade her? Flw was, as I said, a docile creature,

as fragile as a butterfly's wing. The Inspector's projections fascinated her, but Bm Bn's brutality repulsed her. It was not difficult for me to stir up her resentment against the pirate; she agreed to follow me.

The granite excrescence seemed more than ever to be thrust out of the Earth's innards, straining with all its forces towards the Sun. In fact, the part that was most exposed to solar attraction was expanding continually, so that the area below it ended up being reduced to a kind of bottleneck or stalk, hidden in a cone of shadow. We would have to use that as our escape route, sheltered as it was from the midday light. 'This is it!' I said to Flw, and, taking her by the hand, we slithered down the stalk. 'It's now or never!'

I had said these words as a rousing exhortation, without suspecting how literally they corresponded to reality. We had barely swum out of reach of what now appeared to us, seeing it from the outside, as a monstrous extension of our planet, when the Earth and the waters began to shudder and shake. The granite mass attracted by the Sun was uprooting itself from the basalt base to which it had until then been anchored. And a huge boulder of enormous dimensions – the upper part eroded and porous, but underneath still soaking as with the mucus of the Earth's innards, raddled with mineral fluids and lava, and barnacled with colonies of worms – hovered in the air, light as a leaf. The waters of the globe cascaded into the huge crack left agape, thus letting islands and peninsulas and plateaux emerge in the distance.

Clinging on to these emerging plateaux, I managed to save Flw and myself, but I still could not take my eyes off that bit of world that had flown away and had started to rotate in the sky as it moved off. I was still in time to hear Bm Bn's curses coming down from it, as he took it out on the Inspector – 'You and your bloody predictions, you fool . . .' – while already in the rotating movement the rough edges and out-crops were gradually being smoothed down into a sphere with a uniform, lime-white surface. And by now the Sun was moving further away, while the sphere – what from then on would be called the Moon – was overtaken by night, but it retained a reflection of pale brightness shining on it as on a desert.

'They got what they deserved, those two!' I exclaimed, and since Flw did not seem to fully understand that the situation had been reversed, I explained: 'That was not the continent that the Inspector predicted, but – if my senses do not deceive me – this one that is forming underneath our feet.'

Mountains and rivers and valleys and seasons and trade winds were giving shape to the emergent regions. Already the first iguanodons, harbingers of the future, were coming out of the sequoia forests to reconnoitre. Flw seemed to find everything natural: she plucked a pineapple from the branch, broke its skin against a tree-trunk, bit the juicy flesh, and burst out laughing.

That's the way things have gone, as you know, right up to today. Flw, no doubt about it, is happy. She goes out into the night that is resplendent with neon signs, wraps herself softly in her chinchilla fur, smiles at the photographers' flashes. But I wonder if this really is my world.

From time to time I look up at the Moon and think of all the desert, the cold and the void up there which weigh down on the other side of the scales and sustain this poor pomp of ours. If I jumped down just in time on this side, that was just chance. I know that I am in debt to the Moon for everything I have on Earth, indebted to what is not here for everything that is.

The Daughters of the Moon

Deprived as it is of a covering of air to act as a protective shield, the Moon found itself exposed right from the start to a continual bombardment of meteorites and to the corrosive action of the Sun's rays. According to Tom Gold of Cornell University, the rocks on the Moon's surface were reduced to powder through constant attrition from meteorite particles. According to Gerard Kuiper of the University of Chicago, the escape of gases from the Moon's magma gave the planet a light, porous consistency, like that of a pumice stone.

The Moon is old – Qfwfq agreed – pitted with holes, worn out. Rolling around naked through the skies, it gets worn down and loses its flesh like a bone that's been gnawed. This is not the first time that such a thing has happened; I remember Moons that were even older and more battered than this one; I've seen loads of these Moons, seen them being born and running across the sky and dying out, one punctured by hail from shooting stars, another exploding from all its craters, and yet another oozing drops of topaz-coloured sweat that evaporated immediately, then being covered by greenish clouds before being reduced to a dried-up, spongy shell.

What happens on the Earth when a Moon dies is not easy to describe; I'll try to do it by referring to the last instance

I can remember. Following a lengthy period of evolution, one could say that the Earth had by then reached the point where we are now; in other words, it had entered that phase when cars wear out more quickly than the soles of your shoes; beings that were more or less human manufactured and bought and sold things; the cities covered the continents with luminous colour. These cities grew more or less in the same places as now, however different the shape of the continents might have been. There was even a New York which in some way resembled the New York that is familiar to all of you, but much newer, or rather more awash with new products, new toothbrushes, a New York with its own Manhattan that stretched out dense with skyscrapers gleaming like the nylon bristles of a brand new toothbrush.

In this world where every object was instantly thrown away and substituted with another new and perfect replacement, at the slightest sign of breakage or ageing, at the first dent or stain, there was just one false note, one shadow: the Moon. It wandered through the sky, naked, corroded and grey, more and more alien to the world down here, a hangover from a way of being that was now incongruous.

Ancient expressions like 'full moon', 'half moon', 'last-quarter moon', continued to be used but were just figures of speech: how could you call 'full' that shape that was all cracks and holes and that always seemed on the point of crashing down on our heads in a shower of rubble? Not to mention when it was a waning moon! It was reduced to a kind of cheese crust that had been nibbled away, and always disappeared before we expected it to. At the new moon, we wondered each time whether it would ever appear again (did we hope it would just disappear like that?) and when it did reappear again, looking more and more like a comb losing its teeth, we averted our eyes with a shudder.

It was a depressing sight. We went around in the crowds, our arms laden with parcels, going in and out of the big department stores that were open day and night – with our eyes we scanned the neon signs which climbed higher and higher up the skyscrapers, notifying us constantly of the new products that had been launched on the market – and there suddenly we would see it advancing, pale in the midst of those dazzling lights, slow and sick, and we could not get it out of our heads that every new thing, each product we had just bought, could become worn out, fade away, deteriorate, and we would lose our enthusiasm for running around buying things and working like mad, something not without consequences for the success of industry and commerce.

That was how we began to consider the problem of what to do with it, this counterproductive satellite: it did not serve any purpose; it was a wreck, no good to anyone any more. As it lost weight, it started to incline its orbit towards the Earth: it was dangerous, apart from anything else. And the nearer it got, the more it slowed down its course: we could no longer calculate its quarters; even the calendar, the rhythm of the months had become a mere convention; the Moon went forward in fits and starts as though it were about to collapse.

On these nights of low moon, people of a more unstable temperament began to do weird things. There was always a sleepwalker teetering along the edges of a skyscraper with his arms outstretched towards the Moon, or a were-wolf starting to howl in the middle of Times Square, or a pyromaniac setting fire to the dock warehouses. By now these were common occurrences which no longer attracted the usual crowd of rubbernecks. But when I saw a girl sitting, completely naked, on a bench in Central Park, I had to stop.

Even before I saw her, I had had the feeling that something mysterious was about to happen. As I crossed Central Park at the wheel of my open-top car, I felt myself bathed in a flickering light, like that of a fluorescent tube emitting a series of livid, blinking flashes before it comes on fully. The view all around me was like that of a garden that had sunk into a lunar crater. Beside a pond reflecting a slice of Moon sat the naked girl. I braked. For a second I thought I recognized her. I ran out of the car towards her, then stopped as if stunned. I did not know who she was; I just felt that I had to do something for her urgently.

Everything was scattered on the grass all round the bench: her clothes, one stocking and shoe here and the others there, her earrings, necklace and bracelets, handbag and shopping bag, with the contents emptied out in a wide arc, and countless packets and goods, almost as if on her way back from a lavish shopping spree in the city's shops, that creature had felt herself called and had instantly dropped everything to the ground, had realized that she had to free herself of every object or sign that held her bound to the Earth, and was now waiting there to be assumed into the lunar sphere.

'What's happening?' I stammered. 'Can I help you?'

'Help?' she asked, with her eyes still staring upwards. 'Nobody can help. Nobody can do anything,' and it was clear that she was not talking about herself but about the Moon.

We had the Moon above us, a convex shape almost crushing us, like a ruined roof, studded with holes like a cheese-grater. Just at that moment the animals in the zoo began to growl.

'Is this the end?' I asked mechanically, with no idea what I meant.

She replied, 'It's the beginning,' or something like that (she spoke almost without opening her lips).

'What do you mean? It's the beginning of the end, or something else is beginning?'

She got up, walked across the grass. She had long copper-coloured hair that came down over her shoulders. She was so vulnerable that I felt the need to protect her in some way, to shield her, and I moved my hands towards her as though to be ready to stop her from falling or to fend off anything that might harm her. But my hands did not dare even graze her, and always stopped a few centimetres from her skin. And as I followed her like this past the flower gardens, I realized that her movements were similar to mine, that she too was trying to protect something fragile, something that might fall and shatter into pieces, and that needed consequently to be led towards places where it could settle gently, something that she could not touch but could only guide with her gestures: the Moon.

The Moon seemed lost: having abandoned the course of its orbit, it no longer knew where to go; it let itself be transported like a dried leaf. Sometimes it appeared to be plummeting towards the Earth, at others corkscrewing in a spiral movement, at others still it just seemed to be drifting. It was losing height, that was certain: for a second it seemed as if it would crash into the Plaza Hotel; instead it slid into a corridor between two skyscrapers, and disappeared from view towards the Hudson. It reappeared shortly afterwards, on the opposite side, popping out from behind a cloud, bathing Harlem and the East River in a chalky light, and as though caught by a gust of wind it rolled towards the Bronx.

'There it is!' I shouted. 'There, it's stopped!'

'It can't stop!' exclaimed the girl, and she ran naked and barefoot over the grass.

'Where are you going? You can't wander around like that! Stop! Hey, I'm talking to you! What's your name?'

She shouted out a name like Daiana or Deanna, something that could also have been an invocation. And she disappeared. In order to follow her, I jumped back into my car and began to search the avenues of Central Park.

The beams of my headlights lit up hedges, little hills, obelisks, but the girl, Diana, was nowhere to be seen. By now I had gone too far: I must have gone past her; I turned round to go back the way I came. A voice behind me said: 'No, it's there, keep going!'

Sitting behind me on the folded-back hood of my car was the naked girl, pointing towards the Moon.

I wanted to tell her to get down, that I could not travel across the city with her so prominently on view in that state, but I did not dare distract her, all intent as she was on not losing sight of the luminous glow that disappeared and reappeared at the end of the Avenue. And in any case – and this was even stranger – no passer-by seemed to notice this female apparition sitting up on my open-top car.

We crossed one of the bridges that link Manhattan to the mainland. Now we were going along a multi-lane highway, with other cars alongside us, and I kept my eyes fixed on the road ahead, fearing the laughter and crude comments that the sight of the two of us was no doubt prompting in the cars on either side. But when a saloon car overtook us, I nearly went off the road in surprise: crouched on its roof was a naked girl with her hair spread out in the wind. For a second I thought my passenger was leaping from one fast-moving car to another, but all I had to do was turn my eyes round ever so slightly to see that Diana's knees were still there at the same height as my nose. And it was not just her body that glowed before my eyes: I saw girls everywhere, stretched out in the strangest of poses, clinging to the radiators, doors, mudguards of the speeding cars – their golden or dark hair was the only thing that contrasted with the pale or dark gleam of their naked skin. One of these mysterious female passengers was positioned on every car, all stretching forwards, urging the drivers to follow the Moon.

They had been summoned by the endangered Moon: I was certain of that. How many of them were there? More cars carrying lunar girls gathered at every crossroads and junction, converging from all quarters of the city on the place above which the Moon seemed to have stopped. Reaching the outskirts we found ourselves opposite an automobile scrapyard.

The road petered out in a hilly area with little valleys, ridges, hills and peaks; it was not the contours of the land that created the bumpiness, but rather the layers of things that had been thrown away: everything that the consumerist city expelled once it had quickly used it up so it could immediately enjoy the pleasure of handling new things, ended up in that unprepossessing neighbourhood.

Over the course of many years, piles of battered fridges, yellowing issues of *Life* magazine, fused light-bulbs had accumulated around an enormous junkyard for cars. It was over this jagged, rusty territory that the Moon now loomed, and the swathes of beat-up metal swelled up as if lifted by a high tide. They resembled each other: the decrepit Moon and that crust of the Earth that had been soldered into an amalgam of wreckage; the mountains of scrap metal formed a chain that closed in on itself like an amphitheatre, whose shape was precisely that of a volcanic crater or a lunar sea. The Moon hung over this space and it was as if the planet and its satellite were acting as mirror images of each other.

Our car engines had all stopped: there is nothing that intimidates cars so much as their own cemeteries. Diana got down and all the other Dianas followed suit. But their energy now seemed to fade: they moved with uncertain steps, as though on finding themselves amidst those ruins of sharp scrap-iron they were suddenly seized by an awareness of being naked; many of them folded their arms to cover their breasts, as if shivering with cold. Meanwhile they scattered, climbing over the mountains of useless scrap: they went over the top, and down into the amphitheatre, and found themselves forming as it were a huge circle there in the middle. Then they all raised their arms up together.

The Moon gave a start as though that gesture of theirs had affected it, and it seemed for an instant to recover its energy and to climb again. The circle of girls stood with their arms raised, and their faces and breasts turned towards the Moon. Was that what the Moon had asked of them? Did it need them to support itself in the sky? I did not have time to ask myself this question. At that very moment the crane entered the scene.

The crane had been designed and built by the authorities, who had decided to cleanse the sky of such an inelegant encumbrance. It was a bulldozer from which a kind of crab's claw rose up; it came forward on its caterpillar-treads, squat and stocky, just like a crab; and when it arrived at the place that had been prepared for the operation, it seemed to become even more squat, in order to cling to the Earth with every part of itself. The winch spun quickly; the bulldozer raised its arm into the sky; nobody had ever thought that a crane with such a long arm could be built. Its bucket opened, showing all its teeth; now, more than a crab's claw, it resembled a shark's mouth. The Moon was just there; it wavered as though it wanted to escape, but the crane seemed to be magnetized: we saw the Moon being hoovered up, as it were, and landing in its jaws. Its mandibles closed round it with a dry sound: crack! For a second it seemed that the Moon had turned into crumbs like a squashed meringue, but instead it stayed inside the jaws of the bucket, half inside and half out. It had turned into an oblong shape, a kind of thick cigar held between the bucket's teeth. Down came a shower the colour of ashes.

The crane now tried to yank the Moon out of its orbit and drag it downwards. The winch had started to wind backwards: by this stage it needed to make a huge effort. Diana and her friends had stayed motionless with their arms raised, as though hoping to beat the enemy's aggression with the strength of their circle. It was only when the ash from the disintegrating Moon rained down on their faces and breasts that we saw them disperse. Diana let out a sharp cry of lament.

At that point the imprisoned Moon lost what little light it had left: it became a black, shapeless rock. It would have crashed down on to the Earth had it not been held fast by the bucket's teeth. Down below, the contractor's men had prepared a metal net, fixing it to the ground with long nails, all around the area where the crane was slowly lowering its load.

Once it was on the ground, the Moon was a pockmarked, sandy boulder, so dull and opaque that it was incredible that previously it had illuminated the sky with its shining reflection. The crane opened the jaws of its bucket, went back on its caterpillar treads, and almost flipped over as it was suddenly lightened of its load. The contractor's men were ready with the net: they wrapped it round the Moon, trapping it between the net and the ground. The Moon tried to struggle in its straitjacket: a tremor like that of an earthquake caused avalanches of empty cans to slide down from the mountain of refuse. Then all was peaceful again.

The now moonless sky was being drenched by bursts of light from the big lamps. But the darkness was already fading.

Dawn found the car cemetery contained an extra wreck: the Moon that had been shipwrecked there in the middle was almost indistinguishable from the other discarded objects; it was the same colour, had the same condemned look, the same appearance as something you couldn't imagine ever being new. All around, a low murmuring resounded throughout the crater of terrestrial rubbish: the light of dawn revealed a swarm of living things slowly waking up. Bearded creatures were advancing amidst disembowelled lorry carcasses, the shattered wheels, the crumpled metal.

In the midst of the things that had been thrown away lived a community of people who had also been thrown away, or marginalized, or had thrown themselves away of their own volition, or who had got tired of running all over the city to sell and buy new things that were destined to go out of date immediately: people who had decided that only things that had been thrown away were the real riches of the world. Encircling the Moon, throughout the whole amphitheatre, these lanky figures were standing upright or were seated, their faces framed by beards or unkempt hair. It was a tatterdemalion, bizarrely dressed crowd and in their midst was the naked Diana and all the girls from the night before. They came forward, and began to release the steel wires of the net from the nails that had been driven into the ground.

Immediately, like an air balloon released from its moorings, the Moon rose, hovering above the girls' heads, above the grandstand full of tramps, and stayed suspended, held back by the steel net whose wires Diana and her friends were operating, sometimes pulling them, sometimes letting go, and when they all started to run, still holding the ends of the wires, the Moon followed.

As soon as the Moon moved, a kind of wave began to rise from the valleys of wreckage: the old car carcasses crushed like accordions started to march, creakily arranging themselves in a procession, and a stream of battered cans rolled along, making a noise like thunder, though you couldn't tell whether they were dragging or being dragged along by everything else. Following this Moon that had been saved from the scrap-heap, all the things and all the people that had been resigned to being chucked into a corner, started on the road again, and swarmed towards the richest neighbourhoods of the city.

That morning the city was celebrating Consumer Thanksgiving Day. This feast came round every year, one day in November, and had been set up to allow the shops' customers to display their gratitude towards the god Production who tirelessly satisfied their every desire. The biggest department store in town organized a parade each year: an enormous balloon, in the shape of a garishly coloured doll, was paraded through the main street, held by ribbons which sequin-clad girls pulled as they marched behind a musical band. So that morning the procession was coming down Fifth Avenue: the majorette twirled her baton in the air, the big drums banged, and the giant made of balloons representing 'The Satisfied Customer' flew amidst the skyscrapers, obediently following a leash held by girls in kepis, tassles and fringed epaulettes, riding on spangly motorbikes.

At the same time another parade was crossing Manhattan. The flaky, mouldy Moon was also processing, sailing between the skyscrapers, pulled by the naked girls, and behind it came a line of beat-up cars and skeletons of lorries, in the midst of a silent crowd gradually increasing in size. Thousands of people flocked to join the throng that had been following the Moon from the early hours of the morning, people of all colours, whole families with children of every age, especially now that the procession was filing past the most crowded black and Puerto Rican areas around Harlem.

The lunar procession zigzagged around Uptown, started down Broadway, and came quickly and silently down that street to converge with the other procession which was dragging its balloon giant along Fifth Avenue.

At Madison Square one procession met the other; or rather, it became just one single procession. 'The Satisfied Customer', perhaps because of a collision with the Moon's jagged surface, turned into a rubber rag. On the motorbikes now were the Dianas pulling the Moon with multicoloured ribbons; or more likely, since their number had at least doubled, the female motorcyclists had thrown away their uniforms and kepis. A similar transformation had overtaken the motorbikes and the cars in the parade: you could no longer tell which were old and which were new – the twisted wheels, the rusty mudguards were mixed up with bodywork as shiny as a mirror, with paintwork gleaming like enamel.

And behind the parade, shop windows became covered with cobwebs and mould, lifts in skyscrapers started to creak and groan, posters with advertisements on them turned yellow, egg-holders in fridges filled with chicks as if they were incubators, televisions broadcast whirlwinds of atmospheric storms. The city had consumed itself at a stroke: it was a disposable city following the Moon on its last voyage.

To the sound of the band drumming on empty petrol cans, the procession arrived at the Brooklyn Bridge. Diana lifted up her majorette's baton: her friends twirled their ribbons in the air. The Moon made a last dash, went over the curved grillwork of the bridge, tipped towards the sea, crashed into the water like a brick, and sank downwards, sending up thousands of little bubbles to the surface.

Meanwhile instead of letting the ribbons go, the girls had stayed attached to them, and the Moon had lifted them up, sending them flying over the parapet of the bridge: in the air they described arcs like divers and disappeared amidst the waves.

We stood and stared, some of us on the Brooklyn Bridge, others on the jetties on the shore, gazing in astonishment, caught between the urge to dive in after them and our confidence that we would see them reappear.

We did not have long to wait. The sea began to vibrate with waves that spread out in a circle. At the centre of this circle there appeared an island, which grew like a mountain, like a hemisphere, like a globe resting on the water, or rather raised just above it; no, like a new Moon rising in the sky. I say a Moon even though it did not resemble a Moon any more than the one we had seen plunge into the depths a few moments before. However, this new Moon had a very different way of being different: it emerged from the sea dripping a trail of green, glistening seaweed; spouts of water gushed in fountains from fields that lent it the sheen of an emerald; a steamy vegetation covered it, but not with plants. This covering seemed to be made of peacock feathers, full of eyes and shimmering colours.

This was the landscape that we just managed to glimpse before the sphere it covered swiftly receded into the sky, and the more minute details were lost in a general impression of freshness and lushness. It was dusk: the contrasts of the colours were fading into a vibrant chiaroscuro; the lunar fields and woods were little more than contours, barely visible, on the taut surface of the shining globe. But we were just in time to see some hammocks hanging from branches, rocked by the wind, and nestling in them I saw the girls who had led us to that place. I recognized Diana, at peace at last, fanning herself with a feather punkah, and perhaps sending me a signal of recognition.

'There they are! There she is!' I shouted; we all shouted, and the happiness at having found them again was already fraught with the pain of having lost them now for ever, because the Moon rising in the dark sky sent out only the reflections of the Sun on its lakes and fields.

We were seized by a frenzy: we began to gallop across the continent, through the savannahs and forests that had covered over the Earth again and buried cities and roads, obliterating all trace of everything that had been. And we trumpeted, lifting up to the sky our trunks and our long, thin tusks, shaking the long hair of our croups with the violent anguish that lays hold of all us young mammoths, when we realize that now is when life begins, and yet it is clear that what we desire shall never be ours.

The Meteorites

According to the most recent theories, the Earth was originally a tiny, cold body which later increased in size through the incorporation of meteorites and meteor dust.

At first we were under the illusion that we could keep it clean – *old Qfwfq said* – since it was really small and you could sweep it and dust it every day. Of course a lot of stuff did come down: in fact you would have thought that the Earth had no other purpose in its orbiting but to gather up all the dust and rubbish hovering in space. Now it's different, there's the atmosphere; you look at the sky and say: 'Oh, how clear it is, how pure!' But you should have seen what landed on us when the planet bumped into one of those meteor storms in the course of its orbit and could not get out. It was a powder white as mothballs, which deposited itself in tiny granules, and sometimes in bigger, crystalline splinters, as though a glass lampshade had crashed down from the sky, and in the middle of it you could also find biggish pebbles, scattered bits from other planetary systems, pear cores, taps, Ionic capitals, back numbers of the *Herald Tribune* and *Paese sera*: everyone knows that universes come and go, but it's always the same stuff that goes round. The Earth, being small and also swift (because it travelled much faster than it does now), managed to avoid a lot of it: we would see an object

approaching from the depths of space, fluttering like a bird –
then later we'd find out it was a sock – or sailing towards us
pitching slightly, like the time we saw a grand piano; then
it would come to within half a metre of us, and then nothing happened, it would go on its way without even grazing
us: it was lost, perhaps for ever, in the empty darkness
we left behind. But most of the time the meteoric shower
would empty over us, stirring up a thick dustcloud and
making a racket like empty cans; that was the moment
when a convulsive agitation would seize hold of my first
wife, Xha.

Xha wanted to keep everything clean and in order; and
she managed it. Of course she had to keep very busy, but the
planet was still of a size to allow us to carry out a daily check,
and the fact that we were the only two inhabitants – though
it had the disadvantage that there was nobody to give us a
hand – was also an advantage because two calm and orderly
people like us do not create chaos: when they take something
they put it back in its right place. Once we had repaired the
damage done by the meteoric rubble, and dusted everything
properly, and washed and hung out the laundry, which
constantly got dirty, we had nothing more to do.

As for the rubbish, initially Xha would wrap it up in little
packages that I would chuck into the void, flinging them as
high as I could: the Earth had still very little power of
attraction, and in any case I had strong arms and a certain
skill in throwing, so we were able to rid ourselves of items
of considerable bulk and weight, forcing them back into
space whence they had come. With the granules of dustcloud
such an operation was impossible: even if we filled up paper
bags, you could not throw them far enough away for them
not to come back; they nearly always came undone in the

air and we would find ourselves covered again in dust from head to toe.

For as long as it was possible, Xha preferred to get rid of the dust by putting it inside certain cracks in the ground; then the cracks would fill up, or rather they expanded into overflowing craters. The fact was that the huge quantity of accumulated matter made the Earth swell from the inside and these cracks were actually caused by this increase in volume. So she decided to spread out the dust in uniform layers on the planet's surface and let it set into a smooth and continuous crust, so as not to give the impression of a solution that had been only half thought through or abandoned.

The skill and tenacity that Xha had shown in trying to remove every granule that came to disturb the polished harmony of our world were now directed towards making the meteoric crumbs the very basis of this harmonious order, storing them up in regular layers, hiding them under a polishable surface. However, every day more powder would land on the Earth's floor in a veil that was at times thin and at other times thickened by humps and mounds here and there; we would then instantly get to work to establish a new layered surface.

The bulk of our planet was increasing, but thanks to the care which my wife and I – under her direction – lavished on it, it retained a shape that was without irregularities, excrescences or waste, and no shadow or stain sullied its white-naphthalene sheen. The external layers hid even those objects which landed on us all mixed up with the dustcloud and which by now we could no longer send back to the currents of the cosmos because the Earth, as it grew, had set up around itself a gravitational field too strong for my arms to overcome. Where the detritus was densest in volume we buried it underneath tumuli of dust in the shape of beautifully squared-off pyramids, not too high, arranged in symmetrical rows, so that every intrusion of the shapeless and the arbitrary was cancelled from our sight.

When describing my first wife's industry, I would not want to have given you the idea that there was an element of irritability, anxiety, or anything like alarm, in her scrupulosity. No, Xha was sure these meteorite showers were an accident, a temporary phenomenon, in a universe that was still in its settling-down phase. She had no doubts about the fact that our planet and the other heavenly bodies, and everything that was inside and outside of them, had to obey a precise, regular geometry of straight lines and curves and surfaces; according to her, anything that was not part of this pattern was an irrelevant leftover, and trying immediately to sweep it away or bury it was her way of minimizing its importance, even of denying its existence. Of course this is my interpretation of her ideas: Xha was a practical woman, who did not get bogged down in general statements but simply tried to do well what she saw as her duty, and did so willingly.

Every evening, before lying down, Xha and I would walk through this terrestrial landscape that was protected with such meticulous persistence. It was a smooth, glabrous expanse, interrupted only, at regular intervals, by the stark edges of those pyramid-shaped elevations. Above us in the sky revolved planets and stars at the appropriate speed and distance, reflecting rays of light that spread a uniform sparkle over our ground. My wife waved a stick-fan to stir the always rather dusty air around our faces; I carried an umbrella to protect us from any gusts of meteoric rain. A light sprinkling of starch lent a continual freshness to Xha's well-folded clothes; a white ribbon held her hair firm.

These were the moments of tranquil contemplation we allowed ourselves; but they did not last long. In the morning we would get up early, and our few hours of sleep had already been enough for the Earth to be covered again with debris. 'Hurry up, Qfwfq, there's no time to waste!' Xha would say as she thrust a broom into my hands, and I would set off on my usual round, while the dawn turned the narrow, bare horizon of the plain white. As I went along, I observed here and there piles of wreckage and knick-knacks; as the light increased, I would notice the opaque dusting that veiled the planet's gleaming floor. With my broom I would sweep everything I could into a bin or a bag I carried with me, but first I would stop to study the fresh haul the night had brought us: a sculpted bull's head, a cactus, a cartwheel, a gold nugget, a Cinerama projector. I would weigh them and run them through my hands, suck a finger pricked by the cactus, and have fun imagining that these totally incongruous objects were connected by a mysterious link which I was meant to discover. Such imaginings I could indulge in when alone: because with Xha the passion to remove, to obliterate, to throw away was so overpowering that we would never stop to look at what we were sweeping up. Instead now it was my curiosity that became the most powerful urge in my daily inspections, and I would set out every morning almost happily, whistling as I went.

Xha and I had in a way divided up our tasks, agreed which hemisphere each would keep in order. In my hemisphere sometimes I did not remove the stuff immediately, especially when it was rather heavy, but piled it up in a corner, to be collected later in a barrow. So at times there formed what looked like piles or stacks: carpets, sand-dunes, editions of the Koran, oil-wells, an absurd lumping together of knick-knacks that didn't match. Of course Xha would not have approved of my system, but to tell the truth I felt a kind of pleasure seeing these composite shadows looming on the horizon. At times I would even leave the piled-up stuff from one day to the next (the Earth was starting to become so big that Xha was not able to get round it all in one day), and the surprise in the morning was discovering how many new things had been added to the rest.

One day I was contemplating a pile of broken boxes and rusty bins, over which stood a crane holding the distorted wreckage of a car, when on lowering my gaze I saw, on the threshold of a hut built with bits of metal and plywood, a girl busy peeling potatoes. She was dressed, it seemed to me, in rags: strips of cellophane, scraps of frayed scarves; in her hair she had bits of straw and wood-shavings. She was taking the potatoes from a sack and, peeling them with a penknife, she would unroll ribbons of potato-skin which piled up in a grey mass.

I felt the need to apologize: 'I'm sorry, you've found us in a bit of a mess, I'll clean it up at once, I'll clear everything . . .'

The girl flung a peeled potato into a basin, and said: 'Oh, for heaven's sake . . .'

'Perhaps if you could give me a hand . . .' I said, or rather this was said by that part of me that was still thinking in the way it had always thought. (Just the night before, Xha and I had agreed: 'Yes, if we could find someone to give us a hand, it would all be so different!')

'No, you,' said the girl, yawning and stretching, 'you help *me* to peel.'

'We no longer know how to get rid of this stuff that lands on us,' I explained. 'Look at this,' and I lifted up a barrel without a lid that I had just spotted. 'Who knows what's in it?'

The girl sniffed and said: 'Anchovies. We'll have fish and chips.'

She insisted I sit with her and cut the potatoes into thin strips. In the middle of that rubbish-tip she found a blackish can full of oil. She lit a fire on the ground, using wrapping material, and began to fry tiny fish and slices of potato in a rusty basin.

'We can't do this here, it's dirty . . .' I said, thinking of Xha's kitchen utensils, shiny as glass.

'Oh, for heaven's sake, come on . . .' she replied, serving the hot fry-up in parcels of paper.

Later I often asked myself whether I was wrong not to tell Xha that another person had landed on the Earth that day. But I would have had to own up to my laziness in letting so much stuff pile up. 'I'll do a good clean-up first,' I thought, even though I realized that everything had become more difficult.

Every day I went to visit the girl, Wha, in the middle of that avalanche of new objects with which the whole hemisphere was now overflowing. I didn't understand how she managed to live in the midst of that confusion, and let things pile up on top of each other: lianas on top of baobab trees, Romanesque cathedrals on top of crypts, hoists above coal deposits, and more stuff again settling on top of that, chimpanzees on the lianas, sightseeing tour coaches parked on the squares in front of the Romanesque cathedrals, fire-damp fumes in the galleries of the mines. I got angry every time: that wretched girl, her way of thinking was the exact opposite of mine.

Nevertheless, at times I had to admit that I liked watching her move around in the midst of all that, with those careless gestures of hers, as though her every action happened by chance; and the surprising thing was seeing that, each time, everything she did turned out unexpectedly well. Wha chucked the first things she came across into the same saucepan for boiling, for instance, beans and pork rind: who would have thought it? This produced a wonderful minestrone; she would pile up pieces from Egyptian monuments one on top of the other as though they were dishes to wash – a woman's head, two ibis wings, the body of a lion – and out came a wonderful Sphinx. In short, I was amazed to find myself thinking that – once I'd got used to it – I would end up being perfectly at ease with her.

What I could never forgive her for was her absentmindedness, the chaos, the way she never knew where she had left things. She forgot the Mexican volcano Paricutín in the middle of a ploughed field, and the Roman theatre at Luni amidst the terraces of a vineyard. The fact that she subsequently would find them just at the right time was not enough to assuage my irritation, because that was simply another accidental circumstance to add to the others, as if there were not enough already.

Of course my life was not here, it was the other life, the one I lived at Xha's side, keeping the surface of the other hemisphere level and clean. On this matter I was of the same mind as Xha: no doubt about it, I worked so that the Earth could be kept in its state of perfection; I could spend hours with Wha only because I was sure I could go back to Xha's world, where everything worked the way it should, where you understood everything that had to be understood. I should say that with Xha I reached an internal calm underneath constant external activity, whereas with Wha I could maintain an external calm, do precisely what I wanted to do at that moment, but I paid for that peace with a constant anxiety, because I was sure that that state of things could not last.

I was wrong. On the contrary, the most disparate meteoric fragments continued to connect with each other, in however approximate a manner, and to compose themselves into a mosaic, even though it was one with gaps. Comacchio eels, a river source on Monviso, a series of ducal palaces, many hectares of rice-fields, agricultural workers' trade-union traditions, some Celtic and Lombard suffixes, a certain growth index in industrial productivity, were materials that were scattered and unconnected but which fused into a tightly knit network of reciprocal relationships at the very moment when suddenly a river fell to Earth, and it was the Po.

Thus every new object that landed on our planet ended up by finding its own place as though it had always been there, as well as its relationship of interdependence with other objects, and the unreasonable presence of one thing found its reason for existing in the unreasonable presence of the others, to the point where the general disorder started to be able to be considered the natural order of things. It is in this context that one must also consider other facts which I shall barely touch on, since they belong to my private life: you'll have gathered that I'm alluding to my divorce from Xha, and my second marriage, to Wha.

If one considers it carefully, life with Wha also had its own harmony. All around her things seemed to follow her very own style in the way they arranged themselves, joined other things and created a space for themselves; they followed her very lack of method, her indifference towards materials and uncertainty of gestures which culminated in the end, nevertheless, in an instantaneous and clear choice which could not be disputed. In the sky flew the Erechtheum, all damaged by cosmic shipwrecks, and losing its bits: it hovered for a second above the top of Mount Lycabettos, started to glide again, grazed the square by the Acropolis where the Parthenon was later to land, and came gently to rest a bit further on.

Sometimes it just needed a little intervention on our part

to connect the detached pieces, to get the elements in the layers to match up, and in those cases Wha showed that she had a sure touch, even though it seemed she only wanted to fiddle about. As she tinkered, she would crumple the layers of sedimentary rocks into synclines and anticlines, she would change the orientation on the faces of crystals and obtain walls of feldspar, quartz, mica or slate, and between one layer and another she would hide marine fossils at different heights in order of date.

Thus the Earth began gradually to take on the contours you know today. The shower of meteoric fragments still continues to the present, adds new details to the picture, frames it with a window, a curtain, a network of telephone wires, fills the empty spaces with bits that fit together as best they can – traffic-lights, obelisks, bars, tobacconists, apses, floods, a dentist's surgery, a cover from the Sunday edition of the *Corriere* with a hunter biting a lion – and always some excess is added in the execution of superfluous details, for instance in the pigmentation of butterflies' wings, and some incongruous elements, like a war in Kashmir, and I always have the impression that there's something still missing which is just about to arrive, perhaps just two Saturnian verses by Naevius to fill the gap between two fragments of an epic, or the principles that govern the assembly of DNA into chromosomes, and then the picture will be complete, I will have in front of me a world that is precise and abundant, I will once more have Xha and Wha together.

Now they are long since gone: Xha overcome by the dustcloud shower, gone for ever along with her realm of precision; Wha perhaps still crouching for fun somewhere in a hiding place in the packed storehouse of objects we'd found, and herself now unfindable. And I'm still waiting for them to come back – to reappear maybe in a thought crossing my mind – waiting to catch a glimpse of them with my eyes open or closed, but the two of them together, at the same time; all I would need is to have them both together for just one second to understand.

The Stone Sky

The speed with which seismic waves spread inside the terrestrial globe varies according to the depths and discontinuities between the materials that make up the Earth's crust, mantle and core.

You live out there, on the crust, outside – *the voice of old Qfwfq could be heard from the bottom of the crater* – or almost outside, because above it you've got that other covering of air, but still outside for those who look at you from the concentric spheres that the Earth contains, as I do as I watch you while I move in the interstices between one sphere and another. Nor are you interested in knowing that the Earth, inside, is not compact: it is discontinuous, made up of overlapping skins of different densities, right down to the core of nickel and iron, which in turn is also a system of cores one inside the other, and each one rotates independently of the others depending on the greater or lesser fluidity of the element.

You insist on being called terrestrial, but who gave you the right to do so? Your real name should be extraterrestrials, people on the outside: terrestrials are those who live inside, as Rdix and I did, until the day you tricked her and took her away from me into that desolate outside of yours.

As for me, I've always lived inside here, along with Rdix initially, and then on my own, in one of these inner earths.

A stone sky rotated above our heads, one more limpid than yours, but criss-crossed, like yours, by clouds at those points where gatherings of chrome or magnesium collected. Winged shadows rise up in flight: the internal skies have their own birds, accretions of light rock describing spirals, scudding upwards until they disappear from sight. There are sudden changes of weather: when bursts of leaden rain shower down, or when we have a hail of zinc crystals, there is nowhere else to escape except to slip inside the porous holes of the spongy rock. At times the darkness is split by a fiery zigzag: not a lightning-bolt, but incandescent metal slithering down a vein in the earth.

We believed that the sphere that supported us was the Earth, and the sky was the sphere that surrounded that first sphere: in fact, exactly the same as you do, but in our world such distinctions were always provisional, arbitrary, since the consistency of the elements changed continuously, and at a certain point we would notice that our sky was hard and compact, a boulder crushing us, whereas our earth was a sticky glue, churned up by whirlpools, pullulating with bursting bubbles. I tried to take advantage of the flows of heavier metals to get closer to the real centre of the Earth, to the core that acts as core to all other cores, and I took Rdix's hand, to guide her in that descent. But every seepage that headed towards the core undermined other material and forced it to rise up towards the surface: at times as we plunged down we would be caught up in the wave that spurted towards the upper layers, curling around itself as it did so. So we would go back up the Earth's radius in the opposite direction; amidst the mineral layers passages opened up that sucked us in while beneath us the rock turned solid again. In the end we found ourselves supported by another layer of ground and standing beneath another stone sky, without knowing whether we were higher or lower than the point we had started out from.

As soon as Rdix saw the metal of a new sky above us becoming fluid, she would be seized by the urge to fly. She dived upwards, swam across the dome of one sky, then of another, then of a third sky, and would grab on to the stalactites hanging from the highest vaults. I stayed behind her, partly to encourage her game, partly to remind her to take the journey back in the opposite direction. Of course, Rdix was also convinced, like me, that the point to which we had to head was the centre of the Earth. Only once we'd reached the centre would we be able to say that the whole planet was ours. We were the progenitors of life on Earth and for this reason we had to start to make it liveable from its core outwards, gradually extending our condition to the rest of the globe. We were headed towards *earthly* life, that is to say life of the Earth and on the Earth; not towards what pops up from its surface and which you call life on Earth but which is just a mould spreading its spores over the apple's wrinkled skin.

Yours has proved to be the wrong way, a life condemned to remain for ever partial, superficial, insignificant. Rdix also knew this full well: and yet her capacity for being enchanted by things led her to love every state of suspension above all else, and as soon as she was allowed to soar upwards in leaps, in flights, in scaling the funnels of the underworld, you would see her seeking out the most unusual locations, the most extraordinary vantage points.

Border areas, passages between one earthly layer and another, gave her a mild vertigo. We knew that the Earth is made up of superimposed roofs, like the skins of an enormous onion, and that every roof leads you to a roof higher up, and all of them together prefigure the final roof, the point where the Earth ceases to be Earth, where all the inside is left on this side, and beyond there is only the outside. For you this border of the Earth is identified with the Earth itself; you think the sphere is the surface that wraps it, and not its total volume; you have always lived in that flat, flat dimension and you don't even imagine that one can live elsewhere and in a different way. For us at that time, this border was something we knew existed, but we didn't think we could see it without leaving the Earth, a prospect which seemed to us not so much frightful as absurd. That was where everything was flung out in eruptions and bituminous spurts and smoke-holes, everything that the Earth expelled from its innards: gases, liquid mixtures, volatile elements, base matter, all types of waste. It was the world in negative, something that we could not picture even in our minds, the abstract idea of it was enough to give us a shiver of disgust, no, of anxiety; or rather a stunned sensation, a kind of – as I said – vertigo (yes, that's it, our reactions were more complex than you might think, especially Rdix's), into which there crept an element of fascination, a kind of attraction to the void, to anything double-faced or absolute.

Following Rdix in these wandering whims of hers, I found myself in the mouth of an extinct volcano. Above us, beyond a kind of hourglass bottleneck, there opened up the cavity of a crater, lumpy and grey, a landscape not too different in form and substance from what we were used to in our subterranean depths; but what stopped us dead in our tracks was the fact that the Earth ended just there, it did not start to bear down on itself again in a different guise, and from that point onwards the void began, or at any rate a substance that was incomparably thinner than any we had gone through up to that point, a substance that was transparent and vibrating: blue air.

As far as vibrations are concerned, we were ready to accept those that spread slowly across granite and basalt, the snaps, clangs, deep booms moving torpidly through the masses of molten metals or the crystalline walls. Now, though, the vibrations of the air came towards us like a crackle of tiny, sharp acoustic sparks, succeeding each other from all points of space at a speed that was unbearable for us: it was a kind of tickle that led to a restless craving. We were seized – or at least I was: from here onwards I am forced to distinguish my mental responses from Rdix's – by the desire to retreat into the black depths of silence over which the echo of earthquakes passes softly and is lost in the distance. But Rdix, attracted as she always was by what was rare and startling, felt an impatient desire to take hold of this unique thing, whether it was good or bad.

That was when the trap was sprung: beyond the mouth of the crater the air vibrated in a continuous manner, or rather in a continuous manner that contained several discontinuous ways of vibrating. It was a sound that filled out, then faded, then increased in volume again, and in these modulations it followed an invisible pattern that stretched out in time like a succession of full and empty intervals. Other vibrations were superimposed on these, which were sharp and well separated from one another, but they blended into a drone that sounded now sweet, now bitter. As they countered or accompanied the course of the deeper sound, they created a kind of sonorous circle or field or domain.

My immediate instinct was to escape from that circle, and return to the padded denseness: and I slid inside the crater. But in the same instant Rdix had run up the precipice towards where the sound came from and, before I could hold her back, had gone beyond the mouth of the crater. Either that or it was an arm, something that I could imagine was an arm, a sinuous arm, that grabbed her, and dragged her out; I managed to hear a cry, her cry, one that mingled with the previous sound, in harmony with it, in a single chant which she and the unknown singer intoned and picked out on the chords of some instrument, as they descended the external slopes of the volcano.

I don't know if this image corresponds to what I saw or imagined: I was by then plunging down into my darkness, and the internal skies were closing over me one by one: flint vaults, aluminium roofs, atmospheres of sticky sulphur; and the variegated subterranean silence echoed around me with its muffled rumbles, and its sotto-voce thunder. The relief at finding myself far from the nauseating border with the air and from the torture of the soundwaves seized hold of me along with the desperation at having lost Rdix. So there I was, on my own: I had not been able to save her from the torture of being yanked from the Earth, and exposed to the continuous percussion of strings stretched tight in the air with which the world of the void pursues its illusions of existing. My dream of making the Earth alive by reaching its ultimate core with Rdix had failed. Rdix was a prisoner, exiled in the exposed wastelands of the outside.

There followed a period of waiting. My eyes contemplated the landscapes densely compressed against each other that filled the globe's volume: spindly caverns, mountain-chains that were crowded together in splinters and strips, oceans wrung out like sponges: the more I recognized our crammed, concentrated, compact world, the more I suffered because Rdix was not there to inhabit it.

To free Rdix became my sole thought: to force the doors of the outside, invade the external with the internal, reconnect Rdix to terrestrial matter, build over her a new vault, a new mineral sky, save her from the hell of that vibrating air, that sound, that song. I espied lava gathering in the volcanic caverns, the way it pressed up the vertical conduits of the Earth's crust: that was the way.

The day of the eruption came, a tower of lapilli rose black in the air above decapitated Vesuvius, the lava surged through the vines along the bay, burst the doors of Herculaneum, crushed the mule-driver and his beast against the city wall, while the dog imprisoned in his collar uprooted his chain and sought refuge in the barn. I was in the middle of it: I advanced with the lava, the fiery avalanche split into tongues, rivulets, snaking eddies, and in the forefront pushing furthest ahead I was there, running to find Rdix. I knew – something warned me – that Rdix was still a prisoner of the unknown singer: wherever I heard the music of that instrument and the sound of that voice, that was where she would be.

I was swept along by the lava flow amidst secluded gardens and marble temples. I heard a song and an arpeggio; two voices singing alternately: I recognized Rdix's voice – but oh! how changed – as she followed that of the stranger. There was an inscription on the architrave, in Greek characters: *Orpheos.* I broke through the front door, overflowing the threshold. I saw her, just for an instant, beside the harp. The place was enclosed and hollow, deliberately made – you would have said – for music to gather there, as in a shell. A heavy curtain – made of leather, it seemed to me, or rather stuffed like a quilt – hid a window, thus isolating their music from the surrounding world. The minute I went in, Rdix yanked the curtain aside, revealing the open window: outside it stretched the bay dazzling with reflected light, and the city and its streets. The midday light invaded the room, the light and also the sounds: a strumming of guitars rose up on all sides and the uneven rumble of hundreds of loudspeakers, and these blended with a sharp sputtering of engines and a blaring of horns. This carapace of noise extended from there outwards over the surface of the globe, or rather over the strip that delimits your extraterrestrial existence, with aerials hoisted on roofs transforming the invisible and inaudible waves that pervade space, transistors stuck to your ears filling them at every second with the acoustic glue without which you don't know whether you are alive or dead, jukeboxes that store and spew out sounds, and the endless siren of the ambulance collecting hour by hour those injured in your endless carnage. Against this wall of sound the lava came to a halt. Pierced by the shafts from the network of crackling vibrations, I made one more movement forwards towards the point where I had glimpsed Rdix for a second, but Rdix had disappeared, her kidnapper too: the music by which and on which they lived was swamped by the avalanche of noise; I was no longer able to distinguish either her or her song.

I withdrew, moving backwards through the lava flow, climbed back up the volcano's slopes, went back to inhabit the silence, to bury myself.

Now, you who live outside, tell me, if by any chance you happen to catch Rdix's song amidst the thick paste of sounds that surrounds you, the song that keeps her prisoner and which at the same time is itself a prisoner of the non-sound that encloses all music; if you manage to recognize Rdix's voice, in which the distant echo of silence still resounds, tell me, let me have news of her, you extraterrestrials, you temporary winners, so that I can return to my plans to find Rdix again and descend with her to the centre of the terrestrial world, to make life terrestrial from the centre outwards, now that it is clear that your victory is actually a defeat.

As Long as the Sun Lasts

Depending on their size, brightness and colour, stars have a varying evolution that can be classified according to the Hertzsprung-Russell diagram. Their life can be very brief (just a few million years, for the large blue stars) or they can follow such a slow course (ten billion years, for the smaller yellow stars) that before it brings them to old age their life can last (in the case of the reddest and smallest ones) for billions of millennia. For all of them there comes a moment when, once all their hydrogen has been burned, there is nothing more left for them to do except expand and cool down (turning into Red Giants) and from that point they embark on a series of thermonuclear reactions that will bring them swiftly to extinction. The Sun, a yellow star of medium power which has already been shining for four or five billion years, has in front of it a time that is at least just as long again, before it reaches that point.

It was precisely for that reason, to have a bit of a quieter life, that my grandfather came and settled here – Qfwfq said – after the last supernova explosion had flung them once more into space: grandfather, grandmother, their children, grandchildren and great-grandchildren. The Sun was just at that stage condensing, a roundish, yellowish shape, along one arm of the galaxy, and it made a good impression on him, amidst all the other stars that were going around. 'Let's try a yellow one this time,' he said to his wife. 'If I've understood it right, the yellow ones are those that stay up longest without changing. And maybe in a short time from now a planetary system will form around it too.'

This idea of settling with all the family on one planet, maybe one of those with an atmosphere and beasties and plants, was one of Colonel Eggg's old ideas for when he would retire, after all those comings and goings amidst incandescent matter. Not that he suffered from the heat, my grandfather, and as for upheavals in temperature, he had had to get used to such things for some time now, after so many years of service; still, once you've got to a certain age, everyone starts to like a temperate climate around them.

My grandmother, though, immediately butted in: 'And why not on that other one? The bigger they are the more I trust them!' and she pointed to a Blue Giant.

'Are you mad, don't you know what that is? Don't you know about the blue ones? They burn so fast you don't even notice, and barely a couple of thousand millennia go by and you've already got to start packing!'

But you know how Grandma Ggge is: she's stayed young not just in her looks but also in her outlook, never happy with her lot, always craving change, no matter whether it's for better or worse, attracted by everything that is different. And to think that the bulk of the upheaval, in those hasty and panicky removals from one heavenly body to another, always landed on her shoulders, especially when there were small children around. 'It's as if she didn't remember from one move to the next,' Grandpa Eggg would say, letting off steam with us grandchildren. 'She never learns to calm down. I'm telling you, here, in the solar system, what can she complain about? I've been travelling all across galaxies for a long time now, so I've got a bit of experience, haven't I? And does my wife ever acknowledge that?'

This is the Colonel's obsession: he has had plenty to make him happy in his career, but he has never had this one satisfaction, the one he would like above all else: hearing his wife finally say, 'Yes, Eggg, you were spot on about this, I wouldn't have given tuppence for this Sun but you immediately managed to see that it was one of the most reliable and stable stars, one that wouldn't start to play tricks two minutes later, and you were also able to put us in the right position to get a place on the Earth, when it later took shape . . . and this Earth, with all its limits and defects, still offers good residential areas, and the kids have space to play and schools that are not too far away . . .' This is what the old Colonel would like his wife to tell him, indulging him just for once in his life. No chance. Instead, the minute she hears of some stellar system that works in a completely different way, for instance the varying luminosity of the 'RR Lyrae', her cravings begin: there life is probably more varied, you're more in the swing, whereas here we're stuck in this corner, in a dead end where nothing ever happens.

'And what is it you want to happen?' asked Eggg, appealing to all of us as witnesses. 'As if we didn't now know that it's the same story everywhere: hydrogen is transformed into helium, then come the usual tricks with beryllium and lithium, the incandescent layers collapsing on top of each other, then swelling like balloons and getting paler and paler until they collapse again . . . If we could only, while we're in the middle of it all, manage to enjoy the spectacle! But instead each time the great worry is not losing sight of the parcels and packages for the removal, and the kids crying, one daughter with inflamed eyes, a son-in-law whose denture is melting . . . The first to suffer from all this, everyone knows, is her, Ggge; she talks and talks, but when it comes to the actual event . . .'

Those early days were full of surprises for old Eggg too (he told us this so many times): the condensation of gas-clouds, the clash of atoms, matter clumping together and swelling and swelling until it ignites, and the sky swarming with white-hot bodies of every colour, each one seemingly different from all the others in diameter, temperature, density, in its way of contracting and dilating, and all those isotopes that nobody imagined existed, and those puffs and explosions, those magnetic fields . . . one unpredictable thing after the other. But now . . . all he needs is a glance and he's worked it all out: what star it is, what its spectrum is, how much it weighs, what it burns, whether it acts as a magnet or spews out stuff, and how far away the stuff that is spewed out stops, and how many light-years away there might be another star.

For him the expanse of void is like a cluster of tracks in a railway junction: these and no others are the gauges, points, diversions; you can take this or that route but you can't run in the middle or leap over the ballast. The same for the flow of time: every movement is slotted into a timetable which he knows by heart; he knows all the stops, delays, connections, deadlines, seasonal timetable variations. This had always been his dream for when he would retire from active service: to contemplate the ordered and regulated traffic that runs up and down the universe – like those pensioners who go to the station every day to see the trains arriving and departing – and to feel happy that he's no longer the one to be bounced around, laden with luggage and kids, amidst the indifferent comings and goings of those contraptions, each one whirling around on its own . . .

An ideal spot, then, from every point of view. In the four billion years they've been here, they've already settled in more or less, got to know a few people: folk who come and go, of course, that's the kind of place it is, but for Mrs Ggge, who loves variety so much, this ought to be a plus point. Now they have neighbours, on the same floor, Cavicchia they're called, who are really nice people: neighbours who help you out, pleasant neighbours you can rely on.

'I'd like to have seen you,' Eggg says to his wife, 'in the Clouds of Magellan: I bet you'd never have found such civilized people there!' (The thing is that Ggge, in her craving for other homes, even brings up extra-galactic constellations.)

But when someone has reached a certain age, there's no way you can change her ideas: if the Colonel hasn't managed it after so many years of marriage, he certainly won't manage it now. For instance, Ggge hears that their neighbours are leaving for Teramo. They're from the Abruzzi, the Cavicchias, and every year they go back to visit their relations. 'There,' says Ggge, 'everyone's leaving and we're always stuck here. I've got my mother whom I've not been to see for billions of years!'

'When will you ever understand that it's not the same thing?' old Eggg protests.

My great-grandmother, you see, lives in the Andromeda Galaxy. Yes, at one stage she always travelled with her daughter and son-in-law, but right at the point when this clutch of galaxies started to form, they lost sight of each other: she went one way and they went the other. (Even today Ggge still blames the Colonel: 'You should have paid more attention,' she claims. And he replies: 'Oh yes, I had nothing else to do at that particular time!' This is all he says, so as not to point out that his mother-in-law, a wonderful woman, of course, but as a travelling companion, well, she was one of those people specially designed to complicate things, especially at moments of upheaval.)

The Andromeda Galaxy is straight up here, above our

heads, but in between there are always a couple of billion light-years. For Ggge light-years seem like flea-jumps: she hasn't realized that space is a glue you get stuck in, just like time.

The other day, perhaps to cheer her up, Eggg said to her: 'Listen, Ggge, we won't necessarily stay here for ever. How many millennia have we been here? Four million? Well, let's say we must be halfway through our stay at the very least. Barely five million millennia will go by and the Sun will swell up until it swallows Mercury, Venus and Earth, and a series of cataclysms will start all over again, one after the other, at tremendous speed. Who knows where we'll land up? So, try to enjoy this small amount of peace that we have left.'

'Is that so?' she says, immediately interested. 'Well then, we mustn't be caught unawares. I'm going to start putting aside everything that won't go off and is not too cumbersome, so we can take it with us when the Sun explodes.'

And before the Colonel can stop her, she runs into the attic to see how many suitcases are there, what condition they're in, and to check they lock properly. (She claims to be thinking ahead by doing so: if you're flung out into space there is nothing worse than having to gather up the contents of suitcases that have been scattered in the midst of inter-stellar gas.)

'But what's your hurry?' Grandfather exclaims. 'We've still got several billion years in front of us, I told you!'

'Yes, but there are so many things to be done, Eggg, and I don't want to leave everything till the last minute. For example, I want to have some quince jam ready, in case we meet my sister Ddde, who's crazy about it: heaven knows how long it's been since she last tasted it, poor soul.'

'Your sister Ddde? Is she not the one on Sirius?'

I don't know how many there are in Grandma Ggge's

family, scattered here and there throughout every constellation: and at every cataclysm she expects she'll meet some of them. And in fact she's right: every time the Colonel explodes into space, he finds himself in the midst of newly acquired in-laws and cousins.

In short, there's no stopping her now: totally caught up in her preparations, she thinks about nothing else, and leaves the most urgent chores half done, because 'any moment now the Sun will finish'. Her husband is beside himself at this: he had dreamed so much about enjoying his retirement, allowing himself a rest amidst the ongoing conflagrations, letting the heavenly crucibles fry in their different fuels, sheltered from it all, contemplating the passing of centuries as if it were a uniform flow without any interruption, and now look what's happened: just when they'd reached more or less the exact mid-point of the holiday, Mrs Ggge starts getting him all worked up, with the suitcases flung open on the beds, the drawers turned upside down, shirts piled on top of each other; all the thousands of millions of billions of hours and days and weeks and months that he could have enjoyed as if the holiday were endless, from now on he'll have to live through them as though always on the point of leaving, just like when he was in active service, always waiting to be transferred. He won't be able to forget even for an instant that everything around him is temporary, temporary but always repeated, a mosaic of protons, electrons, neutrons, that will fragment and come together again indefinitely, a soup that will be stirred until it cools or heats up: in short, this holiday in the most temperate planet in the solar system is completely ruined.

'What do you think, Eggg, some of the crockery if it's well wrapped up, I think we'll be able to take that with us without it breaking . . .'

'No, what are you thinking of, Ggge, with all the space it takes up, think of how many other things you've got to get in . . .' And he is forced to take part as well, to offer an opinion on the various problems, to share her endless impatience, to live life as though it were always the day before leaving.

I know what this old pensioner is now yearning for, he's told us clearly so many times: to be eliminated from it all once and for all, to let the stars perish and re-form and perish again a hundred thousand times, with Mrs Ggge and all his sisters-in-law in the middle chasing and embracing each other, and losing their hatboxes and umbrellas and finding them and losing them again, and him having nothing to do with any of it, staying at the bottom of matter that has been squeezed and chewed and spat out and is no use for anything . . . the White Dwarves!

Old Eggg is not one to talk just for the sake of it: he has a very precise plan in mind. You know those White Dwarves, those stars that are very dense and inert, the residue of the most violent explosions, searing hot from the white heat of the nuclei of metals that have been crushed and compressed inside each other? The ones that continue to go slowly round forgotten orbits, gradually turning into cold, opaque coffins for elements to be buried in? 'Let Ggge go, let her go,' Eggg chuckles, 'let her get carried away by the spurts of flying electrons. I'll wait here, until the Sun and everything that goes round it is reduced to a decrepit dwarf star; I'll dig myself a niche amidst the hardest atoms, I'll tolerate flames of every colour, as long as I can finally get to that dead end, that siding, as long as I can reach the shore that nobody ever leaves again.'

And he looks up with his eyes already as they will be when he is on his White Dwarf, and when the rotating of galaxies which light up and extinguish blue, yellow and red fires, and condense and dispel rainclouds and dustclouds, will no longer be the occasion for the usual conjugal bickering but something that exists, that is there, that is what it is, full stop.

And yet I believe that, at least in the early days of his stay on that deserted and forgotten star, he will want to continue mentally arguing with Ggge. It won't be easy for him to stop. I seem to see him, alone in the void, as he travels through the expanse of light-years, but still quarrelling with his wife. That 'I told you so' and 'brilliant discovery' that accompanied the birth of the stars, the movement of galaxies, the cooling of planets, that 'you'll be happy now' and 'that's all you ever say' that marked every episode and phase and explosion of their quarrels and of heavenly cataclysms, that 'you always think you're right' and 'it's because you never listen to me' without which the history of the universe would not have for him any name or memory or flavour, that eternal conjugal bickering: if ever it should one day come to an end, what a feeling of desolation, what emptiness!

Solar Storm

The Sun is subject to continuous internal perturbations of its gaseous incandescent matter, which appear as upheavals that are visible on its surface: solar prominences that burst like bubbles, spots of diminished luminosity, intense flares from which sudden jets shoot up. When the Sun emits a cloud of electricized gas and this hits the Earth crossing the Van Allen radiation belts, magnetic storms occur as well as phenomena such as the Aurora Borealis.

There are people for whom the Sun provides a sense of security – *said Qfwfq* – stability, protection. Not me.

They say: 'Here it is, the Sun, it's always been there, it nourishes us, warms us, high above the clouds and the wind, radiant, always constant, the Earth goes round it subject to cataclysms and storms, and what about the Sun? It's always there in its place, calm and impassive.' Don't believe a word of it. What we call the Sun is nothing but a continuous detonation of gas, an explosion that's been lasting for five billion years and still hasn't stopped spewing up stuff; it's a typhoon of fire, shapeless and lawless, threatening constant aggression, totally unpredictable. And we're inside it: it's not true that we are here and the Sun is there; it's all a constant whirlpool of concentric currents with no intervals between them, a single tissue of matter, denser in some places, less dense in others, stemming from the same original cloud that has contracted and caught fire.

Of course, the amount of matter that the Sun chucks down here – particle fragments, shattered atoms – arranging itself along the lines of force of the magnet that passes from one pole to the other, has formed a kind of invisible shell enfolding the Earth, and we can even pretend that ours is a separate world, where causes and effects answer to certain laws, which if we know them we can master them, safe from the maelstrom of chaotic elements whirling around us.

I, for instance, have obtained a long-haul captain's licence and taken command of the steamer *Halley*: in the log I make note of the latitude, longitude, winds, data from the meteorological instruments, radio messages; I have learned to share your confidence in the fragile conventions that govern life on Earth. What more could I want? Our route is certain, the sea is calm, tomorrow we will be within sight of the familiar Welsh coasts, and in two days we will enter the tarry Mersey estuary, and cast anchor in the port of Liverpool, the end of our voyage. My life is regulated by a calendar that is plotted down to the smallest details: I count the days that separate me from the next voyage, and which I will spend in my house in the Lancashire countryside.

Mr Evans, the mate, appears at the door to the bridge, and says with a smile, 'Lovely Sun, Sir.' I nod, because really the Sun has an extraordinary clearness about it for the time of year and the latitude; if I sharpen my gaze (I who have the gift of being able to look straight into the Sun without being blinded) I can clearly make out the corona and chromosphere and the position of the sunspots, and I notice . . . I notice things that it is pointless to tell you people about: cataclysms that are even at this moment shattering its fiery depths, continents that are collapsing in flames, incandescent oceans swelling and overflowing out of the crucible, turning into currents of invisible radiation heading towards the Earth, almost as fast as light.

The choking voice of the helmsman Adams sounds in my loudspeaker: 'The compass needle, Sir, the compass needle! What the hell is going on? It's going round and round like a roulette wheel!'

'Is he drunk?!' Evans exclaims, but I know that everything is under control, that *it is now that everything starts to be under control*, I know that in a second Simmons the radio operator will rush in here. Here he is arriving, his eyes popping out of their sockets: he almost knocks Evans down on the threshold.

'Everything's dead, Sir! I was listening to the semi-final of the boxing match and it's all gone dead! I can't establish radio contact with any station!'

'What shall I do, Captain?' Adams shouts into the phone. 'The compass has gone mad!'

Evans is as white as a sheet.

This is the moment to make my superiority felt. 'Calm down, everyone, we've run into a magnetic storm. There's nothing to do. Commend your souls to whatever it is you believe in, and keep calm.'

I go out on to the fo'c'sle. The sea is still, hardened to enamel by the Sun at the zenith. In this calm of the elements, the *Halley* has become a mass of blind iron that all the arts and genius of man are powerless to control. We are sailing in the Sun, inside a solar explosion where neither compasses nor radios are of any use. We have always been in the Sun's control, even though we almost always managed to forget it and to think that we were sheltered from its whims.

It was then that I saw her. I looked up to the foremast: she was up there. She was holding on to the foreyard, hanging in the air like a flag unfurling for miles and miles around, her hair flying in the wind, and her whole body flowing like her hair because it was made of the same pulviscular substance, her arms with their thin wrists and their ample shoulders, her loins sickle-shaped like a crescent moon, her breasts like a cloud covering the ship's quarterdeck, and the spirals of her drapery mingling with the smoke from the funnel and with the sky above. All this I could see in the invisible electricization of the air; or at times it was just her face, like an aerial figurehead, the head of a monumental Medusa, with crackling eyes and locks: Rah had managed to catch up with me.

'Are you there, Rah?' I said. 'You've tracked me down.'

'Why did you hide down here?'

'I wanted to see if there was another way of being.'

'And is there?'

'Here I guide boats on routes marked out with the compass, I can orientate myself with this compass, my instruments pick up radio waves, everything that happens has a reason.'

'And you believe that?'

From the radio cabin we could hear Simmons's curses, as he tried to pick up any station at all in the crackle of electric charges.

'No, but I like to act as if it was like that, to play the game right to the end,' I said to Rah.

'And when you see that it's impossible?'

'One just drifts. But we're always ready to seize control again at any moment.'

'Are you speaking to yourself, Sir?' It was Evans who was always poking his sallow face in.

I tried to assert myself. 'Go and give Adams a hand, Mr Evans. The oscillations of the magnetic needle will tend to repeat themselves obeying certain constants. One can work out an approximate route, as we wait to orientate ourselves by the stars, tonight.'

At night, the streaks of an Aurora Borealis arched up into the sky's vault above us as though on the back of a tiger. With her flaming locks and sumptuous raiment, Rah paraded above us, hanging from the yards. Finding our bearings again was out of the question.

'We've ended up at the Pole,' said Adams, just to show he had some spirit; he was well aware that magnetic storms can cause an Aurora Borealis at any latitude.

I watched Rah in the night: her gorgeous hair, her jewels, her flashing clothes. 'You're dressed for a ball,' I said.

'I have to properly celebrate finding you again,' she replied.

For me there was nothing to celebrate; I had fallen back under her old spell; my patient plan had failed. 'You do get more and more beautiful,' I admitted.

'Why did you escape? You've ended up in this hole, let yourself get caught in a trap, reduced to the dimensions of a world where everything is limited.'

'I am here of my own free will,' I retorted, but I knew she would not understand. For her our life was in the freedom of space criss-crossed by rays of light, amidst the bursts of solar explosions that constantly buffeted us this way and that, outside all dimensions and forms.

'Still your old game of pretending it's you who choose, decide, determine,' said Rah. 'Your old flaw.'

'And you? How did you get here?' I asked. Was the ionosphere not an impregnable barrier? So often I had heard Rah graze against it like a butterfly beating its wings against the window of a room. 'You still haven't told me how you got in.'

She shrugged. 'A burst of rays, a hole in the ceiling; now here I am down to get you.'

'To get me? But it's you who are trapped. How will you get back out?'

'I'll stay here. I'm staying with you,' she said.

'Disaster, Sir!' Simmons was racing along the deck towards me. 'All the radio installations on board have packed up!'

Evans was hidden behind a hatchway, and he seized the radio operator by his arm; he was saying – I worked this out from his gestures – that it was pointless to turn to me, the magnetic storm had addled my brain, that I talked to myself, staring up at the masts.

I tried to re-establish my authority: 'The ocean is crossed by powerful electric currents,' I explained, 'the tension in the wires increases, the valves go, it's all normal . . .' But by now they were looking at me with eyes that no longer showed any respect for my rank.

The next day the effects of the magnetic storm had ceased to be felt all over the ocean except on board our ship, and for a wide area around. The *Halley* continued to drag Rah along behind it, languidly reclining in the air, hanging on by a finger to the radar, the lightning conductor or the smokestack. The compass was like a fish floundering in a tub, the radio continued to boil like a pan of chickpeas. The ships that had been sent to our aid could not find us: their instruments broke down as soon as they got close.

At night luminous streaks hovered above the *Halley*; it was an Aurora Borealis all to ourselves, as though it was our flag. This was what allowed the aid ships to track us down. Without getting too close in case they got infected by what seemed a mysterious magnetic disease, they guided us into the Liverpool roadstead.

The story began to spread through every harbour: wherever the captain of the *Halley* went, he carried around with him electric storms and an Aurora Borealis. Furthermore, my officers told everyone around that I had links with invisible powers. Naturally I lost the command of the *Halley*, and there was no way of obtaining other captaincies. Luckily, with the savings from my years of sailing I had bought an old house in the country, in Lancashire, where – as I said – I used to stay between one voyage and another, and where I could devote myself to my beloved experiments in the measurement and prediction of natural phenomena. I had filled the house with precision instruments I had made myself, among which there was a monochrome heliograph. Every time I got back on shore, I could not wait to lock myself away with all those gadgets.

So I retired to Lancashire, with my wife Rah. Immediately the televisions of other house-owners started to go wrong, for an area of several miles around. There was no way of getting any broadcast into focus: on the screen black and white streaks whirled around as though a flea-ridden zebra had come on.

I knew there were rumours about us but I wasn't worried: it seemed they were annoyed above all by my experiments; they were still living in the time when my machines actually worked; maybe they did not yet suspect anything about my wife – they had never seen her, they didn't know that in our house no device could work any more, that we did not even have electric light.

Nevertheless, the one thing you could see coming from our windows at night was the light of candles and this gave our house a sinister air: in those days many people stayed up at night to see the flashes of the Aurora Borealis which had become a feature of our region; no wonder suspicions about us increased. Subsequently migrating birds could be seen losing their sense of direction: storks arrived in the middle of winter, and albatrosses swooped down on the moors.

One day I received a visit from the vicar, the Reverend Collins.

'I would like to have a word with you, Captain –' and he gave a little cough – 'about certain phenomena which have been taking place in the parish, you know? And about certain rumours that are going around . . .'

He was on the threshold. I invited him in. He was unable to conceal his amazement at seeing everything in pieces in our house: shards of glass, dynamo brushes, bits of nautical maps, everything in chaos.

'But this is not the house I visited last Easter . . .' he muttered.

I too was for a second seized by a nostalgia for my ordered, well-equipped and fully functioning laboratory, which I had let him visit the previous year. (The Reverend Collins was very careful to keep courteous relations with the local inhabitants, especially with those who never set foot in church.)

I recovered my composure. 'Yes, well, we've changed the layout a bit . . .'

The vicar immediately came to the point of his visit. All the strange things that happened after I had returned to live there, *as a married man* (he emphasized this phrase), were linked in public opinion with my person, or with Mrs Qfwfq (I gave a start), though nobody had yet had the good fortune, he said, to have met her. I said nothing in reply. 'You know what people are like around here,' the Reverend Collins went on, 'there's still so much ignorance, so much superstition . . . One cannot, of course, believe everything they say . . .' And it was not clear whether he had come to apologize for the hostility of his parishioners towards me, or to establish how much truth there was in what they said. 'There are completely groundless rumours. Just imagine what I've heard said: that your wife has been seen at night flying above the rooftops and swinging on the television aerials. "What?" I asked, "and what does this Mrs Qfwfq look like? Like an imp, an elf?" "No," they replied, "she is a giantess who is always stretched out in the air like a cloud . . ."'

'No, that's impossible, I assure you,' I began, though I was not quite clear what I was trying to deny. 'Rah has to lie out because of her physical condition . . . you understand? And that is why we prefer not to socialize . . . but she stays at home . . . Rah is nearly always in the house now . . . If you want, I'll introduce her to you . . .'

Naturally the Reverend Collins leaped at the chance. I had to lead him to the garage, a big, old garage-cum-storehouse which at one time, when this property was a farm, had been used for threshing-machines and for drying hay. There were no windows, light filtered in through the cracks, and you could see the dust-beams hanging in the air. And in the midst of the dustclouds Rah was clearly visible. She took up the whole of the garage, lying on her side, curled up into a ball, one hand holding her knee, and the other stroking a Rutherford coil as though it was an Angora cat. She kept her head down because the ceiling was a bit low for her; her eyes were half closed on account of the sparks that showered from the copper wire of the coil each time her hand rose up to stifle a yawn.

'Poor thing, shut up like this, she's a bit bored, she's not really used to it,' I tried to explain, but it was something else I would have liked to articulate: the pride that filled my heart at that sight. This is what I would have said, had there been anyone able to understand me: 'See how she's changed: when she came here, she was a fury; who would ever have thought I'd be able to live with this tempest, to contain it and tame it?'

Lost in such thoughts, I had almost forgotten about the

vicar. I turned round. He was no longer there. He'd escaped! There he was racing away, jumping the hedges, vaulting over them with his umbrella.

Now I'm waiting for the worst. I know that my neighbours have banded together in armed gangs, surrounding the hill. I hear the dogs barking, people shouting to each other, every now and then the rustling of leaves from a hideout where they are spying on me from a hedge. They are about to attack the house, perhaps to set it on fire: I can see a number of lit torches scattered all around. I don't know whether they are intending to take us alive, or lynch us, or kill us off in the flames. Perhaps it's my wife they want to burn as a witch; or maybe they have realized that she will never allow herself to be taken?

I look at the Sun: it looks as if it has entered into a phase of tumultuous activity; the sun-spots are diminishing; bubbles that are a hundred times more bright are spreading all over it. Now I open the garage and allow the light to stream in. I wait for a more powerful explosion to fling an electric spark into space, and that way the Sun will stretch out its arms all the way here, it will rend the veil that separates us, will come and take back its daughter, and let her return to her headlong runs over the endless plains of outer space.

Soon all the televisions in the area will start working again, the images of detergents and beautiful girls will occupy the screen again, these gangs of persecutors will disperse, everyone will go back to their ration of daily rationality. I too will be able to reassemble my laboratory, go back to the way of life I had chosen, before this enforced interruption.

But do not think that, even with Rah on my back, I have ever strayed from the line of conduct I had set for myself; do not believe that I surrendered at any point, seeing that I could not escape from Rah, that she was too strong. I had come up

with a plan that was even more difficult, to replace the one
that had been forestalled by Rah, a plan that depended on
Rah, or in spite of Rah, or rather because of Rah, or more
accurately a plan created out of love for Rah, the only way
to bring to fulfilment the love between the two of us: to
plan, in the midst of that shattering of instruments, in that
dustcloud of vibrations, other instruments, other measurements, other calculations that would allow us to know and
control the interplanetary sun-storm that pervades and shakes
and judders and conditions us, something beyond our illusory
ionized umbrella. That was what I wanted. And now that
she is rising like a lightning-bolt towards the sphere of fire,
and I am coming back to being master of myself, I begin to
gather the fragments of my machines. This is the point when
I see how pathetic are the powers that I have recovered.

My persecutors have not yet noticed anything. Here they
are arriving, armed with pitchforks and rifles and sticks.

'Are you happy now?' I shout. 'She's not here any more!
Go back to your compasses, to your television programmes!
Everything is in order! Rah's gone. But you don't realize
what you've lost. You don't know what my plan was, my
plan for you, you don't know what Rah's presence might
have meant for us, disastrous, unbearable Rah, for me and
for you who are about to lynch me!'

They've stopped. They don't understand what I'm saying,
they don't believe me, they don't know whether to be afraid
or be encouraged by it. In any case, I don't understand what
I've said either, I don't believe myself, I don't know whether
to feel relieved either, and I'm afraid too.

Shells and Time

Documentation on life on Earth, which is very scarce for the Precambrian period, suddenly starts to become extremely plentiful from about 520 million years ago, for in the Cambrian and Ordovician periods living organisms begin to secrete calcareous shells that will be preserved as fossils in geological strata.

Who do you think admitted you to that dimension in which you are all immersed, so much so that you believe you were born into it and for it, who do you think opened the breach for you? It was me – *Qfwfq's voice could be heard exclaiming, from underneath a shell* – me, a lowly mollusc condemned to my moment-by-moment existence, a prisoner of an eternal present. It's pointless you pretending to understand; you can't guess what I'm talking about. I'm talking of time. If it hadn't been for me, time would never have existed.

Because, listen carefully, I had no idea what time might be like, and I didn't even have any idea that something like time could ever exist. Days and nights crashed over me like waves, all interchangeable, identical or marked by totally fortuitous differences, a toing and froing where it was impossible to establish any sense or norm. However, in constructing my shell, the intention I had for it was already in some sense connected with time, an intention to separate my present from the corrosive dissolution of all presents, to keep it out, to set it apart. The present landed on me with so many different aspects I could not establish any succession: waves, nights, afternoons, ebbs, winters, quarters of the moon, tides, summer heatwaves; my fear was of losing myself in all this, of splitting myself up into as many myselves as there were bits of the present that were dumped on me, layer after layer, and that for all I knew might all have been simultaneous, each one inhabited by a bit of myself that was contemporaneous with all the other bits.

I had to start by fixing some signs in this immeasurable continuum, by establishing a series of intervals; in other words, numbers. The calcareous matter I secreted, making it whirl like a spiral on top of itself, was precisely that, something that continued uninterrupted; but meantime, at every turn of the spiral, it separated the edge of one spiral from the edge of another, so that if I wanted to count something I could start by counting these spirals. In short, what I wanted to construct was a time that belonged to me alone, regulated solely by myself, self-contained: a clock that did not have to report to anyone what it was measuring. I would have liked to construct an extremely long, unbroken shell-time, to continue my spiral without ever stopping.

I went to it with all my strength, and of course I wasn't the only one: at the same time, many others were trying to build their own endless shells. Whether I or someone else succeeded was not important: all it needed was for one of us to manage to make an endless spiral and time would exist, that would be time. But now I come to the most difficult thing of all to say (also the most difficult thing to reconcile with the fact that I am here speaking to you): to talk of time, that thing that never stays up, that unravels, that collapses like a bank of sand, that is as multifaceted as saline crystals, as ramified as a coral reef, as porous as a sponge (and I am not going to tell you which hole, what breach I went through to get all the way to here). The infinite spiral proved impossible to make: the shell grew and grew, and at a certain point stopped – that was it, finished. Another one started up somewhere else, thousands of shells started every second, thousands and thousands continued to grow in every phase of the winding of the spiral, and all of them sooner or later would suddenly stop, and the waves would drag away an empty container.

It was wasted effort on our part: time refused to last, it was a friable substance, destined to crumble into pieces; ours were only illusions of time that lasted as long as the length of a tiny shell-spiral, splinters of time that were detached and different from each other, one here and another there, not linkable or comparable to each other.

And on the remains of our unstinting labour sand would settle, sand which, at irregular gusts of wind, sand-time would lift up and let fall, burying the empty shells beneath successive layers in the belly of plateaux that had emerged and were subsequently submerged when the seas reconquered the continents and covered them with new showers of empty shells. Thus the substance of the world was made up of the substance of our defeat.

How could we have thought that that cemetery of all our shells was the real shell, the one we had tried to construct with all our strength, and thought we had failed to construct? Now it is clear that the construction of time consisted precisely in the very defeat of our attempts to construct it; except that we had not worked for ourselves but for you. We molluscs, who first had the intention of lasting, have given our kingdom, time, to the most volatile race of inhabitants of the temporary, namely humanity: had it not been for us they would never have thought of it. It needed the cross-section of the Earth's crust to throw up our shells, which we had abandoned some hundred, three hundred, five hundred million years before, for the vertical dimension of time to open up to you and release you from the continual cycle of the stars' circuit in which you continue to pigeonhole the course of your fragmentary existences.

I'm not saying that you too don't take some of the credit; after all it was you who discovered how to read what was written between the lines of the Earth's notebook (there, I'm using your usual metaphor of things that are written; there's no getting away from it: this is the proof that we are in your territory now, not mine), it was you who managed to spell out the distorted characters of our stammering alphabet that lay scattered amidst thousand-year intervals of silence, you who extracted from all this a whole coherent discourse, a discourse *about you*. But tell me, how would you have been able to read in the middle of all that stuff, if we hadn't written there, though we didn't know what it was we were writing, or rather, if we, while knowing full well what would happen, had not wanted to write (I may as well continue with your metaphors while I'm at it), to signpost, to act as a sign, to act as a relationship or link between ourselves and others, to be something which, existing as it is in and of itself, is nevertheless happy to be something different for others . . .

Someone had to start not so much to construct as to become, to become something, to come into being in what it was making, to ensure that everything that was left or buried was a sign of something else, the imprint of fish-bones in clay, the carbonized petroliferous forests, the Texas dinosaur's footprint in the mud of the Cretaceous period, the splintered pebbles of the Palaeolithic period, the mammoth's carcass found in the Beresovka tundra with the remains of the buttercups it had grazed on twelve thousand years previously still in its teeth, the Venus of Willendorf, the ruins of Ur, the Dead Sea Scrolls, the Lombard spear-tip that popped up at Torcello, the Templars' temple, the treasure of the Incas, the Winter Palace and the Smolny Institute, the car cemetery . . .

Starting with our interrupted spirals, you have put together a continuous spiral you call history. I don't know if you've got that much to be happy about; I can't make any judgement on this thing that isn't mine: for me this is only time as a footprint, the trace of our failed enterprise, the reverse of time, a stratification of remains and shells and necropolises and registers, of what has been saved as it perishes, of what by stopping has managed to reach you. Your history is the opposite of ours, the opposite of the history of what by moving has not arrived, of what has been lost in order to survive: the hand that modelled the vase, the bookcases that burned at Alexandria, the way the scribe spoke, the flesh of the mollusc that secreted the shell . . .

World Memory

Here's why I called for you, Müller. Now that my resignation has been accepted, you are to be my successor: your appointment as director is imminent. Please don't pretend this is such a big surprise: the rumour has been doing the rounds for some time and I'm sure you will have heard it yourself. Then, there's no doubt that of the young élite in our organization, you are the most competent, the one who knows, you could say, all the secrets of our work. Or so at least it would seem. Allow me to explain: I am not speaking to you on my own initiative, I was told to do so by our superiors. There are only one or two things you don't yet know, Müller, and the time has come to fill you in. You imagine, as does everybody else for that matter, that our organization has for many years been preparing the greatest document centre ever conceived, an archive that will bring together and catalogue everything that is known about every person, animal and thing, by way of a general inventory not only of the present but of the past too, of everything that has ever been since time began, in short a general and simultaneous history of everything, or rather a catalogue of everything moment by moment. And that is indeed what we are working on and we can feel satisfied that the project is well advanced: not only have we already put the contents of the most important libraries of the world, and likewise the archives and museums and newspaper annals of every nation, on our punch cards, but also a great deal of documentation gathered ad hoc, person by person, place by place. And all this material is being put through a reduction process that brings it down to the essential, condensed, miniaturized minimum, a process whose limits have yet to be established; just as all existing and possible images are being filed in minute spools of microfilm, while microscopic bobbins of magnetic tape hold all sounds that have ever been and ever can be recorded. What we are planning to build is a centralized archive of humankind, and we are attempting to store it in the smallest possible space, along the lines of the individual memories in our brains.

But it's hardly worth my while repeating this to someone who won admission to our organization with a project entitled 'The British Museum in a Nutshell'. Relatively speaking, you have only been with us a few years, but by now you are as familiar with the workings of our laboratories as I myself, who am or was the foundation's director. I would never have left this job, I assure you, if I still felt I had the energy. But since my wife's mysterious disappearance, I have sunk into a depression from which I still have not recovered. It is only right that our superiors – accepting what are anyway my own wishes – should decide to replace me. Hence it falls to me to inform you of those official secrets which have so far been kept from you.

What you are not aware of is the true purpose of our work. It has to do with the end of the world, Müller. We are working in expectation of an imminent disappearance of life on Earth. We are working so that all may not have been in vain, so that we can transmit all we know to others, even though we don't know who they are or what they know.

May I offer you a cigar? Forecasts that the Earth will not

be able to support life, or at least human life, for much longer should not distress us unduly. We have all been aware for some time that the Sun is halfway through its lifespan: however well things went, in four or five billion years everything would be over. That is, in a short while the problem would have presented itself anyway; what is new is that the deadline is now very much nearer, we have no time to lose, that's all. Obviously the extinction of our species is not a happy prospect, but crying about it offers only the same empty consolation as when we mourn the death of an individual. (I'm still thinking of my dear Angela, do forgive my emotion.) There are doubtless millions of planets supporting life forms similar to our own; it hardly matters whether our image lives on in them or whether it be their descendants rather than our own who carry on where we left off. What does matter is that we give them our memory, the general memory put together by the organization of which you, Müller, are about to be made director.

No need to be overawed; the scope of your work will remain as it is at present. The system for communicating our memory to other planets is being designed by another sector of the organization; we already have our work cut out, we needn't even concern ourselves whether they decide on optical or acoustic media. It may even be that it's not a question of transmitting information at all, but of putting it in a safe place, beneath the Earth's crust: wandering through space the remains of our planet may one day be found and explored by extra-galactic archaeologists. Nor do we even have to worry about what code or codes will be chosen: there's a sector exclusively dedicated to looking for a way of making our stock of information intelligible whatever linguistic system the others may use. For you, now that you know, I can assure you that nothing has changed, except the responsibility that rests on your shoulders. That's what I wanted to talk over with you a little.

What will the human race be at the moment of its extinction? A certain quantity of information about itself and the world, a finite quantity, given that it will no longer be able to propagate itself and grow. For a certain time, the universe enjoyed an excellent opportunity to gather and elaborate information; and to create it, to bring forth information there where in other circumstances there would have been no one to inform and nothing to inform them about: such was life on Earth, and above all human life, its memory, its inventions for communicating and remembering. Our organization can guarantee that this body of information will not be lost, regardless of whether it is actually passed on to others or not. The duty of the director is to make sure that nothing is left out, because what is left out is as if it had never been. At the same time it will also be your duty to treat any element that might end up causing confusion, or obscuring more essential elements, as if it had never been – everything, that is, that rather than increasing the body of information would generate pointless clutter and clatter. What matters is the general model constituted by the whole of our information, from which further information, which we are not giving or perhaps don't have, may be deduced. In short, by not giving certain kinds of information, one is giving more than one would if one did. The final result of our work will be a model in which everything counts as information, even what isn't there. Only then will it be possible to say what really mattered out of all that has been, or rather what really was, since the final state of our archive will constitute at once that which is, has been and will be, and all else is nothing.

Of course there are moments in our work – you will have experienced them too, Müller – when one is tempted to imagine that the only things that matter are those which elude our archives, that only what passes without leaving any trace truly exists, while everything held in our records is dead detritus, the leftovers, the waste. The moment comes when a yawn, a buzzing fly, an itch seem the only treasure there is, precisely because completely unusable, occurring once and for all and then promptly forgotten, spared the monotonous destiny of being stored in the world memory. Who could rule out the possibility that the universe consists of the discontinuous network of moments that cannot be recorded, and that our organization does nothing but establish their negative image, a frame around emptiness and meaninglessness?

But the quirk of our profession is this: that as soon as we concentrate on something, we immediately want to include it in our files; with the result, I confess, that I have often found myself cataloguing yawns, pimples, unhelpful associations of ideas, little tunes I've whistled, and then hiding them among the mass of more useful information. For the position of director which you are about to be offered brings with it this privilege: the right to put one's personal imprint on the world memory. Please understand me, Müller: I'm not talking about arbitrary liberties or an abuse of power, but of an indispensable element in our work. A mass of coldly objective and incontrovertible information would run the risk of presenting a far from truthful picture, of falsifying what is most specific in any situation. Suppose we received from another planet a message made up of pure facts, facts of such clarity as to be merely obvious: we wouldn't pay attention, we would hardly even notice; only a message containing something unexpressed, something doubtful and partially indecipherable, would break through the threshold of our consciousness and demand to be received and interpreted.

We must bear this in mind: the director's task is that of giving the whole of the data gathered and selected by our offices that slight subjective slant, that touch of the opinionated, the rash, which it needs in order to be true. That's what I wanted to warn you about, before handing over: in the material gathered to date you will notice here and there the mark of my own hand – an extremely delicate one, you understand – a sprinkling of appraisals, of facts withheld, even lies.

Only in a superficial sense can lies be said to exclude the truth; you will be aware that in many cases lies – the patient's lies to the psychoanalyst, for example – are just as revealing as the truth, if not more so; and the same will be true for those who eventually interpret our message. What I'm telling you now, Müller, I'm no longer telling you because instructed to do so by our superiors, but drawing on my own personal experience, speaking as colleague to colleague, man to man. Listen: the lie is the real information we have to pass on. Hence I didn't wish to deny myself a discreet use of lying where it didn't complicate the message, but on the contrary simplified it. When it came to information about myself in particular, I felt it legitimate to indulge in all kinds of details that are not true (I don't see how this could bother anyone). My life with Angela, for example: I described it as I would have liked it to be, a great love story, where Angela and I appear as two eternal lovebirds happy in the midst of every kind of adversity, passionate, faithful. It wasn't exactly like that, Müller: Angela married me out of convenience and immediately regretted it, our life was one long trail of sourness and subterfuge. But what does it matter what happened day by day? In the world memory Angela's image is definitive, perfect, nothing can taint it and I will always be the most enviable husband there ever was.

At first all I had to do was to apply some cosmetics to the

data our everyday life provided. But there came the point when the facts I found myself confronted with as I watched Angela day by day (then spied on her, finally followed her) became increasingly contradictory and ambiguous, such as to justify the worst suspicions. What was I to do, Müller? Muddy that image of Angela at once so clear, so easy to transmit, so loved and lovable, was I to make it incomprehensible, to darken the most brilliant light in all our archives? I didn't hesitate, day after day I eliminated these facts. But I was constantly afraid that some clue, some intimation, some hint from which one might deduce what she, what Angela did and was in this transitory life, might still be hovering around her definitive image. I spent the days in the laboratory, selecting, cancelling, omitting. I was jealous, Müller: not jealous of the transitory Angela – that was a game I'd already lost – but jealous of that information-Angela who would live as long as the universe itself.

If the information-Angela was not to be contaminated, the first thing that must be done was to stop the living Angela from constantly superimposing herself on that image. It was then that Angela disappeared and all searches for her proved vain. It would be pointless, Müller, for me to tell you now how I managed to get rid of the body piece by piece. Please, keep calm, these details are of no importance as far as our work is concerned, since in the world memory I remain that happy husband and later inconsolable widower you all know. But this didn't bring peace of mind: the information-Angela was still part of an information system where certain data might lend themselves to being interpreted – whether because of disturbances in transmission, or some malevolence on the part of the decoder – as ambiguous conjectures, insinuations, slander. I decided to destroy all references to people Angela could have had relationships with. I was sad about that, since there will now be no trace of some of our colleagues in the world memory; it will be as though they had never existed.

You imagine I'm telling you all this in order to seek your complicity, Müller. But that's not the case. I feel obliged to inform you of the extreme measures I am being forced to take to make sure that information relative to everybody who might have been my wife's lover is excluded from the archives. I am not worried about any repercussions on myself; the few years that remain for me to live are a trifle compared to the eternity I am used to measuring things against; and the person I really was has already been definitively established and consigned to the punch cards.

If there is nothing that needs correcting in the world memory, the only thing left to do is to correct reality where it doesn't agree with that memory. Just as I cancelled the existence of my wife's lover from the punch cards, so I must cancel him from the world of the living. Which is why I am now pulling out my gun and pointing it at you, Müller, why I'm squeezing the trigger, killing you.

From *Cosmicomics Old and New*

Nothing and Not Much

'Calculations made by the physicist Alan Guth of the Stanford Linear Accelerator Center suggest that the universe was created literally from nothing in an extremely short space of time: a second divided by a billion billion billions' (from the Washington Post, *3 June 1984).*

If I tell you I remember it – *began Qfwfq* – you will object that in nothingness, nothing can remember anything, nor be remembered by anything, which is one reason why you won't be able to believe so much as a word of what I am about to tell you. Tough arguments to knock down, I admit. All I can tell you is that the moment there was something, there being nothing else, that something was the universe, and since it hadn't been there before, there was a before when it wasn't and an afterwards when it was; from that moment on, I'm saying, time began, and with time memory, and with memory someone who remembered, that is to say myself, or that something that later I would understand was myself. Let's get this straight: it's not that I remembered how I was when there was nothing, because there was no time then, and there was no me; but I realized now that, even if I didn't know I was there, still I had a place I could have been, I mean the universe; whereas before, even had I wanted to, I wouldn't have known where to put myself, and that's a pretty big difference, and it was precisely this difference between the before and the after that I remembered. In short, you must recognize that my reasoning is logical too, and what's more doesn't err on the side of the simplistic like your own.

So let me explain. One can't even say for sure that what there was then, really was: the particles, or rather the ingredients with which the particles would later be made, existed in the virtual sense: that kind of existence where if you're there you're there, and if you're not there you can begin to count on being there and then see what happens. We felt this was a fine thing, and indeed it was, because it's only if you begin to exist in the virtual sense, to fluctuate in a field of probability, to borrow and return charges of energy still entirely hypothetical, that sooner or later you may find yourself existing in reality, wrapping around yourself, one might say, a scrap, be it ever so small, of space-time, as happened to an ever-increasing number of I-don't-know-whats – let's call them neutrinos because it's a nice name, though at the time no one had ever even dreamed of them – bobbing one on top of another in a torrid soup of infinite heat, thick as a glue of infinite density, that swelled up in a time so infinitely brief that it had nothing to do with time at all – since of course time hadn't yet had the time to show what it would later become – and as it swelled it produced space where no one had ever known what space was. Thus the universe, from being an infinitesimal pimple in the smoothness of nothing expanded in a flash to the size of a proton, then an atom, then a pinpoint, then a pinhead, then a teaspoon, then a hat, then an umbrella . . .

No, I'm going too fast; or too slow, I don't know: because this expansion of the universe was infinitely fast yet started out from a beginning so deeply buried in nothing that to push its way out and peep over the threshold of space and time required a wrench of such violence as not to be measurable in terms of space and time. Let's say that, to tell everything that happened in the first second of the history of the universe, I should have to put together an account so long that the whole subsequent duration of the universe with its millions of centuries past and future would not be enough; whereas everything that came afterwards I could polish off in five minutes.

Naturally enough our belonging to a universe without precedent or terms of comparison very soon became a cause of pride, boasting, infatuation. The split-second yawning of unimaginable distances, the profusion of corpuscles squirting all over the place – hadrons, baryons, mesons, a quark or two – the reckless speed of time, taken all together these things gave us a sense of invincibility, of power, of pride, and at the same time of conceit, as if all this was no more than our due. The only comparison we could draw was with the nothing that had come before: and we put the thought behind us, as of something petty and wretched, deserving only of commiseration, or scorn. Every thought we had embraced the whole, disdained the parts; the whole was our element, and it included time too, all time, the future holding thrall over the past in terms both of quantity and fullness. Our destiny lay in more, more and more, and we couldn't think, even fleetingly, of less: from now on we would go from more to even more, from additions to multiplications to exponentials, without ever slowing down or stopping.

That there was an underlying insecurity in this excitement, a craving almost to cancel out the shadow of our so recent origins, is something I have perhaps only recently come to appreciate, in the light of all I have learned since; unless it was already secretly gnawing away inside me even then. For despite our certainty that the whole was our natural habitat, it was nevertheless true that we had come from nothing, that we had only just raised ourselves up from absolute deprivation, that only a fragile sliver of space-time lay between ourselves and our previous condition of being without substance, extension or duration. I would be seized by fleeting but intense sensations of precariousness, as if this whole that was struggling to develop were unable to hide its intrinsic fragility, the underlying emptiness to which we might well return with the same speed with which we had emerged. Hence my impatience with the universe's indecisiveness in taking on a form, as if I couldn't wait for that vertiginous expansion to stop, so I could discover its limits, for better or worse, but mainly so that its existence should stabilize; and hence too my fear, a fear I could not stifle, that as soon as the expansion let up, the contraction phase would begin at once with an equally precipitate return to non-being.

I reacted by leaping to the other extreme: 'Completeness! Completeness!' I proclaimed far and wide; 'The future!' I cheered; 'I want immensity!' I insisted, shoving my way through that confused mill of forces; 'Let potential be potent!' I incited; 'Let the act act! Let probabilities be proven!' I already felt that the barrages of particles (or were they only radiations?) included every possible form and force, and the more I looked forward to being surrounded by a universe populated with active presences, the more I felt that those presences were affected by a criminal inertia, an abnegatory abulia.

Some of these presences were, well, let's say they were feminine, I mean they had propulsive charges complementary to my own; one in particular attracted my attention; haughty and reserved, she would establish a field of languid, long-limbed forces around her. To get her to notice me, I redoubled my exhibitions of excitement at the prodigality of the universe, flaunted a nonchalant ease in drawing on cosmic resources, as if they'd always been available to me, and thrust ahead in space and time as though always expecting things to improve. Convinced that Nugkta (I call her by the name I would learn later on) was different from all the others, in the sense of more aware of what it meant to *be*, and to participate in something that *is*, I tried by every means available to distinguish myself from the hesitant mass of those who were slow to get used to this idea. The result was that I made myself tiresome and unpleasant to everybody, without this bringing me any closer to her.

I was getting everything wrong. It didn't take me long to realize that Nugkta didn't appreciate my extravagant efforts at all; on the contrary she took care not to give me any sign of attention, apart from the occasional snort of annoyance. She went on keeping herself to herself, somewhat listlessly, as though crouched with her chin on her knees, protruding elbows hugging long folded legs (don't misunderstand me: I describe the position she would have assumed if one could have spoken then of knees, legs and elbows; or better still, it was the universe that was crouched over itself, and for those in it there was no other position to assume; just that some, for example Nugkta, did it more naturally). Lavishly, I scattered the treasures of the universe at her feet, but the way she accepted them it was as if to say: 'Is that all?' At first, I thought this indifference was affectation, then I realized she wanted to teach me something, to suggest I assume a more controlled attitude. My wild enthusiasm must have made her think me ingenuous, mindless, a greenhorn.

There was nothing for it but to change my attitude, behaviour, style. My relationship with the universe should be the practical, factual approach of one capable of assessing the objective value of the evolution of any given thing, however immense, without letting it go to his head. That was how I hoped to come across to her, more convincing, promising, trustworthy. Did I succeed? Not a bit of it. The more I banked on solidity, on what was feasible, quantifiable, the more I felt I was coming across as a braggart, a con man.

In the end I began to see the light: there was only one thing worthy of admiration as she saw it, only one value, and that was nothingness. It wasn't that she had a low opinion of me, but of the universe. Everything in existence carried some original defect within itself: being, to her mind, was a depressing, vulgar degeneration of non-being.

To say that this discovery upset me would be an understatement: it was an affront to all my beliefs, my craving for completeness, my immense expectations. What greater incompatibility could there be than between myself and someone with a nostalgia for nothingness? Not that she was without her reasons (my weakness for her was such that I struggled to understand them): it was true that there was an absoluteness about the void, a rigour, a presence such as to make everything that claimed to have the requisites for existence seem approximate, limited, shaky; if one starts to draw comparisons between what is and what is not, it is the poorer qualities of the former that strike you, the impurities, the flaws; in short, you can only really feel safe with nothingness. That said, how should I react? Turn my back on the whole, plunge into the void again? It was hardly possible! Once set in motion, the process by which non-being was becoming being couldn't be stopped: the void belonged to a past that was irremediably over now.

One of the many advantages of being was that it allowed us, from the climax of our achieved fullness, to indulge in a moment's regret for the nothingness we had lost, a moment's melancholy contemplation of the negative fullness of the void. In that sense I could go along with Nugkta's inclinations, indeed no one would be more capable than myself of expressing this feeling of yearning with conviction. No sooner thought than done: I rushed towards Nugkta crying: 'Oh, if only we could lose ourselves in the boundless spaces of the void . . .' (That is, I did something somehow equivalent to crying something of the like.) And how did she react? By turning away in disgust. It took me a while to realize how crude I had been and to learn that one speaks of the void (or better still doesn't speak) with a great deal more discretion.

From then on it was one long series of crises which kept me in a state of constant agitation. How could I have been so mistaken as to seek the completeness of fullness in preference to the perfection of the void? True, the passage from non-being to being had been a considerable novelty, a sensational development, a discovery guaranteed to impress. But one could hardly claim that things had changed for the better. From a state of clarity, faultless, without stain, one had gone to a bungled, cluttered construction crumbling away on every side, held together by pure luck. How could I have been so excited by the so-called marvels of the universe? The scarcity of available materials had in many cases led to monotonous repetitive states, or again in many others to a scatter of untidy, inconsistent improvisations few of which would lead to anything at all. Perhaps it had been a false start: the veneer of what tried to pass itself off as a universe would soon fall away like a mask, and nothingness, the only true completeness possible, would once again impose its invincible absolute.

So began a time when it was only in the chinks of emptiness, the absences, the silences, the gaps, the missing connections, the flaws in time's fabric, that I could find meaning and value. Through those chinks I would sneak glances at the great realm of non-being, recognizing it now as my only true home, a home I regretted having betrayed in a temporary clouding of consciousness, a home Nugkta had brought me to rediscover. Yes, to rediscover: for together with her, my inspiration, I would slither into these narrow passages of nothingness that crossed the compactness of the universe; together we would achieve the obliteration of every dimension, of all time, all substance, all form.

By now the understanding between myself and Nugkta should at last have been clear. What could come between us? Yet every now and then unexpected differences would emerge: it seemed I had become more severe with the world of existence than she; I was amazed to discover in her an attitude of indulgence, complicity I might almost say, with the efforts that dusty vortex was making to keep itself together. (Already there were well-formed electromagnetic fields, nuclei, the first atoms.)

Here it must be said that so long as one considered the universe as the complete expression of total fullness, it could inspire nothing but banality and rhetoric, but if one thought of it as something made from very little, a poor thing scratched together on the edge of nothingness, it excited sympathy and encouragement, or at least a benevolent curiosity as to whatever might come of it. To my surprise I found Nugkta willing to support it, to assist it, this mean, poverty-stricken, sickly universe. Whereas I was tough: 'Give me the void! All glory and honour to nothingness!' I insisted, concerned that this weakness of Nugkta's might distract us from our goal. And how did Nugkta reply? With her usual mocking snorts, exactly as she had at the time of my excessive enthusiasm for the glories of the universe.

Slow as I am, only later would I come to appreciate that once again she was right. The only contact we could have with the void was through this little the void had produced as quintessence of its own emptiness; the only image we had of the void was our own poor universe. All the void we would ever know was there, in the relativity of what is, for even the void had been no more than a relative void, a void secretly shot through with veins and temptations to be something, given that in a moment of crisis at its own nothingness it had been able to give rise to the universe.

Today, after time has churned its way through billions of minutes, billions of years, and the universe is unrecognizable from what it was in those first instants, since space suddenly became transparent so that the galaxies wrap the night in their blazing spirals, and along the orbits of the solar systems millions of worlds bring forth their Himalayas and their oceans according to the cosmic seasons, and the continents throng with masses whether jubilant or suffering or slaughtering each other, turn and turn about with meticulous obstinacy, and empires rise and fall in their marble, porphyry and concrete capitals, and the markets overflow with quartered cattle and frozen peas and displays of brocade and tulle and nylon, and transistors and computers and every kind of gadget pulsate, and everybody in every galaxy is busy observing and measuring everything, from the infinitely small to the infinitely large, there's a secret that only Nugkta and I know: that everything space and time contains is no more than that little that was generated from nothingness, the little that is and that might very well not be, or be even smaller, even more meagre and perishable. And if we prefer not to speak of it, whether for good or for ill, it is because the only thing we could say is this: poor, frail universe, born of nothing, all we are and do resembles you.

Implosion

'Over the last few years, quasars, Seyfert galaxies, BL Lacertae objects, or, more generally, active galactic nuclei, have been attracting the attention of astronomers because of the huge quantities of energy these bodies emit, at velocities of up to 10,000 kilometres per second. There are good reasons for supposing that the central driving force of the galaxy is a black hole of enormous mass' (L'Astronomia, no. 36). 'Active galactic nuclei may be fragments left unexploded by the Big Bang and engaged in a process exactly opposite to that which takes place in black holes, a process, that is, of explosive expansion involving the liberation of enormous quantities of energy ('white holes'). They could be explained as the exit extremities of a connecting link between two points in space-time (Einstein-Rosen's bridges), expelling material devoured by a black hole situated at the entrance extremity. According to this theory, a Seyfert galaxy a hundred million light years away may now be expelling gas sucked in by another part of the universe ten billion years ago. And it is even possible that a quasar ten billion light-years away may have assumed the form we see today by taking in material that reaches it from some point in the future, travelling through a black hole which, as far as we are concerned, formed only today' (Paolo Maffei, Monsters of the Sky, pp. 210–15).

To explode or to implode – said Qfwfq – that is the question: whether 'tis nobler in the mind to expand one's energies in space without restraint, or to crush them into a dense inner concentration and, by ingesting, cherish them. To steal away, to vanish; no more; to hold within oneself every gleam, every ray, deny oneself every vent, suffocating in the depths of the soul the conflicts that so idly trouble it, give them their quietus; to hide oneself, to obliterate oneself: perchance to reawaken elsewhere, changed.

Changed . . . In what way changed? And the question, to explode or to implode: would one have to face it again? Absorbed by the vortex of this galaxy, does one pop up again in other times and other firmaments? Here sink away in cold silence, there express oneself in fiery shrieks of another tongue? Here soak up good and evil like a sponge in the shadow, there gush forth like a dazzling jet, to spray and spend and lose oneself. To what end then would the cycle repeat itself? I really don't know, I don't want to know, I don't want to think about it: here, now, my choice is made: I shall implode, as if this centripetal plunge might for ever save me from doubt and error, from the time of ephemeral change, from the slippery descent of before and after, bring me to a time of stability, still and smooth, enable me to achieve the one condition that is homogeneous and compact and definitive. You explode, if that's more to your taste, shoot yourselves all around in endless darts, be prodigal, spendthrift, reckless: I shall implode, collapse inside the abyss of myself, towards my buried centre, infinitely.

How long has it been since none of you has been able to imagine the life force except in terms of explosion? You have your reasons, I know. Your model is that of a universe born from a madcap explosion whose first splinters still hurtle unchecked and incandescent at the edge of space; your emblem is the exuberant kindling of supernovae flaunting the insolent youth of stars overloaded with energy; your favourite metaphor is the volcano, to show that even a mature and settled planet is always ready to break its bonds and burst forth. And the furnaces that flare in the furthest bounds of the heavens confirm your cult of universal conflagration; gases and particles almost as swift as light hurl themselves from vortex to centre of spiral galaxies, burst out into the lobes of elliptic galaxies, proclaim that the Big Bang still lives, the great Pan is not dead. No, I'm not deaf to your reasons; I could even join you. Go on! Explode! Burst! Let the new world begin again, repeat its ever renewed beginnings in a thunder of cannonfire, as in Napoleon's times . . . Wasn't it that age, by the way, with its elation at the revolutionary might of artillery fire that made us think of the explosion not just as harmful to people and property, but as a sign of birth, of genesis? Isn't it since then that passions, poetry and the ego have been seen as perpetual explosions? But if that's true, then so is its opposite; ever since that August when the mushroom rose over cities reduced to a layer of ash, an age was born in which the explosion is symbolic only of absolute negation. But that was something we already knew anyway, from the moment when, rising above the calendar of terrestrial chronicle, we enquired of the destiny of the universe, and the oracles of thermodynamics answered us: every existing form will break up in a blaze of heat; there is no entity can escape the irretrievable disorder of the corpuscles; time is a catastrophe, perpetual and irreversible.

Only a few old stars know how to get out of time; they are the open door to jump from a train headed for annihilation. At the limit of their decrepitude, shrunk to the size of Red Dwarfs or White Dwarfs, panting out the last glimmering gasp of the pulsar, compressed into neutron stars, here they are at last, light lost to the waste of the firmament, no more than the dark deletion of themselves, ready for the unstoppable collapse when everything, even light itself, falls inwards never to emerge again.

Praise be to the stars that implode. A new freedom opens up within them: annulled from space, exonerated from time, existing, at last, for themselves alone and no longer in relation to all the rest, perhaps only they can be sure they really exist. 'Black holes' is a derogatory nickname, dictated by envy: they are quite the opposite of holes, nothing could be fuller and heavier and denser and more compact, with a stubbornness to the way they sustain the gravity they bear within, as if clenching their fists, gritting their teeth, hunching their backs. Only on these terms can one save oneself from dissolving in overreaching extension, in Catherine wheels of effusion, exclamatory extroversion, effervescence and ebullition. Only in this way can one break through to a space-time where the implicit and the unexpressed don't lose their energy, where the pregnancy of meanings is not diluted, where discretion and keeping distance multiply the effectiveness of every action.

Don't distract yourselves fantasizing over the reckless behaviour of hypothetical quasi-stellar objects at the uncertain boundaries of the universe: it is here that you must turn your attention, to the centre of our galaxy, where all our calculations and instruments indicate the presence of a body of enormous mass that nevertheless remains invisible. Webs of radiation and gas, caught there perhaps since the time of the last implosions, show that there in the middle lies one of these so-called holes, spent as an old volcano. All that surrounds it, the wheel of planetary systems and constellations and the branches of the Milky Way, everything in our galaxy rests on the hub of this implosion sunk away into itself. That is my pole, my mirror, my secret home. It need fear no comparison with the furthest galaxies and their apparently explosive nuclei: there too what counts is what cannot be seen. Nothing comes out of there any more either, believe me: those impossibly fast flashes and whirls are just fuel to be crushed in the centripetal mortar, assimilated into the other mode of being, my own.

Sometimes, of course, I do seem to hear a voice from the furthest galaxies: 'It's me, Qfwfq, I am yourself exploding as you implode: I'm splashing out, expressing myself, spreading myself about, communicating, realizing all the potential I have; I really exist, not like you, introverted, reticent, egocentric, fused in an immutable self . . .'

Then I'm overwhelmed by the fear that even beyond the barrier of gravitational collapse time continues to flow: a different time, with no relation to the time left on this side, but speeding similarly headlong on a road with no return. In that case the implosion I've leaped into would be just a lull I've been granted, a respite before the fate I cannot escape.

Something like a dream, or a memory, goes through my mind: Qfwfq is fleeing the catastrophe of time, he finds an escape route through which to elude his destiny, he rushes through the gap, he is sure he has reached safety, from a chink in his refuge he watches how the events he has escaped gather pace, pities, from a distance, those who are overwhelmed, until, yes, he seems to recognize one of them, yes, it's Qfwfq, it's Qfwfq who beneath Qfwfq's very eyes is experiencing that same catastrophe of before or after, Qfwfq who in the moment he perishes sees Qfwfq save himself, but without saving him. 'Qfwfq, save yourself!' cries Qfwfq, but is it the imploding Qfwfq who wants to save the exploding Qfwfq or vice versa? No Qfwfq can save any exploding Qfwfqs from the conflagration, as they in turn can't pull back the other Qfwfqs from their unstoppable implosion. Any way time runs it leads to disaster whether in one direction or its opposite and the intersecting of those directions does not form a network of rails governed by points and exits, but a tangle, a knot . . .

I know I mustn't listen to voices, nor give credit to visions or nightmares. I go on digging my hole, in my mole's burrow.

A Rewritten
Cosmicomic Story

The Other Eurydice

You have won, men of without, you have recast the stories
to suit yourselves, to condemn us of within to the role you
like to give us, the role of powers of darkness and of death,
and the name you have given us, Hades, is laden with tones
of doom. Truly, if all should forget what really happened
between us, between Eurydice and Orpheus and myself,
Pluto, a story quite the reverse of the one you tell, if no one
at all now remembers that Eurydice was one of us and that
she never did live on the surface of the Earth until Orpheus
snatched her away from me with his deceitful music, then
our ancient dream of making the Earth a living sphere will
be lost for ever.

Even now hardly anyone still remembers what we meant
by making the Earth live: not what you imagine, content
with your dustcloud life set down on the border between
water, earth and air. I wanted life to expand outwards from
the centre of the Earth, to spread upwards through its concentric spheres, to circulate around its metals, liquid and solid.
Such was Pluto's dream. It was the only way the Earth might
have become an enormous living organism, the only way we
could have avoided that condition of precarious exile to
which life has been forcibly reduced, the dull weight of an
inanimate ball of stone beneath, and above, the void. You can
no longer even imagine that life might have been something

different from what now goes on without, or rather, almost without, since above you and the Earth's crust, there is always the other tenuous crust of the air. Still, there's no comparing this to the succession of spheres in whose interstices we creatures of the depths have always lived, and from which we still rise up to throng your dreams. The Earth is not solid inside, but disjointed, made up of superimposed layers of different densities one below the other, right down to the iron and nickel nucleus, which again is a system of nuclei one inside the other, each rotating separately from the others according to the greater or lesser liquidity of its element.

I don't know what right you have to call yourself terrestrial creatures. Your true name would be extraterrestrials, people who live without: we who live within are the terrestrials, myself and Eurydice, for example, until the day you tricked her and took her away from me, to your desolate without.

This is the realm of Pluto, since it is here that I have always lived, together with Eurydice at first, then alone, in one of these lands within. A sky of stone wheeled above our heads, clearer than your sky and crossed, like yours, by clouds, gathering suspensions of chrome and magnesium. Winged shadows take flight: these skies within have their birds, concretions of light rock tracing out spirals that wind upwards and out of sight. The weather is subject to brusque changes: when showers of leaden rain beat down, or zinc crystals hail, there's nothing for it but to worm your way into the shelter of some porous rock. Sometimes a fiery streak zigzags through the dark: it's not lightning, but an incandescent metal snaking down through a vein.

We thought of the Earth as the internal sphere where we happened to be, the sky as the sphere that surrounded that sphere: the same way you do really, except that here these

distinctions were always temporary, arbitrary, since the consistency of the elements was constantly changing, and sometimes we would realize that our sky was hard and solid, a
millstone crushing us, while the earth was a sticky glue of
whirling eddies and bubbling gases. I tried to take advantage
of the downward melt of heavier elements to get closer to
the true centre of the Earth, the nucleus of all nuclei, and I
held Eurydice by the hand, leading her in the descent. But
every downward infiltration that opened a way towards the
centre would displace other material and force it back
towards the surface: sometimes, as we sank down, we would
be caught by the upward gushing tide and whirled along on
the crest of its wave. So we went back up the terrestrial
radius; passages would open in the mineral layers and suck
us in and beneath us the rock would harden again. Until we
found ourselves standing on another soil with another stony
sky above our heads, hardly knowing if we were higher or
lower than the point we had set out from.

No sooner did she see the metal of a new sky liquefy above
us than Eurydice was seized by a yearning to fly. She flung
herself upwards, swam across the dome of a first sky, then
another, then a third, grabbing on to the stalactites that hung
from the highest vaults. I followed, partly to join in her game
and partly to remind her that we were supposed to be
going in the opposite direction. Of course, Eurydice was as
convinced as I was that the place we must get to was the
centre of the Earth. Only by reaching the centre could we
call the whole planet our own. We were the forefathers of
terrestrial life and hence we had to begin to make the Earth
live from its nucleus, gradually irradiating our condition
throughout the globe. Terrestrial life was our goal, a life *of*
the Earth and *in* the Earth; not what sprouts on the surface
and which you think you can call terrestrial life, when it is

no more than a mould that spreads its stains on the wrinkly peel of the apple.

We could already see the plutonic cities we meant to found rising under basalt skies, surrounded by walls of jasper – spherical, concentric cities sailing on oceans of mercury, washed by rivers of incandescent lava. What we wanted was a living-body-city-machine that would grow and grow until it filled the whole globe, a telluric machine that would use its boundless energy in ceaseless self-construction, combining and transforming all substances and shapes, performing, with the speed of a seismic shock, the work that you without have had to pay for with centuries of sweat. And this city-machine-living-body would be inhabited by beings like ourselves, giants stretching out their powerful arms across wheeling skies to embrace giantesses, who, with the rotating of concentric earths, would expose themselves in ever new attitudes giving rise to ever new couplings.

These minglings, these vibrations were to give birth to a realm of diversity and completeness, a realm of silence and of music. Constant vibrations, propagating themselves at varying slownesses, according to the depth and discontinuity of the materials, would ruffle the surface of our great silence, transforming it into the ceaseless music of the world, harmonizing the deep voices of the elements.

This to show you how mistaken your way is, your life where work and pleasure are at odds, where music and noise are two different things; this to show you how even then all this was clear, and the song of Orpheus none other than a sign of your partial and divided world. Why did Eurydice fall into the trap? She belonged entirely to our world, Eurydice, but her enchanted spirit was such that she delighted in every possible state of suspension, and as soon as she got the chance to launch herself in flight, in leaps, in ascents up volcanic vents, you would see her bending her body into twists and turns and curvets and capers.

Boundary zones, the passages that led from one terrestrial layer to another, gave her a keen sense of vertigo. I have said that the Earth is made up of roofs laid one above another, like the skins of an immense onion, and every roof leads to a higher roof, and all together look forward to the final roof, there where the Earth stops being Earth, where everything within is left on this side and on the other there is only what is without. You identify the Earth's boundary with the Earth itself; you believe that the sphere is the surface that wraps around it, not the volume beneath; you have always lived in that flat dimension and you never even imagine that an elsewhere and an otherwise could exist; at the time we knew that this boundary was there, but we didn't imagine one could see it, without leaving the Earth, an idea that wasn't so much frightening as absurd. Everything the Earth expelled from its guts in eruptions and bituminous jets and fumaroles was sent flying out there: gases, liquid mixtures, volatile elements, worthless materials, refuse of every kind. The outside was the world's negative, something we couldn't even picture in our minds, the mere abstract idea of which was enough to provoke a shiver of disgust, no, of horror, or rather, a stupor, yes that's it, a sense of vertigo (certainly our reactions were more complicated than you would imagine, especially Eurydice's), into which would creep a certain fascination, an attraction to the void, the Janus-faced, the ultimate.

Following Eurydice on one of her wandering whims, I was led into the throat of a spent volcano. Above us, the other side of something like the narrow passage of an hourglass, the crusty grey cavity of the crater opened out into a landscape hardly different in shape and substance from those we lived in deep below; but what bewildered us was that the Earth ended here, it didn't begin to weigh down on itself again in another form; from here on was emptiness, or at least a substance incomparably more tenuous than those we had so far encountered, a transparent, vibrant substance, the blue air.

It was these vibrations that lost Eurydice, vibrations so different from those that spread slowly through basalt and granite, different from all the cracks, clangs and dull boomings that shudder sluggishly through masses of fused metal or great walls of crystals. Here, minute pointed sound-sparks darted towards her one after another from every possible direction and at a speed that was unbearable to us: it was a sort of tickling that filled you with unseemly cravings. We were seized – or at least I was seized, since from here on I shall have to distinguish between my own state of mind and Eurydice's – by the desire to retreat into that dark depth of silence over which the echo of earthquakes passes softly and is lost in the distance. But Eurydice, drawn as ever to the unusual and the rash, was eager to make this unique thing her own, regardless of whether it was good or bad.

It was then that the trap was sprung: beyond the edge of the crater the air vibrated continuously, or rather it vibrated continuously but in a way that involved different discontinuous vibrations. It was a sound that rose to fullness, faded, swelled again, and this modulation was part of an invisible pattern it followed, extended across time like a chequer of solids and spaces. Further vibrations were superimposed on these, and they were shrill and sharply separate, yet drew together in a halo, first sweet then bitter, and as they contrasted or followed the movement of the deeper sound, they imposed a sort of circle or field or dominion of sound.

My immediate instinct was to get out of that circle, to get back to padded density and I slipped inside the crater. But that same moment Eurydice had leaped up the rocks in the direction of the sound, and before I could stop her she was over the brim of the crater. Oh, it was an arm, something I thought might be an arm, that snatched her, snake-like, and dragged her out; I just heard a cry, her cry, join with the earlier sound, in harmony with it, in a single song that she and the unknown singer struck up together, to the rhythm of a stringed instrument, descending the outer slopes of the volcano.

I don't know whether this image corresponds to something seen or something imagined: I was already sinking down into my darkness, the inner skies were closing one by one above me: the siliceous vaults, aluminium roofs, atmospheres of viscous sulphur; and the dappled subterranean silence echoed around me with its restrained rumblings, its muttered thunder. My relief at finding myself once again far away from the sickening edge of the air and the torment of those sound-waves was matched only by my desperation at having lost Eurydice. I was alone now: I hadn't been able to save her from the torture of being torn from the Earth, exposed to the constant percussion of strings stretched in that air with which the world of the void defends itself from the void. My dream of making the Earth live by reaching the ultimate centre together with Eurydice had failed. Eurydice was a prisoner, exiled in the roofless wastes of the world without.

What followed was a time of waiting. My eyes studied the closely packed landscapes which, one above the other, fill the volume of the globe: threadlike caverns, chains of mountains stacked in scales and sheets, oceans wrung out like sponges; the more I acknowledged and was moved by our crammed, concentrated, compact world, the more I suffered that Eurydice was no longer there to live in it.

Freeing her became my sole obsession: forcing the gates

of the world without, inside invading outside, reuniting Eurydice with terrestrial material, building a new vault above her, a new mineral sky, saving her from the hell of that vibrant air, of that sound, that song. I would watch the lava gather in volcanic caverns, the upward pressure on the vertical ducts of the Earth's crust: that was the way.

Came the day of the eruption, a tower of lapilli rose black in the air above a decapitated Vesuvius, the lava poured through the vineyards of the bay, burst the gates of Herculaneum, crushed the mule-driver and his beast against a wall, snatched the miser from his money, the slave from his chopping block; a dog trapped in his collar pulled the chain from the ground and sought refuge in the barn. I was there in the midst: I pressed forward with the lava, the flaming avalanche broke up in tongues, rivers, snakes, and at the foremost tip I was there running forward to find Eurydice. I knew – something told me – that she was still a prisoner of the unknown singer: when I heard the music of that instrument and the timbre of that voice, I would have found her too.

I rushed on, transported by the lava flow through secluded gardens towards marble temples. I heard the song and a chord; two voices alternated; I recognized Eurydice's – but how changed! – following the stranger's. Greek characters on the undercurve of an arch spelt: *Orpheos*. I broke down the door, flooded over the threshold. For just an instant I saw her, next to the harp. The place was closed and vaulted, made specially, you would have thought, so that the music could gather there, as though in a shell. A heavy curtain, of leather I had the impression, or rather padded like a quilt, closed off a window, so as to isolate their music from the world around. As soon as I went in, Eurydice wrenched the curtain aside, throwing open the window; outside was the bay dazzling with reflected light and the city and the streets. The midday sun invaded the room, the sun and the sounds: a strumming of guitars rose from every side and the throbbing roar of scores of loudspeakers, together with the jagged backfiring of car engines and the honking of horns. The armour of noise stretched out across the Earth's crust: the cortex which circumscribes your surface lives, with its antennas bristling on the roofs, turning to sound the waves that travel unseen and unheard through space, with its radios stuck to your ears, constantly filling them with the acoustic glue without which you don't know whether you're dead or alive, its jukeboxes with their store of incessantly revolving sounds and the never-ending siren of the ambulance picking up the wounded of your never-ending massacres.

The lava stopped against this wall of sound. Lacerated by the barbs of that fence of crashing vibrations, I made one more move forward to the point where for a moment I had seen Eurydice, but she was gone, and gone likewise her abductor: the song by which and on which they lived was submerged by the intruding avalanche of noise, and I could no longer distinguish either her or her song.

I withdrew, climbing reluctantly back along the lava flow, up the slopes of the volcano, I returned to live in silence, to bury myself.

Now, you who live without, tell me if by chance you happen to catch Eurydice's song in that thick paste of sounds that surrounds you, the song that holds her prisoner and is in turn prisoner of the non-song that massacres all songs, and if you should recognize Eurydice's voice with its distant echo of the silent music of the elements, tell me, give me news of her, you extraterrestrials, temporary victors, so that I can resume my plans to bring Eurydice to the centre of terrestrial life, to restore the realm of the gods of within, of the gods who inhabit the dense compactness of things, now that the gods of without, the gods of the Olympian heights and the rarefied air, have given you all they could give, and clearly it isn't enough.